Keeping Him

USA TODAY BESTSELLING AUTHOR

KENNEDY FOX

Each book in the Bishop Brothers World can read as standalones but if you wish to read the others, here's our suggested reading order.

BISHOP BROTHERS SERIES
Original Bishop Family

Taming Him

Needing Him

Chasing Him

Keeping Him

SPIN-OFF'S
Friends of the Bishops

Make Me Stay

Roping the Cowboy

CIRCLE B RANCH SERIES
Bishop Family Second Generation

Hitching the Cowboy

Catching the Cowboy

Wrangling the Cowboy

Bossing the Cowboy

Kissing the Cowboy

Winning the Cowboy

Claiming the Cowboy

Tempting the Cowboy

Seducing the Cowboy

So if you're gonna break my heart, just break it.
And if you're gonna take your shot, then take it.
If you made up your mind, then make it.
If you ever loved me, have mercy.

"Mercy"
-Brett Young

PROLOGUE
KIERA, 15 YEARS OLD

"Truth or dare?"

"Neither," Jackson responds, groaning as he kicks up dirt with his boot. We're sitting on hay bales we stole from the Bishop's barn and put them close to the firepit to keep warm. It's mid-January, and now that it's night, the temps have dropped. It's been our private hiding spot since we were thirteen. It's on a piece of Jackson's family's ranch, and we hang out here when we want to get away from everyone or secretly drink a bottle of his dad's whiskey.

"You know the rules, Jackson," I remind him, poking his shoulder as hard as I can. He doesn't even flinch, though. His body's made of steel. "You *have* to play."

"Says who? That's a game twelve-year-old's play when they want to get their dicks wet."

"Ew!" I shove my shoulder into his, laughing. "Stop being gross and just pick one."

"*Fine*." He pinches his lips together and moves them side to side as if he's actually pondering the question. But I already know his answer. Jackson picks the same option every time. "Dare."

Even when I want to get the truth out of him. But I've found a work-around.

"Alright. I *dare* you to tell me who your secret crush is." I smile boldly, knowing he's going to make a fuss about it.

"I said dare, Kiera." He groans again, placing his hands behind his head and locking his fingers around his neck.

"Yeah, and I'm daring you to tell me. So spill it," I declare. "You know what happens if you don't…" I taunt.

"You actually leave me the hell alone?" he teases.

"You know I'm not going to tell anyone. Plus, Tanner already told me you have a crush on someone, so don't even pretend you don't."

"When were you talking to him?" He grunts and rolls his eyes, obviously annoyed. Tanner's his best friend, so if Jackson has a crush on a girl, he'd know.

"He stopped me in the hall because he had a sub and skipped," I explain, but by the redness covering his neck and cheeks, I can see he's not happy about it. "He asked if I was going to the stupid Valentine's dance in a few weeks."

Jackson snorts, leaning down and picking up the nearly empty bottle of Crown Royal Reserve. It's his dad's top-notch whiskey, and if we're caught with it, he'll whip us both into next week.

I watch his throat move as he takes a long drink. Jackson loves drinking, and though I hate the taste of it, I like having these moments with him.

"All the chicks at school are annoying."

"Hey!" I swat his arm.

"All the *hot* chicks," he adds with a smirk.

Now I'm the one snorting and rolling my eyes. "That didn't stop you from making out with Bunny Vanderbilt last semester." I call him out. Bunny's one of my friends, and her real name is Barbara, but since she'll jump on anything breathing with a penis, she's been penned the appropriate nickname. "Or Rosa Michels," I add. She's another friend of mine.

As a matter of fact, he's made out with *most* of my friends.

Jackson snickers as if he's reminiscing about his moments with them. Ugh. I really hate him sometimes.

"Who haven't you made out with?"

"You can't ask twice," he deflects.

"Well, you didn't answer my first question," I remind him, taking the Crown Royal bottle from his grip. He's already had way too much.

"I don't have *crushes*, Kiera. I'm not a seven-year-old boy who thinks girls have cooties."

Groaning, I roll my eyes so hard I'm quite sure they're permanently stuck in the back of my head. "So you didn't crush on Bunny or Rosa?"

He shrugs, staring intently at the flames of the fire. "They were decent enough for a few minutes. Nothing to think twice about."

Oh my God. I think I might puke.

Nope. I *am* going to puke.

Turning away, I kneel over the hay bale and empty my stomach over the small patch of grass that isn't dead. Jackson's hand rests on my back, rubbing soothing circles as I dry heave until everything has been purged from my stomach.

"Damn," Jackson howls. "You've gotta learn to hold your liquor."

I turn around and wipe my mouth with my sleeve. "You're such an ass."

"What?" He raises up both hands. "I'm just sayin'. I've had way more than you, and I barely feel it."

"That's because you're a bottomless pit. You're like some weird breed." I situate myself back on the hay, feeling my face flush with embarrassment. Although it's not the first time he's seen me vomit, it's not something I like to make a habit of.

No wonder he makes out with all the girls in school except me.

Jackson makes a fist and punches himself in the gut, roaring loudly into the dark night sky. "Invincible, baby!"

"You are not invincible, Jackson Bishop! You're going to seriously get hurt one of these days," I tell him. "Drinking and being stupid are going to eventually catch up with you."

3

"Stop being a fish!" He pushes my shoulder. "Always going with the flow is boring."

"I am not a fish!" I pout, pushing him back.

"You so are! That's why you care about that stupid dance. All your friends are going, so, of course, you're going too."

"Me wanting to hang out with friends doesn't make me a fish. Gah! I don't even know why I hang out with you."

"Because I'm the coolest person you know, and you know I'm right." He flashes his infamous Jackson Bishop smirk at me, and like always, it turns me to mushy goo. *Damn him!* Why does he have to be charming and arrogant at the same time?

"You wish," I fire back, though the smile I'm failing to hide gives me away. "And if I'm a fish, then you're a seagull. Always squawking and getting into mischief. Sounds just like you."

His head falls back as a crack of laughter escapes his throat while he smacks his thigh over and over. "Oh, Kiera." He's still laughing as though I just said the funniest thing in the world. "This is why I like you. I never know what random shit will come out of that sassy mouth of yours."

He has no idea what those words just did to my heart. The blood in my chest pumps so hard and fast, and my heart is racing as I eagerly wait for whatever else he has to say.

"That's why you *like* me?" I repeat as if I'm offended. I'm determined to finally get to the bottom of this. Jackson's many things, and one thing is for sure—he's confusing as hell. We've known each other since we were in diapers, and as we grew older, we bonded over our love of horses. It seemed inevitable, considering our parents are good friends, but the relationship I share with Jackson has always been different compared to the other Bishop brothers. Jackson has a twin brother, John, and though he can be fun to hang out with, we don't have much in common. They might be identical in looks, but their personalities are as different as they come.

"Like you enough to hang out with you," he taunts with a lazy smile. "You're like a less annoying sister."

Thud.

My heart just jumped and fell flat into a million broken pieces.

"And considering Courtney is an annoying little twerp I can't stand most of the time, you're a breath of fresh air—*mostly*."

"Wow…" I say with fake happiness. "I'm not sure if that's a compliment or not."

"Oh stop being so dramatic. We used to take baths together, and I already know what your chest looks like, so why would I bother trying to look at it now?"

"Jackson Bishop!" I scold, standing and smacking him right across the head. "What's wrong with you?"

He grabs my wrist when I try to hit him again and pulls me forward until I'm forced to sit on his lap. I start laughing when he does even though I'm trying to be mad at him.

"You gonna stop smackin' me?" he whispers in my ear, making my body shiver and my heart beat faster.

My breath hitches, and suddenly, I feel like I can't breathe. Jackson's arm is wrapped around my waist as his hand stays locked on my wrist, holding me securely. His erection is evident in his tight jeans as it pushes into my ass. I try to swallow, but the razor blades lodged in my throat make it impossible.

"Kiera?" he prompts. "I'll release you if you promise to stop hitting me."

I finally find my voice and steady my breathing. "Why?" I look over my shoulder to scowl at him. "Afraid you'll get beat up by a girl?"

"In your wet dreams, Kiera Young!" The next thing I know, I'm flipped to my back on the ground and Jackson is towering over me, pinning my arms above my head. "I'd like to see you try, sweetheart, but you'll be painfully sorry. I could take you down with my pinky while fighting a hangover."

I narrow my eyes at him, trying to wiggle my arms out of his grip. Dammit. He really is too strong for his own good. If I didn't know he was raised on a ranch, I'd find it quite freakish.

"I could take you down with one hit while tipsy," I shoot back, ready to prove him just how right I am, and after that whole sister comment, I'm not even sorry for what I'm about to do.

He barks out a loud laugh, obviously not buying my threat. "Show me whatcha got, *fishy*."

"Wait, your thigh is digging into my side." I arch my back, pretending the discomfort is painful, and when he lifts up slightly, I take my shot.

"Sucker!" Lifting my leg, I aim directly between his legs and feel his erection collide with my bony knee. The moment it happens, I instantly regret everything because the look on his face scares the shit out of me. I'm sure he's stopped breathing, and by the way his face goes pale, I'm certain the air was sucked out of his lungs.

"Holy. Fuck." He drops to the ground, holding his groin and spewing out inaudible noises.

Well, at least he's breathing.

"That was a fucking cheap shot, Kiera," he hisses, squeezing his eyes shut as he breathes rapidly in and out.

"To be fair, I did warn you."

"Stop talking before I…" He pauses midsentence to catch his breath.

"Geez. Does it really hurt that bad?"

"Seriously?" He winces, causing me to do the same. "Imagine your tit being twisted off by pliers, then dipped in lava and forced down your throat."

"Jesus." I shiver. "That's mildly disturbing."

Moments pass while Jackson lies in the fetal position, holding his junk and steadying his breathing. Though the flames of the fire have gone down, I'm pretty sure I see Jackson's eyes watering.

"Are you going to be okay? You're making me feel bad here."

"You feel bad?" He glares at me.

"Okay, I'll shut up now."

Jackson finally moves and sits up, so we're facing each other.

"Probably the best thing you've said all night."

6

Now I'm the one rolling my eyes. "We'll call it even for all the times you've picked on me. That was fifteen years of pent-up revenge," I say matter-of-factly.

"So does that mean you'll get revenge on me again in fifteen years?" He pops a brow, bracing for my response.

I point my finger at him, holding back a laugh at his stupidly cute face. "Don't tempt me."

"Shit, seriously." He groans as he stands and sits down on the hay bale, holding himself. "I'll probably never be able to have kids now."

"Then the world will thank me for not allowing you to reproduce more of *you*." I snicker, standing to sit next to him. "I think you're just milking it now. The pain can't be drawing out this long."

Both of his brows raise instantly. "Let me punch you in the vag and see how you feel in ten minutes."

I giggle, trying to hide the blush that surfaces on my cheeks. "Well, unless a bowling ball is coming out of it, I can confidently say I wouldn't bitch out like you did."

"You're a feisty little firecracker when you drink," he howls. "Can we just make a pact that there'll be no junk or vag kicking from now on? I'd like to feel my dick."

Yeah, I know. With just about every one of my friends.

"Fine," I agree. "No tittie punches either."

He cracks up laughing. "Damn, I was hoping that'd slip through."

"On one condition, though…" I add.

"Huh? You secretly like your titties punched?"

"Jackson!" I'm tempted to punch him in the junk again.

"What? Some chicks dig that!" he exclaims. "Kinky, rough sex is a thing, you know."

How the hell would I know anything about that? I'm a virgin who's barely gone past first base.

Ugh. Maybe I *am* his less annoying little sister.

"You still have to follow through with your dare, or else…"

"You've gotta be kiddin' me. After that junk shot, I shouldn't ever have to play that stupid game again," he protests.

"No way! You said 'dare,' and you know that once you pick one, you *have* to follow through or you face the consequences." I remind him of the rules we made when we were eleven.

"It can't be any worse than what I've already endured, so fuck it." Jackson stands, his dick coming back to life. He reaches behind his neck and pulls off his T-shirt. I gaze down his chest and abs, and though I've seen him shirtless dozens of times, the sight of his chiseled muscles never gets old. Next, he unzips his jeans, and I wait with bated breath for what's coming.

"Hold back your drool," he taunts, looking at me with a devilish grin. Jackson pulls his pants and boxers down to his ankles before quickly kicking them off. I'm certain my heart stops beating completely, and I've now died and gone to heaven.

Jackson's always followed through with his truth or dare to avoid this very consequence, but for some reason, tonight he's determined to actually kill me. *Torturously.*

I pull my lower lip into my mouth and bite down. Jackson stands naked in front of me, his dick getting hard, and he's so close, I could reach out and touch it. Sliding my hands under my legs to keep that very thing from happening, I blink and bring my gaze back up to his mischievous face.

"Ready?" His cocky smile has butterflies twirling around my stomach. He bends his arms and puts his fists into his shoulders, mimicking a pair of wings. He then runs around in circles, flapping his pretend wings as he screams 'bwak-bwak-bwak, I'm a chicken' over and over until I'm bent over laughing so hard, I'm crying.

Jackson looks absolutely ridiculous, but I can't deny how much he makes me laugh on a daily basis. Whether we're screwing around or actually working together, I know it's always going to be a fun time.

"There," Jackson pants, coming to a stop in front of me. "Three minutes of naked humiliation. Happy now?"

I swallow hard, willing myself to keep my eyes above his neck because sneaking a peek lower is far too tempting.

"Mildly," I quip. "Though I've changed my mind."

"On what?" he barks.

"A junk punch isn't enough to get even for all the shit you've done to me."

"Are you kiddin' me? I'm standing naked here. What else do you wanna do to me?"

So damn much. Bad, bad, bad.

I pinch my lips together, flashing an innocent look as I eye the fire behind him. "Gotta get home. Curfew!" I walk out of his reach, moving farther away while he starts to put the pieces together.

"Where are my clothes?" He looks down to where he left them, then searches the rest of the area. "Kiera! Goddammit! Where are they?"

"I decided to bend the rules a little. Felt the consequences were too lenient." I nod my head to the fire that's effectively using his clothes as fuel.

Jackson finally gets the hint and spins around to the large flames. I run faster, putting more distance between us as I look over my shoulder to see whether he's chasing after me.

"You're dead, Kiera Young! DEAD! You know I'm going to get you *so* much worse!" he shouts.

Running, I laugh as loud as I can, knowing he's going to have to walk into his house butt-ass naked. I can only hope Mama Bishop or one of his brothers are still up to add to his misery.

Turning around in his direction, I cup my hands over my mouth and shout back, "Don't worry. Shrinkage is normal in the cold!"

I squeal the moment Jackson comes charging for me. Bolting as fast as I can back to the house, Jackson eventually catches up to me and tackles me to the ground. Our bodies hit the grass with full force, both of us laughing as we catch our breath.

"So, am I still a fish?" I ask, breaking the silence.

"No." He chuckles. "You're a goddamn bull."

"A bull?" I turn toward him with a questioning glare.

"Yeah. A fuckin' savage. Chewed me up and spit me out." He laughs as if he's actually impressed. God, I love the sound of his laughter. He's always looking for a good time, and when he's laughing, I know he's having the time of his life.

"Hmm," I say. "Well, guess that'll teach you—mess with the bull…"

"You get the horns," he finishes for me, rolling his eyes at my proud victory.

"That's right."

I feel Jackson's stare, and when I turn to face him, I catch him looking at my lips, and wonder if this is finally it. I've dreamt of kissing Jackson for as long as I can remember, but instead of making a move, I've watched on the sidelines as he's flirted with and dated all my friends.

"Miss Whitman," he blurts out, taking me by surprise.

"Huh? What about Miss Whitman?" I'm so confused.

"The answer to my dare."

"Your dare? Wait, what? You liar!" I scoff, reminding myself to *not* look at his dick.

"I don't lie, Kiera. You know that."

"You do not have a crush on Miss Whitman, the librarian! She's like fifty!"

"So? She's hot!"

I mimic a gagging noise and lean up on my elbows. "You're a pig."

"You're just jealous," he fires back, and my cheeks instantly burn.

"No, I think you've mistaken my disgust for jealousy. She wears her glasses on the tip of her nose!"

"Yeah, it's sexy as hell." He whistles a catcall.

Leaning over, I shove him. "Stay down in the mud where you belong, *pig*."

"C'mon, you know you wanna join me!" He opens his arms with a mocking smile. "Gotta take off your clothes, though."

I stand, stepping away from him so he can't reach out and grab me.

"In your dreams, playboy!" I continue walking backward, putting much needed space between us.

I'm almost back to my four-wheeler when I hear him yell out once more. "Only the naughty ones!"

CHAPTER ONE

KIERA, PRESENT DAY

I CAN'T BELIEVE it's almost time.

As I stare at my wedding dress hanging in my old bedroom, I know this is really happening. I'm finally getting married, and hopefully soon, we'll have kids and the family I've always dreamed of. Trent isn't a perfect man, but he's sweet, kind, and ready to settle down.

The past two years together have been filled with some great memories. Trent travels a lot for work and often works long hours, but it's part of what brought us together. As an equine vet, he'd been my family's vet for years before we started dating. Since I train horses, I saw him frequently, but nothing happened until we ran into each other at a Bishop wedding two springs ago. He asked me to have a drink with him, and sparks instantly flew between us.

Smiling, I think back to those early days of Trent and me dating. They were so easy and effortless. I was smitten by him so fast that I missed the signs of deception, but we were able to work through them to get to this point. Every relationship goes through hardships, and everyone has their flaws, but I'm ready to move on to the next chapter in our lives.

I'm ready.

"I still can't get over how gorgeous your dress is," my matron of honor and best friend, Emily, says from behind me. The sound of her voice makes me jump since I didn't hear her come in.

"It really is, isn't it?" I beam, glancing at her over my shoulder as she comes to my side. "I could stare at it all day."

"Well tomorrow, everyone's going to be staring at you. You getting butterflies yet?" Emily loops her arm through mine and rests her head on my shoulder. She just married into the Bishop family, which means our friendship has grown even more since college.

"I've had butterflies since the day Trent and I started dating," I admit with a smile.

"Aww…" Emily teases. "I'm so happy for you." Emily turns so we're facing each other; her hands rest on my shoulders. "I want you to have everything you've ever dreamed of and more. You deserve to be happy with Trent," she tells me as if she needs to coach me through this.

"I couldn't have done this without you. After so many decisions and numerous headaches, it's finally here." I chuckle at that last one. "I'm so glad you'll be up there with me."

"I wouldn't miss it for anything in the world, Kiera. You know that." She pulls me in for a hug, and I suck in a deep breath, trying to keep myself together and not cry.

"I love you," I tell her.

"I love you." She pulls back, already tearing up. "You ready to do this? Pastor Montgomery is ready to start, so we need to get lined up."

"Yep." I wipe under my eyes. "Ready as I'll ever be!"

Emily leads us out of my parents' house where my mother has proudly deemed it set up as the wedding party headquarters. Being that we're in west Texas and it's the middle of October, the weather is just perfect for an outside wedding on my parents' ranch. It's not too hot and uncomfortable for us to have the ceremony and reception on top of the hill with one of the best views of the land.

Everyone is huddled together near their trucks, waiting to drive the short path to where the ceremony is being held. Trent spots me and immediately walks toward me with a gorgeous smile on his face. He's tall with brown hair and brown eyes and is the perfect combination of tall, dark, and handsome.

"You look beautiful," he whispers as he cups my face and presses a soft kiss to my lips. My stomach does somersaults every time he says those words because I know how strongly he means them. He makes me feel like the prettiest woman alive by how attentive and sweet he is toward me.

"You're looking mighty handsome yourself. I love this blue color on you," I tell him, wrapping my arms around his neck and pulling him in for another kiss.

"Think we can tell everyone to do the rehearsal without us and sneak away to one of the barns for a quickie?" He winks, licking his lips as his eyes gaze down at my white, curve-hugging dress.

I laugh at his eagerness but swat his hand away as he tries to cop a feel. "Nice try. We'll show up tomorrow having no idea what we're doing."

"Oh, I will. You walking down the aisle to me is all that needs to happen. The rest we'll figure out." He grabs my hand and presses a sensual kiss to my knuckles.

"Alright, lovebirds," Emily cuts in with a knowing grin on her face. "Save it for the honeymoon. It's time to get going."

"You're riding up with your best man," I remind Trent. "Then the other groomsmen are riding up with Jackson."

Trent's face hardens when I mention Jackson's name, though that's his typical scowl whenever he hears it. To say the two don't get along would be an understatement. Trent was the Bishops' vet too, so he had to play nice to keep their business, but it's no secret the two have been frenemies ever since we started dating.

"And you're riding with me and your father," Emily says, grabbing my hand out of Trent's and leading me toward her truck.

I turn around to look at him just as he cups his mouth and shouts, "Love you!"

Smiling wide, I mouth, "Love you!" before I'm spun back around and pushed toward the passenger side.

"You're going to make me nauseous," Emily teases, making a gagging noise. "But I'm *so* damn happy for you guys."

"That means everything, Em. Thank you." I pull her in for a hug and squeeze.

"I'm really happy for *you*. You deserve this more than anyone. I can't wait for you to get pregnant so we can be pregnant together!"

"Wait, what?" I gasp, taking a step back. "You're pregnant?"

"Shh! We haven't told anyone yet."

"Oh my God!" I whisper-shout, giving her another squeeze. "I'm so happy! How'd Evan take the news?" I chuckle. Her husband is also an ER doctor, but he takes life way more seriously than she does, and I always enjoy giving him shit for it.

"He's really excited." She beams. "He's hoping for a boy this time, but I already have a feeling it's another girl." She laughs.

"I hope it's twins!" I chuckle. The Bishops have a history of multiples, which means anyone breeding with a Bishop boy has a chance to have twins or more.

"Oh God, please don't say that. I mean, we'll be happy either way, of course, but I can barely handle Elizabeth and her terrible twos."

I snicker at that because Elizabeth is only eighteen months, but she gives her parents a run for their money with Emily's sassy attitude and Evan's moody behavior.

"Elizabeth is going to have so much fun with a sibling so close in age," I tell her as I open the door and hop in. "When are you announcing it?"

"Probably in a few weeks. I want to get checked out again, and right now is about you, so I don't want to take any excitement away." I'm about to tell her she's crazy considering

Trent proposed to me at her wedding shower, but I know Emily was also behind it. She's been rooting for us since day one.

"That means your baby and River's baby girl will be pretty close in age too!" Rowan was born in June and is only four months old, but I get excited knowing my best friend's kids are going to have cousins close in age. I didn't have much family close by, other than my cousin Addie, which is why the Bishops were an essential part of my life growing up.

"Yep! So many Bishop grandkids." Emily chuckles. "But I'll probably need some help so people don't get suspicious when I'm not drinking anything. I can't say I'm breastfeeding anymore, so I'll need an interference."

"Don't worry. I'm sure I can figure something out." I flash her a wink before shutting the door. My dad hops in the back behind Emily, and once the three of us are buckled, we drive the short distance up the hill.

My bridesmaids are riding together in a couple of other trucks, filling up the flatbeds as they all jump in. Trent's from a large family, and the Bishops have been my family for as long as I can remember, so we ended up with ten bridesmaids and ten groomsmen. Then, of course, Elizabeth is my little flower girl, and she'll be walking down with the ring bearer, Riley, who's three. He's Alex and River Bishop's son, and ever since the two of them have been together, I've grown closer to River, and we've become good friends. Alex is the youngest Bishop brother but, surprisingly, was the first one to get married. River works at the same hospital as Evan and Emily as a pediatric nurse. It's safe to say, everyone knows everyone in this small town.

That also means everyone knows everything about you.

Your secrets, scandals, and drama.

Though it can be stressful at times, I wouldn't have it any other way. I was born and raised here, and I can't wait to raise my own children in Eldorado.

"You nervous, Kiki?" my dad asks, using the childhood

nickname he gave me. He places a hand on my shoulder with an encouraging squeeze.

I cover his hand with mine and smile at him. "A little," I admit. "But I'm really excited it's finally here."

"You're gonna be a beautiful bride but, more importantly, a spectacular wife and mother. I'm so proud of you."

"Dad…" I choke up. "You're not supposed to make me cry before the rehearsal!"

Emily laughs with him, and after a few moments, we arrive at the bottom of the hill where we park.

"River and I made you something," Emily tells me while digging around the backseat. "River wanted to incorporate some of her Midwestern wedding traditions, so she made you a rehearsal bouquet with all the ribbons and bows from your bridal shower gifts."

She holds it up, and it's actually really awesome looking. Strings of ribbon hang like vines, and then big, fat bows mimic flowers on top. "That is the coolest thing ever!" I grab it from her and hold it to my body. "I love it! Thank you!"

"Thank River. It was all her idea! In fact, she made me dig through five trash bags to grab them all after your party." She shivers as if the memory makes her cringe.

I tilt my head back and try to hold myself together. "Y'all gotta stop giving me reasons to cry."

With my dad standing next to me, he holds his arm out and smiles. "Ready, Kiki?"

I loop my arm through his with a bright, cheeky smile. "Ready."

My wedding coordinator, Jessica Hart, flags me down with my mother, and Pastor Montgomery is next to her. Jessica's glowing at five months pregnant and has a huge smile on her face. I met Jessica four years ago when she moved here from Florida to be with Dylan, who works on the Bishop's ranch. She's an event coordinator and was dying to help me with wedding plans as soon as we got engaged. Since we only had six months to get everything together and she did such a great job with Emily's wedding, I was more than happy to have her help.

"Kiera! You look amazing as always." She pulls me in for a hug. "I think everyone's here, so we should get started soon. There's a lot to go over."

"Sounds good to me," I say just as a loud muffler roars behind us. I see Jackson's truck pulling up with a handful of groomsmen in the bed of the truck. They've all more than likely been drinking, which I know is going to piss off Trent.

They jump out and are shoutin' and hollerin' like a bunch of idiots. I spot Trent walking up with his parents and head toward them.

"I thought you were going to talk to him," Trent immediately says in a hushed voice, his jaw clenching with anger. "If you insist on him being in the wedding, he needs to act like a fucking adult."

"Trent…" I whisper. "I will."

"When? You're running out of time," he reminds me.

Inhaling a deep breath, I nod. "I will at dinner, okay? Promise."

Jessica rounds everyone up, and as I look around noticing how many people are here for us today, it makes me want to tear up all over again. We're so blessed to have these people in our lives, supporting Trent's and my relationship. My mother has already handed out handkerchiefs, knowing the majority are criers.

"Mom," I say with a low groan.

"I've been crying all day; I can't help it." She dabs under her eyes, and I feel like an emotional mess right along with her.

"Well, you're going to cry yourself dry if you don't slow down," I tease. "Plus, you're supposed to be in the front row, waiting for Dad and me."

"I know. I'm goin'."

"Alright, let's get the bridesmaids and groomsmen in order

and lined up," Jessica announces with a notebook in her hand. "Emily and Todd, you're at the very end."

Trent's oldest brother stands next to Em, and the rest of them follow Jessica's instructions until all twenty of them are lined up correctly. Next, Jessica tells Trent and his parents when they'll walk down and lead them to the end of the aisle with Pastor Montgomery.

Riley and Elizabeth stand in front of me, both of them getting antsy and tired. My father kneels to their level and distracts them, making my heart soar at how great he is with kids. Since I'm the only child, my parents have been waiting on me for grandchildren.

"When the first couple is about halfway down, the next couple in line will start walking and so on. The matron of honor and best man will be the last ones down before the ushers roll out the aisle runner. Then Riley will walk Elizabeth to where Mrs. Bishop will be waiting in the second row and seat them. Once everyone's lined up in the front, the music will switch, and that'll be your cue, Kiera." Jessica steps closer toward me. "I'll make sure your train is straight and tell you when to go." She winks at me.

The butterflies in my stomach are swirling around rapidly, and I know it's just nerves. The moment I walk down and see Trent waiting for me, it's all going to finally set in that we're really getting married.

"Okay, let's do a first run!" Jessica snaps her fingers and goes to the head of the line. "The orchestra will start playing, and that'll be the first couple's cue to go. Take small steps, loop your arms into the guys', holding the bouquet with your other hand, and remember to smile!"

I chuckle at Jessica's overexcited tone, but she's done such a great job, and it's taken so much stress off my plate. My dad and I stay back as we wait for our turn. From down here, I can't see the aisle, so I know when I take those steps upward, I'll see Trent eagerly waiting for me.

"Jackson!" Jessica scowls, grabbing my attention. Oh God.

What'd he do now? I peek around Emily and see him causing a scene. My heart races as I think how he must be handling all this right now. I know I shouldn't worry about how he feels, considering all the opportunities he's had to confess his own feelings, but I know him well enough to know he's using whiskey as his normal coping habit.

Honestly, when I was a teenager and dreamed of my wedding day, I always imagined Jackson would be at the end of the aisle waiting for me. I had the whole thing planned out in my mind, but I was young and obviously naïve. I will always care deeply for Jackson, no matter what, but a part of me wonders how my life would've turned out had we crossed those boundaries.

"Jackson, straighten up, or I'll have no choice but to call Mrs. Bishop down here." Jessica's threat makes me chuckle because everyone knows Mama Bishop calls the shots 'round here. "And stop licking Faith's cheek."

"You got it, ma'am." Jackson throws her his infamous wink and cheesy grin, but he's a fool to think it'll have any effect on her.

"Just go." She rolls her eyes and motions for him and Mila to walk down.

I knew asking Jackson to be in our wedding party was a risk, but he's been a part of my entire life, and it didn't feel right not having him involved. Of course, Trent was against it, but he knew it was important for me to have his support, so he eventually gave in. However, now I'm wondering if it was the worst idea ever. Jackson barely makes eye contact with me anymore and always has a smartass comment to say about everything I do. I know getting engaged was a shock to him, considering the night Trent proposed he ended up in jail for being his normal idiot self, but as I've been saying to myself since the day Trent and I started dating, Jackson's had his chance. He had fifteen years to express his feelings or ask me out, or hell, make a damn move. I don't think my feelings for him have exactly been a secret, but instead of doing something about it, he

21

dated all my friends instead, making me think I wasn't good enough for him.

I couldn't wait forever, I remind myself when I start getting overwhelmed with emotion. I love Trent so much, and I know he's going to make me happy. He's sophisticated, smart, and has been up front about his feelings for me since day one. Trent loves me, and I love him.

"Okay, Kiera," Jessica says when it's just my father and me standing. "The orchestra will finish playing as soon as everyone's in place and ready. When the 'Wedding March' plays, everyone will stand, and that's when I'll motion for you to walk down."

"Got it." I smile, squeezing my dad's arm tighter. With the fake bouquet in one hand and my other arm looped through my dad's, we make our descent down the aisle. My eyes lock on Trent's, and we hold gazes until we make it to the end.

Pastor Montgomery walks us through the rest of the ceremony. I look around and try to soak this all in, but it all still feels so surreal. In twenty-four hours, I'll officially be Mrs. Trent Laken, and we'll be celebrating our love with our family and closest friends.

"Then I'll announce you as husband and wife, Trent will kiss his bride, and when the orchestra starts playing, you'll walk back down the aisle."

"You'll grab your bouquet first," Jessica reminds me. "That way the photographer can get the first shots of you two as husband and wife." She smiles.

Jessica insists on running through everything one more time. As we all walk down the hill to line back up, I pull on Jackson's arm and tug him toward me.

"Hey!" He stumbles, nearly tripping over his feet. As soon as he sees my face, he straightens and adjusts his shirt. "What?"

"What is wrong with you? How could you show up drunk?" I whisper-hiss, crossing my arms over my chest. Jackson notices the way it pushes my breasts up, and his gaze lingers there. "You better get your shit together. Or don't even bother showin' up tomorrow," I snap, walking away before he can respond.

Thirty minutes later, we're finally done rehearsing and back at my parents' house for the dinner. They set up tables inside and out on the patio to accommodate everyone.

As the night goes on, I've cried at least three times from people giving toasts and saying the sweetest things about Trent and me. It's really starting to sink in. This is my last night as a single girl. Tomorrow, I'll go to bed as a married woman.

"Let's go for a walk," a gravelly voice whispers in my ear from behind me, and I know it's Jackson before I even turn around and face him. He looks defeated as if he realizes everything is about to change. I furrow my brows and try to read his face, but all he offers is a nod toward the door and his hand.

Looking over my shoulder, I see most of our guests are outside sitting around the bonfire and drinking. The sun has set, and the stars and moon are the only sources of light.

"Okay," I agree, taking his hand.

We walk in silence as Jackson leads me down the path to one of the horse barns. I've always felt the electricity between us, and even falling for another man hasn't stopped that. I honestly don't think anything will at this point. Jackson has a piece of my heart, whether he wants it or not.

"Where are we goin'?" I ask, breaking the silence that's fueling my anxiety.

"Almost there," he says. A few minutes later, we're rounding the barn on the side that gives us the most privacy. My parents' house can't be seen from here because the trees and bushes obstruct the view.

"You're freaking me out, Jackson," I tell him when he stares down at the ground. "What is it?"

He finally lifts his head, his lower lip stuck between his teeth, and when I peer in his eyes, I see hunger and agony.

"Are you sure about this, Kiera?"

My eyes nearly pop out of my head. "What? Am I sure about

getting married?" I step back, needing the space between us before I do something stupid.

"Are you sure about marrying *him*?"

"Why are you asking me this?" I whisper. "I wouldn't be doing anything I didn't want to do, Jackson. You don't need to baby me."

He steps forward, closing the gap between us. I swallow at the closeness, needing the space from him, especially when I can smell his scent—a blend of whiskey and mountain spring soap.

"Are you happy?" he whispers. "I just want you to be happy. It's all I've ever wanted."

Jackson's confession has tears surfacing, and as much as I try to hold them back, they pour out. This is the side of Jackson he's only ever reserved for me. His softer, kinder side. The side that shows how much pain he's in. A pain he won't let me heal.

Jackson brings his hands to my face and brushes my tears away with the pads of his thumbs. He's cupping my cheeks so intimately, I almost forget to breathe.

"Answer me," he demands. "Are you happy?"

My hands wrap around his arms, and my nails dig into his skin as I silently plead for him to stop asking me that question. Jackson leans in and presses his forehead to mine as our breath mingles together.

"Jackson…" I say, trying to gain control of my emotions. "What are you doing?"

He swallows, pausing a moment before leaning back and looking into my eyes as if he's searching for an answer. "Something I should've done a long fuckin' time ago."

Without another breath, Jackson brings our mouths together in a heated and desperate kiss. His lips crash to mine, and I don't have enough willpower to push him away. I fist the fabric of his shirt and pull his body against mine until we're molded together. His warm lips taste like whiskey and beer, a dangerous combination, and when he swipes his tongue along my lower lip, I open for him.

Jackson pins me against the barn with his hands and hips, letting me feel his erection straining in his pants. It wouldn't take much for him to lift my dress and feel my arousal, knowing my panties are soaked with desperation and hunger. Moans and gasps echo through the air as over fifteen years of pent-up feelings surface and take over my emotions. This kiss isn't sweet and soft; it's rough and needy, just like him. Jackson's hand slides down to my breast and squeezes it in his palm, and I release the most unladylike moan that only encourages his hand to slide farther down.

Flashes of Trent and me circle in my mind, and I finally realize what I'm doing. What I'm doing to him. It's not right.

This is wrong.

"Jackson, stop…" I press my hands on his chest and push him back. He looks at me questioningly, his lips red and swollen from mine. "I can't do this."

He brushes a hand through his hair before scrubbing both hands down his face. "I shouldn't have done that. I'm sorry."

"You're sorry?" I mimic, my brows shooting up in disbelief. "How could you kiss me like that? On the night before my wedding?" My voice grows louder with anger. "What is wrong with you?"

"I-I said sorry. Jesus. You didn't exactly put up a fight," he shoots back at me.

"Well, my head is swirling with a variety of emotions right now. I wasn't thinking straight."

"Really?" He raises a brow. "And what about now?" He crosses his arms over his broad chest. I hate how he looks so damn good right now. And smug.

"I'm seeing clearly for the first time in a decade," I snap. "You're a selfish, egotistical, arrogant asshole," I spit out. "You wait till *now* to kiss me. Only a self-centered person would do that, knowing this should be one of the happiest moments of my life, and you needed to make it all about *you*. You're supposed to be my best friend! Well, you know what, Jackson Bishop? It's too late." I point my finger at him and dig it hard into his chest. "You're too fucking late."

Walking around him, I don't look over my shoulder as I make my way back to my parents' house, and then I wait until I'm alone in the shower to cry out fifteen years' worth of heartache.

CHAPTER TWO

JACKSON

I FUCKING hate standing in weddings.

I'm so sick of everyone getting married and forcing me to dress up or walk down the aisle with a smile on my face. The only good thing about attending is the free booze and drunk bridesmaids.

I love my family, but this wedding business is too much sometimes. First, my sister, Courtney, married Drew several years ago, then my youngest brother Alex and River got hitched two years ago, then Evan and Emily just this past summer, and now Kiera and Dr. Douchebag are getting married too.

Thank God John and Mila decided to elope over the summer, and I didn't get stuck with preparations or cleanup duty. They met earlier last year when Mila came to help him with baby Maize, then fell in love and got engaged last Christmas. She was hired as his nanny, but things heated up between them pretty quickly. We all fell in love with her, and she easily became a part of the family. I'm happy for them but so damn glad they didn't go through all the trouble of planning a wedding. I've seen firsthand how much stress it can cause.

Reaching into my vest for my flask of whiskey, I take a long sip and enjoy the burn as it coats my throat. I hate everyone in this room, and the only way I'm getting through it is if I'm loaded. When Kiera asked me to be in the wedding party, I laughed in her face, but then realized she was being sincere. After smacking me for laughing, I reluctantly agreed. I find it hard to say no to her after all these years of being friends.

Friends.

That's all we've ever been, and I know I'm to blame for that. Kiera made her feelings for me obvious years ago, but I wouldn't let myself act on them.

Instead, I dated and fucked every other girl. Including most of her friends.

Her leaving for college was supposed to be my saving grace. I'd hoped to be able to get over my feelings for her once and for all, but it did nothing to dull the ache I feel every time I think about her.

Kiera has always deserved so much more than me—so much more than I could ever provide her. The last thing I wanted to do was hurt her, and I knew if we crossed the boundaries of friendship, I'd ultimately end up ruining what we had, and our friendship would forever be jeopardized. I needed her too much to risk it, and if that makes me a selfish bastard, then so be it. Having Kiera in my life is a necessity, and whether it's her calling me out on my shit or just sitting around and talking, I wasn't willing to give that up because of how I've always felt about her.

Kissing her last night was long overdue, and I know she felt it just as strongly as I did even if she pushed me away.

But now it's her damn wedding day, and I'm standing in a room with her soon-to-be husband, Trent, and all the other groomsmen that consist of mostly his brothers and cousins. Thankfully, I know most of the bridesmaids, so I won't be alone for long. I'm walking down with my sister-in-law, Mila, and I plan to get as wasted as I can before the end of the I Do's.

"Can we do a few photos before y'all have to head out?" the wedding photographer, Lindsey pops her head in and asks. She's a stunning redhead, and I quickly glance at her left hand for a ring. Empty.

"I'm already dressed, but if you insist, I don't mind undressing for you." I speak up before anyone else has the chance. All heads turn toward me, but the only reaction I'm concerned about is Trent's, especially considering we're not on very good terms. Kiera told me he hired her, and she's a longtime family friend, which I'm pretty sure means former fuck buddy. Though I know he'd deny it if I asked.

Maybe I should ask just to see his jaw clench. It's quite amusing to rile up the tool bag.

"Watch your mouth, Bishop," Trent growls, and I smile in victory before flashing a wink at Lindsey. His face turns red as if he's contemplating on giving me a black eye, though he knows better.

I knew it.

"Let's do some in front of the barn since the ladies are still getting ready," Lindsey interrupts, plastering an awkward smile on her face.

The barn. The same barn I kissed Kiera against last night.

I needed one opportunity to see if she had any lingering feelings for me, and though my timing was shitty, I now know she does. Anyone who kisses another man the night before their wedding isn't as in love as they claim. I know I'm not being fair. I'm just as selfish and self-centered as she says, but it's for a good reason. Kiera isn't the type of girl you hit-it-and-quit-it with. She's the forever type, and I've known that since we were fifteen years old. I've never been able to give her what she needs or deserves, but that doesn't mean I haven't thought about it. Keeping my distance all these years gave me the Guinness World Record for blue balls.

"Okay, if you could all stand in one straight line and face me," Lindsey instructs, waving her finger around. "Trent in the middle and five of you on each side."

I line up as directed, thinking how stupid we all look in these vests. Trent's wearing a tan vest while the rest of us are wearing brown ones. They're paired with dark wash blue jeans and long-sleeve, button-up white shirts underneath. And if that's not country enough, we're all wearing tan cowboy hats.

At least we're not dressed up as penguins, so I can't complain too much. Still, I hate it.

"Alright, everyone look up here. Going to take four shots. Ready?" Lindsey holds her hand up, counting down, and then starts snapping away. She then directs us to make a V shape so Trent's in front, looking like a smug asshole. He deserves to have his face punched in, but I'm really trying to be on my best behavior for Kiera's sake.

"Great. Just a couple more," Lindsey announces. "Just the groomsmen for one shot and then Trent and the best man."

As I walk toward the other guys, I lose my balance and trip on a rock sticking out of the ground. I'm quick to catch myself, but not before Trent blurts out a comment.

"I knew you'd be a drunken mess. Should've never let Kiera invite your ass."

My hands ball into fists, the temptation to push him and put him in his place rising every second I'm forced to be near him.

"You wanna handle this like men, Laken? Or you gonna be a big ole pussy?" I step closer, ready to get in his face before a hand wraps around my wrist to pull me back.

"Walk away, Jackson." Mila's voice is soft but stern. If she wasn't my sister-in-law, I'd jerk my arm out of her grip and maul Trent's ass right here and now. That guy has been pushing me ever since he proposed to Kiera. It's as if he thinks he owns her now and tries to tell her what she can and can't do, and the thought pisses me off to no end. "It's time to head to the ceremony and get lined up," Mila informs me.

"We can take the rest of the shots after," Lindsey blurts out to break the tension.

I turn and face Mila whose arms are crossed over her chest, looking moderately pissed.

"What?" I furrow my brows.

She makes a big show of slapping her arms to her sides and huffing. "Really? You gonna give the groom a bloody nose before the wedding? What're you thinkin'?"

"That he'd look much better in red." I smirk.

"Let's go, alright? Jessica wants us to start heading up, and unless you want to watch her head explode, we better do as she says." Mila starts walking toward the row of trucks parked in the driveway, and I follow, knowing I'm supposed to drive half the groomsmen up there.

Once I'm to my truck, Mila pulls on my arm before I'm able to hop in the driver's seat. "Jackson, wait."

"What?" I turn and look at her, studying her face of concern.

"Give me your flask." She holds her hand out like she's scolding a child.

"Not happening."

"Jackson Joseph Bishop," she blurts out, and I have to do a double take to make sure Mama didn't just walk up. "I know you've been drinkin', so just hand it over."

"Just because you married my brother doesn't give you the right to treat me like a kid. I'm not giving you my flask, so just put your little hand away and leave." Opening the truck door, I hop in and close it behind me before she can get another word out.

When I think she's left, I roll my window down and wait for the groomsmen to hop in the back.

"Kiera's really nervous," Mila says, showing back up. She rests her arms inside the window frame and gives me a look. "So if you're planning on doing anything stupid, just…don't. Okay?"

"What makes you think that?"

She cocks her head and narrows her eyes at me. "Best behavior, Jackson. I mean it."

"So…what, were you voted as my babysitter or something?" It all starts to click since she's the one I'm walking down with and isn't pregnant and emotional. She has no problem warning me.

"I lost a bet," she teases. "No more drinking until after the ceremony. Got it?"

Turning the key and revving the engine, I rest my elbow on the window frame and raise a brow. "No promises." Once the truck bed is full, I take that as my cue to leave. "See ya up there, Peaches."

She rolls her eyes at the new nickname I gave her. She's from Georgia, so it's only fitting, but I say it mostly to get a rise out of her.

I put the truck into reverse and drive up the gravel road that leads to the location of the ceremony. Dust and pebbles are all I can see in my rearview mirror. Five minutes later, we make it to the bottom of the hill.

Hordes of people flood the place, and I know Kiera well enough to know the massive guest list wasn't her idea. She's always said she wanted something small and intimate with close friends and family only. Kiera doesn't need to show off or pretend she's something she's not, which means this was all Trent's doing, and she probably gave in to make him happy.

Fuck. Another reason I should've punched him.

Grabbing my flask, I take another long swig. As the time approaches, I'm finding the courage I had to watch her get married to another man dissolve.

"Alright, y'all. I need you to line up just like we practiced," Jessica orders. "The ceremony will begin in about ten minutes. So don't run too far."

"Jackson, you clean up nice when you're not rolling around in the hay," my sister, Courtney, teases, giving me a side hug. "You reek of whiskey. Did you shower in it or something? Geez." She wrinkles her nose to emphasize her disapproval.

"Well you reek of baby poop, but you don't hear me complainin'."

"You're so rude!" Courtney swats me with a smile.

"Just doing my big brother duties." I try to give her a noogie like I used to when we were kids, but she's quicker than me and steps out of my reach.

"Do not touch my hair!" She points a threatening finger at me. "It took me two hours, and the last time I spent that much time on my hair was at my own wedding."

"Really? Could've fooled me," I taunt. Riling her up is the distraction I need right now.

"Jackson…" I hear Mila's warning tone behind me.

Oh c'mon.

"Yes?" I turn around too fast, and the world starts spinning.

"Everyone is seated, and it's about to start," she informs me, coming to my side. I look and see Emily lined up with Trent's brother. River and Courtney and everyone else are standing and ready to start as soon as Jessica gives us the go-ahead.

"I'm here, aren't I?"

"Just checkin'. Better not hurl on my dress either," she quips while giving me a death glare as if she actually thinks I would.

"Trust me, I haven't had nearly enough whiskey for that. Check back in a few hours, though." I wink, and she rolls her eyes at me. Speaking of which, I reach for my flask again and take another swig. Then another. I'm gonna need it to get through this.

The orchestra changes songs, and that's when I see Trent escorting his mother up the hill to walk her down the aisle. His father is behind him; they're both looking at their son like he's made of gold.

"You're crying already?" River teases Emily who's standing behind me. I look over my shoulder, and sure enough, Emily is tearing up.

"I'm just so happy for her. She's waited her whole life for this moment." Emily's words slice right through my heart, and that's when it really hits me.

Fuck. I can't do this.

I can't watch her marry this guy.

The alcohol is rushing through my veins, and I know I'll do something stupid if I see her up there with him. My heart is

33

beating so hard and fast, I can feel it thumping in my chest like it's going to explode any second.

"Kiera and her father are going to come out shortly, so the guests don't see her beforehand," I hear Jessica tell one of the bridesmaids. "Okay, first couple. Once the orchestra transitions to the next song, that'll be your cue to go."

My palms start to sweat, and I feel like I can't breathe. My heartbeat is drumming in my ears now, and I know I can't go through with this. I'm pretty sure I'm having some kind of anxiety attack and will pass out if I don't catch my breath.

"Jackson, stop fidgeting," Mila whispers. "We're walking down in less than two minutes."

"I can't," I hiss, undoing the buttons on my neckline. "I can't do this."

Stepping out of line, I walk toward my truck with Mila in my shadow. As soon as I make it to the gravel, I walk faster to my truck and jump in.

"What are you doing?" Mila asks with urgency and concern. "Are you insane?"

"Tell Kiera I'm sorry. I can't watch her get married." I shut the door and start the engine and back out before she can respond.

CHAPTER THREE

KIERA

I CAN'T BELIEVE it's almost time.

My heart is racing so fast with nerves and excitement, but I know the moment I see Trent standing at the end of the aisle waiting for me, the anxiety will vanish.

Or so I hope.

I woke up this morning feeling like I could sleep for twenty hours because I was far too excited to get any rest. From the moment we got engaged, we started planning the details of the wedding. The past six months have been consumed by wedding favors, cake flavors, and catering dishes. Now the day is finally here.

I slept over at my parents' house last night in the same bedroom I grew up in, and I'm pretty sure that's part of the reason I couldn't sleep well. I'm used to being in bed with Trent and hearing his cell go off at random times for emergencies. But it was only for one night, and after today, we'll spend every night together.

"Kiki." I hear my dad's voice and three soft knocks on my door. "Can I come in?"

"Yeah, Dad."

He opens it and smiles. "I made breakfast. Your favorite."

"Eggs Benedict with smoked salmon?" I ask.

"Of course! Would I make my Kiki anything else?"

Smiling, I walk toward my dad and wrap my arms around him. "Thanks, Dad. That sounds so good right now." I laugh, knowing I won't have time to eat much throughout the day between getting ready, taking pictures, thanking the guests for coming, and then, of course, the dance.

"You ready for today?" he asks as I walk with him to the kitchen. I'm still in my pajamas, but I know Jessica and Emily will be here shortly to start getting ready.

"I think so…I'm excited. Anxious and nervous, too. But it feels surreal that today is the day," I admit, taking a seat at the table.

Mom comes barging in, rushing to give me a hug. "You're going to break a bone, Mom," I tease, willing her to loosen her grip.

"You're glowing." She kisses my forehead. "I can't believe my baby is getting married and going to have babies of her own soon."

"Mama…" I warn with a grin. "Can we get through the honeymoon first before you start naming my future children?"

"I'll give you through breakfast. That's it." She makes three plates before setting them down in front of us. "Make sure you fill up. I barely ate on my wedding day," she reminds me like she has a handful of times already.

"I will. It smells delicious." I smile at my dad, thankful for these last moments with my parents before the house is jam-packed with the wedding party.

Since the ceremony is on the hill, the bridesmaids are coming here to finish getting ready and help me get dressed. The groomsmen will show up dressed and ready to go, but they'll most likely do some pre-ceremony drinking and take pictures beforehand. But as per tradition, Trent and I won't see each other until I walk down the aisle.

After I get out of the shower, Emily and Jessica come over and start gushing about every little detail. I just want to sit back and soak it all up.

My hairdresser and makeup artist arrive shortly after. I decide to have my hair pulled back in a modest low bun with some loose strands framing my face. The veil is pinned into my bun and drapes down my back.

"Oh my goodness," my mother squeals. "That veil looks stunning on you." She leans in to kiss my cheek.

"Thanks, Mama." I smile sweetly, knowing she's so proud of me. "I already know you're going to be the most beautiful bride in the world."

Her comment makes me laugh, but I thank her anyway.

My makeup artist applies a more natural look, but she gives me red lips and puts a glowing bronzer on my cheeks.

"Now…" Katie says, flicking an eyeshadow brush between her fingers. "Do you trust me?" I want to say yes, but the mischievous grin on her face tells me otherwise.

"I'm not sure…" I tease hesitantly. "Why?"

"Well, I want to do a purple hue for your eyes. It's a great color for green eyes, but I'll blend it nicely with a cream shadow. I promise it'll look elegant with a small pop of color."

"Ooh, I love that idea!" Emily blurts out. "That'd look so pretty with your hair too."

I sigh, knowing I won't win a battle with these two anyway. "Okay, I trust you!" I smile. "Purple is my favorite color anyway, so let's do it!"

Katie finishes my makeup, and soon everyone is freaking out, eagerly waiting for me to put on my dress to complete the whole look.

"Okay, I'm coming out," I announce from the bathroom.

I open the door, lifting my dress slightly to step out and wait for their approvals.

"Wow…"

"Oh my God!"

"Stunning!"

A round of compliments echo throughout the room, and I'm close to tearing up at the way they're all admiring me.

"I can't believe it," I say when I study myself in the full-length mirror. "It's really happening."

Emily wraps her arms around my waist and hugs my back. "You deserve all the happiness in the world, Kiera. I'm so excited for you."

I place my hand over hers and squeeze. "I love you. Thank you again." We smile at each other in the mirror.

"Oh! I need my garter. Would you mind grabbing my purse from my truck?"

"Yeah, absolutely!" She pats my shoulder. "Don't forget your boots," she reminds me.

I head back to the bathroom where I left them and wait for her return. "Here ya go." She hands me my bag. "Want help?"

"No, I got it. Would you mind giving me a minute, though?" I ask, needing a few to myself before it's time to go.

"No problem, babe. Holler if you need me."

Reaching to the bottom, I dig for the garter I stuffed in there last night and pull it out along with a cream envelope I didn't know was inside. I quickly slide the garter over my boot and up my leg to my thigh before I settle it into place.

"What is this?" I mutter to myself. The envelope is sealed, and only my name is written on the front. For a moment, I wonder if Trent slipped it in here before I left yesterday as a surprise.

Once I rip it open and pull out the note, I glance over the handwriting and know it's not from him.

Dear Kiera,

This letter is long overdue, but now that you're engaged, I have no choice but to let you go. I know you've never been mine, but you've been my best friend for as long as I can remember, and it feels like an era is about to end.

When we were just teenagers and Tanner asked you out, and you looked at me before telling him yes, I knew then that you'd always have my heart, no matter what. Tanner had you, but you were always mine. He was the best fit for you—I always knew that—but it didn't make things easier especially seeing you two together all the time. It killed me. I loved you, but he was the better pick for you.

Tanner and I had a history. He was one of my best friends too, but he's always had a better head on his shoulders. Straight-A student, never in trouble, from a family of doctors and therapists, and was already writing his valedictorian speech two years before graduation. Hell, I think he already wrote his college essays before our sophomore year of high school. He was exactly the type of guy you deserved, so I never intervened. I watched on the sidelines as Tanner took you out on dates to dances and special romantic dinners. I helped him plan most of them because I knew all your likes and dislikes. Every gift, every movie suggestion, every birthday card he wrote you—I helped him because you deserved the best.

You still deserve the best, Kiera.

I knew growing up that all I'd amount to is being a rancher. It's all I've known, and I've always been passionate about horses and riding. I love what I do, so I don't regret the choices that led me here, but in my heart, I knew you deserved more than I could ever offer. You deserved to be shown the world, to travel and explore, to live a life without reservations.

A struggling, overworked rancher would never be able to give you that, Kiera. I'm a selfish man; I realize that, but there was always one thing I couldn't be selfish about, and that was you. Even at fifteen years old, I knew that. You'll always be the one that got away, and I'll always be the dumbass who let you.

I want nothing more in life than for you to be happy. Your happiness is all that's ever mattered to me, and if marrying Trent makes you happy, then I'll know I did right by keeping my distance.

I hope you know how much I love you, how much I've always loved you, and that everything I did was always for you, even if it seemed like the opposite at times. I've done a lot of stupid shit and things I'm not proud of. Getting into fights, one-night stands, being arrested, caught stealing, driving without a license—but hurting you will always be my biggest regret. I did most of that stupid shit to numb the pain I felt, and though it's no excuse, I'm still so fucking sorry I ever hurt you. There were times when the disappointment was so evident on your face that I wanted to drink a six-pack of beer and then hit every empty bottle over my head until I passed out. It was the only way to keep you from having feelings or waiting for me, and I hated myself for it.

I know I've rambled a lot and as you can probably guess, I've had a few beers and shots, but it was the only way I could let myself be vulnerable enough to write this.

It's time to let you go. I need to. You're not mine, but I'll always be yours.

My heart will absolutely shatter watching you marry another man, but I've earned it. You deserve all the happiness, Kiera. Even if I'm not the reason for it.

I was never the right guy for you, but you were always the right girl for me.

I will always love you, Kiera.

—Jackson

Most of the letter is covered in my tears before I even finish reading the last word.

My throat is burning while I try holding back the sobs that are threatening to release.

I can't believe this. I can't believe him.

How? *Why?*

I don't know how to feel. I want to be so mad at him right now. But a part of me—the part that's always been reserved for him—is breaking. I've waited over fifteen years for Jackson, and before that kiss last night, I was certain the feelings weren't mutual.

Some part of me had always wished and wondered while dissecting every little sign. Then he'd have another random girl on his arm, and I figured I imagined it all.

But that kiss.

I'd never been kissed like that before. It was nothing like our first kiss, which was sweet and a little awkward. No, this kiss had every built-up emotion over the past decade poured into it. It was intense and filled with hunger. I've dreamt about his lips and hands on me for as long as I can remember. Even when I tried to stop loving him, dated other guys, fell in love with other people, left for college to get over him—it never worked. I continued to fantasize about how it'd feel to just have Jackson for one night. I knew I'd be risking my heart, but a part of me always believed I'd rather have experienced him once than not at all.

Except after he kissed me against the barn last night, I felt anger. Anger that all those feelings were bubbling to the surface again. Anger that he could still have that effect on me after the way he's treated me. Anger that I didn't stop it sooner but also because I stopped it at all.

My feelings are so fucking messed up that I can't sort them out anymore.

God. How could he do this to me? I don't know when he wrote this letter, but he mentions me being engaged, which means it was within the past six months. How could he say all these beautiful things and say he wants me to be happy, but then drop this bomb the morning of my wedding day?

Just like I said last night, he's a selfish, self-centered, asshole. Why wait until this moment? Doesn't he know he's hurting me now more than ever?

My heart rate pulsates in my wrist as I hold the letter tightly between my fingers. The mixed feelings and emotions flowing through me have me feeling nauseous.

"Kiera, you okay in there?"

"Just feeling a little queasy. I'll be okay. Be right out."

"What's wrong?" Emily barges in without knocking, and I quickly scramble to fold the letter up.

"Nothin', just needed a few minutes alone. To calm my nerves and all." I keep my eyes locked on hers in hopes she doesn't notice how weird I'm acting.

"What's that?" She reaches for the envelope that has my name written across it. Before she can grab it, I hurry and shove it into my boot.

"What's goin' on?" She folds her arms over her chest and narrows her eyes at me. "You look strange."

"It was just a letter from Trent," I lie, hating that I'm being dishonest to my best friend, but I can't get into this with her right now. Not minutes before we're supposed to leave.

"Aww…that's sweet! Better be all about how damn lucky he is to be marrying you while promising you the world," she teases, smiling wide with pride.

"It was." I choke back a sob as I think about the letter and the truths it held. How am I supposed to do this right now?

"Okay, I need to go meet everyone up the hill. You okay? Want me to stay behind until you have to come up?" Emily asks.

"I'm great! I promise! It's just really starting to settle in, and I'm getting emotional, but I swear I'm ready." Standing up, I grab my handkerchief and dab under my eyes. "You go ahead. Dad and I will be up shortly."

"Okay." Emily smiles, placing her hands on my bare shoulders. "I love you. Enjoy this moment, okay? Everything goes by so fast, but it's all going to be beautiful and perfect."

Her words are music to my ears and just what I needed to hear. "I love you too. Thank you again. I'm so lucky to have you by my side for this."

She pulls me in for a tight hug before releasing me and grabbing her bouquet. "Meet you up there," she says over her shoulder, giving me an encouraging wink.

After taking a few minutes to calm my nerves, I stand and head out of the bathroom.

"Kiki…" My dad's deep voice startles me as he opens my bedroom door. "You look stunning, sweetheart."

"Thank you, Dad." I smile. "It's hard not to feel beautiful in this dress."

"I wasn't talking about the dress." He winks. "You ready for your chariot to take you up? Your groom is waiting." He holds his arm out for me to take.

"I'm ready."

My mother comes in and smiles. She's so damn happy. Inhaling a deep breath, I walk with Dad to his truck and hop in with Mom behind me to stuff my dress inside.

"Meet you up there, baby. I love you." Mom kisses my cheek before shutting the door. She's driving up with my uncle who's going to usher her down the aisle before the wedding party.

Dad starts the truck and drives us there. Butterflies swarm in my stomach, and my nerves are so intense, I hope I can calm down before the "Wedding March" starts playing.

As soon as we park, I see Emily and Trent's brother getting ready to walk down. Riley and Elizabeth are with Jessica, and as soon as she directs them to start, I know that's my cue to get ready.

My dad and Jessica come to my side and help me out. "You look amazing," she tells me, and I smile in return. I'm not sure any words would come out even if I opened my mouth and tried.

Jessica hands me my bouquet, and I grip it tightly, feeling my palms sweat as she fans out my train and brushes her hands along the skirt. The orchestra is still playing, and I know once the next song starts, it'll be my turn.

"You ready for this?" Jessica whispers.

"Yeah, I'm good." I suck in a deep breath.

I link my arm through my dad's and watch as Jessica motions for the orchestra to wrap it up. The "Wedding March" begins, and my heart drops. It's time.

As we make our way toward the front, everyone stands, and

as soon as my eyes land on Trent, a wide smile spreads across my face.

He looks so damn handsome, and the nerves start to slowly fade away as he focuses all his attention on me. I try soaking it all in and smile as we walk toward Trent. My attention is glued to him while our guests watch me. My dad clasps my hand that's on his arm, and when I look up at him, and our eyes meet, I can see how proud of me he is.

As I stand next to my dad at the end of the aisle, I lock eyes with Trent again and see a smug expression I don't understand. It's then that I look at the groomsmen lined up and notice Jackson isn't there.

Oh my God.

The kiss. The letter. And now he's not here.

My throat goes dry and tight. *Where the hell is he?*

The pastor speaks as soon as the orchestra finishes, but I don't hear what he says because my mind is spinning out of control. Why would Jackson do this to me? Why would he wait for *this* moment to tell me his true feelings? I can't sort these thoughts out, and when my father speaks up to give me away, my heart thumps so damn hard in my chest as if to protest it all. Deep down, I know this isn't right. My gut instinct over the past few months hits me harder now more than ever. I've ignored a lot of it, hoping the stress of the wedding planning was giving me these doubts, but now I know for sure.

Once I pass my bouquet to Emily, Trent takes my hand and leads me to the front where the pastor is standing. I start to panic as the realization that *I can't do this* hits me. I can't do this without Jackson here.

John's standing with Maize in his arms, and he's watching me. Our eyes meet, and I give him a questioning look, and as if he knows exactly what I'm silently asking, he shakes his head with a frown and shrugs.

Pastor Montgomery directs the guest to be seated with a smile.

"Welcome to the nuptials of Trent Laken and Kiera Young. It's a gorgeous day for a wedding and an outside ceremony. I can feel the love surrounding this couple, and I have no doubt that even if was raining out, they'd be up here exchanging their vows. Now, me, on the other hand, I'd be requesting a rather large umbrella."

The guests' laughs echo throughout, but I can barely process his words. I should be thinking about Trent and our future together. Instead, all I'm thinking about is Jackson and how much of a mistake it'd be to marry Trent when I'm not one hundred percent positive this is what I want.

"I'm sorry…" I blurt out over the pastor's words.

"What?" Trent's head snaps toward me. "What's wrong, Kiera?" he whispers.

Blinking, I look at him before releasing his hands, and my arms fall to my sides. "I'm so sorry, Trent. I can't do this." The words roughly come out as I try to hold my composure and not cry. I can't believe what I'm saying right now.

"Kiera, what are you talkin' about?" he firmly asks, leaning in so the guests can't hear our words.

I lick my lips and inhale a deep breath. "I can't marry you."

Before he can respond, I grab ahold of my dress and walk away.

I can feel everyone's gaze on me as I run down the aisle, and it's not until I hit the bottom of the hill that the tears roll down my cheeks at the realization of what I just did.

"Kiera!" I hear Emily yell behind me. "Kiera, wait!"

I look over my shoulder and see a panicked and worried Emily as I rush toward the gravel driveway. She's going to kill me for this; I already know. What I just did is unforgivable, but I couldn't follow through with it without talking to Jackson first.

"Kiera, take my keys," she shouts. Turning to face her, she rushes toward me and hands me a set of keys. "Take Evan's truck. It's over there." She points behind me.

"How'd you know?"

"I knew the second I saw your face in the bathroom, and then when Jackson left…let's just say I had a gut feeling." She flashes a small, sympathetic smile. "I'll take care of everything here. Don't worry."

"Thank you." I quickly wrap my arms around her, then run over to the truck before guests begin to leave. I'm sure Trent and my family are humiliated, and I know I'll have to deal with that soon enough, but right now, I need to find Jackson.

CHAPTER FOUR

JACKSON

EIGHT MONTHS BEFORE THE WEDDING

I ROLL out of bed and realize I'm late *again*, which means if John is feeling better today and is at the B&B, I'm going to hear him bitching at me like he's our father. I'm used to it, though, considering we're twins and have worked together all our lives. Since he's always been the much more responsible and boring twin, his ass chewings barely faze me anymore. His words go in one ear and out the other—according to him and my brothers— because I don't care what they have to say. Ever since John found out he was a dad last year, he's moved to a whole new level of responsible. I'm trying my best to tread lightly with my tardiness, but it's pretty much impossible.

I brew a pot of coffee, needing something to jolt me awake. I drank too much whiskey and tossed and turned for the past four hours, so I feel like a zombie—a hungover one at that.

As I'm standing in the kitchen wanting the coffee to hurry the hell up, my phone buzzes, and I look down and see a text from John saying he's still sick with the shits and throwing up.

Jackson: I can bring some adult diapers over for you.

John: Bring something. It's coming outta both ends.

Jackson: Doesn't it usually?

Jackson: Will do. Feel better.

I smile, knowing I'll get to give his assistant hell this morning after all. It's one of my favorite pastimes, especially this early in the day. She's not a morning person, which cracks me up considering she works at a B&B that requires her to be here before the sun rises.

Once I pour some coffee in a travel mug, I head outside and start my walk over to the B&B. Each time I exhale, my warm breath creates a cloud of smoke, and with each step, the frost crunches beneath my boots. The sun hasn't even woken up yet, and I'm already behind on my daily tasks.

When I moved out of my brother Alex's house a couple of years ago, I promised myself I'd finish remodeling the old cabin close to the B&B that was in disrepair because I needed a place of my own, but then I moved in with John and didn't worry with it. Relationships were never our thing, and I thought we'd live together for a few years at least. Then life happened, and things changed, especially when a baby was brought into the picture.

So I moved into the ranch hand quarters, which was like a frat party every night. After not getting sleep for a month, a fire was lit under my ass to finish my house. I *almost* felt guilty bringing women back to the ranch hand quarters, considering a bunch of guys live there, and they're not always the cleanest. Still, I continued to sneak chicks in and out like I did when I was a teenager. As long as they kept quiet, we wouldn't get caught, except it was easier said than done, especially while in my bed.

My house is a little farther away from the B&B than John's, but it's still within walking distance. I could drive, but the morning chill helps wake me up before I start my chores, especially when I've been up drinking all night.

Soon I'm walking up the back steps of the B&B, and my exhaustion feels like it's finally caught up with me. My restlessness and wandering mind have made me a hot ass mess, which is the norm these days. The only person to blame is Kiera Young. Lately, she's been driving me fucking crazy and has for as long as I can remember. But now that she's getting serious with her boyfriend—who I hate with a fucking passion—our friendship has changed, and it's been bothering the shit out of me.

Once inside the B&B, I notice how eerily quiet it is. The guests are still sleeping soundly, which gives me time to drink my coffee. I complete some of John's morning duties to help Nicole out a bit before she gets here. Once the coffee's dripping and the breakfast area is set, I see Nicole sneaking in through the front door. At first glance, I know she thinks I'm John, and I take the golden opportunity to give her a hard time.

Crossing my arms, I look at the clock on the wall, then back at her.

"You're late." I keep my tone dry, perfectly pulling off John's demeanor.

"I thought you weren't coming in today?" She looks confused, and I almost think my cover is blown, and that maybe she realizes I'm fucking with her. John must've texted her too. Of course, his responsible ass did, or he didn't trust me to actually tell her.

"I changed my mind. Feeling a lot better, actually. Also, the next time you're late, I'm writing you up. Don't you understand the importance of being on time? We have a job to do here, Nicole. Guests to attend to." I try to think back to all the times John has given me his boring ass speech about running a business and *blah, blah, blah.*

"Yes, sir. I'm really sorry. The fog was terrible this morning, and I didn't want to hit a deer or something," she explains.

After I catch a glimpse of the serious look on her face, I burst out into laughter. "I'm just shittin' you, Nic."

Nicole walks up to me and punches me as hard as she can in the arm.

"You're a dick, Jackson. I swear. Practically gave me heart palpitations."

"I don't know how, after all this time, you can't tell us apart. I'm the better lookin' brother. It's obvious."

"I really hate you," she says with a laugh, shaking her head as she walks toward the office, and I take it as my cue to go. Nicole has been working at the B&B for the past few years and was a godsend when John had to take time off after Maize showed up. We have an unspoken agreement that she does what she's supposed to do, and I'll do the bare minimum at the B&B, and we won't get in each other's way. So far, it's worked out perfectly when John needs off.

After she's got a handle on what needs to be done, I walk down the path that leads to the barn and find some of the horses waiting impatiently in their stalls to be fed. Their fur is thick, and they love the cool weather. It sure beats the summer temperatures.

Once I've lined the buckets and filled them with grain, I let out a loud whistle, and a few horses trot in from the pastures. I slip a pair of leather gloves on my hands and grab the metal handles on the buckets. I walk around, pouring feed into the troughs and stacking the empty buckets on top of one another. Once the horses eat, they mosey their way out to the pasture. Considering today is slow as far as lessons and trail riding, I do the not-so-glamorous work of cleaning and oiling the saddles until Kiera shows up to pick up a gelding we purchased from auction.

I've been waiting for this day all week. Though we don't hang out as much as when we were teenagers, I'm grateful I get to see her for work. It's the highlight of my week, though once she started dating Trent, she often acts like it's more of a chore. Her smartass mouth has only gotten worse over the years, and she's become fiercer with age, which only makes her more attractive and off-limits. I've come to the conclusion she wants her wild horse spirit tamed, and I'm convinced her pussy ass boyfriend won't be able to do it.

As soon as I hear the rumble of her truck traveling down the rock driveway that leads to the barn, I lean against the opening of the door and wait. I study her as she climbs out of the truck, lost in her own world, not even realizing I'm watching her every move. Her strawberry blonde hair is pulled up into a high ponytail, and she's wearing tight jeans that hug all her curves. As if she's teasing me, she stands on the bumper of her truck and bends her body over the tailgate, showing off her perfectly round ass. If I could take a picture right now, I would. Before she notices me staring, I walk out to meet her at the truck.

"Mornin'." She hops off the bumper with a smile and throws the extra lead ropes over her shoulders. When I make eye contact, I notice she's even wearing makeup.

"Got dressed up for me?" I ask, teasing her.

She playfully rolls her eyes, and I see the hint of blush hit her cheeks. "Trent's taking me out to lunch later. We're heading out for a Valentine's Day getaway tomorrow. I can't wait."

Just the sound of his name on her lips puts me in a bad mood, and I'm sure she notices my blood boiling. I swear she mentions him just to get a rise out of me.

"I don't know what you see in that loser. There's somethin' about him I don't like," I tell her as I turn around and walk toward the barn, not giving her a second glance. But damn, she smells so pretty.

"He's a nice guy, Jackson. Isn't that what you said I always needed? A *nice* guy. Someone who treated me right?" I look at her, and for a moment, I see the girl who used to drink stolen whiskey with me in our spot by the makeshift firepit surrounded by hay bales. Those days are long gone.

"Trent *isn't* a nice guy. He's a snake in the grass waiting to strike. He looks at you like you're a piece of goddamn meat," I tell her, though she's still following me.

"At least someone does," she mumbles under her breath, and I'm sure those words were meant for me. I stop and turn around and take four steps forward until the space between us is gone. Her breath hitches as we stand face-to-face. I can smell the sweetness of her soap and shampoo, and if I weren't such a chicken shit, I'd finally make a move.

"You deserve better than him. We both know that," I say matter-of-factly.

"By your standards, no one will ever be good enough for me, and I'll die single and alone with fifty horses," she says, looking into my eyes, and I swear she can see right through me. Not able to stand there another second, out of fear of doing the unpredictable, I turn on my heels and head through the corral toward the barn that's set in the back. I hear her groan behind me, and it actually makes me smile that she gets just as frustrated as I do.

Once we're inside the barn, Kiera falls in step beside me. We walk to the last stall where I locked up the new horse that needs to be trained, and I lean over the stall door and give Kiera the rundown on him.

"He's almost three years old and was doing halter training with his previous owners. His name is Chief, and he's pretty good at longing. I haven't tried to saddle him yet, so I think that's probably where you'll want to start after building that trust," I explain, but she already knows all this. Though I'm more than capable to train the horses on the ranch myself, I send them to Kiera because she's good at what she does, and it allows me to see her. Plus, I don't have a lot of time with helping run the bed and breakfast, giving lessons and trail riding, then acting as a backup for the ranch hands when Dad is shorthanded.

She glances at Chief, then back at me. "I love quarter horses."

"I know." I smile, but I don't dare tell her that's the reason I keep buying them.

Kiera opens the stall, walks in, and holds out her hand where she's tucked a treat. Chief immediately zeros in on it and lazily walks over to her. Once he's close, she runs one hand over his fire engine red coat and says sweet things as he takes the treat from her free hand.

"You're gonna be a good boy, aren't ya?" She clips the lead rope on the bottom of his halter and looks over at me and smiles.

"How long do I have?" she asks, opening the stall door.

"As long as you need to do your magic; you know that."

"I can him ready in a few months as long as he cooperates," she tells me as she leads Chief out of the stall and through the barn. I follow on the other side of the horse, wishing our time wasn't so rushed and we could go back to the way things used to be, but that's wishful thinking.

Once we're across the pasture and walking through the main barn, I go to the horse trailer and open the door. Kiera leads Chief inside with no problems.

After he's situated and Kiera comes out, I lock the door while she wipes her hands on her jeans and lets out a deep breath. It's awkward for a moment as neither of us really knows what to say. Ever since she started dating Trent last year, it's been like this between us. The tension is so thick it could be cut with a dull butter knife.

"Okay then. Well, I guess I'll call you if I need anythin'," Kiera finally says, but before she walks away, I grab her arm and pull her back to me.

"Do ya love him?" The words slip out of my mouth before I can stop myself. My heart races as I search her face, and I wait with bated breath. She hesitates for a moment, and it feels like the world around us freezes. I want her to say no. I want her to tell me she's just dating him because I'm too much of a bastard to admit how I feel, how I've *always* felt about her. I want her to tell me the truth because when I look into her eyes, I know it. I know she doesn't love him. Not the way she could love me.

She sighs and then almost forces herself to smile. "I do."

I give her a look, begging her to admit the truth.

"You really do? You see yourself being with him for the next fifty years? Trent's your future?"

She stands there and tucks her hands into her back pockets. She pinches her lips together and nods.

I shake my head. "If he ever hurts you, I'll fuckin' kill him," I add, before walking back toward the barn. Moments later, I hear the truck start and the rattle of the horse trailer making its way down the gravel, and all I can think is how I deserve to see her with another man. That's what I get for believing she'd be by my side, and that maybe one day, she'd be mine.

The rest of the day, I'm in a piss-poor mood, and to make matters worse, Alex gets the same stomach bug John has and is puking his guts up, so I have to go fill in for him after lunch.

As I make my way over to my parents' house where Dad is gonna pick me up, I look up at the dark clouds rolling in. I park the truck and get out and walk inside. Mama is rocking Riley to sleep. She sees the scowl on my face and shakes her head.

"Now what?" she asks quietly.

"Nothin'," I sharply tell her. "I don't wanna talk about it."

She lifts her eyebrows. "This have somethin' to do with Kiera and Trent?"

Bingo. Mama can see right through my moods. "No."

"I love you, son, but you're an awful liar." She loves calling me out on my shit.

I plop down in the recliner and wait for Dad to arrive, hoping he'll get here before Mama dissects my heart to pieces.

"You're so damn stubborn, Jackson. I don't know why you don't just finally admit how you feel before it's too late. We've been tellin' you this for about two decades, and you've done nothing but deny it. You're not a teenager anymore. Denying crushes isn't cute. If you keep it up, she's always gonna be known as the one who got away. You know her mama called me the other day and told me Kiera still talks about you?"

My interest is piqued, but I try to seem uninterested, though I'm failing. "Yeah? What'd she say?"

"What do you think she says?" Mama rolls her eyes at me, stands, and gently places Riley down on the couch with a blanket. She sits and puts her hand on him, so he stays right where he is.

"You should come to the cakewalk at the church on Valentine's Day."

I shake my head. "Not happening. I'd rather shovel shit for twelve hours straight."

"I might be able to make that happen," she gets in right as Dad opens the front door. I've never been so happy to see him. I give Mama a smile, Dad gives her a wave, and we make our way down the front steps.

"Imma need some help branding all the new calves over on the east side. You up for it?" Dad asks with a grin. I give him a head nod and don't speak on the ride over. It's okay, though, because Dad isn't a man of many words, which I'm happy about at the moment.

I stare out the window and think about all the times Kiera and I rode four-wheelers all over the ranch when we were teenagers. We spent every single day together, attached at the hip and inseparable, but all that seemed to change when she started dating my best friend, Tanner.

She had picked *him*, or it felt that way. Even though I never came out and told her about my true feelings or made a move, I thought about it many times. The three of us were all friends, and as soon as they got together, things got awkward and tense. *How could she pick him over me?* I thought, but deep down, I knew. She deserved a guy like him.

Tanner came from a family of unlimited money and could afford to do the nicest things for her. His parents took them on ski trips to Colorado, flew them to New York City to explore Times Square, and on expensive dates— all things I'd never be able to do. After I saw how happy she was with him and because he was my best friend, I'd considered her forbidden territory. I'd never be good enough for Kiera and denial took over. Hell, it's still here. After they broke up, she left for college, making it impossible for me to tell her how I felt. I'd never be the man to hold her back from her dreams, and her happiness is all I've ever wanted. Even she knows that.

Before I can get too lost in my thoughts, we make it to the east side of the property where the cattle and calves are being held in an open, fenced-off space. There are over a dozen people on horses keeping them within the perimeter. We started doing it this way instead of corralling so the herd would be less stressed.

Shadow, a large Arabian horse Courtney trained before she moved to California, is saddled and waiting for me. If I didn't know better, I'd say Alex played hooky because he knows I'm better at roping cattle than any of them, but then again, branding is what we live for. I've been so lost in my own world lately, I totally forgot this was happening. They've been getting up close to three in the morning to get this done and will for the next few days. I secretly hope he's sick tomorrow, too, so I can come out here again.

Once we're parked, Dad gives me a head nod, and I get out of the truck and walk over to the horse and check the cinch strap to make sure it's tight. Once I confirm it is, with one swift movement, I put my foot in the stirrup and grab onto the horn, then position myself on the saddle. Dad walks over and hands me some leather gloves, and I thank him because I don't want my hands to be torn up from the lasso. There's a handful of ranch hands scattered all around. Some are on horses, and others are branding the calves with the ranch logo, which is basically like a return address if these little assholes wander off.

As I look at my surroundings, a smile covers my face because I'm happy to be here doing this. It's part of that cowboy culture I crave every once in a while. It's easy to take this all for granted, but when I'm helping brand, it reminds me of old ranch traditions Dad keeps alive. It makes me so damn proud to be a Bishop.

One of my good friends, Colton, makes his way over to me wearing a shit-eating smirk. He's been working on the ranch for the past year, and we've gotten into plenty of trouble together. It all started when I moved into the ranch hand living quarters. He was the Robin to my Batman, and we drank enough to drown Gotham City.

"Wonderin' when I was gonna see ya again, ya bastard," he says with a chuckle. He's probably still pissed about all the whiskey I made him drink at my last party.

"The only bastard I see here is you," I throw right back at him with a grin. I lean down. "Are you the one who smells like shit out here or what?"

He grins. "Get off that horse and say it to my face, ya pussy."

My head falls back, and I burst out into hearty laughter before shrugging. "I am what I eat."

Once he's called over to help wrestle a calf to the ground, I get to work. Riding through the herd, I rope calf after calf with beautiful loops. I pull them out into the opening, and they're branded in less than a minute and running back to their mamas. This process goes on for hours, and I lose track of time, thinking about nothing but this. Thankfully, it's the only thing that gets Kiera off my mind—for now.

CHAPTER FIVE

KIERA

EVEN AFTER ALL THIS TIME, Jackson continues to get under my skin. As Trent sits in front of me at the diner, all I can think about is Jackson's question.

"Do you love him?" His words echo in my head.

Of course, I love Trent. We've been living together for seven months, and he's quickly become my other half. But when Jackson asked me, I hesitated, and I don't know why I would even pause for a second.

Ever since Alex's wedding, Trent and I have been inseparable. Though I wasn't looking for a relationship at the time, I gave him a chance. I walked out to the old barn with him just to chat, and all we did was discuss horses as we lay on the grass. Honestly, I did it to make Jackson jealous at first, hoping he'd see me leave with someone else, but what I didn't realize was he didn't even notice I had left. *Figures.* But that night, Trent and I shared something magical under the stars at the Bishop ranch. For the first time since returning from college nearly a decade ago, I let go of the *what-ifs*, and I ended up meeting the most perfect man in the whole state of Texas.

Trent treats me the way I've always deserved, and it's hard not to be madly in love with him. Somehow, he manages to say all the right things at all the right times, making me feel as if I'm the center of his universe. And he's not afraid to tell me how he feels, which is completely the opposite of Jackson. Without a doubt, Trent's the one for me, and one day, I hope to get married and start a family with him. However, even as I sit here, trying to think of all the happy moments Trent and I will make together, I can't stop thinking about Jackson and the way he looked at me today. My skin still burns from where he pulled me back to him—and has all morning. I try really hard to push Jackson out of my thoughts as I twirl the spaghetti on my fork, but it's useless.

"Are you okay?" Trent asks as he takes a sip of coffee. He's been talking for the past five minutes about a horse, and I feel guilty that I haven't listened to a word he's said, so I hurry and give him a smile.

"Yes, of course. Just thinking about all the things I need to do back at the ranch. The horses that were recently boarded, the ones that need rehabilitation therapy, and those that still need training. Making a mental list, that's all."

He places his hand on mine and squeezes.

"Have I told you that I love you today?" he asks with a wink. He tells me every morning when I try to sneak out of bed for work. Since I need to be at the ranch around five in the morning to help feed the horses, I'm usually up before him, unless he has an emergency call. But starting and ending our day with an *I love you* has become our routine since I moved in with him.

"I love you, too. Thank you." I squeeze his hand back.

"For what?" he asks, noticing how disinterested I am in my food.

"For always keeping me grounded."

He gives me a smile, then continues talking about a horse and putting shoes on, and this time, I really try to pay attention to him as I finish eating. He'd already eaten before arriving and just drank coffee the entire time. Once he pays, we get up to leave, and he takes my hand. Trent walks me out to the truck and pins me against it, his hot lips mingling with mine. I melt into his kiss as my back presses against the cool metal. Moaning against his mouth, he takes it as a cue and tugs at my bottom lip, then sucks on it.

"If you keep that up, you might miss your next appointment," I tease, feeling his growing erection against my stomach. All he does is chuckle.

"Mrs. Hanson would call my mama if I canceled. See you tonight around seven. Love you." He gives me one more kiss before he forces himself away. I lean against the truck as I watch him walk to his, reminding myself that this gorgeous man is mine and perfect for me.

"Love you, see you then," I tell him before I hop in my truck. As he backs out of the diner, I blow kisses at him, and he pretends to catch them. I crank the truck, turn on the heat because it's cold as hell, and sit there thinking about my day. It's gone from bad to good in about thirty minutes, and I'm half tempted to drive over to the Bishop ranch and kick Jackson in the balls because he deserves it for making me second-guess everything. Anytime I'm around him, this happens, and I hate it. He always throws me off my axis, and I have to figure out how to turn it off—how to stop him from affecting me. Trent and I have been together for almost two years, and while we've had our ups and downs, it's been nothing short of a fairy tale.

After five minutes have passed, I decide to call my cousin, Addie, to have her talk me off the ledge. She's been by my side for as long as I can remember and knows all my history with Jackson. If anyone understands my frustrations, it's her—she's heard them all.

The phone rings, and she picks it up after one time. Last year, she got married to the love of her life and found out soon after she was pregnant. She only has a few weeks until the baby is due and has been put on bed rest until then, which means she's available anytime I need a quick chat.

"Thank God. I've been wanting to call you all morning," she says breathlessly.

"So why didn't you?" I ask her, wishing she would have.

"I looked down at my vag, and I swear to God, Kiera. It's a fucking jungle down there. I can't take it anymore."

I burst into uncontrollable laughter, and I'm so happy I'm not driving because by how desperate she sounds, I might have lost all control. "Then shave it. It's simple."

"I had to use a mirror to see if I still had one. How the hell am I supposed to shave it? My stomach is so big there's no way I could even reach it very well. I need it waxed, *today*. And I need you to help me."

"Nope. No way. I love you like my sister, but there's no way I'm getting that close to your lady bits. No, ma'am. You better ask Landon." Now I'm the one with the serious tone. Her husband needs to help her out. It'd be too weird for me.

Addie starts laughing.

"What?" I finally ask her.

"I don't need you to help me *actually* do it. I need you to drive me there. I made an appointment at three. Pretty, pretty, pretty please. If I don't go, I may transform into Cousin It, but the pube version."

My mouth falls open. "The visual I just had, so disgusting."

"I'm desperate. So desperate. I'll even pay for yours too."

I stare out at the gray colored sky. "I've never done it before. Does it hurt?"

She giggles. "Only the first strip. I used to get them done religiously; like it was on a calendar just like my cycle, but then I got pregnant, and everything has been thrown off. Please? Pretty please. Like I will love you forever. I'm almost willing to promise you my firstborn."

I let out a sigh. "Okay. I gotta run back to the house and change clothes, and then I'll be over. Deal?"

"I love you. Oh my God. I love you so much." She makes kissy noises in the phone before we let each other go. I'm usually not scared of anything, but getting my crotch waxed kinda scares the crap out of me. I have to try everything once, I suppose.

After I make my way back to my house, I text my assistant trainer, Alexis, and let her know I'll be gone the rest of the afternoon. She's really great at making sure everything runs smoothly when I'm out on calls and understands and accepts my hectic schedule. Thankfully, Trent's house is pretty close to everything. Once I drive up the road and make it home, I hurry and wrap my hair up in a tight bun, then jump in the shower and change into some fresh clothes. Addie and Landon recently built their dream home close to my parents' ranch, so we're practically neighbors now. As soon as I turn down the dirt road that leads to her house, my heart begins to rapidly beat. This happens to me anytime I randomly think about Jackson, and there's one person to blame. Just the fact he still affects me makes me hate him. It's so frustrating.

As soon as I put the truck in park, Addie is out the front door, walking toward me. When I see her baby bump, I start smiling. She climbs inside and lets out a deep breath as she buckles.

"What?" she asks with a grin.

"You're so adorable."

Instantly, I get the evil eye. "I cannot wait until you're knocked up. Any day now."

"Do not jinx me. Wedding first, then seven babies." I let out a laugh before putting the truck in reverse and heading toward San Angelo. I'm quiet on the drive over, and Addie notices.

"What is it now?" She looks at me as if she's reading my mind.

I sigh, hating that she knows me so well. "Jackson asked me today if I loved Trent," I finally tell her. "It's been bothering me."

"For crying out loud," she says. "He had his chance. Why does he even care?" Addie has been telling me to get over him since I left for college, and I'm pretty sure I convinced myself I had, but every once in a while, doubt rears its ugly head.

"I don't know. But the look on his face. It's like he almost…"

"He wasn't going to tell you anything, Kiera. He's too stubborn, and he knows you're with Trent. Jackson's an asshole

62

most of the time, and he hates Trent with a passion, but he'd never disrespect you while you're with someone. His mama taught him better than that," she tells me just as she has time and time again.

"I know. Why do I keep going back to this?" I want to slam my head against the steering wheel.

"Because every time you see him, it's a constant reminder of what you two didn't have. I'm sure it's not easy."

"But he was my best friend in the whole world, and there were years when we didn't spend a day apart. *Years*. It's hard to forget someone who's such an integral part of your childhood. We're friends, and I could never just cut him off," I admit.

"Friends who want to fuck and who have wanted to for the past fifteen years."

I huff. "I don't think I like the pregnant version of you. That tiny filter you once had has disappeared. Addie's filter, oh where have you run off to?" I glance over at her and smile.

"Landon's told me the same thing. It's the baby. I swear, it's just made me insensitive." She laughs.

"Do you think I'm going crazy?" I ask her.

"I think your relationship with Trent is getting more serious, and you're freaking out about it. That's the honest truth." Addie grins, and when I look over at her, she gives me a wink.

"You're right. I just feel like he's planning on proposing anytime now, and while we've been together for almost two years, and I'm ready to move to the next level, it just seems as if everything is going by so fast. Like, when did you know Landon was the man for you?"

Her eyes get all dreamy as she thinks about Landon, and I love that she found love. "You just know deep down inside who you're supposed to be with. You can feel it in your bones. Every time I look at Landon, there's not a single doubt in my body that he's my soul mate. It's weird. Like we've known each other forever," she continues. "I'm sure you feel that way about Trent."

I smile and nod. "I do, but…"

"Don't you dare add a 'but' to that sentence," she playfully warns as I pull into the parking lot of the salon.

"You don't even know what I was going to say!"

Addie stares at me. "You were going to say you feel that way about Jackson too."

I sit silently for a moment. There's no fooling her. "No, I totally wasn't."

She turns her body toward me. "Then what?"

"It's stupid. Enough about Jackson. Time to take care of your jungle." I smile, and she claps her hands.

"Finally! Here, take this." Addie hands me an ibuprofen.

I look down at it.

"It's to help with the pain." I expect her to laugh, but she doesn't.

"You are seriously making me not want to do this."

She rolls her eyes, and I take the pill with a sip of water, then we get out of the truck and walk inside the salon. They lead us to a back room, and Addie asks me to stay for hers to see if I want to get one too. Considering I've never been, I agree.

"You're not some freak who gets off on pain like this are you?" I ask Addie, and she chuckles. All I do is shake my head.

Once she's undressed and is situated on the table with a covering, an older lady walks in with a grin. It's hard not to smile at Addie's cute belly.

"So what are we doing today, dear?" she asks as she puts on some rubber gloves.

"I want a Brazilian. I want it all gone," Addie tells her, and the woman isn't fazed by this, though I'm pretty sure my eyeballs are ready to fall out of my head. She told me a bikini wax, but a Brazilian is completely bare.

"Perfect, honey. Is this your first time?" The woman smiles at her. Strangely enough, she reminds me of my mother.

"I should have a trophy for how many times I've had it done," Addie tells her, just as the woman puts wax on a popsicle stick and removes the covering. I place my face in my hands as soon as

I hear the wax being ripped from the skin because I can't watch. Glancing up at Addie, she acts as if nothing happened, and I'm pretty sure she doesn't feel a lick of pain. Once she's done, Addie turns to me. "Now it's your turn."

My face goes red, and I'm halfway tempted to chicken out, but I don't. The older woman walks out of the room, and I look at Addie.

"It doesn't hurt that bad." She laughs. "Don't be a chicken."

This is cousin peer pressure at its finest, but I do it. Luckily, I haven't shaved in a while, so my hair is the length it needs to be as noted in the pamphlet I tried to memorize while Addie was being waxed. Another woman walks in, and she's just as nice as the previous lady.

"So this is your first time?" she asks with a grin, and Addie bursts into laughter.

I nod, and she explains exactly how it will work, then asks me what type of wax I'd like. Considering I can feel Addie's judgy eyes on me, I go for the Brazilian too. The woman removes the covering and places the hot wax on me, then in two seconds, she rips it off. I scream out, and I'm sure every person in the entire salon heard me. If I wouldn't look like I had a reverse mohawk on my crotch, I'd tell her to stop, but I take a few deep breaths and allow her to continue.

"Okay, it looks like we're done. Just need you to flip over," the woman instructs.

I sit straight up on the table and look at her. "Do what?"

"She has to get your butt crack," Addie adds. She doesn't even pull away from her phone.

"My what?" My brows lift, and my mouth falls open. I didn't get to that part in the pamphlet.

"It's the last step," the woman ensures me. I roll over onto my stomach and do exactly what she says, and surprisingly enough, the only thing that hurts is my ego. It's such a weird place to get waxed, and I try to erase it from my mind as soon as it happens.

She places the soothing lotion on my body and gives me some care instructions, and we're sent on our way.

"You look like someone just stole your puppy," Addie says as we walk through the salon.

"The only thing that was stolen back there was my dignity."

She pays and sets up two appointments for next month at the same time.

"You've lost your mind." I shake my head and laugh.

"Trent will thank me later." Addie gives me a wink and a smile.

"I'll thank you when my crotch stops burning." We get in the truck and head back to her house. I don't dare bring up Jackson again and hope I can keep him off my mind for the rest of the day. It's easier said than done, though, especially after the way he looked at me today.

CHAPTER SIX

JACKSON

SIX MONTHS BEFORE THE WEDDING

TIME IS FLYING BY SO QUICKLY. I can't believe it's April already and we're having Emily and Evan's co-ed bridal shower. It feels like only yesterday when they met, and now she's officially going to be my sister-in-law. She practically is already. I roll out of bed and am actually surprised I don't have a hangover considering my night.

I've been living in my new house for almost a year now, and the Friday night whiskey parties have continued on its regular schedule. I wake up and shuffle my feet to the kitchen to make some coffee because even though we have a family event today, the horses still need to be fed. There are no days off when you work on a ranch. Every day's a work day—rain or shine.

Once I'm in the kitchen, I walk past the couch and see Colton sleeping. He still has on his boots, and his cowboy hat is on the coffee table. Beer cans and red Solo cups are everywhere, and it looks like a damn frat house.

That's it. I'm going to have to start making some rules at my parties—clean up after your damn self.

I lean over the couch to nudge him, but he swats me away. He obviously drank way more than I did.

"Colton, you need to get the fuck up. You're late for work. Dad is gonna rip your balls off," I tell him.

He bolts awake, sitting straight up and glares at me. "Shit. What time is it?"

I look at the clock on the stove. "Six thirty."

"Fuck!" He hurries to stand but loses his balance. I place my hand on his shoulder to steady him as I shake my head.

"Somehow, I know this shit is gonna get blamed on me," I say.

He shrugs with a smile. "You're a bad influence. Even your folks know."

Colton tries to smooth down his messy hair, but it's no use. He walks to the kitchen, chugs a glass of water, then heads out the door. I'm pretty sure he's not walking in a straight line, but that's going to be his problem when he shows up to work for my father; not mine.

Once the coffee finishes brewing, I pour a cup, set it on the counter to let it cool, then get dressed. After I'm ready, I grab my mug and head toward the barn. On the walk over, it's completely still outside. The wind isn't blowing, and in the distance, I can hear the roosters crowing by the barn, but other than that, there's not a sound.

I think about Evan and Emily, and then my mind instantly goes to Kiera. She'll be there today, of course. We haven't really spoken too much, other than to discuss business, and I honestly miss her. She was my best friend for a long time, and though I have other friends, with her, it's different. Kiera understands me on a level most people don't.

As quickly as I can, I distribute feed to all the stalls, then head back to the house. I spend the rest of the morning trying to clean up the damn mess my friends left for me. The floor is sticky as hell, and I fill an entire trash bag full of bottles. I like a good party, but damn, this is ridiculous. After I take several bags of trash out and mop all the spilled alcohol from the floor, I jump in the shower. Everyone's going to be at this thing, so I make sure to clean up as nicely as I can. I intentionally wear nicer clothes, knowing that she'll see me, and I put on the cologne she loves.

Though I want to tell Kiera to leave that asshole she's dating, I know it's useless. They moved in with each other last summer, and from what I've heard from everyone, their relationship has gotten serious. More than anything, I want her to be happy. It's all I've ever wanted, but I always wanted her to be with someone who deserves her. Trent has always rubbed me the wrong way. I'll have to figure out how to support it, even though the thought of it makes me fucking sick to my stomach. It's like he wears this façade around everyone that I can see right through. Most people like him, but I see the mask he wears, trying to cover all his ugliness. One time, he made a comment to me under his breath about Kiera, and I almost decked him right between the fucking eyes. The only reason I didn't was because I knew he'd turn it around as if I attacked him for no reason at all. He's such a douche.

Considering Evan and Emily's party is around brunch time, I don't eat before I go.

Realizing it's time, I grab my keys and head out the door. The drive into town doesn't take long, but it's enough time to get lost in my thoughts. When I park, I spot Kiera walking in and see stupid Trent following her with his hand on her back, as if he's telling the whole world she's his. I sit in the truck and wait for them to walk out of my view. The last thing I want to do is talk to him or have to look at his smug face. I give myself a pep talk, telling myself I can be around the two of them together. I've avoided it at all costs.

Once I make it inside, I'm stopped and told how this wedding game called Put a Ring On is played. Apparently, the goal is to get as many plastic rings as possible, and I make it my mission to win. I just have to remember not to say the words wedding or bride. *Easy.*

I spot my sister Courtney and her husband, Drew. Across the

room, I see Mama with the triplets. They're getting so big and almost three years old now. As soon as Courtney sees me, she waves me over, and I go to her, giving her shit as always. I love my sister with all my heart, but it wouldn't be the same if I didn't pick on her about something. At this point, I know she looks forward to it.

"Dang, lil' sis. Didn't know you were bringing the gun show to the party." I glance at her sleeveless shirt. Of course, being the complete ham she is, Courtney starts flexing and balling her hands into fists like she's ready to fight me.

"If you don't watch it, you might get shot." I'm almost convinced she's going to sock the shit out of me, but I pull her into my arms and give her a big hug instead. Court and I get along so great, and I hated when she moved to California. I think out of all of us, I'm the closest with her, and we share a special relationship. I was the big brother who kicked all her boyfriends' asses if they made her cry, the one who taught her how to throw a sucker punch and how to ride. Sure, I pick on her as much as I can, but no one else was ever allowed to. I was protective of her. We've always had each other's backs, and always will, simple as that. Just as we break apart, Evan walks over.

It's the happiest we've all been in a long time, being together. Thankfully, it didn't take a holiday or funeral to make it happen. Of course, seeing the opportunity, Mama hurries over with the triplets and Dad, and asks someone to snap a photo.

Being the bad influence, I bend down until I'm eye level with the triplets. Delaney gives me a hug, and my heart melts. She's adorable and reminds me of Courtney when she was that age with curly blonde hair and blue eyes. There's no doubt that any of them are Bishop kids.

"Okay, so here's the thing. We're going to make really funny faces," I tell them quietly. Anderson hooks his fingers in his mouth and sticks out his tongue. "Yes, just like that. Y'all got it?" I look at all their little faces, and they nod their heads as if they understand exactly what's happening. I chuckle as I straighten up, standing behind them, and get my ridiculous pose ready. The woman with Mom's phone begins the countdown, and we make the silliest faces we possibly can. Mama looks over at me with a stern look.

"Can we take a serious one now?" she asks, only adding fuel to the fire. Right before the photo snaps, I make a farting noise with my mouth and everyone bursts into laughter while making their funny faces too. Mama knows that's the best she's gonna get and decides to give up while she's ahead. I give the triplets high fives before they take off running toward the cake.

Eventually, Emily and Evan open their gifts, and watching their eyes light up at one another makes me so fucking happy for them. Evan deserves true happiness—actually, all my brothers do —and as I look around, I realize I'm the only person left who hasn't found love. Well, that's not true. I've found love; I just haven't acted on it. Guilt washes through me again, and I glance over at Kiera who's watching Emily with bright eyes. She's wearing a cute shirt over her dress, and I love watching her so excited. They're best friends and have always had each other's best interest in mind, and I know she's loving this as much as the bride-to-be is. I swallow hard, trying to bring my attention back to Emily and Evan, though it's hard when I have a straight shot of Kiera. She's beautiful without even trying.

I look down at the ground, trying to bring my mind back to reality, and see all the plastic rings I've managed to steal from people. Just as the thought fills my mind, I hear someone close to me say bride, and I ask the woman to hand over her plastic jewelry. I could basically stand here and not say a word and probably win this game.

After we've had cake and are forced to play more ridiculous wedding games, I see John and Mila chatting. Kiera is standing really close to them, and Dr. Douchebag isn't anywhere near her. I suck in a deep breath and walk across the room. Once I'm close, I notice Kiera has at least ten plastic rings on her fingers, and my new goal is to get all of hers.

John and Mila are whispering about something, and I interrupt them. I instantly pull out my shit-eating grin. "You're falling behind a little, brother," I tell John, and he rolls his eyes.

"Looks like you are." Mila walks up to me and bumps me with her hip, nearly making me lose my balance.

I watch Kiera from my peripheral vision, and she notices me close. A feeling of excitement spreads through me when she walks over, finally giving me some sort of attention. The hint of a smile hits her lips when she sees my rings, or maybe it's the cologne she smells. I've been wearing it for her for the last decade.

Kiera is standing close enough that our arms brush together. Electricity streams through me when we touch, and I wonder if she feels it too, but I don't dare say shit when I know Trent is twenty feet away.

I lean over and whisper, "You're goin' down," as my lips brush across the shell of her ear. I hear her breath slightly catch, and it's the confidence booster I need. Right now, it's just her and me.

"You better stop it, Jackson Bishop," Kiera tells me, but her eyes say otherwise. She's enjoying this just as much as I am. The stolen glances are almost too much for even me to handle. Kiera steps close, and she's laughing.

"I've been kicking your ass at games since we were five. What makes you think this'll be any different?" she asks with a tinge of attitude, but her smile is big and genuine.

"Oh really? Is that a dare? You know how I feel about that game," I warn her playfully. She's openly flirting with me, and it gives me all the hope in the world that maybe she and Trent aren't doing as great as everyone says, and we'll eventually have a chance together. I realize Mila and John are watching us and pretend to go toward Mila to get her rings.

"Don't even think about laying a pinky on her or I'll break all your fingers off," John warns with a smile, but I really don't think he's joking.

I turn back to Kiera, who's watching me intently. I look at her from head to toe, lingering on all her curves—her hips, her flat stomach, perky breasts—until my eyes trail over her lips and finally meet her eyes that are watching me. I basically just imagined her completely naked, sitting on my face, and by the way she's looking at me, she noticed.

I walk closer to her, standing only inches from her body. "Emily's sure gonna make a beautiful…"

She flips her strawberry blonde hair over her shoulder, acting like a priss. "You're not tricking me out of this prize." Kiera reaches out and places her hand on my chest, and I'm half tempted to grab her and kiss her right here in front of everyone. If I would've taken a few shots before drinking all these mimosas being served, I just might have. I'm not drunk enough for that yet, though. Before she removes her hand from me, Trent walks up behind her, and I hear him whisper the word 'wedding' in Kiera's ear. She lights up, knowing she's about to get another ring. I'm fucking livid that he ruined our moment, but never in my life would I have imagined what he does next.

The rest happens so fucking fast that my head spins. Trent drops to one knee, gives this cliché ass speech that I'm pretty sure was ripped off from a movie and asks Kiera to marry him. People crowd around the happy couple, and I watch as she covers her mouth with her hands. My heart shatters into a million pieces when she says *yes*. At that moment, as he slides the ring on her finger, I feel like the biggest fucking idiot in the world for allowing her to get away. Regardless if I've always felt like I didn't have a chance, I didn't even try.

My hands are balled tightly into fists, and I don't even notice until my fingernails cut into my palm. I feel as if my entire world is crumbling, and I can barely breathe. It was never supposed to be like this, especially at my own fucking brother's party. Rude as fuck. I shake my head, thinking about how she deserves someone better than him, better than this, a special engagement, not riding off my brother's coattail. I'm furious, and I want to strangle Trent.

As more people fill in to congratulate Kiera, I take a few steps back, needing to find my escape as quickly as possible. As I stand there in a daze, John walks up to me. It's as if my soul called out to him, or he knows I'm five seconds away from pulling Trent into a choke hold in front of the entire town.

"Are you okay?" he asks. He looks at me with sad eyes.

"Is he fucking kidding? It's rude and tacky to propose during someone else's party. Kiera deserves better than that. I should go over there and punch his pretty boy face in." My voice cracks, and I know my emotions are getting the best of me. I see nothing but red, but all I feel is sadness and pain. I don't know how I'm ever going to get over this.

John squeezes my shoulder and gives me the comfort I need right now. "Emily knew and even helped with the plan."

I feel so betrayed.

I can't even really explain it.

I know they're best friends, and Emily wants the best for Kiera, but it just seems wrong to me on so many levels.

I meet John's eyes, and I feel like I'm suffocating in the room as I watch everyone crowd her and hear Kiera's voice in the distance. "I need to get some fresh air."

"Want me to come with you?" he offers, but I really need to get the fuck out of here before I make a scene and embarrass myself and my family.

"Nah. I need some space right now." I look over at Kiera and take a mental snapshot of how happy she is as she shows everyone the rock he gave her. I slowly let out a breath, knowing I could never give her that—knowing that she was never mine, and we were never meant to be. Not able to be there any longer, I head straight toward the door and walk across the parking lot.

Once I'm in my truck, I slam my fist against the steering wheel so many times that my knuckles throb in pain, and some disturbing thought inside me tells me I deserve to see her happy with someone else.

As the anger rocks through me, I start the truck and drive

around for hours. John keeps calling me, and I keep ignoring him. I don't want to talk to anyone. I just want to be in my head for once so I can work out how I feel. Eventually, before it gets dark, I drive out to the spot on the ranch where Kiera and I used to drink whiskey and bullshit after school. We used to steal bales of hay and stack them around an old ring firepit I took from the ranch hand quarters. All that's left in the ring is dust these days. I sit there for almost an hour staring at nothing, thinking about her.

I'm a damn fool. I'm a goddamn fool. She could never love you anyway, the negative voice in my head keeps repeating, and I just want it to shut up.

I think back to all the times I almost told her how I felt. All the chances I had to get it all out there. Now, she's marrying that asshole. I wouldn't be surprised if he tries to get her pregnant as soon as he can before she realizes what a fucking snake in the grass he really is. I don't trust him, and so help me God, if he ever hurts her, he's a dead man.

I'm tempted to go home first and grab a bottle of whiskey, but considering my state of mind, I wouldn't be able to drive back. Once the sun goes down, I decide I want some interaction, so I drive to a little private members bar tucked in one of the side streets in town.

As soon as I walk in and plop down on the barstool, the bartender Kandi greets me with a beer. The room is dark and old-time rock and roll plays in the background. It's a place where an older crowd hangs out, and if Mama knew I was in here, she'd bust in and pull me out by my ear because nothing but trouble parties here. Right now, I *am in* trouble.

"Why so sad?" Kandi leans over, giving me the perfect view of her big, fake tits. She sticks out her lower lip and pretends to pout. She's at least fifteen years older than me but still looks good for her age. Though I hate to admit it now, I've slept with her in the past. She was a good fuck, but I can't say I've had a bad one. I've always heard the only way to get over one woman is to crawl

in bed with another. No one has ever been able to fuck Kiera out
of my head, and I doubt anyone ever will.

She gives me shot after shot after I explain it's woman trouble.
She offers to take me home with her, and I consider it, but I've
found it's best to only be with someone once. More than that and
they get attached, regardless if I tell them I'm not looking for
anything other than sex. They always turn into crazy stalkers, or
maybe I don't have the best luck. These days, I'm dodging more
women in the grocery store than I'd like to admit and pretending
I'm John when it doesn't work. I've got his personality down to a
T. Definite perks of being a twin.

Just as I'm almost willing to give in to Kandi's flirtatious
advances, a tall, skinny blonde walks in. At first, I think of Kiera
and force myself to push her out of my mind. The woman sits
right next to me at the bar, and I smile. She smiles back. Soon
we're flirting, and I almost ask her to go back to my truck, until a
man sits beside her. At this point, I'm too fucking drunk to care,
and the flirting continues.

"Hey asshole, keep your dick in your pants. This is my
woman," he warns in a gruff tone, leaning across the bar
toward me.

I roll my eyes at him and continue talking to her, not paying
him any attention. The next thing I know, he's standing up and
tapping me on my shoulder. I rise to my feet and meet him eye
to eye.

"You need to back the fuck down before I beat your ass," he
tells me.

All I do is laugh in his face. "I don't think a little bitch like you
could beat anything—not even your little pecker."

When he notices the woman holding back her laughter, he
rears his fist back and punches me right in the face. That's when I
lose control. Screams echo, and I hear Kandi calling the police
when the guy picks up a barstool and tries to hit me with it, but
misses. The guy hurries to grab a beer bottle and cracks it on the
edge of the bar before he grazes my arm with it, causing a long

scrape. I might've had way too much to drink, but all the anger I've been harboring all day releases. I feel no pain as I slam my fist into his face while imagining it's Trent. It takes three older guys to pull me off the dumbass. Blood drips from my busted lip, and I'm gonna be so fucking pissed if he blacked my eye, which I can already feel is starting to swell.

The guy stands up just as two police officers and the deputy sheriff walk in. I roll my eyes and whisper under my breath when I see Deputy Pettigrew walk in with his big handlebar mustache and an ego the size of Texas. I am literally fucked because I know he's gonna tell Mama I was fighting in a bar she's warned me not to enter since I was sixteen. And, unfortunately for me, I don't know how to shut the fuck up when I've been drinking.

"What the hell happened here?" Deputy Pettigrew looks around at the mess in the bar. There's broken glass, knocked over barstools, and Kandi, who's glaring at the two of us like we deserve to be arrested.

"That dumbass decided to punch me in the face," I tell him. Pettigrew narrows his eyes at me in disbelief that the other guy threw the first punch. The deputy used to catch me and Tanner doing stupid shit when we were teenagers, and ever since the cow tipping incident, he's made it his mission to make my life hell. So far, he's succeeded.

The guy starts yelling nonsense across the bar. "He hit me first. He threw the first punch. I was just defending myself."

I'm ready to beat his ass all over again. "He's lying, Pettigrew. He's a fucking liar."

"You need to calm down, Bishop. And quit all that cursing in front of women. It's rude, and I know your mama taught you better than that."

My face goes hot when he mentions Mama. Yep. The whole town is going to know about this before the sun rises tomorrow.

The guy continues yelling. "He sexually assaulted my girlfriend."

And that's when I lose it *again*. I take off running, breaking free from the two guys holding me back and charge at the guy. My body slams against his, and we both fall to the ground, throwing punches all over again.

Almost immediately, the two of us are taken into custody. Pettigrew shakes his head at me after he roughly cuffs me. He gives me the stinkiest ass look before he walks over to Kandi, who I hope will tell him the truth.

I'm half tempted to head butt this dumbass standing close to me, but luckily, there's a rookie officer keeping us separated. The alcohol swims through my body, and I don't feel anything other than annoyed. I was having a good time until this dick decided he didn't want anyone talking to his girlfriend. Not my fault she was more interested in me than him. I watch the blonde talk to Pettigrew, too, and I assume he takes a statement from her. Once they're done speaking, the woman walks up to us and slaps her boyfriend across the face. This only causes me to burst out into laughter.

"That's for being over controlling," she says. They have a heated exchange, and it ends with her breaking up with him, which makes me laugh even harder. I can see he's boiling in anger, and even more so when she walks over to me and slips a piece of paper in my front pocket. "Call me."

I give her a smirk. "I will as soon as I get out of these cuffs, darlin'." I wink just to piss the guy off even more.

She glares back at her now ex-boyfriend and walks out of the door.

He leans over, trying to break free, and the cop tells him to stop.

"I'm going to kill you," he tells me, and I can't stop laughing. I am not scared of this guy one bit, and if I were out of these cuffs, I'd beat his face in until tomorrow. There's too much aggression inside me to give a shit about the consequences.

Eventually, Pettigrew comes over to us.

"So I've gotten everyone's statements, and it looks like you're going to jail, buddy," he tells the guy.

"Don't be sad. You might actually get some prison pussy tonight," I tell him, and he lurches toward me again. Pettigrew places his hand on the guy's shoulders to stop him.

"If you don't shut the hell up, Bishop, you'll be riding along with us," he warns.

"Oh okay. Yes, sir. I'll shut up like a good boy, the way you want me to." I should stop, but when I start drinking, it's like my mouth brings on a personality of its own.

"Bishop, you're making me lose my goddamn patience," Pettigrew warns, turning toward me.

"It's not the only thing you've lost over the years." I raise my brows and glance up at his thinning hairline, and I know this pisses him off more than anything else.

"Son. Shut your fucking mouth."

"No can do." I really want to, but I think it might physically hurt me if I don't have the last word with him. "Maybe you should watch your mouth in front of the ladies." The words continue flowing from my mouth, and I'm unable to stop, knowing it drives him crazy.

Pettigrew releases a deep, gruntal moan. "He's coming along too," he tells the rookie officer. I can't remember his name because he's so much younger than me, but he shakes his head and leads me outside.

"Why didn't you just keep your mouth closed?" he asks me as he's walking me to the car.

The more I walk, the more I feel the alcohol. Drinking that much was a really bad idea. "Because the old man needs someone to push his buttons every once in a while. He's been riding my ass for over a decade."

I see his name badge says Fawkes as he steps out of the way to place me in the back of the patrol car. "He wasn't going to bring you in, though."

I laugh. "Well, then I guess I'll have time to think about it in jail."

He nods. "You'll have plenty of time, Bishop."

As we drive to the police station, I fall asleep. My eyes are heavy, and the alcohol has taken over. When I wake up, I'm slightly confused as to where I am until I feel the handcuffs and am pulled out of the car and booked into the jail. They stick me in a room so I can sober up, and after a while, they let me call someone. I stand at the phone for a long time wondering who'd be the best person to get me out, and the only person I know who can keep a secret is John, or at least that's my drunk logic for calling him. I don't even know what time it is, but when I hear his voice, I know it's late.

"John?"

"Yeah? What's up?" His voice is heavy with sleep, and I feel guilty for waking him up for this, especially when he has a baby at home.

I try to think about what I'm going to say. Clearing my throat, I lower my voice. "I need you to bail me out of jail."

There's worry in his voice, and it's probably because I've ignored his calls and texts all day. "What? Are you okay?" I don't answer him, and he asks again. "What happened?"

I let out a deep breath. "I'll tell you when you get here. Just promise you won't tell Mama."

After hanging up, I'm escorted back to my holding cell. I kick my feet up on the bench and fall asleep.

Sometime later, I'm being woken up by the sounds of the door unlocking. An officer escorts me down a long hallway, and I have to sign some paperwork. On the other side of the door, I look at my brother as he looks me over.

"You look like shit. What the hell happened?" he asks as we walk outside and cross the parking lot.

"Bar fight at Silver Spur," I explain, my head already pounding. "Pettigrew threw me in jail."

John starts laughing. "You told me not to tell Mama, but if Pettigrew picked you up, you're already fucked."

I groan as I hop in the passenger seat and buckle up. "How much do I owe you for bailing me out?"

John cranks the truck. "Nothing. Apparently, you were only being detained for being intoxicated. You should be happy Pettigrew dropped you off. Might've gotten a ticket or something otherwise."

I lean my head against the cool window and close my eyes.

"If you look like this, I hate to see what the other guy looks like," John says, shaking his head. As the alcohol wears off, my face begins to pound. I drop the visor in the truck to look in the mirror and squint as the bright light shines back.

"Fuck," I mumble and slap it back up. A busted lip and a black eye; there's no way I'm going to be able to cover this up. I close my eyes and drift off to sleep as John drives us back to the ranch. At least I got the distraction I was begging for.

CHAPTER SEVEN

KIERA

I'm a nervous wreck getting ready for Emily and Evan's bridal shower, especially since I'm her maid of honor, and I want everything to be perfect. She's finally getting her fairy-tale wedding to her real-life Romeo, and the thought alone makes me smile. We've all come so far over the past few years.

I slip on a navy dress that falls right above my knees, and it shows enough cleavage not to be too revealing while still hugging my curves in all the right places. Spring is in full effect, and the weather is perfect today.

As I'm putting on some dangly earrings, Trent comes up behind me and kisses my neck. I lean into him, wishing we had more time to spend together. I look at him over my shoulder and see he's dressed in a nice button-up shirt and black slacks. I turn in his arms and pull him closer to me, giving him a proper kiss.

"Mmm, you smell so good." He holds me in his arms, and I look up into his brown eyes.

"You do too." He smiles, smacking another quick kiss on my lips. Today has been perfect so far. Trent woke up and cooked me breakfast after he fed the horses, and we ate out on the back porch overlooking acres of green grass. The weather is still brisk enough in the morning to wear a light jacket, but the coolness was perfectly paired with a steaming cup of coffee with cream. Trent smiled and looked at me while I ate in such a way that it made me want to devour him instead of the food in front of me. Being with him is so easy and carefree, and I always look forward to our mornings together spent on the back porch.

"We need to leave here in fifteen minutes if you want to be early," he says as I hurry and put on my favorite red lipstick. I begged Mama Bishop to let me help set up, and she refused, saying she had it all taken care of. Instead of arguing with her, which I've learned over the years is a losing battle, I agreed. She wanted me to be able to spend time with Emily beforehand, which was sweet of her, but I feel guilty for not helping since I'm the maid of honor.

The morning passes quickly, and soon, we're walking out to Trent's truck and driving into town to the old bank building where the reception is being held. Of course, I arrive early and find the bride-to-be as Trent chats with Evan. The first thing I do is wrap my arms around her, and we exchange big hugs.

"I'm so happy for you," I tell her as she walks me around the venue. She's wearing a white dress that's cinched at the hips and flares out with some bright red high heels. I laugh, thinking back to the non-sexy, don't-even-look-at-me dress she almost wore the night she met Evan.

"I'm excited for *you*." She turns and gives me a wink, and I remember the past couple of years and how much has changed in such a short amount of time.

"Huh, why?" I ask her as she shows me all the wedding games we're going to be playing.

"Because weddings are magical and contagious." She laughs.

"And so are babies. I swear if Trent doesn't pop the question soon, my ovaries are going to shrivel up and die, and I'll never have kids." I look over my shoulder at him, and he looks so damn handsome standing there all regal talking with Evan, who looks just as handsome. But then again, those Bishop boys can make rags look like riches.

"Don't worry about it. He's over the moon about you," she says, encouraging me. I smile because I know he is; there's no doubt about that. I feel exactly the same way about him too, but sometimes, that little voice of doubt whispers in the back of my head, and I'm not sure why.

"We've been living together for almost a year in July, and we're coming up on two years of dating. I was already wary about moving in before we got married—or at least engaged—because I always hear about those women who move in with their boyfriend, who then realizes he's already living the married life without all the responsibility and commitment, and then never proposes." I keep my voice low, but it's been bothering me for a while. I was convinced he would propose at New Year's, but it never happened.

"I don't think Trent is that kind of guy." She playfully laughs. "You're worrying too much about it. Trust the process, babe." She flashes a reassuring smile, and I know she's right.

"I know. Always so smart," I tease.

"So I have something for you," she says with a smile, reaching for a gift bag.

"What's this for?" I ask as she hands it to me.

Emily smiles. "Just open it."

I unwrap the paper, and inside is a shirt that has Maid of Honor written across the front. I give her the biggest hug and slip it on over my dress. "It's a perfect fit."

"You don't have to wear it now," she jokes.

"I'm totally going to. I want everyone to know I'm your number one." I smile proudly. I don't even care how weird it looks over my dress. "Well, aside from Evan and Elizabeth."

"Looks great on you!"

Emily shows me the cake Mama Bishop made next, and I'm blown away by the intricacy of the ribbons made from icing. It

KEEPING HIM

looks too pretty to eat. Mama Bishop has seriously taken care of everything, and I hope when Trent and I do finally get married, she'll help my mama do everything because she's one of the best party planners in the area.

I look at Emily and put the attention back on her because this is her day, after all, and I want it to stay that way.

"Are you nervous?" I ask, watching her bite her bottom lip.

She looks over at me. "Just a bit. Though I don't really know why. You know, I can handle a hospital full of sick, bleeding, complaining, even dying patients, but as soon as I'm the center of everyone's attention, I get anxious as hell. Plus, Mama Bishop insisted on inviting the whole town. Then my parents invited their friends. Then we had to invite our co-workers from the hospital too. I really wished we could've eloped and just got it over with."

I grab her hand and lead her over to the bottomless mimosa bar. I take two from the tray and hand one to her before sipping mine. "And this is exactly why we scheduled it for brunch time." We clink our glasses together and drink up. We both burst out into giggles as we finish our first glass, feeling less nervous by the sip. "I'm excited for this next chapter of your life." I grab her hand and squeeze. "You're officially going to be a Bishop." Emily quietly squeals, then her eyes go sad. I tilt my head at her. "What is it?"

She shakes her head and pinches her lips together.

"You better tell me right now. I'm not opposed to kicking your ass, regardless if today is your day," I threaten lightheartedly.

"Fine." She groans. "I just, I dunno, I know you always wanted to be a Bishop. I halfway feel like I'm living the life you've always wanted. I know how much you love the family, and I can't help but feel guilty about that."

I force a smile, hating that she'd even feel an ounce of guilt. I haven't thought about Jackson all day, until now. I actually haven't thought about him much since the last time I saw him

85

two weeks ago when I dropped off a horse. I've learned that as long as I'm not around him, I don't think about him as much, so I've been keeping my distance. It hurts to do that, but he's not making an effort either, so why should I continue to be the only one who cares?

"No, no. Don't you dare feel guilty. We both know Jackson never wanted me that way. It's not your fault." My eyes dart back and forth between Emily and Trent because I don't want him to hear this conversation at all.

Her voice goes low. "I don't think it's the fact that he didn't or doesn't want you, K. It's a deeper issue than that. A few weeks ago, Jackson came over drunk and upset. I overheard him chatting with Evan on the porch, and something was mentioned about him feeling as if he'd never be good enough for you and how you always deserved so much more. I don't think Jackson even knew I could hear them, but they were so damn loud I didn't even have to try."

My eyes go wide, and my mouth slightly falls open. "What? That's fucking ridiculous. Actually, it makes me want to kick him in the balls. He knows better than that."

"But does he? I didn't even want to mention it because it's so trivial at this point because I know how you feel about Trent."

Her words echo in my ears. "Exactly. Jackson had years to make a move or tell me how he felt. He obviously doesn't want me that way, and I can't keep waiting around. I want a happily ever after, and I know Trent is my future. He doesn't play games with my heart."

Emily finishes her mimosa and grabs us two more. "Did something happen between you and Jackson? I don't know why he would think that, considering the way you've always felt for him. I've been trying to figure it out. I even asked Evan, and he told me he didn't really know. Just said you were always off-limits because you dated one of Jackson's best friends."

I suck in a deep breath and drink the rest of my mimosa in one large gulp. "Tanner? Seriously? Emily, that was when I was sixteen. We broke up before I left for college. I've been off-limits for the past fifteen years because of a high school relationship? How fucking stupid is that?" Heat rushes to my cheeks, and blood swiftly pumps through my body. There's no way that's his real issue here, and I try to push it away, but I'm holding onto every word she's saying as if I might not hear her speak again. I know they were close friends, but there has to be more to this story. Though I'd love to march up to Jackson and demand answers, it no longer matters. Trent is the one I'm with, and he makes me happier than ever.

Emily opens her mouth to continue, then closes it when I hear Trent and Evan walking up. This conversation isn't done, and I have to know the whole story, even if it's to let Jackson go one last time. Something I feel like I've done a lot of lately. When Trent takes my hand and leans over and kisses me, I try to soak in the feeling of him, his smell, every little thing about him, hoping it will erase the thoughts of Jackson that are ripping through my mind. Eventually, he and Evan walk away, and I look at Emily.

"Forget I said anything, okay? Promise me. You're over Jackson. You're with Trent. You'll eventually get married and have a million kids and a barn full of horses. It's just I'm unsettled right now, and I've been playing investigator, which Evan told me to stop doing, but I can't. I'm naturally curious, and if I had a chance to pull Jackson to the side and ask him my damn self, I would. But he's been closed up in a tight ball lately. He still makes lighthearted jokes, but he hasn't been himself."

I shrug. "I haven't seen him in two weeks, so I wouldn't know."

Her eyes light up as if she's put two puzzle pieces together. "That's probably why he's been an uber asshole then. Explains it all. Mystery solved." She grabs my hand and pulls me over to the mimosas where we both grab another one. If we keep this up, we'll both be shit-faced before the party even starts, but by the way I feel at this moment, I'm all for it.

"Promise me you won't say a word, and you'll forget I even mentioned it. Okay?"

I roll my eyes at her.

"Promise me." She grabs my hand tighter and squeezes.

I stare at her for a moment and smile. "Okay. But only and I mean *only* because you're my best friend. And because it doesn't change a thing."

"Exactly. I knew you'd understand." She glances over at Trent who's helping himself to a mimosa with Evan. "Our men are sexy as hell."

I look at Trent, and a smile instantly fills my face. He sees me and nods, and I'm broken away when Mama Bishop wraps her arms around me.

"There's one of my favorite daughters," she says, and I hold on to her.

"Hey, Mama B." I smile. She's insisted I call her Mama, too, since she practically helped raised me. Jackson does the same for my mom, too.

"Lookin' gorgeous, Kiera. Love that dress on you." She pats me on the shoulder, then turns to Emily.

"Honey, the photographer is about to be here and wanted to get some photos of you and Evan and you and Kiera beforehand. You up for that?" Mama asks her sweetly, though Emily doesn't really have a choice.

"Yes, ma'am." Soon, Emily and Evan are walking toward the photographer, and I go to Trent and give him the biggest kiss I can.

"What's that for?" he asks with a grin.

"That's because I love you," I tell him as I see how happy Emily and Evan are. It makes me excited for my own future—the one I'm focusing on.

"I love you, too, baby." He kisses me again, and then I'm being waved over to Emily.

We pose together with our mimosas, and the smiles on our faces are as genuine as can be. The alcohol swims through me, and I know I can't have another drink without getting some food in my stomach.

Soon, the guests are arriving, and I greet many of them, asking Mama if there's anything I can help with, but she just tells me to be with Emily. For the first hour, I walk around with her and greet church members, hug her family like they're my own, and even meet people she works with at the hospital. I'm not even the one getting married, but damn, I'm exhausted already. I see Courtney and Drew entering, and as soon as Courtney lays eyes on us, she runs up to Emily and me, pulling us into her arms.

"Court! Oh my God, girl. You look amazing!" I tell her. We used to have slumber parties once a month, and she always tried to get me to admit I had a crush on Jackson. I was pretty stubborn, though, and kept it to myself, though I suspected she knew the truth anyway.

Courtney talks about California and the triplets, who are running all around the building. They stop when Mama captures them and shows them off to all the church ladies. They're absolutely adorable.

"Ever think you'll move back, Court?" I ask her, and she smiles.

"If I could capture my best friends and make them move to Texas, too, I would. Viola and Travis would never move here, though. I might be able to talk Logan and Kayla into it. Just tell Kayla she can adopt ten dogs." We burst into laughter as she talks about her best friends who all came for a visit a couple of years ago.

"I wish you would move back here. Mama Bishop chats about how she has ten acres set aside for you by the main house," I tell Courtney, who glances at her husband, Drew.

"She's the boss. I do what she wants." He smirks. "But I wouldn't mind it," he adds. "I could just work on the ranch with your brothers and dad."

Courtney instantly starts laughing. "I don't think you could handle it."

He looks at her with a popped eyebrow. "I handled you just fine."

Her mouth falls open, then she shuts up and playfully nods her head. "We'll see."

"Oooh. Now you're in trouble," I tell Drew, and he shrugs with a smile. We give Courtney more hugs before a few ladies from church grab us and happily explain the main game we'll be playing today.

"So all I have to do is capture people's rings who say those two magic words?"

"Yes. Wedding and bride aren't allowed," the older woman says, handing over my plastic ring. It's pink and fits my finger perfectly. I'm so competitive with games like this that I'm determined to win. Emily shakes her head at me because I know she can see the fire lit in my eyes.

Each time we walk around the room and talk to someone, at least one person mentions one of the words, and I happily take their rings. I almost feel as if I'm cheating, but hey, rules are rules.

Soon Emily and Evan are pulled away to take a family photo, and I finally catch up with Trent, who's chatting with my parents, but they all look guilty when I walk up to them.

"What y'all talking about over here?" I ask, trying to read them.

"The weather, mainly," Dad says, but I have a feeling he's lying. Mom just gives me a smile.

"We're about to open gifts. Afterward is the cake. I can't wait!" I quickly change the subject since they're all acting strangely.

River and Alex pass me, and I stop River to see how she's doing since she's almost six months pregnant.

"This baby is going to be bigger than the last one." She groans, referring to Riley, their three-year-old. "And he was huge. These Bishop babies are like birthing cattle, I swear."

Alex gives me a side hug. "Hey, Keira."

"Hey, you. Make sure you're giving her everything she needs, or I'll kick your ass," I warn him with a smirk.

"Yes, ma'am. When she says jump, I literally ask how high," Alex says. He thinks the world of River, which is obvious just by the way he looks at her. I see Mama Bishop waving Emily over from the other side of the room, which means it's time to open presents.

We make our way to the front of the crowd, and people giggle when they finally see my shirt. I pose for a few photos before I start handing gifts to Emily. As she opens them, Mama writes down who they're from.

I almost feel like Vanna White as I hold everything up so people in the back can see. The guests let out *oohs* and *aahs* over towels and Tupperware, which makes me giggle.

Soon we're cutting the cake, which tastes like heaven, and then we're forced to play more cheesy bridal games. Everything goes by so quickly, but I know everyone's having a great time.

At this point, I dare anyone to say the magic words around me because I have so many plastic rings on my fingers that it's almost painful. There's no less than ten, and I've actually started placing them in the single pocket in my dress.

Just as we wrap up the last game, I see Jackson walking toward Mila and John. I have so many questions for him after Emily mentioned him this morning, but there's no way I'd ever have the courage to bring it up here. Once he's close, I overhear him bragging about all the rings he's stolen from people. I take it as my cue to join their conversation because I want every single ring he has.

As soon as Jackson sees me, he gives me a sexy smirk. The light in his eyes return, and my heart begins to pound hard in my chest. I swallow hard as he openly flirts with me, not giving a fuck who sees. I just hope Trent doesn't. It's hard for me not to flirt back when he's like this—easygoing and fun like old times. His arm touches mine, and it sends goose bumps across my body. We're close—closer than we've been in a long time—and he smells so damn good. I always loved the way he smells especially when he puts on that cologne. I'm sure it drives all the ladies wild, though, because that's Jackson; it's the effect he seems to have on everyone.

He whispers in my ear, and his mouth barely grazes across my skin. My breath hitches as my heart pounds, and it's like no one else is in the room but us.

"Emily's gonna sure make a beautiful…" he says, trying to bait me, and I eye all the rings on his fingers. If I had all his, there'd be no way anyone could catch up with me, and I'd be declared the winner without a doubt.

Jackson's standing inches from me, and when I look into his blue eyes, I find myself falling, getting lost. Those old emotions I've been able to push away for so long reignite, and I feel guilty and torn and even pissed. All I need is a sign, something to show me these old feelings should be buried away.

Before I get lost in my thoughts, I feel strong hands around my waist and smell Trent. He leans in and whispers the word *'wedding'* in my ear. I know he has a few plastic rings, so my face lights up, and when I turn on my heels with a big smile, he drops to one knee. It's the sign I was begging for.

Then it all happens so fast.

"Kiera, my love. I've waited my whole life to find a woman like you. You make the bad times good and the good times better. You're beautiful, caring, and my other half—my true soul mate. You make me want to be a better man, and being loved by you is my greatest accomplishment. I can't imagine my life without you in it, and I want to spend the rest of my days with you. Kiera Young, will you marry me?"

I feel as if I'm living a dream as Trent looks up at me, smiling, holding the black box open in his hand. I go to him as tears of happiness run down my cheeks. I drop down to kiss him with everything I have in me, and I basically fall on top of him. I hear laughter and applause behind me. As soon as I stand and he places the ring on my finger, Emily comes to me and hugs me tightly. I'm shocked and surprised, and I hope Trent had enough sense to ask Emily if this was okay. I'd never ever want to take away from her special moments.

"Were you in on this?" I ask her, searching her face.

"The whole time." Emily smiles, understanding my question and the meaning, and looks over at Trent, who thanks her for helping again.

He gives her a side hug. "I couldn't have done it without Evan's and your help."

"You're both so sneaky!" I look back and forth between them and give Emily another hug, thanking her for everything, for being my best friend and for loving me. I'm over emotional, and I try to reel it all in.

The ring feels foreign on my finger, but as I glance over at Trent, I know this is meant to be—how it was always meant to be. Trent interlocks his fingers with mine and presses a kiss to my knuckles so damn sweetly. His parents walk up and give me huge hugs, and then my parents do the same. I knew they were acting weird earlier, and it all makes perfect sense now.

The rest of the afternoon flies by. All the Bishops come over to look at the ring and congratulate us. We all exchange love and hugs, and before the party wraps up, I find myself looking around the room for Jackson as Trent wanders off. I go to Emily and take her off to the side.

"Have you seen Jackson?" I whisper.

She gives me sad eyes. "He left, apparently."

My heart drops. "Why?"

She just shakes her head. "I think he was just as shocked as you."

"Well, what did he expect me to do? Wait another fifteen years for him?" I let out a sarcastic laugh and force my emotions down, so they don't bubble over.

"And that's exactly why I gave Trent permission to propose." She grabs my hands and squeezes.

Eventually, Trent pulls me away from Emily, and I ask Mama if I can help clean up, but I already know the answer is no.

"Super happy for you, honey." She gives me another tight squeeze before we leave. "I know you've wanted this for a long time."

"Yes ma'am," I tell her with a smile.

By the time Trent and I make it home, we can barely keep our hands off each other. I need him like I need water, and apparently, he's just as parched as I am. Soon, we're undressing one another and making love. I feel complete in every sense, and love knowing that Trent and I will be spending our lives together forever.

After dinner, we drink a glass of wine and watch a movie. Halfway through, Trent's phone rings, and he excuses himself to answer it. I try to get lost in the movie, but I'm too busy thinking about my life and how it's the way I've always wanted it to be. I let out a sigh and take a sip of wine.

Mila texted me earlier and told me that they haven't heard from Jackson since the party, and I'm beginning to get worried. I'd text him, but I'm sure I'm the last person he wants to hear from right now.

Trent comes back in and runs his fingers through his hair.

"Who was that, babe?"

He fidgets for a minute before responding. "Oh, it was Mrs. Miller. She's concerned about her pregnant mare who's not eating, and I might need to drive out there in the morning to check on her." He sits next to me and pulls me into his arms. "Nothing you need to worry about, babe." Trent kisses my temple, and I snuggle closer. I love that he cares about horses just as much as I do. It's a passion we share, and even though emergency calls sometimes take him away from home in the early hours, I know it's because he wants to help and give the owners peace of mind.

Eventually, we go to bed, and I fall asleep wrapped in his strong arms. Though I instantly fall asleep, hours later I'm woken up by my cell phone buzzing on the nightstand. I glance at the home screen and see it's just past one. I get up to pee and take my phone with me and unlock it as soon as I step into the bathroom.

Mila: Jackson got arrested. John just went to bail him out of jail.

I close my eyes and shake my head, hoping he's, at least, okay.

CHAPTER EIGHT

JACKSON

"You dumbass." Colton laughs at my expense when I slip and fall in a pile of horse shit.

"Takes one to know one, fucker. Gonna help me up or what?"

"You think I was born yesterday? The minute I grab your hand to pull you up, you're gonna pull me down with you." He crosses his arms over his chest and smirks at me. Dammit. He's right.

"Fine, but the second I'm on my feet, your ass is grass," I threaten, managing to get up without getting more shit on me.

"What the hell did I do?"

"You shoved me!" I chase after him as soon as he runs toward the barn. I spot Evan and Alex in the distance, working in the pasture, and I hear one of them shouting to knock it off. My guess is it's Evan, but I ignore him. Since he has a few days off from the hospital, Dad put him to work.

"Don't you dare," Colton says, turning around with a pitchfork aimed at me. He must've grabbed it from the side of the shed.

"Pussy," I tease.

"You can come back when you change your damn clothes."

Colton's laughing, and just when I turn around, I see Evan and Alex riding up on four-wheelers.

"You two gonna get your work done today or continue messin' around?" Evan glares, wrinkling his nose. "What the hell? Who reeks?"

"Asshole over here," I say, pointing at Colton, "pushed me in horse shit."

Alex bursts out laughing, and when I shoot him a death stare, he clamps his mouth shut. "You've pushed me in shit more times than I can count, so I don't pity you one bit."

"Yeah, whatever." I wave them all off. "I'm heading home to change. I have a horse delivery coming soon."

Thoughts of Kiera surface. I haven't seen her since she got engaged two weeks ago when I ended up getting into a bar fight. Mama reamed me a new asshole when she found out. Of course, it took all of twelve hours for the news to spread around town. Today will be the first time Kiera and I have seen each other since then. Thankfully, my busted lip is no more, and my black eye is almost gone.

Once I drive home, I peel off my jeans and shirt, searching for clean clothes in the dryer. Unfortunately, it's empty, so I sniff some dirty clothes in the hamper and decide they'll do for now. Just as I get my jeans and boots on, I hear Kiera's truck pulling the trailer down the gravel road in the distance. Deciding to leave my shirt off, I grab my cowboy hat and wrap my shirt around my neck as I drive toward the horse barn.

Kiera's unloading the horse when I arrive, and as soon as I'm within hearing distance, I whistle loudly to get her attention. The big rock on her left ring finger doesn't go unnoticed, but I continue to pretend it doesn't bother me.

"Did ya forget to do laundry again?" She arches a brow, holding the horse's lead rope as she waits for me.

"I was changing when I heard you pulling in."

"So you rushed out?" She noticeably glances at my chest and tattoos before her eyes meet mine.

"Well that, and yeah, I need to do laundry," I admit, chuckling. "If my six-pack offends you, I can put my shirt on." I wink, and as usual, she rolls her eyes at me.

"When are you gonna grow up?"

I follow her into the barn and open the stall door. "What're you talkin' about now?"

Kiera walks Daisy into the stall, unclips the rope before walking out, and I shut the gate behind her.

"I heard you got thrown in jail a couple of weeks ago," she finally says, and my face drops. I didn't think she'd bring it up, but I guess I really shouldn't be that surprised. Kiera lives to bust my balls.

"The dickwad hit me first," I say slowly, emphasizing my words for her. I don't know what she's heard, but I'm sure it's all bullshit. "What'd you like me to do? Stand there and be a punching bag?"

"So what'd you do to antagonize him in the first place?" She crosses her arms, giving me a look like she already knows the answer.

"I guess I just have a face guys like to punch," I say, annoyed at her accusations.

"Well, I heard you hit on his girl and kissed her in front of him, so if that's the case, you deserved it."

I scoff, barking out a laugh. "If that's what the rumor mill is saying, then I guess it's true." I walk away, pissed off.

"Jackson!" Kiera yells, but I ignore her and walk back to my truck. I start it and drive off, not wanting to discuss it because I feel like she wouldn't believe me anyway. There used to be a time when she'd ask for my side of the story instead of placing blame or believing the town gossip. She's changed—we both have—and I wish the days of us being close friends weren't a distant memory.

Being together was an essential part of our younger years. Kiera and I were always hanging out, even after she started dating Tanner. It's hard to think of my childhood without Kiera.

Between my two closest friends, I have a crap load of memories, including the one of Kiera's and my first and only kiss.

"You get any closer, your hair's gonna catch on fire or you're going to fall in," I warn her, but as usual, Kiera's too stubborn to listen to me. We've been drinking out here for hours, but I can hold my alcohol much better than she can, which is why she's way more blitzed than I am.

"Stop being such a funsucker," she teases, walking along the firepit ledge we made a couple years ago.

"Okay, we'll see how much fun you're having when you're burnt and bald." I roll my eyes, though I love this free-spirited side of her. When we drink together, it's just her and me. All our worries fade away and nothing else in the world matters. It's fast become a tradition of ours every Friday night; though she's dating my best friend, she never makes plans with him on our nights.

"Fine." She groans, but instead of hopping off like I expect her to, she lifts a knee and balances on one foot.

"What the hell are you doin' now?" I step closer, ready to catch her clumsy ass. "Kiera, you're going to fall in the damn pit."

"You worried 'bout me, Cowboy?" she taunts, holding out her arms to steady herself.

"Well, I'd rather not have to explain to your father why your ashes are the only remaining parts of you." She starts laughing as if this is the funniest thing in the world. "You're so drunk."

"I am not that drunk," she denies. "I only had a couple sips."

I burst out laughing. "Yeah, and I'm a virgin. Get your ass down."

Reaching for her arm, she jerks it away quickly before I can grab her, and she loses her balance. In one swift movement, I wrap my arms around her waist and pull her toward me. We both fall to the ground with her body on top of mine.

"What're you doing?" she squeals, laughing as we collapse. She wrapped her arms around me as soon as I grabbed her, but when we fell, she tightened her hold.

"You're so trashed," I say, loving the way she feels in my arms. "You

better not vomit on me," I tease, embracing the moment and wrapping strands of her gorgeous strawberry blonde hair behind her ear.

"Can you keep a secret?" she asks, slurring her words.

I roll us over to the side, but we don't break contact. "Do you even have to ask that?"

She giggles and brings herself impossibly closer to me. "I think I drank too much whiskey." She laughs again, resting her forehead on my chest.

"That's it?" I chuckle. "Pretty lame, if you ask me."

"No!" She laughs again, and it's the most perfect sound I've ever heard. Looking up at me, I watch as she moves her gaze down to my lips. I've dreamt of kissing her for as long as I can remember but have never crossed that line.

"What's your secret, Kiera?" I whisper softly, watching her eyes lingering at my lips and then moving to my eyes as if she's contemplating something.

"You're my best friend, Jackson," she finally says.

"I already know that." I smirk. "Was that it?"

"No, not quite." She bites down on her lower lip, which always drives me crazy. Then she leans in as if someone is around to overhear us. "I'm not wearing any panties."

My cock immediately twitches, and my eyes widen in shock. That's definitely a new one.

I hold back a chuckle, hoping she can't feel the way my body is reacting to her right now. "Why is that, Kiera?"

"Because I wanted to be able to have a secret…a dirty one."

"You're not very good at keeping your own secrets," I tell her, laughing. "But that is a very dirty secret. Making it a bit hard for me to think about anything else now," I admit with a grin so she can't see the real truth behind those words.

"I have another one I haven't told anyone. Not even you."

Attempting to angle my lower body away from hers since my cock is now awake and well aware of her going commando under her shorts.

"Is that so? I bet it's a juicy one," I tease, hoping she'll tell me.

"Oh, it's sooooo juicy. Not even Courtney knows."

Well if it happens to be about me, I sure as fuck hope she hasn't told Courtney anything. That's the last thing I'd need. My sister has a loud mouth.

Before I can respond, Kiera tilts her head and angles our mouths inches from one another. She's never been this brave before, and I can't help but think it's due to the excessive amounts of whiskey she's had, but I can't seem to push her away.

Her throat moves as she swallows hard, and it's then when all my resolve crumbles. Wrapping a hand around the back of her neck, I pull her the rest of the way until her mouth lands on mine. Within seconds, her arms and legs are mingling with me, and I pull her body up until she's straddling my lap.

Sitting up, I hold her in place as her knees fold around my legs and our hips are grinding against one another. Kiera is the most gorgeous girl I've ever laid eyes on, and we've been friends for as long as I can remember, but we've always kept our distance—until now it seems.

Just when I'm about to loop my fingers in her shirt and pull it up, Tanner's face pops into my head, and the realization of what we're doing hits me hard in the gut.

"Kiera, wait…" I reluctantly push us apart. "You've been drinking. We shouldn't be doing this."

She looks at me, and I see the hurt in her eyes. "Why? Am I not easy enough for you like all the other girls at school?"

Her words are a smack in the face, and I nearly stumble to reply. "What? No!" She's completely wrong if that's what she really thinks.

Kiera climbs off and starts walking away. I quickly jump up and chase after her. "Kiera, wait!" I plead, grabbing her arm and spinning her around to face me. When I see her, I want to punch myself in the junk because tears are falling down her cheeks.

"Just leave me alone, Jackson!" She tries to pull away, but I'm bigger and stronger. I tighten my hold on her and make her look at me.

"Not until you listen to me," I demand. "I didn't stop because I wanted to. I stopped because you're dating Tanner, and he's my best

friend, and it's not fair to him. I don't have many real friends, but the ones I do have, I want to keep. You can't date him and kiss me, Kiera. That's not fair."

She pauses for a moment, listening to my words. Her anger crumbles before my eyes, and her shoulders relax. "You're right, it's not. I don't know what I was thinking." Her words are true, but they still sting. Her tone is harsh and filled with regret, and I hate that we've crossed this line, and we can never undo it.

"You've been drinking. We weren't thinking clearly." I try to comfort her because the last thing I want is for her to beat herself up over it.

"Yeah, that's clear to me now more than ever." She yanks her arm out of my grip. "Let's just pretend this never happened, okay? Better for us both if we just erase it from our minds forever."

And with that, Kiera walks away.

That memory has haunted me since the night it happened. Kiera walked away, and we never talked about it again. We had a silent agreement that we wouldn't bring it up or discuss it. Neither of us wanted Tanner—or anyone for that matter—to find out. Being from a small town, rumors would fly in no time, and at school, Kiera would be called a slut or worse, which is something I'd never want.

Tanner never did find out. Or if he did, he never mentioned it. It's a secret we've kept for years.

I drive across the property, back to where Evan and Alex were working. I somehow push the thoughts of Kiera away and park.

"Colton…" I shout after jumping out of my truck and walking toward him.

"You missed me already?" He flashes a cocky grin.

"You wish. But we're going out tonight, so put on your drinkin' pants."

"My drinking pants are *no* pants," he says, making us both laugh.

"As long as it's not your birthday suit." I snort.

Colton raises his arms and starts swaying his hips from side to side, popping his groin and pretending to grind against me.

"Listen, I told you last time, and I'm tellin' you again, you ain't my type, so put your dick away."

CHAPTER NINE

KIERA

I DON'T KNOW why we thought having the bachelorette party two days before Emily's wedding was a smart idea, but I'm definitely paying for it now. I can't remember feeling this way since my college days. Hungover and bloated.

"I tried this dress on less than two months ago." I groan, trying to zip it up and suck in at the same time. Emily's sitting and laughing as she watches me struggle.

"You sure you're not pregnant?" She winks at me with hopefulness in her eyes.

"First, I hope not because I've been drinking a lot. Second, Trent and I decided we'd wait until closer to the wedding to start really trying. Third, I think the dress just shrunk."

Emily snickers, shaking her head at me.

"Fine, it didn't shrink. This is your fault, though. All your wedding events and drinking and eating amazing food made me pack on an extra ten pounds." I complain.

"Well, if it'll make you feel any better, I plan to get knocked up as soon as possible, so I'll be pregnant and fat for your wedding."

I snort-laugh at her admission. "You have five months, so even if you got pregnant yesterday, you'd still be adorable with a cute little baby bump."

Finally, Emily takes pity on me and helps me with the zipper. "Ready?" she asks, and I nod. "Inhale."

I do as she says, and after a couple of deep breaths, she gets the zipper up. "There. How does it feel?"

"Like a seam is going to burst if I move."

"But you look hot, so that's all that matters." She flashes me a wink, and I know she's only trying to make me feel better.

"After this weekend, I'm going on a strict pre-wedding diet. No more fried chicken and booze." I smooth my hands down my dress, hoping I don't pass out from the lack of oxygen.

Emily snorts, not believing me. She knows I love fried chicken.

"If you want, I'll do it with you. We'll go on a juice cleanse! Then only eat greens," she says matter-of-factly.

I groan inwardly. "That sounds awful actually. Maybe I'll just get one of those maternity wedding dresses, so it stretches."

Mila overhears the conversation and starts laughing. "And another reason eloping sounds like the best idea ever," she says smugly. She and John got engaged in December and haven't decided when they're getting married yet.

"I can't wait for you and John to get pregnant," River chimes in. She's glowing at nearly eight months pregnant, and we're all so excited to find out what they're having.

"Maize is a handful enough for us right now," she says with a smile. "But…" She chews on her bottom lip. "I can't wait to have John's baby and give Maize a sibling. We're enjoying just the three of us right now, though. There's no rush."

"I can't believe Maize's eighteen months already," Emily adds. "I swear, the time has just been flying. Elizabeth turning one a couple of months ago blows my mind. She was this tiny precious baby girl, and now she's a walking, talking sass machine."

We all laugh, knowing they have their hands full with the kids at their ages. Elizabeth and Maize are so much fun to watch when they play. Their little personalities are coming out so strongly.

"Ladies!" Jessica, a family friend who's Emily's wedding

coordinator, comes in clapping her hands. She's married to one of the ranch hands, Dylan, who works for the Bishops. "How are we doin' in here?"

Even though Emily is having a large wedding, they wanted to keep the wedding party small. She's not particularly close with her sister and brother, but she's included them in some of the events. However, it's just River, Mila, and me as her bridesmaids.

"I'm too fat for my dress. River is sweating already, and Mila looks stunning." I give her a recap, still sucking it in. "Oh, and the bride is gorgeous and flawless as usual." Everyone turns and looks at me. "What?"

They burst out laughing, and Jessica quickly goes through the itinerary for the day. Emily got her hair done early this morning, and we're waiting for the makeup lady to arrive and finish the look before she slips into her wedding dress.

After Emily is ready to go, we help her put on her dress and admire the finished product. It makes me so excited for my special day, but I'm happy to be here with her right now celebrating hers.

"Want some perfume?" I ask before we head out.

"Oh yes, grab my blue one, please. It's Evan's favorite," Emily responds with a beaming smile.

She holds her arms out for me, and I spritz her lightly on the wrists and neck. Emily rubs them together, and moments later, Jessica is gagging behind us.

"Excuse me, sorry…" She runs toward the bathroom with a hand over her mouth.

Furrowing my brows, I follow to check on her. "Jess, you okay?"

I hear her emptying her stomach and try to give her some privacy. When the faucet starts running, I tap lightly on the door before opening it.

"I'm so sorry," Jessica says, looking flushed.

"Oh gosh, don't be!"

Emily, River, and Mila all stand behind me as we check on her.

"I'm sensitive to smells, and that perfume just set off a button, I guess." She rinses her mouth and pats her face with a towel. Then it hits me.

"Oh my God," I whisper-squeal. "Are you pregnant?"

Jessica clamps her mouth shut with wide eyes, looking guilty.

"Jessica…" Emily taunts, egging her on.

"Fine!" Jessica waves her arms up before letting them slap to her sides. "We just found out and haven't even told our parents yet! I didn't want to say anything because this is your day," she directs to Emily with a frown.

The four of us engulf her in a hug and squeal with excitement.

"Are you kidding? I'm so excited for you and Dylan!" Emily gushes. "Now I really need to get knocked up ASAP. There must be something in the water, and I'm ready to drink up!"

We laugh and smile, congratulating Jessica on her first baby. She and Dylan have been together for as long as River and Alex, and I know they've been trying to get pregnant ever since they got married.

"So what you're saying is I need to buy triple filtered bottled water in bulk?" Mila teases, and we all laugh.

The wedding is what fairy tales are made of. Emily walks down with her father, and Evan tears up the moment he sees her. She's wearing a strapless lace gown with a gold sash around her waist. It hugs her curves just right and makes me so excited to go dress shopping. I know I need to find one soon.

I'm paired with John since he's Evan's best man, but Jackson is with Mila, and they've been placed in front of us. Of course, he cracks jokes the entire time, making me laugh. He's in a chipper mood, and even though he knows I'm here with Trent, it doesn't stop him from flirting and touching me every chance he can. It's like the last time we talked didn't even happen. I should apologize for making assumptions about the fight that got him thrown into jail, but I've been around him long enough to know there's always more to the story, and I should've given him the benefit of the doubt. The ceremony was beautiful, and after more pictures are taken, we head over to the tent where the reception is being held.

I order a drink from the bar, swearing I'll start my diet tomorrow.

"Truth or dare?" I feel Jackson behind me as he whispers in my ear, his body way too close to mine.

Looking over my shoulder, I hold back a smile as I rake my eyes over Jackson's perfectly fitted tuxedo. I love that Evan and Emily did a traditional wedding theme since most people around here don't, but then again, Emily didn't grow up in the country. She's originally from Houston, and they both work in the city, so this definitely suits them.

"I don't trust you," I whisper back, not wanting to draw any attention to us. Evan and Emily are sharing their first dance, and everyone is watching them as they slow dance with Elizabeth on Evan's arm.

"Good. You shouldn't." I hear the smile in his voice. He knows exactly what he's doing.

"Then I'm not answering," I fire back softly.

"Why not? Afraid of the consequences?" he taunts.

"The newlyweds invite everyone to come out and dance with them," the DJ announces, and couples start flooding the dance floor.

"Fine," I say, looking around for Trent and am slightly annoyed I can't find him or that he isn't looking for me. I'm afraid to say *truth*, knowing he'll probably ask me something I don't want to answer or admit. He's smart enough not to make me do anything too embarrassing at Emily's wedding—at least I hope.

"Dare." I shrug.

I see him smirk from the corner of my eye and immediately regret playing along.

"I'm not giving you my panties!" I whisper-hiss, turning to face him.

Jackson places a hand over his heart as if he's wounded. "Only amateurs would have to dare a girl for her underwear. I'm much more skilled than that." He winks, sending butterflies to my stomach, which irritates the hell out of me.

I roll my eyes, crossing my arms over my chest, and when his gaze lowers down to my breasts, I realize how pushed up I just made them. Unfolding my arms, I inhale a deep, exaggerated breath. "Alright, then what is it?"

Jackson flashes his boyish grin at me and holds out a hand. "Dare you to dance with me."

Narrowing my eyes, I study him for any signs of deception. He looks genuine, and knowing what he'd make me do if I don't follow along, I place my hand in his and agree. "Okay."

Jackson confidently leads us out onto the dance floor with the other couples and swings me around until I'm flush against his chest. He snakes his hand around to the small of my back and holds me in place while his other hand folds into mine. I wrap my free arm around his shoulder and let him lead as our bodies find a rhythm.

I rest my head on his chest and follow along to his movements. Jackson's an amazing dancer; he always has been, whether he admits it. Dancing with him takes me back to the past when we first danced together and the same feelings surface. The way he securely holds me, his rapid breathing in my ear, the rising and falling of his chest—it makes me feel like a teenager again.

The song changes, and I'm ready to pull apart when I hear "Never Stop" by SafetySuit come through the speakers. Jackson doesn't skip a beat and continues to dance with me.

"This is my favorite song," I tell him. I used to listen to it on repeat when I'd train for a show or needed something to pump me up in the early mornings.

Jackson looks at me with a glimmer of pride in his eyes. "I know." He winks before wrapping his arm around me tighter.

I furrow my brows at him, trying to read him. "You requested this song?"

Jackson nods, keeping his eyes glued to mine.

"How'd you know I'd pick dare?"

The corner of his lips tilts up in a knowing smirk. The bastard knows me way too damn well. "Was a gamble, but I had a gut feeling."

Jackson starts singing the lyrics to me, the words holding so much meaning yet so much pain. The song talks about how the guy will never stop trying, never stop losing his breath every time he sees the girl, and how she still makes his heart race. It's a beautiful song, but the lyrics are what drew me to it all those years ago. It's a song I'd always hoped Jackson would read into and realize he was all that to me.

Everything around us fades to black.

I don't see or hear anyone else, and the thoughts surrounding my head are dangerous ones. This Jackson is why I fell in love with him, even as a naïve teenager, because it's little things like this that remind me he cares. He notices my quirks, my likes and dislikes, my qualities, and weaknesses. Jackson knows everything about me, inside and out, and no amount of distance could ever change that. We share too much history.

"If I remember correctly, you have pretty lame *truth* questions," I tease, needing to break the intense tension.

"Looks who's talking, Pippi Longstocking." Jackson wraps his hand along my throat, dragging his finger down to my collarbone, leaving goose bumps behind. He hasn't called me that in years, and though I used to hate it as a kid, I grew to adore it as a teenager. It always made me feel special that he had a secret name just for me. "Too bad you don't wear your hair in braids anymore. They always looked so cute hanging down your neck."

I chuckle, breaking the spell he could so easily put me under. "Got sick of a certain someone pulling on them all the time."

Jackson rolls his eyes with a smile. "Then why'd you keep wearing them?"

Because I knew you loved them, I want to say but hold back. Before I can respond, Trent comes into view with a displeased look and his lips in a firm line.

"Excuse me." Trent interrupts our moment, and I feel guilty the second I think those thoughts. "May I intervene and dance with my fiancée?" Trent asks in a non-question tone, telling me how unhappy he is to find me dancing with Jackson.

Jackson looks at me for confirmation, and when I nod, he frowns.

"Of course." Jackson releases me, and my body immediately feels cold without him. He steps back, allowing Trent to take his place. I force a smile, but deep inside, I want to beg Jackson to come back. I know I'm marrying Trent, and I should be more than happy to dance with him right now, but Jackson and I have been through quite a bit of a rough patch lately. I want our friendship to be back to where it was, but I worry that'll be impossible now.

CHAPTER TEN

JACKSON

FOUR MONTHS BEFORE THE WEDDING

"WHISKEY, NEAT."

"You got it, handsome." Tessa winks at me as she reaches for the bottle. I shouldn't be drinking, but after the day I've had, it's necessary.

"You started without me?" Tanner smacks me on the shoulder before he sits down next to me.

"Barely." Tessa sets my glass down and turns toward Tanner, placing a napkin in front of him.

"What can I get for ya?"

"I'll have whatever he's having."

"Sure you can hang with the big boys?" I taunt, bringing the amber liquid to my lips.

"Yeah, yeah. Suck a fat one, Bishop." Tanner slaps a fifty on the bar. "I grew up with you and survived, didn't I?"

"Here you go, sweetie." Tessa places the drink down, then leans on the bar, pushing her tits out like they're an art display.

She's a huge flirt, but I've learned that's where the fun stops. Tessa is the definition of a cock tease. She loves to make you feel special, and her little touches indicate she's looking for more, but she's knocked my pegs down more times than I like to admit. She's working this job to pay her way through college, and flirting is what gets her the big tips.

"Thanks, doll face." Tanner winks at her with a smug grin on his face. Poor bastard has no idea the trap he just walked into. "So how're things?" Tanner finally brings his attention back to me once Tessa walks to the other end of the bar to help other customers.

"Fine, I guess." I shrug. "Everyone's either knocked up or gettin' hitched."

Tanner takes a sip, keeping his eyes on me. "And where's that leave you?"

"Well, I'm not changing dirty diapers at two in the morning." I snicker. "But I'm in my thirties and pretty sure I'm about to lose the woman I love for good. She's never been mine, not really, but even our friendship has changed over the past few years."

"You're not kids anymore," Tanner says. "Of course friendships and relationships change; it's natural. Though I'm still shocked you two never hooked up or dated. Boggles my mind."

I give Tanner a look, and he arches a brow. "It boggles your mind?" I snort at his choice of words. "You asked her out and dated her for over two years."

"So?" He shrugs. "That was when we were in our teens. Once we both left for college, we went back to just being friends."

"You're a dick for asking her out in the first place."

Tanner rolls his eyes, tilting his head back to finish off his drink already. "I did that for you, jackass."

"How so?" I scoff and empty my glass in one big gulp. Raising my glass to get Tessa's attention, she nods to let me know she'll be right over.

"I knew you liked her. I wasn't blind. Asking her out was to light a fire under your ass so you'd protest or finally ask her out yourself."

"And how did that end up dating for two years and taking her virginity?" The displeased tone in my voice doesn't go unnoticed.

"Well I liked her, but you were the one in love with her. We grew closer, and I fell in love with her, too. We shared a lot of firsts, and when we decided to end things, I was devastated. We both knew going to different colleges would add more burden and stress to our relationship. Plus, I always suspected you'd swoop in and mend her broken heart. Guess you pussied out."

"Dude, fuck you."

Tessa refills our glasses, and I immediately swallow it down.

"Why the hell wouldn't you tell me this shit before? I never made a move on her out of respect for *you*."

"How was I supposed to know you were going to have morals?" He grins. "Sure, I might've been pissed about it at first, but I always knew she had feelings for you. Kiera talked about you nonstop. It was sickening." Tanner mimics a gagging noise, making me laugh.

"Uh, well because you were my closest friend, and there was an unspoken bond that you don't hook up with each other's girls," I explain. "I didn't want girls to get between us after all these years. I may be a dick, but I'm a loyal friend."

"Well, in that case, Kiera was the only girl left for me to hook up with." He smirks, implying I hooked up with all the other girls. I won't deny there's been a lot of them, but I had my reasons for that too.

"Seriously, though. I wouldn't have cared. You should've told me that was why you stayed away. I had moved on within my first year of college."

"Man whore," I tease, both of us knocking our glasses together after Tessa refills them again.

"College was an eye-opener, that's for sure," Tanner admits. "But I'm glad I did it. I had to get away and focus on getting my degree. But that doesn't mean I didn't enjoy living the college experience," he gloats.

I shrug, the whiskey blazing through my veins at fast speeds. "It doesn't matter anymore anyway. She's with Dr. Douchebag, and they're getting married."

"Does she know how you feel?" Tanner asks me seriously. "Like…how you *really* feel? Or did you just give up?"

"I think she knows," I admit. "I've never said it to her face, but it should be obvious how I feel."

"Because you're so transparent?" Tanner mocks. "And sleep with different chicks?"

"That was so she wouldn't like me," I say. "You were always the type of guy I saw her with, and that's why I didn't intervene when you two dated. Even at eighteen, you always had your shit together. She wanted the whole white-picket fence, two-and-a-half-car garage, two-story house with three kids and a horse ranch. You were well-educated, wealthy, and a straight-A student. That's what she wanted and deserved."

"Tessa," Tanner calls. "We're gonna need some stronger shit. Pity party for one happening over here."

"You're such a dick," I say, laughing. "Trust me. I did the right thing by staying away."

Tanner shakes his head, disagreeing with me. Though I'm sure he's not the only one who thinks that. Being in love with Kiera doesn't change the fact that I'm all wrong for her.

"Self-loathing startin' early, boys?" Tessa teases as she hands us four shots of tequila. "These are on me." She winks before walking away.

"Better call us a ride," I say, grabbing a shot in each hand and downing them both in seconds.

"Do you remember that time we snuck onto the Miller's farm and nearly got killed by their cows?" Tanner asks, laughing the whole way through his question. I nod in response, remembering it way too well.

"And then you dared me to tip it," I add.

"That was all Kiera!" he exclaims. "I just agreed."

"Yeah well, that cow nearly took a chunk of hair out of my head. She was pissed!"

"And if it weren't for Mr. Miller hearing all the commotion, it would've chased me right into the electric fence," I say, remembering more of the details. Tanner's laughing so hard he's crying.

"That was one of my best summers," he says.

It was mine, too. It was the summer Kiera and I kissed. The kiss we never spoke of again. Anytime someone asked me if anything had ever happened between us, we both denied it.

"I need to get over her. Let her go for my sake so I can find some closure and move on," I say mostly to my half empty glass of beer I changed to an hour ago.

"If that's what you think is right, then yeah, you do. She's not married yet, though." He raises his brows as if he's implying I could do something about it now.

It's well past midnight before John picks up our drunk asses. He looks less than amused, but I know he's at least glad we called for a ride instead of passing out drunk in the back of my pickup.

"So what's the occasion this time?" John asks as he pulls out onto the road.

"When has there ever needed to be a reason?" Tanner jokes. "But I guess you could say we needed to catch up."

"Kiera," John says simply. "Amiright?"

I say no at the same time Tanner says yes. John looks at me, and I roll my eyes.

"She's getting married," I tell him.

"I know," he replies.

"To Dr. Douchebag." I groan. "I hate that guy."

John laughs and shakes his head. "You're drunker than usual."

"Tanner ordered us the hard shit. Then I switched to beer."

"It was that, or you were about to start singing a sad love song." Tanner cracks up laughing, and I nudge him with my fist.

"You suck." I grunt. "You both suck."

After we make it back to the ranch, John walks into the house with us and sits on the couch while I stumble to take off my boots. "I need a cure," I tell him, though he hasn't said anything.

"Who knew Jackson Bishop was capable of being pussy whipped by one he's never had?" Tanner slaps me on the back, jerking my body over.

"You're such a dick, you know that?"

"You need to get over Kiera if you don't plan on doing anything about it. Like I said before. Either say something or move on."

"Tanner's right," John chimes in.

I glare at them both. "You're both exhausting."

"You should write her a letter," Tanner suggests.

"Yes, and then you should fold it into a triangle and pass it to her during first period geometry." John laughs, and if the room wasn't spinning right now, I'd lean over and punch him.

"Write her a letter that's for you," Tanner clarifies. "Like a goodbye, I'm letting you go, want you to be happy, blah, blah, blah. It's a therapeutic exercise. When someone has something they need to get off their chest, it helps to write it out instead of holding it all in, which you've been doing for over a decade."

"So I wouldn't actually give it to her," I say, thinking he might be onto something.

"Not unless you wanted to, but most people don't. They just usually feel a lot better afterward."

I shrug, contemplating it. "Okay. I'll give it a try."

"You want to do it now? You can barely open your eyes," John says, cracking up.

"Okay, maybe after I drink a pot of coffee."

Tanner pours me a third cup of coffee as I continue writing on a piece of notebook paper. It's the longest note I've written in years, and though I don't typically go for this sort of stuff, I trust Tanner enough to try his method.

"Do we get to read it?"

"Fuck no."

"We're helping you sober up, and we don't even get to read it?"

I eye John and Tanner who are sitting at the table with me. "So you can use it against me later and give me shit? I'm not stupid."

"What if we swear to never bring it up after this night?" Tanner asks. John nods in agreement, and I'm not sure whether it's the buzz or the caffeine high, but I give in.

"Fine, but not until I'm done."

Tanner and John wait with me for another hour as I finish writing it. I didn't expect it to be this long, but I shouldn't be surprised either. Years of pent-up emotions are spilling out of me, and while it hurts to write it, I do find some relief in doing it.

"Okay, I think that's it." I put the pen down and look through the pages. "You sure you wanna read it?"

"Hell yeah." They both reach for the letter and start reading. I take the opportunity to get up and get myself a glass of cold water. It's so damn late, but after drinking coffee, I feel wide-awake yet tired at the same time. It's a fucked-up combination.

"Why the fuck am I mentioned so much in here?" Tanner teases.

"Wow…" John says. "This actually doesn't suck."

"I'm not just a pretty boy, ya know?" I smirk, sitting back down.

Once they're done reading, John and Tanner slowly look up at me and grin. "What?" I ask.

"I think you should give it to her," John says. "It's good."

I swipe it from his hands before he can put it out of my reach. "No way. She doesn't need to read this letter. She's getting married in four months."

"Exactly," Tanner says. "You still have time to tell her."

I shake my head. "It's too late. This will only ruin our friendship, or she'll accuse me of being jealous and only doing it for attention or some shit. She has dreams much bigger than what I could give her anyway. I just want her to be happy."

"Sometimes I wonder how we can be twins, considering how different we are, but then at other times, I see a lot of myself in you and remember we have more in common than I realize," John says.

"What's that mean?" I ask.

"It means that I actually understood what you just said. I could feel the pain in your words as I read the letter. Like, my heart feels the ache you're feeling right now. It's…weird."

"Some twisted twin connection," Tanner blurts out with a chuckle. "That's actually very common for identical twins. Like when one twin gets into an accident, the other can often feel their pain when it happens."

"Well, whatever it is, I get it. When Mila left to go back to Georgia, and I thought I'd lose her forever, I felt similar pain. It's an ache that harbors in your chest and feels so damn heavy and weak at the same time. I actually think I understand now." It's the sincerest thing I've ever heard him say about me.

"Hurts, doesn't it?" I frown. "But at least Mila came back. I'm happy she did."

"Me, too."

The three of us sit awkwardly, and after a few minutes, I fold up the letter. "I'm going to bed. Y'all can see yourselves out." Standing, I take the letter with me and toss it into the trash before walking to my room and passing out.

CHAPTER ELEVEN

KIERA

AFTER WORKING with a couple of new horses all day, I need a drink or two to wind down. I head home, take a long, hot shower, and pour myself a glass of wine as I wait for Trent to finish up his day so we can begin dinner.

I click on the TV and close my eyes. I've been feeling overworked lately. Between all the wedding planning and extra horse training I've had, I doze off and don't hear him come in. My eyes flutter open, and his back is to me as he walks around. I begin to sit up until I notice how he's speaking quietly to the person on the other line. Not wanting to give myself away, I close my eyes and lie there, listening to every word that comes from his mouth that's filled with venom. He's shaking his head, and I'm so thankful I can't see the look on his face because I know he's wearing a scowl.

"I told you to stop fucking calling me," he whisper-shouts as if he's mad but trying to keep his voice low.

My heart races and pounds hard in my chest, but I somehow steady my breathing.

"No. Stop. Just stop it. If you need more money, you need to contact my lawyer. I'm not having this conversation right now." He pauses for a short moment. *"Listen. To. Me,"* he continues, seething between gritted teeth. I hear him pacing, then the front door snaps closed.

The breath I was holding escapes from my lungs, and my eyes open wide as I replay every single word he said. I can still hear him outside talking, but I have no idea what he's saying. Who the fuck is he talking to? Who does he owe money to? And why didn't he feel like he could tell me about this?

I wish I had my phone, so I could text Addie and tell her what I just heard, but I left it in the bedroom. Sucking in a deep breath, I stand and find the courage to open the front door instead. Trent immediately turns around and forces a smile.

"Okay, well we'll deal with this later. I'm glad she's doing better. Alrighty. Bye," he says quickly, then steps toward me.

"Hey, baby. I was going to let you sleep." He pulls me into his arms and kisses my forehead.

I look up at him and smile, keeping my tone light and fluffy. "Who was that? Everything okay? You sounded upset." I add the last part, hoping he'll tell me what's going on because when I opened the door, he was yelling. By the surprised look on his face when he saw me, he knows I heard him.

He leans down and kisses my lips as if it were nothing at all, though I've not seen that side of him…well, ever. "Oh, that was Mrs. Parsons. She was wondering if I could come to check on one of her horses that's limping pretty badly. Bad horseshoes or something. I really can't stand it when people don't have the experience to put on shoes but do it anyway. Apparently, she allowed her nephew to do it, and now the horse is in pain."

I smile, but when I look at him, I have a feeling he's lying straight to my face with a long-exaggerated story. It's unsettling, but I force it away for now. I'm trying to give him the opportunity to be honest with me, but he's not taking it. Or maybe I'm overreacting, and he really was talking to Mrs. Parsons, but my gut instinct tells me otherwise. Not to mention the money conversation that's still lingering in my head. We have separate business accounts and created a joint bank account when I moved in with him to put money in for our monthly bills. I've refused to fully depend on him and want to take care of my share. "Are you ready for dinner? I was going to put some burgers on the grill tonight." He easily changes the subject.

"Yeah, that sounds perfect." I keep the smile, not allowing it to falter, but it's hard. Somehow I keep it together, not wanting to make a big deal out of something that might not actually be anything. *Wedding jitters*, I remind myself. That's all this is.

Trent takes my hand and leads me inside. I grab my empty wineglass and pour it to the top as he washes his hands. He looks over his shoulder at me and gives me a wink as he takes the hamburger patties from the fridge and seasons them. Once they're ready, I follow him outside to the back porch, and we chat about our day as he grills.

Purple and dark pink streaks of clouds paint the sky, and I find myself lost in my thoughts as Trent chats about horses.

"I ran into your parents today at the grocery store," he tells me.

"Yeah? I'm supposed to have lunch with my mama tomorrow."

"Your mom mentioned something about Mrs. Bishop baking our wedding cake." He looks over his shoulder, giving me a pointed look.

I smile, but I can tell by the look on his face that he's not thrilled about it.

"Yeah, she usually does that for people at the church," I remind him. "She made Emily's cake for the bridal shower, and you said you liked it."

"We don't need anything from the Bishops. Not a damn thing." Trent keeps his back to me, and I suck in a deep breath. Lately, he's been like this about anything to do with the Bishops, and it's starting to wear on me, considering he knows the relationship I have with all of them.

"They've been family friends since before I was an apple in my mother's eye, Trent. You're gonna have to get over this. But while we're on the subject, I want Jackson to be in the wedding party. We've talked about your cousins and sister, and I think it's important that one of my best friends is as well." Now seems as good a time as ever to bring it up since it's been on my mind for the past two weeks, but I just hadn't found the opportunity to mention it. When I talked to Emily about it, she warned me Trent would probably flip out but encouraged me to do it if that's what I wanted, which I do.

He sets the spatula down on the side of the grill and turns around. He's seething, but I refuse to allow it to bother me.

"I don't think so," he tells me, crossing his arms over his chest. "I don't want him to be there at all."

I mirror his stance, not willing to back down. "This isn't a negotiation, Trent. Jackson is one of my closest friends, and I want him in the wedding party. Getting married is something I've dreamed of my whole life, and it's important to me that he's up there. So I want to ask him the next time I'm at the Bishop ranch."

I'm not trying to start an argument with him, but I'm putting my foot down.

"I don't understand your obsession with him." He huffs, shaking his head, then turns around as he continues to speak. "But do whatever you want. Seems like you're going to anyway."

Now, I'm pissed.

It's always something between the two of them, and I don't know why. Trent has no reason to be threatened by Jackson, considering he's the one I'm marrying. Instead of taking this to a level it doesn't need to be, I calm down and walk over to Trent. I snake my arms around his waist and rest my head against his back.

"I love you, Trent. I love you so damn much, even when you're stubborn as hell. Don't forget you're the man I'm marrying, okay? If you don't want him to be there, then I'll do what *you* want, but it's important to my parents too. I'll just let them know you said you'd prefer him not to be there."

He stills for a moment, then turns around and pulls me into his arms. His demeanor completely changing.

"No, it's okay, babe. I know you're marrying me, and you'll be mine for the rest of our years. If you want him there, then I'm okay with it."

I look up into his eyes, and he leans down and kisses me. It's almost frightening how he can change from being pissed to happy in all of five seconds. Maybe my words affected him?

It's been almost a week since Trent and I had our discussion about Jackson being in the wedding party. A few days ago, I asked Jackson, and he gave me shit about it, but hesitantly agreed. Before he did, though, he asked what Trent thought about it, knowing they have a mutual hatred for one another. I gave him a smile and told him Trent didn't mind, though I'm sure he didn't believe me. The truth is, I need Jackson there.

Growing up, he was my number one support system when big decisions were made, and without him being there on a day that I've dreamed about since I was a little girl, I didn't know if I could do it. Though, when I used to think about getting married, it was to him, but now I know he's not the marrying type of man, so it would mean everything to have his blessing.

After rinsing my hair in the shower, I turn off the water and reach for my towel. Trent and I are going on a date night. He was recently hired by a large rancher in the town over and wanted to celebrate, so we're going out for a fancy steak dinner in San Angelo as soon as he gets home.

Just as I finish drying off, I hear my cell phone ring and hurry to the bedroom where I left it. Once I reach it, I see it's my mother. She's been enjoying the wedding planning process, but considering there's so much to do in such a short amount of time, I ended up hiring Jessica to help.

"So, we set up the rental for the tent for the second weekend in October, if that's firm."

I smile. "Yes, Mama. That's the date we're planning on. It's going to be here so soon."

She's giddy with all this, and it makes me so damn excited. "I spoke with Rose yesterday, and she said she could round up all the boys to help set up the tent so we wouldn't have to pay to get it done. Apparently, they've had lots of practice with all the Bishop weddin's they've been having."

"That sounds great, Mama." I set my phone down and put her on speaker as I get dressed.

"All we really have left is to pick out the flowers and order them, decide on the food so we can let the caterers know, and finalize your last dress fitting. Oh, before I forget, I spoke with Tracy, the lady who has that string quartet at church, and she said they need a deposit to schedule your date. Since I know how adamant Trent was about paying for them, I'll just need to get a check from you. I'm supposed to see her tomorrow if you can drop it off tonight," she says.

"Oh right, hold on one second," I tell her, grabbing my phone so I can send a text to Trent.

Kiera: Hey babe. Mama needs a check to book the orchestra. Do you have any extras? I think I used the last one for the chair rental deposit.

Trent: Yep. In my desk, top drawer. Should be a checkbook right on top. Almost done here. I'll see you in thirty minutes. Love you.

Kiera: Thank you! Love you too.

I smile, then go back to my phone call. "Yeah, Mama. I can bring you one in the morning before I feed the horses if that's okay. Trent and I are going out for dinner tonight."

"Sure, sweetie. That'll be fine. Just put it in the mailbox. I know you'll be at the ranch early or if you wanna drink coffee with your dad in the morning."

"I just might," I say.

"Well, I'm gettin' another call, Kiera. I'll see you first thing tomorrow. Love you."

"Love you, too, Mama."

I end the call, grab my wet towels and throw them in the hamper, then go into Trent's office. It's tidy inside, and he usually spends a few hours in the afternoon catching up with paperwork once he's back home.

Equestrian books line the walls along with different award-winning horses he's owned over the years. I sit in the big executive chair and slide the drawer out. Right on top just as he said is the checkbook. I open it and see both of our names on top and know it will eventually say Trent and Kiera Laken. I rip out a check before placing it back. As I'm about to close the drawer, I catch a glimpse of an envelope with another bank name on it, one that isn't familiar. I sit there for a moment, but then curiosity gets the best of me, and I open it.

Studying the statement, I don't recognize any of the information except his name at the top. Deposits are made monthly, and then on the first of each month, a direct withdrawal of a thousand dollars gets taken out. My heart races as I look in the drawer and find a stack of these statements, all with the same transactions, dating all the way back to four years ago. Immediately, my mind goes to the worst possible place. Who is he paying this money to, and why does he feel he needs to hide this from me? I think back to the conversation I overheard earlier this

127

week, and every terrible scenario fills my mind. Is he cheating on me? Is he addicted to drugs? Is he living a double life?

With shaky hands, I put the envelope and statements back where I found them, then put the checkbook on top of it all. I place the check on the kitchen counter and go to the bathroom.

I'm in complete shock and don't know what to think. This month marks a year we've lived together, and it's frightening to know there are still things I don't know about him. I halfway doubt everything, our relationship and the foundation of trust it was built on, and I know deep down something isn't right. He's hiding something.

I don't know what to say or how to start the conversation, so when Trent comes home, I don't say anything at all. I pretend as if everything is fine because I'm afraid I'd sound accusatory if I bring it up now before I have time to really process it.

As always, he pulls me into his arms and tells me how beautiful I look before he plants a kiss on my lips.

"I'm so hungry, but I need a shower," he says with a smile before walking to the bathroom. "I'll be quick."

"You better!" I call out, plopping down on the couch and allowing my mind to wander. I text Emily, giving her the details of what I found.

Emily: I'm going to stay neutral on this, but maybe you should bring it up?

Kiera: I can't tonight, not right now, but I'm going to have to before the wedding.

Emily: All I have to say is he better tell the truth. We're four months away from a wedding. If he's seeing someone else, you kinda need to know now.

I sigh, because I know she's right.

Kiera: I don't think he's cheating.

Emily: For his sake, I hope he's not. There are too many Bishops that would kick his ass and go all big brother on him.

Her words make me smile.

Emily: Not to mention me bitching that ass out too.

Kiera: And we all know how fierce you can be when it comes to your bestie.

I can imagine her smiling and laughing. When I hear the water stop running, I tell her I have to go.

Emily: Please keep me updated.

Kiera: You'll be the first to know once I find out.

Trent walks into the living room dressed in a button-up shirt and nice slacks. His hair is parted to the side, and he looks really handsome. We head outside and get into the truck, and on the drive to the restaurant, I try to push the thoughts away, but they continue to haunt me. All I know is, I will get to the bottom of this, especially if I plan on spending the rest of my life with this man.

CHAPTER TWELVE

JACKSON

After my lunch break, I head back to the barn for a few riding lessons John scheduled. I'm happy the weather is nice because this morning the clouds looked gray and angry. Summer storms can happen at the drop of a hat in July and can be so unpredictable. Considering my students today have zero riding experience, we're going to start from the very beginning.

I look over the waiver and study their information. Three students, ranging from twelve to sixty-five years old. All beginners. No health issues. *It should be an interesting day*, I sarcastically think, but then again, I love introducing people to the saddle for the first time.

I grab a few helmets from the tack room, along with saddles, then round up the horses who are gentle enough for infants to ride. After the horses are brushed and ready, I walk back to the B&B where they're all waiting.

"Howdy, y'all." I greet them with a smile. It's important to be able to read them, and I can tell they're nervous, except for the kid, who seems to be more excited than anything.

"Today, we're going to learn how to ride. We'll start with the basics, then we're going to ride a short trail around the ranch. It's going to be a fun day, but remember safety is always first. If at any point, you don't want to ride anymore, just let me know, and we'll stop. But the goal is for you to feel confident in the saddle." I study their expressions, then lead them out to the barn. I give a little history lesson about the ranch, how many acres we have, and how many generations it's been in the Bishop family. We walk inside the barn where the horses are saddled and ready to go, all tied to metal rings. I turn to face them, and watch as their eyes light up.

"Okay, so first we're going to learn the basics of the saddle." I explain the horn, stirrups, and the importance of having the cinch tight enough on the horse, then allow them to ask questions.

"So what happens if, when we're on the trail, the horse just runs away with me?" Janelle, an older woman, asks.

"Trust me when I say that won't happen. Since you're all beginners, we're using the friendliest horses on the ranch. Nothing spooks them. They're gentle enough a two-year-old could ride without being led."

Her shoulders relax.

"When can we start riding?" Matthew asks. He's twelve and excited to get going. I remember being his age and completely enthralled with riding. It makes me recognize how lucky I've been to be able to do this almost every day of my life.

"How about we practice getting on and off first?" I grin.

He claps his hands, and I go over to where the helmets are and hand them out based on the sizes I think they are. After their helmets are secure, I lead Yancy, one of the tamest horses we have, outside to the open space. I keep my grip on the lead rope as I demonstrate how to pull themselves up using the horn and stirrup, then how to dismount. After I do it once more, I have each one of them try it a couple of times. I lead each person around the corral, letting them get a feel of being in a saddle on a moving animal.

"Good job, y'all. You'll be naturals by the time the lesson is over." I wink, trying to build their confidence.

Soon, I'm explaining how to use the reins and how to guide

the horse, left and right, and how to stop. Once they all have a grasp of the concept, I lead each horse that will be ridden today out to the posts outside the barn and tie the lead ropes around metal hooks. I tell everyone to practice getting on and off their horse for about five minutes while I explain the trail.

"It's short, only two miles long, and will take us around an hour. The horses have taken it so many times, I'm pretty sure they could walk it in their sleep. If any of you would prefer not to go, now's the time to speak up. There are no jumps or climbs, just a flat trail with beautiful views."

I look at each of them, and they all nod with smiles on their faces. I've never had a person tell me no when it comes to riding. I like to make sure everyone is comfortable and work with those who are struggling. The hardest part for most new riders is getting on. I climb up and sit in my saddle and turn toward everyone, waving them on to follow.

We stop at the random points I've laid out on the trail, and I discuss different plants, birds, and animals that roam the ranch. There's a lookout on the trail with a perfect view of the valley, and one can see for miles. No issues happen on the ride, and by the time we make it back, they're all asking me when they can sign up again.

"Probably can fit you into tomorrow's lesson. Might need to check back with my brother at the B&B and see."

"The one who looks just like you?" the little boy asks.

"Yeah, that's the one," I tell him, patting him on his back. "Y'all take care. I'll see you soon," I say, giving them handshakes and high fives.

After the lessons, I take the saddles off the horses, then brush them all down. The rest of my afternoon is clear, other than Kiera dropping off a horse, so I plan to clean the stalls and check back in with John to get the rest of my schedule for the week. Just as I'm walking through the barn, my phone vibrates in my pocket. I unlock it, and as soon as I see Kiera's name flash across the screen, a smile fills my face.

Kiera: I'm not gonna be able to make it out today. Got caught up in training. I can drop Chief off tomorrow if that's okay.

I glance at her message and read it again. My heart sinks because I was looking forward to seeing her this afternoon. Instead of cleaning stalls, I decide if she won't come to me, then I'll go to her. It's been a while since I've been over there anyway.

Jackson: I'll come pick him up if that works better for you.

Kiera: Yeah, sure. That'd be fine. See ya soon.

I head back to the house and change into some clean pants and a button-up shirt. I spray on some cologne, run my fingers through my messy hair, then grab my keys. I walk across the pasture and down the path that leads to the B&B. Once inside the B&B, I find John chatting with some guests and wait until he's done. A younger woman looks back and forth between the two of us and smiles with dreamy eyes. It's a common reaction.

"Howdy, ma'am." I tilt my hat at her, and her cheeks go pink.

John shakes his head, then narrows his attention to me. "Can I help you?"

"I'm heading over to the Youngs'. Gonna go pick up Chief," I tell him, just in case he plans something last minute for me.

"No problem." He gives me a nod and a smile, probably because I'm going to see Kiera, but I ignore him. I walk out of the back door of the B&B, knowing I just passed up the perfect opportunity to give him shit in front of guests. The thought makes me laugh because I can imagine how worked up he would've gotten if I started flirting with the woman who was giving me googly eyes.

After I say my goodbyes, I go to my truck, back it up to the horse trailer, and latch it down on the hitch. Considering Kiera lives maybe ten minutes away, it feels like I fly there. The thought of her completely takes over, and then I think of Trent, and I'm instantly in a bad mood. Ever since they got engaged, things have been different between us. There's been a shift, and I fucking hate it.

As soon as I pull onto the Young ranch, a smile touches my lips. I haven't been out here in a while, but it brings back tons of memories as soon as I cross under the wrought-iron gate with the Lazy Y logo. While driving down the gravel road, it doesn't take long before I see Kiera on the saddle, her hair pulled up into a messy ponytail, running a horse around barrels. I park, get out of the truck, and lean against the wooden fence, watching her. The woman has zero fear and takes the barrels at such a high speed that it looks as if the horse is sliding into home base. Once she's completed her run, she waves at me and rides over, smiling.

Damn. The afternoon sun beams down on her skin, and I can't help but think how absolutely stunning she is.

"Hey, you." Kiera looks me from head to toe with a smile, and I notice.

I lift an eyebrow and watch as she chews on the corner of her lip. I don't give a shit who she's marrying. I know she still thinks about me, about what could've been, especially when she looks at me the way she is right now.

"New horse?" I ask, breaking the building tension. I stand on the bottom board of the wooden fence and reach over to pet the chocolate-colored quarter horse.

"Nah, one I'm training for Mrs. Johnson's daughter. They're gonna be travelin' around in the next few months barrel racing and want to take several horses. This is Hershey. He's a sweetheart."

I search Kiera's face, knowing she always wanted to travel and race but gave up the dream when she went to college. We haven't talked about it in years. "You know, it's not too late."

She laughs it off as the horse digs his hoof in the dirt, kicking up dust. "It kinda is."

"Hell no. If that's still your dream, you should go for it. You're good at what you do. How fast is your run?" I ask, knowing she's one of the best. She can have a new horse trained in a few months, and many of them have beat records.

"I've gotten him down to sixteen seconds, but I know we can do better. We're right there. In a few weeks, we'll be at fourteen with no issues." She leans over and runs her hand over his coat.

"Seeing is believing," I playfully tease, knowing damn well she will.

"I know I can, and when I do, I'm handing him over to her. This boy is gonna win her lots of money and possibly a barrel racing title, too."

I give her a smirk, and she acts like she's immune, but I know better. "You should go again. But this time, let go of all the stress you're holding because it's literally holding you back."

"I'm not under any stress, Jackson." She tries to lie, but I see right through her.

I tilt my head. "Really? You're wound up so damn tight right now. I can see it in your shoulders."

She rolls her eyes at me.

"Let me ride him then," I tell her, climbing up over the fence. "Let me see how fast he can go."

Her eyes light up, and she's smiling at me. When we were teenagers, I taught Kiera how to compete and train horses to race. It was a time when we bonded the most. I know if she would've kept it up, she could've been one of the youngest women in Texas to win a championship title.

"Seriously?" she asks.

I nod, and she lifts her leg over the saddle and drops down right next to me. She slightly loses her balance and falls against my chest. I grab her tight, holding on to her. She tilts her head up, looking into my eyes as if she's sending me a silent plea. I smile at how breathtaking she looks and hear her breath hitch.

"Careful," I say softly as my heart races. I know this is my moment. I could easily lean in and kiss her,—right here, right now—because she's so close. I can smell the sweetness of her skin mixed with the sweat of the day, and I just want to hold her as close as I can and never let go. But the reality is, I'm too chickenshit to even go there—especially now. Instead, I take my hands from her arms, and she steps aside. My heart is at a full sprint, galloping along, and I slip my foot in the stirrup and pull myself up on the saddle.

Kiera looks up at me. "If you beat my time, I'm gonna be pissed."

"Get ready to get pissed, sweetheart." We're both so damn competitive when it comes to things like this that I can't help but chuckle as I turn the horse around and trot toward the starting point. Kiera resets the clock she had built for practice and training that hangs at the end of the arena.

I'm right out of the gate, and as soon as I hear the buzzer, I gently dig my heels into the horse, and we take off at a full sprint. With a tight core, and my arms close to my body, we round each barrel, so closely that I almost feel my pants brush against the metal. We're going at a full sprint back to the finish line when I hear Kiera let out a loud woohoo.

When I turn around and see the time's in the thirteens, I pump my fist in the air. It felt right going around the barrels, running at full sprint.

She's got her hands on her hips and is walking toward me with a smile, but her eyes are narrowed.

"How the fuck did you do that?"

I loop my leg over the saddle and hand her the reins. "I told you. You're stressed. It's obvious."

"No, I'm not."

I cross my arms over my chest. "Really? You seem like you're as tense as a virgin on prom night, Kiera. As long as you're riding with stress, you're not ever going to make your time. The horses know. You know that. Come here," I tell her, and she does. I turn her around and place my hands on her shoulders and begin to squeeze, trying to loosen the built-up tension. Her head goes limp on her shoulders, and it makes me smirk. Just touching her like this, as harmless as it is, drives me fucking crazy, and I know I should stop. But when I notice her chest rising and falling and hear the moan escape from her lips, I'm only encouraged to keep going. Once her muscles are loosened, I pat her on the back, and she turns around and looks at me, rolling her shoulders.

"Better?" I give her a shit-eating grin.

"Actually yeah. Can you come by every day and do that after lunch?" she asks with a laugh.

"Only if you dare me," I tease.

She walks past me, leading the horse with her, and climbs back on. Before she does the run, she resets the clock, takes a deep breath, then shoots me a wink. Kiera is so damn fearless. She rounds the barrels closely, keeping her core tight, and as soon as she crosses the line, I see the time. Thirteen seconds. She gallops back, hops off the horse, then runs toward me. Kiera's smiling from ear to ear, screaming out in happiness, as she practically knocks me over. Her arms wrap around my neck, and I stumble to catch her. It all happens so fast as I pull her into my arms.

"I knew you could do it. I told ya so," I tell her, swinging her around.

She's giddy with excitement, and it covers her from head to toe. Eventually, she releases me, taking a step back as if she just realized how close we were. Her breaths are ragged, and I swallow hard, looking at her. We haven't had a moment like that since before she started dating Dr. Douchebag.

"We should do this again sometime. I miss you," she finally says.

I clench my jaw, wanting to tell her everything I'm feeling at this moment, but settle for barely anything. "I miss you too. I miss my best friend."

She turns and looks at me. "We'll always be best friends, Jackson Bishop. Don't you ever forget that, okay?"

"And that's a promise?" I ask, climbing over the wooden

fence, knowing we'll need to load Chief up soon because she'll need to get back to work.

"I promise you with everything I am." Her words circulate around in my head, and when I look at her face, I know she means it.

I might not have her the way I want, but at least we'll be friends forever, and that'll have to be good enough for me.

CHAPTER THIRTEEN

KIERA

RUNNING that horse at thirteen seconds was unbelievable. Everything felt right, and having Jackson encouraging me like old times was amazing. He's always been my lucky charm. Another reason he has to stand up in my wedding.

I ride around the barrel racing area toward the barn where Chief is waiting in a stall. I had my assistant, Alexis, get him washed and brushed for Jackson since he decided to pick him up. After I dismount, I tie Hershey to a post and meet Jackson at the entrance of the barn. The way he looks at me is so damn intense, I can barely stay focused on my surroundings. All I can see is him looking at me, and it's as if he can read my thoughts and knows all my secrets. Well, he basically does.

Back there in the arena, we shared a moment, and I feel as if the invisible wall that's been keeping us apart since I started dating Trent is finally starting to crumble. I'm so happy to have my best friend back—or at least that's what it feels like—even if it's only a temporary feeling.

"I'm so proud I could teach you everything you know," Jackson gloats, shoving his hands in his pockets.

"Oh shut it." I laugh. "But yeah. I do kinda have you to thank for all this."

Jackson smirks and nods. "You're welcome."

When we were fourteen, Jackson taught me how to be a better rider and have more confidence in the saddle. Him being the one to teach people who stay at the B&B was the best choice. I wouldn't be where I was now without him.

"It only took falling off and getting back on about a million times." I smile back at him.

"But the real question is, did you die?" Jackson lets out a soft chuckle.

"It felt like I did," I say truthfully. When I first started riding, I'd fall off all the time. I've been bucked off, had the breath knocked out of me, and even broke my arm once. Jackson was conveniently there for all my riding mishaps. Then one day, my parents bought me a horse that wasn't broken. Jackson spent the entire summer with me, teaching me everything I now know. He was always so patient. Starting with the basics, he'd spend every free moment he had with me. Of course, years of experience with horses helped get me to where I am today, but Jackson laid a solid foundation, and he really wanted me to be successful. But even looking at him right now, standing in front of me, I know he's a million times better than I am. I've begged him to train professionally, asked him to join me in my ventures, but each time, he denied, staying true to his family and the B&B. I know he can train all the horses he sends to me, but he claims he doesn't have time. Personally, I think it's just an excuse, but I don't mind. It gives me extra work and a reason to see him, even if sometimes it's painful.

"Chief didn't give you any issues, did he?" Jackson asks as we walk side by side toward the barn.

"No, not at all. He's going to be a great horse. Has a little wild spirit to him, though. Sometimes he gets stubborn when we're galloping and wants to keep going. Eventually, he stops, though. I think I wore him out more than he did me." I laugh.

"I don't doubt that one bit," he says.

Our arms brush together as we walk to where Chief is. I lean over the stall door, feeling Jackson's eyes on me. I glance over at him with a smirk, and when our eyes meet, it's as if everything around us freezes. My breathing increases, and I notice the faint smell of his cologne. It brings back so many memories of our teenage years. Jackson lifts his hand and tucks loose strands of hair behind my ear. Instinctively, I grab his hand.

"Please don't," I whisper with our eyes locked.

"Don't what?" he asks, searching my face, but he's wearing his infamous shit-eating grin. He knows exactly what he's doing.

"Don't make me question everything." The words fall out of my mouth before I can stop myself, and even I'm shocked by them.

He places his hands in his pocket and focuses on the horse who's lazily eating hay. Things get awkward too quickly, and everything is quiet. There are a million words I want to say but can't find the courage to do it. Instead, I'm lost in my thoughts, trying to distract myself, but everything about him surrounds me. The only sound I hear is my heart pounding in my ears.

"Kiera, you can't force Trent into a mold, okay? You want him to be someone he's not. Someone he'll *never* be…"

Heat hits my cheeks, and my mind is spinning. He doesn't finish the rest of his sentence. He doesn't dare say what he's insinuating—Trent will never be *him*.

Jackson turns, resting his back against the stall door, and crosses his arms over his broad chest. I notice his bulging biceps, his dark, messy hair, and then I find myself focusing on his lips. *Shit*. What the fuck am I doing? Why does he still have this strong hold on me? I'm getting married in four months, and I'm practically undressing him with my eyes. I place my back against the stall door as well, taking my focus off him and pushing the thoughts out of my head.

"Do you remember when we were seventeen and snuck out to go skinny-dipping in the pond during the winter?" he asks.

I burst out laughing. "And you were convinced that the more whiskey you drank, the less your balls would shrivel up."

We both laugh, reminiscing. Jackson glances over at me with a ghost of a smile playing on his lips. "Do you remember what you told me that night as we sat by the fire trying to warm up?"

I think back, replaying our conversations from over a decade ago. Lately, I've noticed I've been doing that a lot. To be a teenager again, when all we worried about was our weekend plans and what we'd spend our summers doing. So much has changed and life isn't as carefree as it used to be. I suck in a deep breath, remembering it all. The times we spent together flash by like photographs, and while those memories make me happy, they make me sad too.

"I said I'd never settle," I finally answer.

"That's right. And somehow I can't help but think you are." He doesn't look at me this time.

I swallow hard. "You're not being fair, Jackson."

All he does is shrug, which frustrates the fuck out of me.

"Look at me," I demand, reaching for his hand. "Why are you being like this? Why can't you just be happy for me and support my decision?"

He sucks in a deep breath and looks down at my hand holding his. When his eyes finally meet mine, I feel like I'm falling deeper. And it's not fair—I shouldn't feel this way anymore. He opens his mouth to say something, but it's interrupted by a voice behind me.

"What the fuck is going on in here?" Trent shouts at the entrance of the barn. I release Jackson's hand and immediately turn around, forcing a smile on my face.

"Hey, baby!" I say, pushing my shock away.

Trent's jaw ticks, and he's staring at Jackson like he's ready to beat his face in. I glance back at Jackson and notice his tight fists at his sides. Honestly, if the two of them were to get in a fight, I know Jackson would destroy Trent. He's been fighting his brothers since he could walk. Not to mention, Jackson has so much built-up rage that he would scare the shit out of anyone who dared to fight him.

I suck in a deep breath, wishing they could get along, but I know that'll never happen. Trying to dissolve the situation, I walk toward Trent with a smile, but he only glares at me in return.

"What the fuck is going on in here?" he asks again, quieter this time.

"Jackson's just picking up a horse. And what are you doin' here anyway? I thought you had a call in San Antonio today?"

He lets out a deep breath and speaks between gritted teeth. "It was canceled, and I wanted to surprise you, but it looks like I'm the one who's surprised here. We'll talk about this when you get home tonight."

"About what?" The fact he's treating me as if I did something wrong pisses me off.

"About you and *him*." He looks over my shoulder toward Jackson. I turn around and glance at Jackson who's wearing the biggest grin ever. He's not intimidated by Trent at all, which doesn't help the situation. I shake my head at Jackson and turn my attention back to Trent.

"Is it always going to be like this, Kiera?" Trent asks, scowling.

"Like what?" I whisper, searching his face.

Trent shakes his head and turns around to walk back toward his truck.

"Trent!" I shout, but he just lifts his hand up in the air and keeps walking. I watch as he gets inside his truck, pulls out of the driveway, then takes off down the gravel road. My heart is racing, and I'm so fucking pissed about all of this. Trent treated me like I was cheating on him, which is something I'd never do. Maybe he shouldn't be so fucking insecure about our relationship and lose his temper like a child. It only encourages Jackson when he acts this way.

Footsteps come up behind me, and Jackson stands next to me, watching Trent drive off the property.

"And that was my point being made," he sneers. "Fucking settling for Dr. Douchebag."

I turn and look at Jackson as he walks to the tack room, grabs a lead rope, then goes to Chief. The lead rope clicks, and soon, Jackson is leading Chief through the barn past me. My hands are shaking as I try to get ahold of my emotions.

"Jackson, wait!" I yell, and he stops and immediately turns toward me.

"What, Kiera?" He pauses, then continues when I don't speak up right away. "Notice who doesn't keep walking when you say their name? Surely wasn't your fiancé, the man you're supposed to be spending the rest of your life with. I almost feel sorry for you, but then I remember that you chose this—*he's* what you want."

I stomp my boots toward him, ready to give him a piece of my mind about staying out of my personal business, but once I'm beside him, he starts walking again, and I know he's pissed, too.

"You better be glad I didn't beat his fucking face in for disrespectin' you like that." Jackson hands me the lead rope and opens the door to the horse trailer. I walk in, loading Chief inside, and feel my emotions bubbling.

When I step out, Jackson locks the door. I run my hands over my face before tucking them into my pockets.

Jackson studies me, and his face softens. "Are you okay?" he asks, his voice softening.

I just stare at him, because the truth is, I'm not okay. Trent has never just walked away from me like that. He didn't even give me a second thought before he drove off.

I nod, trying to cover up what I'm feeling.

"No, you're not." Jackson comes to me and wraps his strong arms around my body and holds me. That's when my emotions take over, and the tears start to fall.

Jackson gently holds me, and we stand there for several minutes while I let it all out. Once I suck it up and wipe my face, he places his hands on my shoulders and forces me to look into his eyes. For a moment, it's like we're sixteen again, and he's comforting me over something stupid. He's witnessed all my

144

moods and been there through all my ups and downs. Jackson has never left my side.

"If he ever hurts you, I swear to you, he's a dead man. One tear is one tear too many. But I'm trying hard to respect your decision regardless if I know it's a bad one."

I exhale, relieved. "Thank you."

"That's what friends are for," he adds, reminding me of where we stand—where we've always stood. Before he walks away, he squeezes my shoulder. "If you need a couch to sleep on, mine is always available to you."

I let out a laugh. "I don't think it's gone that far. But thanks."

He shrugs and smiles. "One can only hope."

"Don't be an ass," I scold him.

"Too late." He walks to his truck and gets inside. Jackson rolls down the window and gives me a wink. "Don't let it bother you. He's just jealous of us."

"I know," I admit. "I don't care, though. You're my best friend, Jackson Bishop. You'll always have a place in my heart."

His eyes soften, and I watch him swallow hard. "You too, Pippi."

The nickname makes me smile. Jackson gives me a head nod, places the truck in drive, and I watch as he disappears in the distance. I suck in a deep breath and let it out slowly. Today turned into a shitshow really quick, one I didn't expect when I woke up this morning.

I walk back to Hershey, untie him, and decide we're done training for the day. My headspace isn't right, and that's the number one way to get hurt. I've learned that the hard way over the years. After I unsaddle him and brush him down, I lead him back to the open pasture and let him loose. As soon as he's free, he rolls around in the dirt, bucks a few times, then gallops off. I burst into laughter and walk back toward the barn.

I decide to send Trent a text, but when that goes unanswered, I call him but am sent straight to voicemail. Instead of focusing on how he's treating me, I spend the rest of the day cleaning stalls and doing bitch work, because it helps to keep my mind busy, which is what I need right now.

Once the sun begins to set, I drive home with a racing heart. Trent still hasn't answered any of my texts or returned my phone calls. You'd think he walked in on Jackson and me having sex by the way he's acting.

By the time I make it home, he's already there. His truck is parked in the driveway, and all the lights are on in the house. I sit in silence for a few minutes before gaining enough courage to walk inside.

As soon as I open the front door, I see him exiting the bathroom with a towel wrapped around his waist. He glances over at me but then continues to the bedroom as if he can't be bothered by my presence. I'm trying my best to calm down because I really don't want to argue about this. It's stupid and petty. So instead of following him and begging him to speak to me, I start cooking dinner. I'm not the type of woman to apologize when I haven't done anything wrong. Never have been, never will be.

I stand in the kitchen and decide to make tacos tonight. I take out the meat, taco seasoning, and all the extra toppings. By the time the meat is cooked, Trent enters.

"Hey," he says as he grabs a bottle of water from the fridge.

"Hey," I reply, trying to keep my tone as flat as his. "Dinner is ready."

"Great." He grabs plates from the cabinet, and we scoop food onto them.

As we sit at the table and eat, the silence draws on, and it basically devours me. There's so much spinning through my mind, not only from today but from the past couple of months.

Once we're done eating, I finally cave and say something. "So, are we going to talk about what happened today or keep pretending everything is fine?"

Trent looks at me. "All I'm going to say is don't let that shit happen again, Kiera," he warns, immediately sending me into a rage.

"What *shit*? What are you talkin' about? Me being with a customer? Me being with my best friend?" I snap. "Jackson and I are only friends. Been friends our whole lives. I've told ya that a hundred times."

"I don't care, Kiera. I don't like it. I don't like the way he looks at you. I don't trust him. If I catch you together—alone like that again—it's not gonna be pretty." His jaw clenches, and he stands, taking his plate with him and placing it in the sink.

"Alright, first off—" I begin, not waiting for him to face me or come back to the table. "Don't talk down to me like a child. Secondly, if you wanna fight, which you obviously do by the way you're acting, let's put everything out on the table then and discuss the statements I found in the top right drawer of your desk. Statements from a bank I've never seen or heard of before."

"What the hell are you talkin' about?" Trent walks back, folding his arms as if he's gearing up for battle. "And why were you snooping through my desk?" His question comes out accusatory, even though if he had nothing to hide he shouldn't care what I see or where I look.

"I wasn't snooping. I asked you for a check for the orchestra, and the statements were right there. I didn't recognize the bank name, and when I saw a thousand dollars get taken out every single month for the past several years, well, I got curious. I thought we shared a joint checking for our personal stuff and we each had our own business accounts. So yeah, why don't you tell me as long as we're traveling down this road?"

My breathing shallows as my chest rises with adrenaline. I've never been this mad at him before, and it feels all kinds of wrong, but a fight happening like this has been inevitable for some time now. Considering the stress of the wedding and our intense work schedules, the spark between us has dimmed, and I'm left wondering if the honeymoon period is over before it even had a chance to begin.

"Is that why you've been acting so crazy lately? You think I'm cheatin' on you or something?" His tone is harsh, and it causes my blood to boil.

The thought of him having a side woman crossed my mind, or perhaps a debt he didn't want me to know about, but then his face goes soft and sweet, making me second-guess ever having those assumptions. Trent is way too kind and widely liked and adored across the county. He'd never want to tarnish his reputation; not to mention he was brought up with the right morals and values from a traditional, Southern family.

"I'm not sure what I thought," I reply. "I had a few scenarios floating through my mind, but I'd be lying if I said I wasn't hurt when I saw it. I thought we didn't keep secrets from each other, especially since we're open about our financials and business income. It was a shock, and I wasn't sure how to bring it up."

"Babe, look…" He steps closer. "I'm so sorry you found it and thought I was intentionally keeping something from you. Honestly, it's one of those things that I just forgot about, and I promise you it's nothing bad. It's an old checking account that I autopay my student loans from, and I just never switched when I opened a new checking account in town. I auto transfer the money from my main account so there's enough for the withdrawal, and it's just something I forgot to bring up. That's it. I keep the statements as receipts for tax purposes." Trent closes the space between us and reaches for my hand. "That's all it is, sweetheart. You have nothing to worry about."

Ten pounds lift from my chest as he tenderly explains it all. Truthfully, I should've just asked him about it right away instead of letting it bottle up, but a tinge of doubt made me worry about knowing the truth.

"Okay," I say, releasing a deep breath. "I was just surprised, ya know? The only way this is going to truly work is if our communication is open and we're honest with each other."

"Of course, darling. I want it all with you." He winks, wrapping a hand around my waist and pulling me into his chest.

"I'm sorry for how I acted with Jackson." He looks down and sucks in his bottom lip as if he needs to dig deep to find the courage to say his next words. "I have a hard time understanding your friendship with him, and I don't like sharin', Kiera. I want you to myself."

"You have me, Trent. I'm marrying *you*," I remind him for the hundredth time. "You're going to have to accept our friendship or things will continue to be rocky between us, and that's not fair. We were friends long before I knew you, and we've always been close. It's just how things have always been, so you don't have to feel threatened."

"I know. Deep down, I know y'all are just friends, but that doesn't mean I like the way he looks at you."

"All that matters to me is how *you* look at me, so stop being a stubborn ass," I tease with a smile. "You two could get along and be friends if you'd both stop letting your egos get in the way."

He snorts, shaking his head. "Fat chance of that ever happening, baby. But for you, I'll try harder at being understanding and try to play nice."

I lean up on my tiptoes and give him a kiss. "Thank you." He leans down to give me a second kiss. "So…dessert?"

Trent bends, reaching under my thighs and hoisting me up until my legs wrap around his waist. I squeal, locking my arms around his neck and laugh.

He flashes a smug smile. "I was thinking the same thing."

CHAPTER FOURTEEN

JACKSON

THREE MONTHS BEFORE THE WEDDING

"Is there a reason you're always here?" I hear John behind me and picture him crossing his arms with a scowl.

I finish filling my mug with coffee before turning around with a shit-eating grin. "What can I say? You have the best brew."

He rolls his eyes and shakes his head. "That's for the guests," he reminds me.

"And employees," I correct with a smug grin. "You're here early." I look at my watch and see it's barely six. "Trouble in paradise for the newlyweds already?" I laugh, enjoying giving him shit at all hours of the day.

"Maize ended up in our bed, and after the third junk shot, I gave up. Left her and Mila to sleep and decided to come in and get a head start instead," he says, filling up his own cup. "And no. We're fine, thanks. Going to take her on a surprise *real* honeymoon in a few weeks, so keep your damn mouth shut."

"Wait…does that mean I'll have to pick up your slack again? Or will Nicole actually do her job?"

John scoffs and rolls his eyes. Nicole's been his assistant

manager for several years, and he's has always warned her away from me, but I know it's only a matter of time before we cross that line. She hasn't exactly kept her advances on the down low.

"I've picked up your slack for years. You owe me." He sips his coffee and walks to his office.

"I like to think it's been fifty-fifty," I protest, following him.

John snorts and takes a seat at his desk, resting his cup on top. He pushes his chair in and wiggles the mouse to wake up his laptop. The ring on his left hand looks foreign, and I'm still getting used to the idea that he and Mila eloped last week.

"So is this a real surprise, or do y'all plan to come back pregnant?"

"Don't jinx me," he says way too seriously. "I'm not ready for another one yet, and by how some of Mila's students act, I'm not sure I'll ever be."

I chuckle at his expense, anticipating Mila will get knocked up within the next year. The Bishop DNA is known for many things, but the top two are: strong work ethics and reproducing.

John proposed over seven months ago, so I'm not that surprised they finally got married, but I am shocked they didn't want to go all out with a big over-the-top wedding ceremony like everyone else around here. Dad nearly had a stroke, and River almost went into labor when we all found out. I think it's cool as hell that it was just the two of them. Small and intimate and no fuss.

Mama and Courtney, on the other hand, were blazing pissed.

John told everyone he was surprising Mila with a weekend away and left Maize with Mama. They left early Friday morning and returned late Sunday night with brand-new rings on their fingers. Apparently, that "surprise" trip was to Vegas where they "spontaneously" got hitched by an Elvis impersonator. It's as fucking cliché as it sounds, but I've never seen my brother so damn happy. They spent the rest of their time there honeymooning—walking down the Strip, getting couples massages, going to shows, gambling, and drinking. In fact, I'm quite sure when they returned, they were still a little tipsy.

Although I definitely saw Mila as a glam girl and was stunned she didn't want the whole wedding shebang, it actually made sense for them. Between John working at the B&B, Mila getting her daycare off the ground, and Maize, the two of them are insanely busy keeping up with it all, and she constantly mentioned how stressful planning a wedding would be.

Before I can respond, my phone dings with a text message at the same time as John's. We both look at each other and reach for our cells.

Alex: On our way to the hospital! River's been in labor all night, so it's finally time! Dropped Riley off with Mama, so I'll need you to cover my chores for me. I'll update y'all when I can.

Fuck that. I'll make Colton do them.

"Damn, looks like another Bishop is about to be born," John says, smiling.

Jackson: I'll take care of it. Let us know when we can come up! Go Team BOY!

I smile when I send the text, eager to find out what they're having. Since they wanted the gender to be a surprise, we've all been taking guesses, and just to rile him up, I've been saying it's going to be a boy and they're going to end up with four boys just like Mama and Dad.

"Well, I better go make sure Colton's ass is awake. I have lessons this morning, so we better get started on chores now." I slide my phone back into my pocket and finish the last of my coffee. "Let me know when you guys head to the hospital so I can ride with ya."

"Okay," he says as I start walking out. "But you're paying half for gas this time!" he calls out when I'm close to the front door. I shake my head and smirk, knowing he saw right through that one.

The hospital is an hour away, and diesel is expensive, so I try to bum a ride here and there.

Once I'm back at my truck, I call Colton and hear his sleepy voice on the other end.

"Get your ass up, Langston. Alex's wife is having the baby, so you're my bitch today." I start my truck and pound on the gas as I make my way to the other barn.

"Fuck off, Bishop," he grumbles.

"Don't make me come over there and spray you with my hose," I warn, revving up my engine.

"There ain't no fuckin' hose over here," he scorns as I hear shuffling and movement on his end.

"Not a water hose, you dumbass. Now, unless you enjoy golden showers, you better be up and ready by the time I get there."

"Shit...give me ten minutes, okay? Jesus," he hisses. "Sorry babe, I gotta get to work," I hear him whisper.

"You have a chick over?" I'm dying laughing. "Even better."

"Shut your mouth."

"No can do. Be there in five minutes." I hang up before he can respond, thinking of all the ways I could fuck up his day. Colton's become a good friend of mine since he started working here, but that doesn't exempt him from getting hazed like a rookie.

I arrive exactly three minutes later, thanks to speeding most of the way to the ranch hand quarters. When I realize his front door is locked, I begin pounding as loudly as I can, banging my fist against the wooden door.

"Colton! You small dick, open up!"

"I'm going to fuckin' kill you," Colton says as soon as he whips open the door.

I raise my brows when I see him wearing red silk boxers with black knee socks. "Dude…" I keel over laughing. "What the hell are you wearin'? You look like fuckin' Santa Claus."

"I hate you. Get out." He tries to slam the door in my face, but I'm too fast for his slow ass and stick my boot out.

"Not a chance, Kris Kringle. Horses need to be fed, watered, and brushed, gotta shovel shit, move hay, fix a few fences, oil the saddles, and pull some weeds by the B&B," I explain, listing it all out for him and laughing at how annoyed he looks right now. "Oh, and that's just half the chores since Alex isn't gonna be here. So go find your plush red suit and let's go."

"You're such a dick. I said I needed ten minutes." He leaves the door open and walks away.

"And I gave you three, so tick tock."

"Oh, hello…" A sultry, sweet voice comes from the kitchen as soon as I walk in and help myself to a bottle of water. Turning, I see Colton's date for the night wearing nothing more than a baggy T-shirt, and no coincidence it's red, which is so not helping his case right now.

"Ho, ho, ho…" I snort, but before I can tell her I'm joking, Colton comes up behind me and smacks me across the head.

"C'mon, Dana. Let's go take a shower. It'll be faster." Colton grabs her hand and starts leading her down the hallway, but before he does, he looks over his shoulder and mouths, *"Motherfucker."*

"Seven minutes!" I call out. "Or I'm coming in and joining."

Dana giggles, and I have no doubt she'd probably like that.

Seventeen minutes later, he finally returns fully dressed and ready to go. I'm sitting at the table with my leg crossed over my knee, and when I look down at my watch, he rolls his eyes and moves past me.

"Ten minutes late," I tsk. "That's comin' out of your lunch break," I taunt, sliding the chair back and standing up to follow him out.

"And it was totally worth it," he says, grabbing his hat off the coat rack and placing it on his head. "Sweet ass to share my bed with beats food any day."

Laughing, I shake my head at him as we get into my truck. "Shit, if I didn't know any better, I'd say you're worse than me. Guess Christmas is the most magical time of year after all."

"Or you could say Christmas came early…" he adds, smirking proudly.

"You're a nasty fuck." I chuckle.

I go through our chores again, then Colton and I go our separate ways, trying to get as much done as possible. The morning quickly transitions into afternoon, and the sun is blazing hot, causing sweat to drip down my face and neck as I finish the majority of the day's chores. I had three lessons this morning and then cleaned the barn to get ready for a ranch tour. I like to keep the barn as organized and tidy as possible, unlike my personal life, because it's my second home. I spend every day with the horses, and even though I like to pretend I don't get attached, it's too easy to not. Kiera takes the new ones for a few months at a time, and I find myself missing them even when they're huge pains in the asses before they're trained.

Alex sent an update a while ago saying River would deliver soon, and I'm waiting on pins and needles to find out the gender and that everyone is healthy and okay. She had an emergency C-section with Riley and is now trying for a VBAC for baby number two. Since she's a pediatric nurse, she knows a lot about the health benefits to at least try, which is why they didn't schedule one for her.

Mama already took Riley up there to wait and be there as soon as he or she arrives, but the rest of us will wait to arrive when they're ready for visitors.

"Heard you're gonna be an uncle again soon," Nicole sweetly says the minute she sees me walking into the B&B. I'm sweatin' balls, yet that doesn't seem to bother her one bit. "Congrats!" She smiles wide, holding her gaze on me as I head to the kitchen for a tall glass of cold water.

"Thanks. Still waiting for the news. Hopefully soon."

"Well, I have off tomorrow if you want to hang later tonight. I was going to maybe have a couple of drinks on the back patio and relax out there for a change."

Since the B&B runs seven days a week, Nicole works a lot, and although she's been around for the past few years, she's kept her distance for the most part. Until lately, it seems.

"Maybe," is all I say. I down the large glass of ice water.

"Well, you know where to find me." Nicole winks as I walk toward John's office.

"You know it, babe." I flash her my panty-melting smirk that all the chicks go nuts over. I shouldn't be laying it on this thick, considering she works with John, but it's just too tempting sometimes.

Just then my phone goes off, and I'm relieved when I see it's Alex with another update.

Alex: Baby GIRL is here!! She and River are doing amazing. Y'all can come up anytime.

I smile wide, excited to hear the news. Though I was wrong about it being a boy, I'm genuinely happy for my little brother.

Jackson: Congrats, bro. Glad to hear it! I'll be riding up with John in about an hour. See you soon!

"I'm gonna shower, then I'll be ready to go," I say into the office where John's sitting. "Alex texted me the exciting news."

"Sounds good. Mila said they'll be ready in about thirty minutes, so meet us at the house if you want a lift."

"I will."

After an hour drive to the hospital, spending two hours there meeting the new baby and unwillingly overhearing the birth story, and another hour to get home, we're finally back at the ranch, and I've never been more grateful to be a man. Though

River took everything like a champ, the detailed images that are flooding my mind have me thanking God for not having a vagina.

Deciding to take up Nicole's offer, I head to the B&B with a six-pack of beer and am surprised when I'm greeted by Colton who's already drinking and sitting on the back porch with her.

"Thought you'd be crying in a bottle of whiskey after all the bitchin' you did today," I say to Colton as soon as he spots me.

"You must be mistaking me for yourself because I kicked ass today."

I snort, shaking my head and taking a seat. "Is that why you pussied out before noon? Can't play with the big dogs, huh?" I grab my beer and twist off the cap before handing one to Nicole.

"You motherfucker," he spits, punching me in the arm.

"You might want to head in early since you'll be doing it for the rest of the week while Alex is gone."

He groans loudly, making all of us laugh.

"So what did they name the baby?" Nicole asks, breaking the playful tension.

"Rowan," I answer. "She looks just like River, too. Dark hair and dimples. She's a cutie."

"Aw, I love that name! I can't wait to meet her. I bet Riley is excited."

I laugh, remembering what Riley said. "Actually, he said he didn't want her to come home with them because she cries and smells."

Nicole laughs, placing a hand on my arm to emphasize how funny she thinks I am. Though I was only repeating what happened, the act doesn't go unnoticed. We continue talking about the baby and Riley, and soon Colton is forgotten.

"Well…since I'm the awkward third wheel here, I'm gonna head home and update my Tinder profile picture."

I snort at his obvious butt hurt tone. Though I love giving him shit, he's good company and a hard worker. But there's no competition when it comes to getting a girl's attention. I don't have any say in that most times anyway.

"Don't make me have to give you another wake-up call, Mr. Claus," I taunt as he steps off the porch.

He gives me a one-finger salute and mutters for me to fuck off.

Once we're alone, Nicole and I finish off the six-pack, and I invite her over to my place for another drink. I only have whiskey and beer, so as soon as we walk in, I pour us each three shots.

The rest of the night is mostly a blur.

"Fuuuuuuuck," I groan as my alarm goes off. I squint to find my phone and turn off the beeping noise. My head is pounding, which isn't unusual for me early in the morning after a night of drinking, but it literally feels like I fell asleep ten minutes ago.

I try rolling over but am blocked by another body and soon realize I'm not alone. An arm snakes around my waist and flashes of the night before surface. Nicole's hand slides down my stomach until she reaches my dick and grabs it.

"Mmm…is that morning wood or are you just happy to see me?" she asks lazily, pouring the seduction on heavily.

I snort, trying to hold back my laughter at her pathetic opening line. "Sorry, darlin'. Gotta get ready for work." I peel her hand off me, but she tightens her grip as if that'll suddenly change my mind. "I think you're still drunk," I tell her, maneuvering out of her reach. "Stay here and sleep it off." Swinging my legs to the side of the bed, I find my shorts on the floor and quickly put them on.

158

Having slept with her is going to make things awkward really quick. I continue my daily duties, hoping she realizes it was nothing more than a one-night stand. Considering I don't remember the before conversation, I'm not sure if I really drove that fact home. Hopefully, I did.

After my morning lessons, I walk inside the B&B and check in with John, but first I grab a cup of coffee because I need caffeine and a possible wake-up call.

"Is there a reason my assistant manager is asking for a raise?" John's voice booms behind me, and I know without a doubt he knows.

I turn around, flashing a smug grin. "Probably because she works sixty hours a week, and lately, the coffee hasn't been that great. Might want to check on finding a new distributor or—"

"Cut the shit, Jackson," he interrupts, closing the gap between us. "You should know more than anyone that you don't shit where you eat. Now she's asking for a raise and claiming she'll file a sexual harassment suit if she doesn't get one."

"What?" I shriek, taking a cautious step back. "That's blackmail. Not to mention, she's lying considering she had her hand tightly wrapped around my dick this morning before I even got out of bed."

"Jesus fuck, Jackson," he hisses. "How many times have I told you not to sleep with any of my employees, friends, or anyone who'll come back to bite me in the ass? If she files a sexual harassment suit with the Department of Labor, we'll get investigated, and I don't need that shit around here. This is one of our busiest times of the year."

"She's bluffing," I say, trying to calm his ass down. "I know it, and she knows it. She has no proof I harassed her."

"And you have no proof that you didn't. That's why they'd bring an investigator in and interview the other employees. You really want to take your chances?"

Fuck. I hadn't thought about that. "Look, I'll talk to her, okay?

Figure out what it is she wants and get her to leave you and the B&B out of this."

"You better, Jackson. Or your ass is out of here. I mean it." He walks away, slamming his office door behind him.

Well shit. That escalated to a level I hadn't seen coming.

CHAPTER FIFTEEN

KIERA

"OH MY GOSH, RIVER!" I squeal, reaching for baby Rowan and holding her to my chest. "She's so cute and tiny!"

I decided to skip out on work this afternoon and have a girls' lunch with River and Emily. Fifty percent to gush over the new baby and the other fifty to discuss the wedding. The only one missing is Mila, and she had to work.

"I love her name," I tell her. "She's seriously so sweet!" Sitting down on the couch, I look down at her wrapped in a plush pink blanket and think about how I can't wait to hold my own baby someday. Hopefully soon.

"Baaaaaabyyyy…" Elizabeth points at Rowan, and the three of us squeal in a round of aw's. She's getting so big, too, which makes my heart melt.

"Elizabeth, don't you want to be a big sister?" I ask, smiling at Emily.

"Baaaaaabyyyyy," she repeats, pointing at Emily's stomach. River and I give her a pointed look, waiting to see if she needs to tell us something else. They got married nearly four months ago, and I know she wanted to start trying right away.

"Something you want to announce?" I raise a brow in her

direction, eyeing the glass of wine I poured for her earlier, but she has yet to drink.

"No, not yet." She laughs. "Still trying." Emily sighs. "Between work schedules, an energetic toddler, and on-call room quickies, we haven't gotten pregnant yet."

"Well damn." I wrinkle my nose. "Wait for me then. I want to be knocked up by Christmas!"

River and Em laugh, knowing how badly I want to start a family. I hope it doesn't take too long. My parents were only able to have one child, and they didn't have me until their early thirties. I worry my window to reproduce is getting smaller and smaller.

"Don't stress. I've known plenty of honeymoon babies. As long as you're off the pill and actively trying, I think you should get pregnant pretty quickly. Assuming there are no medical issues of course," Emily concludes.

"Medical issues, like…my eggs have all dried up, and I'm unable to bear children?" I snicker, but really frowning at the thought.

"You aren't that old," she says, laughing. "I'm the same age as you, have a one-year-old, and am hoping to have more, so stop worrying. Stress and anxiety can affect getting pregnant too. So, tell Trent to start giving you nightly massages."

I snort at the thought. "Oh please. Massages will lead to sex."

"Isn't that the whole purpose?" River chimes in with a chuckle.

"Well yes, but I'm still on the pill. I don't plan to go off it until the end of September so that it's fully out of my system after the wedding."

"If you want my advice," River interrupts. "Getting drunk for like two weeks straight is what knocked me up the first time."

We all start laughing, and I wish I was able to lighten up a bit about the subject. River is younger and already has two babies, so it's hard for me not to feel as if I'm late to the game.

"Oh yeah, I've seen plenty of drunken one-night stand

pregnancies too," Emily says. "Probably because you're pretty damn stress free when you're wasted."

We laugh, and I snuggle Rowan tighter, trying to capture all these sweet and tender moments. They all grow up so fast, and I find myself wanting to sink it all in while I can. The three of us are close, but we all get so busy and wrapped up in our lives that we sometimes forget to slow down and really enjoy times like this.

"So I heard John and Jackson had it out," River says after a couple of minutes. "Alex didn't tell me all the details, but I figured one of you know why. He thinks because I'm hormonal and breastfeeding that I'm a fragile little bird who needs to stay inside and be a round-the-clock milk machine," she says with annoyance in her tone.

We chuckle at her overdramatics, knowing she's been stuck in the house ever since they returned from the hospital. Her VBAC was a success, but she's still sore and recovering from the birth.

"Wait, they did?" I ask, just processing her words. "About what this time?" I snort because it's always something between them. They live to give each other shit.

Emily's eyes lower, not meeting mine, and I know it's not good.

"What?" I ask, nudging her. "What'd I miss?"

"Yeah, spill it, Em," River encourages.

"Well, Jackson…" Emily pauses for a moment. "…hooked up with Nicole a couple of weeks ago, and later that day, she told John she wanted a raise or she's filing a sexual harassment suit."

"Oh my God!" River blurts out, and I'm thinking the same thing. Except I have a few more colorful words to add. First, Nicole of all people? Jackson has never slept with someone who works on the ranch, so I'm more than a little shocked. Though, maybe that means he's doing fine with me getting married and is continuing his man whore ways. Well, minus the harassment suit.

"So, did she sleep with him just to get the raise or did she get her feelings hurt and is now crying wolf?" I ask a little too defensively. Jackson would never force himself on anyone. He doesn't need to. Girls willingly flock to him. Hell, they basically take off their clothes before giving their names.

"That's what they're arguing about. John's pissed he crossed the line, and Jackson's pissed she used him. Though it's probably a bit of both. I'm sure Jackson wasn't Mr. Cuddles the next morning, and she got all butt hurt over it," Emily explains, which makes a lot of sense. "John said he better figure it out or his ass is out of there."

"What does that mean?" I ask.

"I guess he won't be allowed to help at the B&B anymore," Emily says with uncertainty. "Or maybe he just said that because he was pissed at the time. Either way, it's created some tension, and of course, Evan told them both to stop being assholes."

"So what happens if she does file a claim?" I ask. I'm honestly surprised something like this hasn't happened sooner, but I don't say that aloud.

"I guess a whole investigation happens, which will look bad for the B&B, and Mama would shit bricks." Emily sighs, and we all know it to be true. "I'm guessing John's going to give her the raise to keep her quiet."

"That's serious bullshit. I'd fire her ass for extortion," I snip. "Makes me want to go over there and give her a piece of my—"

Before I can finish, Riley comes barging into the living room wearing only his Spiderman undies and climbs up the couch to lie next to River.

"Hey, buddy. How was your nap?" she asks him, and I know our adult conversation is over.

Looking down at Rowan, I think about Jackson and what he must be going through. But then I remind myself it's not my problem to worry about his personal business or his irresponsible behavior that constantly gets him into trouble.

"So I'm thinking I'm going to need to go and get my dress taken in. I'm hoping by the wedding, I'm back to my pre-pregnancy weight. Or at least my post-Riley weight." River laugh-pouts, and I shake my head at her for being so worried. The wedding is over two months away, which gives her plenty of time to adjust her dress. I still think she was all baby anyway, but now that she's had two pregnancies, she's concerned about her stomach not going back as swiftly as the last time.

"If you're that worried, we can add a cute belt to cinch at your waist. That way it'll still be loose and flowy without it looking like a maternity dress."

"I love that idea!" Emily exclaims. "That way if I get pregnant before then, I won't have to worry about being bloated and feeling fat."

Giving her a side-eye, I smirk at her eagerness. "You wouldn't even be showing."

"Second pregnancy showing is so much different than the first!" River jumps in. "When I was pregnant with Riley, you couldn't tell until the second trimester. With Rowan, I popped overnight at like two months. Your muscles stretch so much faster after the first one."

"So what you're saying is maternity dresses for everyone?" I ask laughing, and they both laugh with me.

"Did you guys choose your flowers yet?"

"Ooh, did you guys decide on a wedding song?"

"Also, the rings. Is he picking his out, or are you surprising him with one?"

River and Emily are bombarding me with questions—ones that I should easily have answers to—but all I can think about is Jackson and how he knows exactly the kind of wedding I'd want.

Small, intimate, charming.

Trent has a large family and a wide customer base, so as the guest list grew, so did everything else in terms. Now it's a big, extravagant ordeal.

As the stress of the wedding wears me down, our relationship seems to be dwindling, too. Finding those bank statements in his desk, though he explained the reasoning for them, still has me second-guessing, and my gut instinct still tells me something is off. I'm not sure if it's just nerves or the uneasiness I feel when he gets upset over Jackson. The way he talks about the Bishops is a red flag that makes me wonder if I've overlooked the type of person he is all this time because he was so amazing in the beginning. He was so sweet, thoughtful, caring. Being with him felt so right, and the way he acted was what made me fall in love with him in the first place. I've wanted the whole fairy tale relationship for so long that now I'm scared I've ignored the obvious.

But maybe the stress of the wedding is taking a toll on him, too, and we're both taking it out on each other?

I hope so anyway because I've waited over thirty years to find my happily ever after, and I'll be damned if I let it slip away.

After leaving River's house and make a mental note of everything that still needs to be done for the wedding, I drive to the ranch to check on the horses and finish the chores I missed earlier.

I clean the stall Chief was in before Jackson picked him up, and it makes me think of him again. I shouldn't be upset, or hell, even surprised he slept with Nicole, but I can't help feeling jealous over it. He's always had an adventurous and carefree personality, and his one-night stands have been part of the Jackson package since we were in high school. However, it doesn't make it easier to be told specifics. When it's just the two of us hanging out and having a good time, it's easy to forget that side of him and pretend we'll someday end up together.

Except that dream died years ago, and the only thing I can hope for is keeping him as my best friend.

Kiera: Heard you got yourself into some trouble…when ya gonna learn??

Jackson: I learned chicks were crazy years ago, but this wasn't my fault.

I roll my eyes and snicker.

Kiera: You always say that.

Jackson: What can I say? I'm a magnet for trouble :)

Kiera: How you haven't knocked up someone yet is beyond me. You must be shooting blanks.

Jackson: Pfft! Just because I ride bareback doesn't mean I let girls ride me bareback ;)

Kiera: GAG. You're relentless.

Jackson: You love me.

Kiera: Debatable.

Jackson: Coming to visit me soon? It gets lonely out here.

Kiera: Sure, I can stop by tomorrow. Want to check on Chief anyway.

Jackson: Okay, see you then, Pippi.

I don't know why my heart races every time he calls me that, but it does. I find myself wishing for those careless, fun, adventurous days again.

"Alright, guys. Be good," I tell the horses after cleaning their stalls and putting out some hay. I want to surprise Trent with a nice dinner tonight, so I head out early and will get back to training tomorrow.

Before I pull into the driveway, I check the mail and am surprised to see a large manilla envelope inside with Trent's name on it. Once I walk into the house, I flip through the letters and set it all on the counter except the large one for Trent. It doesn't have a return address, and a part of me wants to rip it open and look inside.

Instead, I decide to take a shower and get dinner ready. I wash the day away and think back to the conversations I had with River and Emily. There's so much left to do for the wedding, and I suddenly get overwhelmed.

After I'm dried and dressed, I head to the kitchen and dig out the ingredients for tonight's meal. As I'm sautéing the onions, I glance over at the envelope again, and temptation pulls me toward it. It might be work related, but something tells me it's not.

Picking it up, I try to guess what could be inside. It's thin and might be papers, but the fact there's no return address has me overly suspicious. Knowing I should trust Trent and respect his privacy, I go against everything in my head and run my finger along the tab to rip it open.

My heart races as I shove my hand inside and pull out the contents.

What the hell?

Blinking, I look at four pictures of a little girl. She has to be no more than ten years old. They're all professional photos, and when I turn one around, I see handwriting.

Maggie Laken, 9 years old.

I know he doesn't have a niece named Maggie, so unless one of his siblings has a child I never met, this can only mean one thing—she's his.

Studying the picture, I notice she looks just like him. Same dark hair, brown eyes, and her facial features are nearly identical to his. Her hair is up in a half ponytail, and she's smiling wide as if someone just told her a joke. She's absolutely adorable.

It could be a family member I've never met or heard of before, but if that's the case, then why is there no return sender or letter, and why does it feel like my life is crumbling all around me?

The door opens and shuts behind me, but I don't move.

I can't.

I can barely breathe.

The realization that Trent could have a kid and never told me hits me right in the gut.

"Hey, darling." I hear him in the hallway. "Something smells amazing."

The sound of his boots grows louder as he moves closer to the kitchen, and I'm too shocked to say anything.

"Kiera?" he says my name behind me, and I finally blink. "You okay?"

I taste salt on my lips and hadn't even realized I was crying. Turning around, I'm greeted by Trent's warm eyes, and as soon as he sees my face, his expression contorts.

"What's wrong, babe?" He steps closer, but I hold my hand out to stop him.

"Do you have a child?" I blurt out, keeping my eyes locked on his so he knows I already know the answer. "A daughter?"

"Kiera, what are you talking about?" He moves closer, but I yell at him to stop. "What the hell?"

"Don't lie to me, Trent," I shout. "Who is this?" I reach behind me and grab one of the pictures for him to see.

He swallows and blinks.

"Is she yours?"

"Kiera, let me explain—" He brushes a hand roughly through his hair, and I can see his mind is spinning as fast as mine.

169

"Just tell me the truth," I interrupt his words, my heart racing. "Maggie. She's your daughter?"

Trent inhales a deep breath before answering. "Yes. Where'd you get that from?"

"They came in an envelope. Her name is written on the back. She's nine years old."

"Yes." He picks up the envelope and sees the other three pictures on the counter. "Why were you opening my mail in the first place?"

"That's what you think is important here?" I screech. "I had a feeling, and I guess I was right. I can't trust a damn thing you say." I push against his chest, needing to get the hell out of here.

"Kiera, don't…" Trent grabs my wrists and locks them tightly to his chest. "It's not what you think. Just let me explain."

"How can you explain not telling your soon-to-be wife that you have a daughter? You've lied to me for two years!"

"I've never met her," he says, shocking me further. "Her mother and I had a one-night stand, and she moved away before she found out. Once she claimed it was mine, I got a paternity test. After it was confirmed, I started paying child support, and that's the extent of the relationship."

"Wait…" I drop my arms. "The bank statements." The pieces start falling together. "That's what those are?"

Trent's shoulders drop as if he's defeated, and it makes me want to punch him in the face.

"Were you ever going to tell me? Or just keep me in the dark like a fool?" My blood is boiling, and I can't remember a time I've ever been this mad.

"It wasn't like that, Kiera," he insists, but I'm not buying it. "It's a part of my past I'm not proud of, okay? I slept around a lot in my twenties, and I was reckless. That's not the person I wanted you to know. When we first met, and things were so great between us, I was worried it'd scare you away. Then as time went on, I wasn't sure if it'd change how you felt about me, and I couldn't risk it. Not after falling so madly in love with you."

"You seriously think that little of me? That I couldn't handle your past and the truth? We aren't talking about a dog here. You had a child with another woman and neglected to tell me. For two years. How could you do that?" The tears pour down my cheeks, and I can't even look at him.

"I fucked up, Kiera. I know that, okay?" he says, his voice pleading for me to understand.

"How could you not be in her life?" I ask abruptly. "You financially support her, but have never met her?"

"I told you; her mother moved away, and we weren't dating."

"That's your excuse?" I raise a brow, unable to believe him right now. "You've never wondered in nine years what your own child was like, how she was doing, or even wanted to get to know her?"

"Sometimes," he says, shrugging. "I don't know."

"The phone calls, the money, and now this. I can only handle so many of your lies, Trent." I walk away and grab my purse and keys off the table. "I'm staying at my parents' tonight."

"Kiera, please don't go…"

Looking over my shoulder, I say my last words before leaving. "You've left me no choice."

CHAPTER SIXTEEN

JACKSON

TWO MONTHS BEFORE THE WEDDING

I WAKE up in a good mood. I feel great, invincible almost, and it might be because Mama invited Kiera over for lunch, and I'll get to see her without Dr. Douchebag interrupting again.

Feeding the horses goes by quickly, and so do my morning horse lessons. At some point, Trent shows up to look over a horse that's been sick the past week. Our conversation stays short and straight to the point, and we don't dare make eye contact. Every time he comes to the ranch, it gets more awkward between us.

Before he started dating Kiera, I didn't care for his condescending attitude, and since he's been with her, I dislike him on a whole new level. However, he's decent at what he does and has always been good with the horses. I've told Mama I wanted to start using the other vet in the area, but Dad refuses to allow me to do that, considering my family knows I don't like him because he's dating Kiera. I hate the way Trent treats me as if I'm below him and an inconvenience. It's obvious he hates Kiera's and my relationship, and by the way he looks at me, I know he wishes I'd just go away, but that's not happening anytime soon. Being around him only makes me think of Kiera even more, and knowing his sleazy lips and hands have touched her puts me into a rage, but I somehow find the strength to push it away. I don't know what she sees in him anyway.

Eventually, he leaves, and I finish cleaning the first two stalls before heading out. After I'm done, I hop in my truck and head to my parents' house. I know Mama is trying to keep Kiera close since our relationship has been rocky the past few months, which I actually don't mind. Mama has always seen her as a second daughter, and any time I get to be around her is time well spent.

As I park the truck, I see Kiera is already inside, and the smile I had this morning when I thought about her returns to my face. Sucking in a deep breath, I mentally prepare myself before opening the door and heading inside the house. As soon as I'm through the front door, I hear Kiera's laughter from the kitchen. John's voice echoes throughout the house, and I smile wider when I realize he's chatting about Maize and her antics.

As soon as I enter the room, Kiera's eyes meet mine, causing my heart to lurch forward. I give her a wink, but Mama distracts me before I can go talk to her.

"There he is," Mama says.

"Whatcha cookin', Mama?" I give her a side hug, noticing the pasta on the stove.

"Made Kiera's favorite. Fried chicken and my special macaroni salad." Mama gives me a knowing grin.

I take off my cowboy hat and sit at the table in front of Kiera. She's smiling at me like a crazy person.

With a smirk, I lean over the table, and whisper, "Isn't it a bit too early to be drinkin'?"

She laughs. "I'm not drunk, Jackson. You have shit in your teeth."

John glances over at me and bursts into laughter. "Looks like pepper from the eggs you ate at the B&B this morning."

"Well shit! I've talked to so many people today, and not one person said a damn thing," I say, lifting a fork and trying to see my teeth in the reflection. "I even had four lessons this morning."

And I saw Trent, so I'm sure he had a good laugh knowing pepper was between my two front teeth. I let out a groan and try to get it out. It's the size of fucking Texas.

Alex and Evan walk in and sit at the table arguing about cows and fences. Dad follows them, and I give him a smile. He smiles back, but he looks exhausted.

"None of that fussin'." Mama places homemade biscuits, fried chicken, and the macaroni salad on the table, glaring at Alex and Evan, so they stop talking about work.

I finally manage to get the huge ass speck of pepper out of my teeth but am almost tempted to leave it there because Kiera thinks it's hilarious. I'm pretty sure I even talked to John this morning after I ate. Bastard.

"How's the wedding plannin' going so far?" Mama asks Kiera once we all sit down to eat, but I wish she wouldn't have mentioned it. It seems as if Kiera doesn't want to discuss it either and keeps her answers short and to the point. I'm halfway hoping she'll come to her senses and call the whole thing off, but then she starts gloating about how perfect Trent is, and I have to physically stop myself from groaning aloud. I pretend to throw up in my mouth instead, and Mama shoots daggers at me. It's so damn hard for me to keep my side comments to myself, but for once I do, though I have a million different things I want to say.

Kiera goes on and on about Trent as if she wants us to fall in love with him, too, which will happen over my cold, dead body. However, as she continues, I study her while she speaks. There's doubt in her eyes, it's as plain as day, and maybe I'm the only person who can see it because I know her so well. Though I hear the words coming out of her mouth about how much she loves him, I wonder if she's just paying lip service to their relationship because that's what everyone expects to hear. Or if she's trying to talk herself into being with him long term.

Why is she marrying him if she seems so unsure?

Or could my mind be playing tricks on me?

Hell no. Her uncertainty is so goddamn blatant it gives me a glimmer of hope she'll pull the plug on it. Though I hope she wouldn't marry the bastard just to appease everyone, but considering she's already this far in, I worry she might feel that way. Either way, I have to get to the bottom of this.

I narrow my eyes at her, and she notices as she finishes her conversation. Thankfully, she doesn't say another word about Trent for the rest of our lunch. To fill the silence, Evan tells Mama a funny story about Elizabeth, making all of them laugh.

I shake my head at Kiera. Of course no one notices, but her. "What?" she mouths.

"I see you," I whisper. "I see straight through you."

She rolls her eyes and continues eating. Soon all our plates are cleared, and Mama pulls a homemade apple pie from the oven.

"Oh, Mama." Kiera groans. "I promised myself I'd stick to my diet until the wedding, which I broke the moment I took a bite of your delicious chicken."

Mama lifts an eyebrow at Kiera. "Are you sure? I'm not gonna pull your arm and force ya, but I won't tell anyone if you eat a piece." Mama flashes her a wink, and I already know she won't be able to resist.

Kiera chuckles, staring at the pie as the scent fills the room. "Screw it. Give me a slice."

After lunch, Kiera and I give Mama hugs and thank her for a great lunch. John stays behind and helps Mama clean the kitchen as Kiera and I head out the door.

"What was that about?" she asks, and when I give her a look, she continues. "That back there at the table?"

She's always been so blunt that it doesn't surprise me she asks.

"Nothing. Nothing at all. I've got my suspicions about something, but only time will tell," I explain, holding back what I really want to say.

"You better tell me, Jackson!" she demands with her hands on her hips.

I tilt my head at her and scoff. "I'm going to the barn. I've got some things to do."

"Can I come?" she asks. "I have a few hours before I need to be back at the ranch."

I let out a chuckle. "You know I'm not gonna tell you no."

Kiera's in a good mood, and I like seeing her like this. I get in the truck and smile as I look in the rearview mirror and see her following me. We park on the side of the B&B, and when I get out of the truck, she's already waiting for me.

"Truth or dare?" she asks as we walk side by side toward the barn. Kiera glances at me, and there's enough sass in her tone to make me want to pull her into my arms and kiss the attitude right out of her.

"I don't want to play," I say with a grin.

"That's not how the game works, Jackson," she reminds me. I look at her, and that's when I notice she's wearing a tank top, cut-off jean shorts that show off her toned legs, and cowboy boots. Standing in front of me is every man's wet dream, and I have to force my jaw shut so it doesn't hit the ground. I swear she wears this shit just to get under my skin, like always.

I finally let out a deep breath, knowing, either way, I'm fucked. "Truth."

Her smile widens, and her eyebrow pops up. "Somehow I knew you'd say that."

I lick my lips. "It's because you know me, Pippi. You know everything about me."

Kiera watches me. "What did you mean back there, during lunch, that you could see straight through me?"

I shake my head. "I don't want to talk about it right now." Or ever.

"You have to. You know the rules. Just tell me." Her eyes soften, making me want to be open and honest with her, but instead, I keep my lips sealed.

Giving her a smirk, I reach for the top button of my shirt and take my time undoing each and every one as I keep my gaze on her. Kiera covers her mouth and shakes her head.

"Jackson, don't do this. It's daylight. Someone could see you." She tries to reason with me, but I refuse to discuss her and Trent when she's happy like this. It brings the mood to a dark place and ruins our moments together.

I drop my shirt to the ground and peel off my undershirt.

"Better take a picture, it'll last longer," I tease when I catch her staring at my abs and the tattoos across my chest.

When I reach down to unbuckle my belt, she places her hand on my arm. "Jackson. Don't. Okay, I take it back."

My eyebrow pops up. "You know the rules, Pippi. No take backs allowed."

I watch her cheeks turn pink as she drops her arm. This only encourages me to keep going. The belt drops with a clank on the ground, and Kiera takes a step forward and places her hands on my shoulders just as I reach for the button of my jeans. She's so fucking close I can smell the sweetness of her soap, her skin, and everything about her completely envelops me. Her hands against my bare skin almost burn, and my breath hitches when I look into her green eyes.

"Jackson, please," she begs. I find myself staring at her lips, and I don't care if she notices.

"Don't do this. You're going to get in trouble. Someone could see you. Mama will beat your ass black and blue, and I'll feel guilty as hell."

"Trouble is my middle name," I remind her with a wink.

"No. That's just the persona you want everyone to see. I know better."

I chuckle, bringing my hands back to the top button of my jeans. She hasn't moved an inch, and the temptation to place my arms around her waist and pull her closer to me—making us as close as we can be—is evident and strong. Kiera places her hands on my cheeks, forcing me to look into her eyes again, and that's when I hear yelling coming from behind her. My brows furrow, and I look around her and see Trent charging toward me.

"What the hell? You motherfucker!" he yells. Kiera turns around and sees him coming at us.

"Trent. Stop," she says softly, but he pushes past her, nearly knocking her down.

I instantly see red.

"Keep your dirty fucking hands off my fiancée," he yells, pushing me with all his body weight, but I was ready for him. I stumble but gain my footing and put my fists up to block his attempt to hit me. I almost laugh at how mad he is right now.

Trent throws his cowboy hat on the ground and swings again but misses. Kiera runs up to him, trying to pull him away and yells at him that he *promised*. What that means, I don't know. Trent's too caught up in trying to beat my ass, he misses me and hits her. Kiera takes a step back and hunches over, covering her face. Instead of stopping to see if she's okay, he zeros in on me, and that's when I completely lose it. It's evident the asshole doesn't give two shits about her.

I allow all the anger and hurt I've felt since they got together surface and tackle him at the waist, bringing him to the ground. I know that when fighting, you should always expect the unexpected, and by the look on his face, as he tumbles down, I know he didn't anticipate me doing that. My fist connects with his face, over and over.

"Don't ever fucking hurt her again, you bastard," I hiss as my fist connects with his nose and jaw. He tries to block me, to get me off him, but I'm much stronger than him. Trent covers his face with his arms, and Kiera tries pulling me off him.

"Please, Jackson," she begs, tugging on my bicep, and it's his only saving grace.

Heaving as I stand, I look at her to see if she's okay. I place my finger under her chin and get a better look at the eye that's already starting to turn. Kiera lowers her eyes, unable to even look me in the face.

"I ought to kill his sorry ass," I growl, trying to catch my breath.

"It's not worth it. It's just a big misunderstanding."

Kiera tries to help Trent up, but he gives her the cold shoulder and nudges her away.

"Don't you ever fucking step foot on my property again acting like that, Trent. Next time, you won't be so lucky," I threaten, my jaw clenching in anger.

"Stop, Jackson," Kiera says, just as Trent gets up off the ground and comes after me again.

That's the point when I lose my resolve. I hear screaming in the background as we're rolling around on the ground, and moments later, I'm being pulled off by someone who's much stronger than me. When I look up and see Deputy Pettigrew, I instantly know I'm fucked. Out of all the men they could've sent out here, it had to be *him*. Next, I see John standing next to Trent.

"What the hell are you doing, son?" Pettigrew asks, looking me up and down, then glancing over at Trent who's in the worst shape. Though I want to smile and rub his face in his own shit, I don't.

"He hit me first," Trent says, spitting out blood. "I wanna press charges."

My mouth drops open, ticking with anger. "You're a goddamn liar, Laken. You threw the first punch."

Trent wipes the blood from his lip with the back of his hand. "Who's he gonna believe? Someone who's educated and respected within the community or a fucking troublemaker who gets in fights all the time?"

Pettigrew looks at me, and instead of running my mouth this time, I bite my tongue even though I'm ready to beat Trent's face in for that comment.

"Can someone here tell me what the hell happened—someone who isn't either one of them?" Pettigrew asks loudly. Guests from the B&B step out onto the back porch to rubberneck the situation, and I know that if this doesn't dissipate soon, Mama will be down here to solve it herself. Trent and I are separated and both placed in handcuffs, and all I can think is how this time, I haven't even had a drink, and I'm going to jail.

"Kiera, you're gonna have to tell me what happened here," Pettigrew says, pulling her off to the side. I hate that he's asking her, putting her word between the both of us, but I hope to hell she tells him the truth. None of this was my fault this time.

I overhear another officer getting a statement from Trent and most of what he says is bullshit, except for the part of why he's here in the first place. Then again, that could be a lie too. I make a mental note to check the stall where the horse is that he saw earlier because apparently, he forgot something in there. If I didn't know better, I'd say he caught wind of our lunch today and allowed his jealousy to lead him back to the barn.

I don't know why he's making a big fucking deal over her being around me. We've known each other much longer than they've been together, and we have a history together that no one, not even him, could replace. After all, Kiera is marrying *him*, but it's as if he won't be happy until she agrees to never talk to me again. I hope it doesn't come to that, but I have a feeling that's where it's heading.

Pettigrew walks over and grabs me by the arm, just when I see Mama pulling up in her Cadillac.

"Oh, fuck," I whisper, but Pettigrew doesn't say a word. I'm sure he's thinking the same thing.

Mama parks and slams the car door, and it's as if everyone feels her wrath because all chatter stops. She glances over at the guests standing on the back porch and nicely tells them to go inside. I notice her fists are in tight balls as she walks up to us. What's even more frightening is she doesn't say a word to me, just gives me the evil eye, and walks straight up to Trent.

"You're fired, Dr. Laken. Coming onto my property, making a scene like that, and disrespecting my family. I outta call your mama right now and tell her what you've done."

I let out a snort, wanting to give Mama a standing ovation.

Mama then turns to me with a scowl. "And don't think you're clear of any of this, Jackson. So keep your damn mouth shut." She hardly ever curses, so I know she's at a dangerous level of pissed off, and that's a force I don't want to reckon with.

Trent doesn't make eye contact with Mama when she turns back around and glares at him. After a moment, she looks at Pettigrew and thanks him for calling her.

"You're a sellout," I whisper. He lifts an eyebrow at me, tempting me to keep running my mouth, but I shake my head instead.

Mama walks past me without saying another word and goes straight to Kiera. She grabs her hand and leads her to the car, and they drive off. My heart is racing. I want to ask Kiera if she's okay and make sure Trent didn't hurt her too badly, but I already know her eye is going to have a shiner.

"Well, son," Pettigrew says, removing the handcuffs from my wrists and looking me up and down. I'm filthy from rolling around on the ground, and there's blood from my busted knuckles. Other than that, I'm fine.

"Kiera told me what happened, and you better be damn glad because I would've booked you so fast your mama's head woulda spun," he informs. "But I realize Laken lied, and you weren't responsible for this. Now, I need to know what you'd like to do."

I let out a deep breath, relieved Kiera told the truth. "I wanna press charges for assault."

"You sure about that?" I hear John ask from behind as he walks toward me. He's always trying to be the voice of reason, but I'm not going to change my mind about this. Trent needs to learn not to fuck with me.

"Absolutely." I look at John and confirm with Pettigrew. This bastard isn't going to get away with hitting Kiera and trying to kick my ass. He earned every fine he'll get, and I don't feel a tad guilty about it. Fuck him.

CHAPTER SEVENTEEN

KIERA

MAMA BISHOP PICKS me up from the B&B, and I'm so fucking mad I can't speak. My eye has already swollen shut, and the way I feel inside doesn't compare to the pain of being punched in the face by my fiancé.

"What happened, child?" Mama Bishop looks over at me and searches my face once she parks the car.

My lip quivers. "Trent punched me," I tell her, cringing at how it sounds aloud. Her brows shoot up, looking ready to drive back there to give him another piece of her mind. "On accident," I add quickly. "He drove up and saw Jackson and me, then lost control. I tried to break it up but happened to be in the wrong place at the wrong time and got hit in the crossfire."

She places her hand on my shoulder, her eyes softening. "So he attacked Jackson first?" she asks, and I know if it were the other way around, he might not live to see another day.

I nod. "I told Pettigrew as much too. I'm not going to lie for Trent. Not now, not ever." My voice cracks at the end, and she notices. I hate to be put in a position to have to choose between them, but being honest is ingrained in me. Too bad it's not ingrained into him.

"It's gonna be okay. Men talk with their fists. I've learned that firsthand." She sighs as if she's been through this more times than she can count. "Let's go inside and get some ice on that eye. Then I'll get you a cup of coffee and a piece of cake." She smiles.

I follow Mama inside, and once she gets me an ice pack to stop the swelling, I willingly eat a piece of chocolate cake as she brews a pot of coffee. Though I've been trying to stay away from sweets and carbs so I can easily fit into my wedding dress, I figure today's an exception.

Once the coffee's brewed, Mama sets the mug down in front of me along with a bottle of hazelnut creamer. I thank her and pour some into my cup before stirring it.

The house is quiet, but it's exactly the same as it was when I was a kid running through the hallways chasing Jackson or playing with Courtney. It's always felt like home here, and I hope it always does.

"Anything you want to talk about?" she asks as she sits down. I'm too embarrassed to make eye contact and feel as if my whole world is crumbling. I've never seen Trent lose complete control before, and considering we've talked about Jackson and our friendship, I thought it was an issue we already worked through. He promised me he'd be on his best behavior and would play nice. He went against his word. It worries me how much I don't know the man I'm marrying, but I don't dare speak my doubts into the universe or even hint them to Mama Bishop. Instead, I shake my head and force a smile.

"You know what's best for you, honey. That's all I'm gonna say."

I'm thankful for the silence as I eat my cake and drink the coffee. It helps settle my nerves just enough. Once there's nothing but crumbs left, Mama takes the empty plate and sets it in the sink, then hands me two ibuprofen. "You're gonna need these."

I laugh, keeping the ice pack to my face. "Yeah, with a shot of whiskey and a bottle of courage. Because this is going to get dealt with today when I get home."

Mama looks at me with an arched brow. "If he lays a hand on you, Kiera, or if you're unsafe—"

"I'm not," I snap but don't mean to. "I'm sorry, I didn't mean for that to sound so rude. I've never seen that side of Trent before, so I'm just a little rattled."

"Honey, it's fine." She covers my hand with hers. "If you ever want to talk, though, I'm always here. No judgments."

I appreciate that more than she realizes. "Thank you, Mama. You've always been sweet to me."

She flashes me a wink and smiles. "It's because you're my second daughter. Want me to take you back to your truck? I think enough time has passed that everyone has probably left."

I glance at the clock on the stove and give her a smile. "Yeah, that'd be great."

We head to the car, and the ride over to the B&B is filled with silence as I hold the ice pack on my face. It's giving me slight relief at least, and I can only hope it keeps the bruising down too. She grabs the steering wheel with white knuckles when she sees Jackson, and I know he's in trouble. Mama shakes her head at him.

"I can't talk to him right now. I might actually whip him like he's a kid again for not keeping a level head. I always taught him to fight back if someone threw the punch first, but it's his ego and attitude that gets me every time." She laughs, but I know she's not joking. "Take care, Kiera." She squeezes my arm with a sympathetic smile. "If you need anything, don't hesitate to call, okay, dear?"

"Yes ma'am, I will."

She turns and gives me a hug, and it makes me smile. After we break our embrace, I get out of the car. Jackson walks across the pasture toward me. His button-up shirt is open, showing off his muscular body again, and I swallow hard. I look at his face and notice his lip is busted, but other than that, he doesn't have a scratch, which doesn't surprise me.

"I'm sorry." It's the only thing I can say.

"For what? You didn't do this, Kiera. The only thing I'm sorry about is not kicking his ass the way he deserves." Jackson reaches out and removes the ice from my eye. I cringe slightly, hating all the thoughts that must be running through his mind right now. He gently places his finger under my chin so he can get a better look. "He got you good."

I sigh and look into his eyes. "He didn't mean to."

"But he did," he whispers.

I shake my head. "I've got to go. I'll see you later."

Jackson grabs my arm and pulls me back to him. "If you need a place to stay. If you feel unsafe, my couch is always available."

I jerk my arm from his grasp. "Why does everyone keep saying that to me? It's really starting to piss me off."

His mouth falls open, and he closes it. His sad eyes bore into me, but I push it away. "I've gotta go."

I don't look back at him. I can't. Instead, I keep walking to my truck. I get in, crank it, and drive down the B&B driveway without taking a glance in the rearview mirror.

As the silence draws on, the tears begin to fall. My eye hurts so damn bad. I can't help but think how Trent and I had finally gotten to a good place after our last blowout. Finding out he had a daughter who he gave up and hid from me from the beginning hasn't settled well with me. Watching him lose control today and have him push me, then hit me, regardless of it being an accident, is too much.

Eventually, the road leads me home, and I pull up to the house and stare at it. Trent isn't around, and I'm unsure of where he is. I double-check my phone to see if he's texted or called, and there's nothing. It's as if all communication has been cut off completely between us. I hate when he gets like this, which has been happening a lot lately.

Sucking in a deep breath, I go inside and walk straight to the bathroom to look in the mirror. I'm a fucking mess, and my eye has already started to bruise. I'm sure by tomorrow everyone in Eldorado will have heard about what happened, and unfortunately, there's no way I can hide my face from the world. Basically, I'm going to have to live with what happened and hope I don't get too many side glances or comments when I'm in public. The reality is Trent lost his shit over nothing, and now I have to deal with it. It's only a matter of time before the rumors start flying.

I walk through the house and feel as if I'm suffocating inside. Not able to take it any longer, I walk outside and sit on the steps of the porch. Moments later, I see Trent's truck pull around the corner, and it causes my heart to race. He parks and gets out, slamming the door. He doesn't look at me as he walks past me. All I can do is stare up at the cloudy sky. The way he's acting is breaking me down. I place my face in my hands and let it all out. Every emotion streams through me from sadness to anger, and that's when I fucking lose it.

I stand, pull up my big girl panties, and walk inside. Trent stands in the kitchen with a beer in his hand. Both his eyes are blackened, and his nose looks broken, not to mention his busted lip. Jackson really beat the shit out of him, and I'm taken aback by how bad he looks. I stop walking. Everything I was going to say slips my mind.

He chugs his beer and sets the empty bottle on the counter. "What?"

"We need to talk about this," I tell him, not even knowing where to start.

"Yeah, we do." He's being short, and his anger isn't lost on me.

Trent grabs another beer and pops the top. "So, are you fucking him or what?"

My mouth falls open. "Are you kidding me right now?"

"Just wondering if I'm marrying a lying, cheating whore or not."

My nostrils flare, and he pushes me to a level of angry I've never felt before. My hand trembles, and I feel like I'm going to explode. "The only person who has secrets around here is *you*.

Don't you fucking forget that, Trent. Jackson and I are just friends.
We've never crossed the line, and I have nothing to lie about or
hide. You owe me an apology for blacking my damn eye too. You
did this, Trent. Remember that. You did this because you're so
goddamn insecure with yourself." I stare at him, and my words
don't even affect him. "It's like I don't even know you anymore."
I grab my keys off the counter and walk toward the front door.

I can't stand to look at him.

I can't stand to be around him when he's like this.

I hear his footsteps behind me, and then he grabs my arm,
stopping me. His fingers dig into my skin, and he's holding me so
tight pain shoots down to my fingers. Trent forces me to turn
around and look at him. "Do you still want to marry me, Kiera?"

"Let. Go," I demand. "You're hurting me."

"No. You're going to answer me right now."

With everything I have, I jerk my arm from his grasp. "I'm not
doing this. Not with you so mad."

He crosses his arms over his chest. "If you leave, the wedding
is off."

"Don't threaten me."

"I'm not. But I'll tell you this much. That son of a bitch pressed
assault charges against me, and based on the statement you gave
the police, there's nothing I can do. So thank you for that, Kiera.
Thanks for choosing him over me."

"It wasn't about choosing sides; it's never been about that. I'm
not going to lie for you, Trent. I'm not going to compromise my
integrity because you can't control your anger and jealousy." I
feel sick. I didn't realize Jackson did that. Pressing charges is a
serious allegation, and I wish I could take it all back. I wish I
wouldn't have followed Jackson back to the B&B or asked him
truth or dare, so then when Trent drove up, I wouldn't have been
there, and none of this would've happened.

Trent clears his throat, bringing me back to reality but doesn't
say a word, and that's when I turn and grab the doorknob and
walk out. He doesn't chase after me. He doesn't beg me to stay.

Somehow, I didn't expect him to either. I text Addie, needing to speak to someone, to talk about what's going on, because I can't keep it all inside.

Kiera: I need to chat. It's important.

Addie: Why don't you come over? Baby is taking a nap. I was trying to catch up on Netflix.

Kiera: I'll be there in five minutes.

I'm so grateful for my cousin and how she's always been there for me. I'd call Emily, but I know she's working a long shift today, and I don't want her to worry about me. I'm sure she'll hear all about it when she gets home anyway. I drive over to Addie's, and as soon as I park, relief sweeps over me. She meets me at the door with a smile on her face, but I watch it fade away when her eyes meet mine.

"Oh my God, Kiera! What happened?" She searches my face. "Are you okay?"

I force a smile. "Truthfully? No."

Stepping aside, Addie opens the door and lets me in. Her house smells like cookies, and I see *Stranger Things* paused on the television. I sit on the couch, and she immediately comes to me and stares at my black eye.

"Jackson and Trent got into a fight. I got into the middle of it." I motion toward my face as an explanation.

Her mouth falls open.

"I know." We sit in silence for a moment.

"Why were they fighting?" she asks.

"Because I was touching Jackson when Trent pulled up. I guess. He's been so jealous and insecure when it comes to Jackson. Now it's just getting out of hand."

She lets out a huff. "Do you blame him, though?"

I glance over at her. "What do you mean?"

"Isn't it obvious?" She laughs. "You look at Jackson like he'll rope the moon for you. Even after everything, even with that ring on your finger. I'm sure Trent notices it, too, because everyone else does."

"Jackson and I aren't anything. You know that."

She nods. "I know. But switch positions with Trent. What if there was a woman who everyone knew he had a thing for, and he was constantly around her, touching her, seeing her every week. Don't you think you'd be pissed about it too? I can't blame him. Add in some testosterone and fighting over you is the only solution."

I roll my eyes at her. "Whose side are you on anyway?"

She chuckles. "You didn't deserve to be punched in the face, but I'm sorry, I kinda have to take Trent's side on this one. Play devil's advocate a bit."

The silence draws on, and I think about what she said. I try my best to put myself in his shoes, to reverse the situation, and I do understand where he's coming from, but there's more to it than just that.

"The fact that I'm marrying Trent and will spend the rest of my life with him should overrule anything else. It should be enough. I don't ever plan on getting a divorce. I want to have kids right away. When things are good between us, they're *really* good, like the stuff fairy tales are made from. But when they're bad, it's like a nightmare, because it's to the extreme."

Addie gives me a small smile. "Who are you trying to convince here? Me or yourself?"

I need to hear this, all of this, because I've been so caught up in my perspective that maybe I haven't given Trent's a second thought. Guilt washes over me.

"What should I do?" I look around the room at the pictures of her and Landon together. They're happy, carefree, and the love and admiration they have for each other just oozes from the frames. What she has is relationship goals.

"Girl, I have no idea what you should do. Maybe think about

Trent when you're around Jackson. Remember why you're marrying him in the first place. If you two keep on down this path, there's no way this marriage will end happily. Trent isn't a monster. He's a nice guy, good-looking, has his shit together, and not too long ago, he was everything you ever wanted. So my question to you is what happened between now and then?" She stands up, goes to the kitchen, and comes back with a plate of cookies. I smile and grab one, though I feel like I've been eating sugar all day. But it's definitely what you do in the South. Offer cookies and cake. Though what I really need right now is a drink.

I think about her question and replay everything that's happened this year.

"A lot," I answer truthfully, taking a bite. They're still warm. "I haven't told a single soul about this. But he apparently had a kid with another woman, and I just found out about it, after being together for two years. I honestly don't think he would've told me if I hadn't stumbled across some things. I thought he was living a double life. Money was disappearing every month. I'd overheard strange phone conversations. So I'm still having a hard time dealing with the secrecy of it all because now it's created trust issues. We were working through that, and then this happened."

Addie stops chewing. "What?" she asks with her mouthful. "A kid? Oh my God. So does he see his kid at all?"

"No. He just writes a check each month for child support. If it were up to him, he'd rather pretend it wasn't a thing and just ignore it altogether." I watch her face contort from confusion to anger.

"Now I'm speechless." She hands me another cookie. "It's like everything I thought about him—"

"I know," I interrupt her, not wanting to hear the rest of her sentence. I've been feeling the same way, that maybe everything I knew about him is a lie, an act, that maybe the man I fell in love with isn't reality, and I've been blinded by his charm all this time.

"Do you still love him?" she asks.

Reluctantly, I nod. "Yes, without a doubt," I say. "Even through all the deceit, lies, and fighting—I do love him. We have history, and I care for him deeply," I admit. "We're going through some rough patches, but I think we can get through them. I hope at least."

She smiles sincerely. "No relationship is perfect. You just have to decide if it's worth fighting for."

"Yeah, you're right. It's a lot to process." I grab another cookie and know if she doesn't take them away, I'll eat them all. I think back to the night of our fight when I learned about Maggie. It still hurts, knowing he kept it from me, but I also know he wouldn't intentionally hurt me that way. The past few months have seriously tested our relationship, and with each test, I can only hope it brings us closer at the end. We've been together for two years, and there will still be things to learn about each other for months and years to come.

The day after our big blowout, I told him I needed time to trust him again. We waited until we were both calm to sit down and talk it through without getting angry with one another. I asked him to tell me everything, and he walked me through all the events from how he found out about his daughter to why he never tried to have a relationship with her. It's hard for me to comprehend, so it's something we still disagree on, but I have to let him live with his own choices on that one. It's something we'll have to continuously work through, and I'd hoped we were moving forward, but now that he blew up on Jackson for just being around me, I'm not sure where this'll take our relationship.

Eventually, Addie changes the subject, noticing I don't want to discuss it anymore and turns on the TV. We sit and watch an episode of *Stranger Things* though I have no idea what's going on. As soon as the baby starts crying, she stands, and I do too. I give her a hug, and she squeezes me tightly.

"Thank you so much for listening and talking it out with me."

"Anytime." She releases me and smiles. "If you want to do

another wax session before the wedding, let me know. My treat." She winks, and I snort in response. Fat chance of that happening.

"I'm going to head out. I need to talk to Trent. And hopefully, he's cooled down by now."

"I'm sure it'll be fine."

On the drive back home, I take in everything we talked about. Addie's smart, levelheaded, and doesn't always take my side. If I want Trent and me to work out—which I do—I'm going to have to meet him halfway on his feelings, and I realize I haven't been.

His truck is still parked in the driveway, and my nerves get the best of me. I swallow hard, gaining the courage I need to walk up the porch and go inside. As soon as I open the door, I see him on the couch sleeping. I go to him, bending down until I'm close to his body. His eyes flutter open, and he just stares at me.

"I'm so sorry." My voice seems small and insignificant.

"I am too," he says, opening his arms and pulling me into them. "I'm so damn sorry. I love you so much and am afraid of losing you."

"I love you too." A sob escapes me, and I look up into his eyes and kiss him. He pulls me onto his chest and holds me.

"I'm not giving up on us," he says, wrapping his arms around me tightly.

I lay my head against his chest and listen to his heart beating. "I'm not either."

CHAPTER EIGHTEEN

JACKSON

A FEW WEEKS have passed since the fight with Trent, and I haven't seen Kiera since. I can't help but think she's written me off for good, and Dr. Douchebag has finally gotten his wish. Things between us are tense, and the last horse that was supposed to be delivered was brought by Alexis. She's avoiding me at all costs, and I'm half tempted to drive over to the Lazy Y Ranch and see what's going on, but I don't. If this is what she wants, so be it. I can avoid her too.

After my workday is over, my mind is all over the place. Knowing I can't sit around, I grab a bottle of whiskey and tuck a few logs into a backpack. I hike the mile to our secret spot, drop the wood into the metal fire ring, and light it. Once the wood is popping, I sit on the ground, crack open the whiskey, and watch the flames dance.

My mind wanders back to a different time, and I replay the memory like it was only yesterday.

Kiera is dancing and singing as loud as she can to a Dixie Chicks song talking about a runaway bride. Lately, she's been bringing a little radio with her out here to help drown out the silence. I actually like the sound of nothing; it relaxes me, but she insists it gets boring, and I always agree to whatever she wants—which is why I'm listening to this crap. It makes her happy, so I can't complain. She's wearing shorts and a T-shirt and her favorite cowboy boots. As she dances around, I can't take my eyes off her. The song finally ends, and she plops down next to me.

"That song is horrible," I tell her.

"No, it's not. It's my favorite song in the whole wide world," she says, smiling.

"But have you listened to the words?"

Kiera giggles. "Yep. She's gonna be ready to ditch that weddin' and have some fun. Every girl's dream."

My face contorts. "Whatever. When I marry someone, they better not run away like that. Can you even imagine?"

She snort-laughs. "I don't see you ever getting married, Jackson."

"Same about you, Pippi. Not with how gross your farts are!" I lift her braid and let it fall down against her back.

Kiera rears back and socks me in the arm, and it actually stings. "Ow, fuck." I rub the spot.

"You deserved that one!"

"I'll hit you back." I joke with her, but she knows I'd never do that. I'd never hurt her, and I'd beat up any boy who does. I'm protective of her, just like I am of my sister, and everyone at school knows it, too.

"Whatever. When I'm older, I'm going to marry a rich guy who can buy me everything I want. Expensive barrel racing horses and real leather boots that match my saddles. I'll have a minimum of one hundred horses, and I'll hire all these trainers to live on my property to train them and keep all my horses fit and in good shape. Then I'm going to have a huge horse trailer with sleeping quarters and travel around America winning championships and beating records with all my horses. And I want like six kids when I'm old, like twenty-five." She laughs. "I hope he's a doctor and really hot. And mega rich. Wouldn't that be cool?" Her eyes light up, and she seems as if she's lost in this make-believe dream world.

Even though I'm fourteen, I know I'll never be a doctor or have tons

194

of money. I plan to work on the ranch just like my dad and maybe train horses when I grow up. It's my future and what I was born to do.

The sun is starting to set, and I put some more wood on the fire to keep the area lit. Kiera glances over at me, and I feel something in my body. I swallow hard, thinking how pretty she looks, but I know I shouldn't think those things. She's supposed to be like my sister, but my thoughts about her aren't very sisterly.

"What about you?" she asks. "What kind of girl do you want to marry?" Kiera takes her hair out of the messy braids. She tucks the waves behind her ears and stares at me.

"I'm never getting married," I joke. "But when I meet the girl of my dreams, I'll know."

I already do.

She playfully rolls her eyes. "Well, if for some reason, when we're like forty and if both of us are single, we should just get married to each other. That way we won't be old hermits with all of our horses. Deal?"

I smile. "You'd marry me?"

"Only if I were old and desperate," she says, giggling. "It'd be like marrying my brother or something, and that's kinda gross." She doesn't even have a brother.

"Gee, thanks." I place my hands behind my head and lean back and watch darkness fall. Kiera does the same. We lie there until the fire dies out, listening to the soft sounds of the country music playing in the background. When we finally sit up, I can't help but feel like I'll never be good enough for Kiera. I'll never be able to make her happy, and she deserves every silly thing on her list.

I take a huge gulp of whiskey, trying to push the thoughts away. I've always felt like I wouldn't be good enough for her, and her being with Trent is proof that I'm not. I guess she got her doctor after all.

Leaning back, I place my hands behind my head and stare at the bruised sky. Soon it'll be dark, and hopefully, I'll be drunk enough for all these thoughts to disappear.

I close my eyes, and Kiera's face is all I see. And the thought of her hurts.

"What the hell are you doin' out here?" I hear a voice behind me. I sit up on my elbows, realizing how much whiskey I had when the world slightly shifts.

"Shut up, Colton," I say, but my speech is slightly slurred.

"I've been lookin' for ya everywhere."

"Why?" I ask. "I'm enjoying the peace and quiet."

He stands over me. "Looks like you're drinking yourself stupid thinking about Kiera."

"Pfft." It's all I can say.

"Wanna talk about it?" Colton genuinely asks, but over the years, I've found it better to just pretend there's no issue.

I smile and wave him away, but I think he sees through it.

"Come on, let's go out," he suggests.

I look up at him and let out a huff.

"It'll be fun. And I'm buying."

He tucks his hands in his pockets, and I feel bad for not wanting to be his wingman tonight. "Fine. But you have to swear on your balls that if you do decide to go home with some chick, you're bringing me home first or getting me a hotel room to sleep off the hangover."

He chuckles. "That's a lot of damn demands."

I stand and stumble. "My way or the highway."

Colton steadies me, so I don't fall. "Fine. That's a deal, boss."

"Then let's go. I'm ready to drink your entire paycheck." I point toward the sky and let out a loud yeehaw.

"Fuck," Colton whispers under his breath, realizing what he just agreed to.

After throwing some dirt on the fire, we walk back to my house. I change out of the clothes I've been wearing all day, then I grab a beer out of the fridge and chug it before Colton leads me out the door to his truck.

"Where we goin' exactly?" I ask.

"To the Honky Tonk. Apparently, it's ladies' night. And I'm looking for a lady."

I groan. "That's all the way in San Angelo. You might as well go ahead and rent two rooms in the motel next door."

Colton smirks. "Probably will."

It takes almost an hour for us to get there, and by the time we arrive, I'm hungry. But as soon as I see all the pretty ladies wearing blue jean skirts, I couldn't care less about food.

"I knew that'd get your attention," he tells me, opening the door to his truck and stepping out. I follow him into the bar, and the place is packed. Instantly, coming here doesn't seem like such a bad idea after all.

Colton grabs us two beers, and we scope out the place. The dance floor is full of couples, and so is the bar top. Eventually, some people leave at the end of the bar, and I walk over and take a seat. Colton joins me, but soon, he's approached by a pretty redhead, which seems to be his weakness these days.

I'm left alone to my thoughts until someone comes up beside me and takes Colton's seat.

I look over at the blonde who's showing enough cleavage to be scandalous and classy at the same time. She smiles at me. "Hey."

"Hi," I tell her and look back at my drink. She reminds me of Kiera with her strawberry blonde hair, and I hate how the thought crosses my mind. I must be broken because I don't even feel like chatting with her because their features are so similar. Why couldn't she be a brunette?

"Why so sad, cowboy?" she asks, then orders a drink from the bartender.

"Who said I was sad?" I ask.

"Are you?" She gives me another smile.

"No. Just tired and hungry, and I'm playing wingman for my friend." I turn around and spot Colton on the dance floor, two-stepping.

She shrugs. "Do you dance?"

"Not really," I lie. The last time I danced with someone was Kiera at Emily's wedding. I swallow hard, thinking about how she looked at me and how she felt securely held in my arms. Fuck, I need to get her off my mind.

"A cowboy who doesn't dance. You're a rare breed." She takes a sip of her pink drink and looks at me with sparkling blue eyes.

"I might dance." I smirk, remembering my old motto of the only way to get over someone is to fall into someone else's bed. Maybe this woman is exactly what I need tonight after all.

"Change of heart. I like that." She stands and goes to walk away but then stops. "Are you comin' or not?"

I smile, chug the rest of my drink, then follow her onto the dance floor. Within moments, she knows I was lying about dancing. I pull her tight little body into my arms, and we two-step across the room. She holds on to me and allows me to take the lead, and I realize she's not too bad of a dancer herself. The song ends, and she's gleaming at me.

"What's your name, cowboy?"

I lift an eyebrow at her as we continue dancing to the next song. "Jackson." I was halfway tempted to give her John's name, but I stopped doing that in my early twenties, and now that he's married, it might not be a good idea. Mila is fierce and might actually hurt someone.

"I like that. I'm Kelsey."

I spin her around and pull her to my chest. "Nice to meet you, Kelsey."

She asks me more questions about myself, and while I don't typically give women so much personal information, at this point, I have nothing to lose. I'll probably never see her again anyway. Eventually, the song ends, and we go to the bar and take a few shots, compliments of Colton's open tab. It's actually the only way I know he's still here, considering I haven't seen him in a while. Pretty soon, I'm seeing double of Kelsey, and when she invites me back to her room, I can't say no. Still not able to find Colton, I shoot him a text and tell him which room and hotel I'm going to. Though I'm off tomorrow, I still need to feed the horses at a decent time, but I kinda don't give two shits about it at the moment.

As soon as we walk into the room, our lips crash together. But each time I kiss her, I think of Kiera. She almost smells like her, too, and when I close my eyes, that's who I imagine. One thing leads to another, and soon we're naked between the sheets. After we're both satisfied and panting, I pass out.

The next morning, I wake up before the sun does with a splitting headache. I roll over and see strawberry blonde hair, and my heart drops. Where the fuck am I and who the fuck am I with? The night comes back in flashes, and I recall leaving the bar with someone, but the rest is a blur. I let out a sigh of relief when I see the condom wrappers on the nightstand. Picking up my phone, I see I have a message from Colton telling me which room he's in. I'm so fucking happy he didn't leave me. Being as quiet as possible, I try to get dressed, but when the woman in the bed rolls over and feels for me, knowing I'm not there, her eyes flutter open. I still, wishing I could disappear.

She smiles. "Sneaking out so early?"

Busted. "I have tons of shit to do back at the ranch. Gotta feed the horses."

Sitting up, she pulls the sheet over her breasts. "One question, Jackson."

I button up my jeans and start to slip on my boots. "Sure."

"Who's Kiera?"

My heart drops, and my brows pinch together. I finish putting on my boots, then grab my shirt and button it up. I try to ignore her question, but I know that's not happening because she's staring at me, waiting for my answer. "Why?"

"Because for some reason, you kept calling me that all night."

Heat rushes through my body as the realization hits me in full force. It's gotten to the point where I can't even have a one-night stand without thinking about her. Now I'm saying her name too?

I'm more fucked than I actually thought.

CHAPTER NINETEEN

KIERA

ONE MONTH BEFORE THE WEDDING

WARM HANDS WRAP around my body, and I somewhat remember Trent kissing me goodbye this morning. Lately, I've been exhausted with all the horses I've taken on, which probably wasn't a good idea, considering the wedding is in a month. Eventually, my alarm buzzes, and I fumble for the snooze button, though I know it's a wasted attempt, but I seriously need five more minutes. Soon my phone is screaming for me to get up, and I force myself out of bed. I place my feet on the floor and unlock my phone, turning off the five alarms I set, and notice Trent still isn't home. He left super early this morning, so I give him a call, but of course, he doesn't answer. I notice I have a few text messages and open them one by one.

I open Mila's first, and my eyes widen.

"No," I whisper. I close out of her text message and open River's, then Emily's. Each of them letting me know there was a fire at the Bishop ranch and were all sent two hours ago. I rush out of bed and get dressed as fast as I possibly can. As soon as I'm walking out the door, I call Emily, knowing she's awake at this ungodly hour.

"What happened?" I ask as soon as she answers, thinking the worst.

"Well good morning to you," she says, amused.

"Is everyone okay?" There's panic in my voice, and she instantly tries to calm me, but I'm already dressed and out the door, driving toward the ranch.

"Someone set the equipment barn on fire. No one was hurt. However, everything's a complete loss. But get this, the firemen are speculating it was intentional, and since the Bishops wouldn't set their own barn on fire, it has to be arson. There's no electricity to that barn, and they found a gasoline trail of where someone scattered it everywhere. There'll still be a full investigation done, though, because of having to claim on insurance."

"Oh my God! Who would do something like that?" I turn onto the country road and travel as fast as I can over there.

"Not sure. Whoever did it is a total asshole. Hundreds of thousands of dollars' worth of equipment lost," Emily says.

"Thank God for insurance, but seriously, it's going to take time to replace everything. I hate that Mr. Bishop has to go through that," I tell her.

"I know. Evan said his dad is distraught. But hey, I gotta go. Call me this afternoon, okay?"

I swallow hard, thinking about my second family. "I will. Have fun at work. Save some lives or something."

She laughs. "Trying!"

A few moments later, I'm making a right turn on the gravel road that leads to the B&B. It's not even six yet, and I have a million things to do, but everything else can wait. As soon as I pull up to where the equipment barn is, my heart sinks. The barn has completely collapsed, and the wood is nothing more than smoking ash. All the tractors, backhoes, bulldozers, and other farming equipment are destroyed. My mouth falls open as I stare at it in shock.

After I park the truck, I get out and see a group of ranch hands and the volunteer fire department huddled around

Jackson as he points to different areas of the barn that are still burning. When he turns around, he spots me and gives me a quick wave.

It's been a few weeks since I've seen him. Not that I've wanted to purposely avoid him, but I've found it best while Trent and I work on mending our relationship, especially after our last big fight. Though from what I've heard, it's not like Jackson has even noticed.

He says something to the guys standing around, then tucks his hands in his pockets and walks toward me. My heart immediately stammers in my chest. Instead of his normal cowboy hat, he's wearing a baseball cap. I've always liked the way they've looked on him.

"Hey," he says, making direct eye contact.

"Is everyone okay? Your dad?" I ask.

Jackson licks his lips and turns to look back at the disaster area. "Some of the stuff that was in that barn isn't replaceable. An old tractor that my great grandfather used to farm. It held a lot of memories for him. There was some other antique farm equipment that was passed down to like four generations too. It's all a total loss."

The tension between us is almost too much. "Do y'all know how it started?"

"With gasoline. I think it was doused around the barn. I found a line on the grass where it was started." His jaw ticks. "I don't know who would do something like this to my family, but it's real personal."

I let out a deep breath. "Yeah, I can't imagine."

"Why are you here, Kiera?" He finally turns and meets my eyes again.

My face contorts. "What does that even mean? Y'all are like my second family, Jackson. Wanted to see for myself that everyone is fine."

"We're fine." He's being short, and I don't like it.

"Okay. Well looks like you got it all under control, I guess."

A moment later, Colton walks up with a big grin smacked across his face.

"Hey Kiera," he says, walking over and giving me a big hug. Jackson watches us, but his face stays straight. We haven't talked about the fight, and I've been keeping my distance since then so everyone can cool down. It's awkward, but I didn't expect it to be like this. Jackson and I have had arguments before, but we always work through them. Honestly, though, I don't know what the hell I expected. I didn't think when I rushed over, and maybe I shouldn't have come at all.

"Still marrying that douchebag?" Colton asks, and I slap him and roll my eyes.

I narrow my eyes at his rude comment. "Trent isn't a douche, and yes, the wedding is still on," I tell him. All he does is shrug.

"Just know, I've got a fifteen hundred dollar bet on it not happening, so make me a rich man." Colton pokes at me.

"You're the worst." I groan, trying to keep my attention on him. "Who's the bet with?"

Colton points at Jackson. "That asshole right there. He shook that it's happening. I'm not convinced yet."

"The wedding is in a month. Pretty sure you're gonna lose this one, Colton."

He shrugs, but the smirk on his face doesn't falter. Turning my head, I look at Jackson who's as still as a statue. He makes eye contact with me for a moment before he turns and walks back to the group of firemen who are still trying to put out the burning wood.

"He's in a mood today," Colton says. "Don't worry about him."

The smile that was on my face falls. "I just don't know if it will ever be the same between us."

Colton gives me a small shrug. "What will happen, will happen. You can't worry about that."

"You're right. So any idea on who'd do such a shitty thing?" I search his face.

"No clue. Someone has it out for the Bishops, though. Kinda makes you second-guess everyone and everything. They're one of the most respected families in the area, so I don't get it." He shakes his head. "I better get going. Take care of yourself, Kiera. Leave that d-bag." He laughs.

"You really didn't bet all that money, did you?" I ask before turning to leave.

"You better believe I did," he says, chuckling.

"Just when I thought you couldn't get any stupider." I playfully roll my eyes at him and walk back to my truck. I sit there for a few minutes, taking in the scene, and watch Jackson, wishing I could be there for him. But by the way he acted, I don't feel too welcome. Instead of worrying about it, I chalk it up to him being stressed about the situation, then place the truck in reverse and head to my ranch to check on things. To know someone would do this to them makes me feel uneasy.

After I quickly help feed the horses, I feel my phone vibrating in my back pocket and hurry to answer it when I see Trent's name.

"Hey, babe! I've been trying to get ahold of you all morning," I tell him with a smile.

"I know. Got an emergency call because Mrs. Miller's mare was finally giving birth. Went over and helped deliver. You know how babies are; they come when they're ready." I can tell he's smiling.

"That's true. Did you hear about the Bishops' barn being set on fire? They lost everything inside."

There's silence.

"No, I didn't. Is everyone okay?" he sincerely asks. I know even mentioning them is often a sore subject, but Trent is trying, and I can see and appreciate that.

"Yeah, they are. Apparently, someone purposely did it. Who would do such a terrible thing?"

Trent lets out a deep breath. "Probably Jackson so he could get some sympathy from everyone."

"Trent…" I warn.

"I'm just kidding. I don't know. I hope they find whoever did, though. Oh babe, can you run to the store and grab some bacon? I'm in the mood for breakfast before I head back out for the day. You should come join me too. I miss you."

It's moments like this that I remember why I'm marrying him. He's thoughtful. "Yeah. I sure will. I'm actually pretty hungry."

"I'm heading home now, so I'm going to jump in the shower. See you when you get here. Love you."

"Love you too." I end the call and hurry to finish putting everything up before I head to the grocery store. My stomach growls the entire drive over because I left so quickly this morning. I didn't grab anything, so breakfast together is a great idea.

I enter the store and say hello to the ladies who've been working there since I was a kid. Just as I make my way to the back where the bacon is, I run into Mrs. Miller. My face instantly lights up when I see her.

"Hey, Kiera, honey. Just got your invitation in the mail. How's your mama doin'?" She gives me a big hug.

"Mama's doin' good. Keepin' her busy with all the wedding planning. How's your little baby doin' this morning?"

Mrs. Miller looks at me like I've grown a third eye, which confuses me. "What are you talkin' about, dear?"

I keep the smile on my face. "Trent told me he helped deliver a colt this morning over at your property."

Mrs. Miller shakes her head. "Are you sure? I don't have a pregnant mare. I actually haven't seen Trent since the beginning of the year when he came out and gave shots to the horses."

I'm trying to recall all the conversations we've had over the past few months about Mrs. Miller. I know for a fact, he was talking about her. There are no other Millers in the area.

"Honey, are you okay?"

I nod and smile. "Yes, of course. He must've meant someone

else, or I misheard him," I say, but I know that's not right. I swallow hard and plant that fake smile on my face.

"Well, tell your mama I said hello. Good seeing you, Kiera. I'll be at the weddin'. Can't wait. It's coming up real soon."

I give her another hug. "Yes, ma'am."

After she walks away, I stand and stare at the bacon for at least five minutes. My mind is racing a million miles per minute. If Trent didn't deliver a horse early this morning, where the hell was he?

I can't concentrate, so I quickly grab a slab of bacon, go to the checkout line and pay, then head home. My heart is thumping in my chest as I pull up to the house, and I know I need to calm down before going in.

I grab my grocery bag and walk inside, busying myself in the kitchen. A few minutes later, I hear the water stop, and soon, Trent's warm fresh body is pulling me closer to him. I turn around, and we exchange a kiss. When we break apart, he's smiling.

"I wish you could've been there this morning to see Mrs. Miller's colt. He was so cute. I stayed around until he took his first steps. There's nothing like watching life being born."

"Really? That's amazing," I add, searching his face, knowing he's lying. It's almost frightening how he does it with so much ease. I want to believe him. I want to believe every word he's saying as he continues going on and on about the foal and even went as far as describing how it looked.

"So," I say, finding a tad of courage, "I actually ran into Mrs. Miller at the grocery store."

Trent zeros in on me. "Really?" he asks with raised eyebrows.

I nod as I scoop eggs and place bacon on plates for us.

"She had no idea what I was talking about when I asked about the colt," I tell him.

In a snap, the charming smile returns. "Oh, Kiera…" He lets out a laugh. "It's the Millers in San Angelo."

Relief floods me, but I'm pretty sure I would've known of

more Millers unless they're newer clients. Considering they're in the town an hour away, it's possible. I push the thought away, taking his word for it. "Oh." I laugh nervously. That explains it.

He stands and comes to me and kisses me. "You act like you don't trust me or something."

I shake my head. "No, babe. I trust you. She just acted like I was crazy. I was confused, that's all."

"Sorry, I should've mentioned that. It's why I had to leave so early this morning so I could get there early."

I look up into his eyes. "Wish you would've snapped a photo for me. Can't wait to start a horse family of my own," I say.

"I can't wait to start a family with you." He kisses me again, and it calms my nerves.

"Me too."

We sit at the table and discuss our weekend plans along with last-minute wedding stuff. The rehearsal dinner is finalized along with all the fine details of the wedding. I've already picked up my dress and shoes, and everything seems to be finally sliding right into place, though we still haven't decided on our honeymoon.

"I was thinking Key West. Alex and River said it's amazing," I say between bites.

"What about Hawaii? Or Australia?" he asks with a cute smirk.

"I don't have a passport, so Australia is a no. But Hawaii is a thought. Or how about you surprise me?" I wink at him.

"Deal." The mood turns slightly serious. "I want to talk to you about something."

I finish chewing and stare at him.

"I know you want to start a family as soon as possible, and lately, that's all I've been able to think about."

I nod. Listening to his every word.

"What if we started trying now?" he asks.

I chew on my bottom lip. "I have a confession to make too."

He studies me.

"I stopped taking my birth control a week ago." I'm trying to get rid of the wedding day jitters and all the nervousness I've felt about our relationship the past few months. It hasn't been perfect, but Trent has proved to me time and again that he loves me dearly. He's trying, and I can see that. We'd agreed we wanted to start a family as soon as possible, and when my prescription ran out, I didn't get it refilled. I know once the wedding is over and we aren't consumed by planning it, things will go back to normal between us.

"Kiera." He stands and comes to me, kissing me, pouring all his emotions out. I stand and wrap my arms around his neck. We break apart, our foreheads touching. "That's the best news I've heard all day."

"I know it takes time to get pregnant sometimes, so I wanted to make sure nothing was holding us back."

"I love you so fucking much. I can't wait to make you my wife and start our family."

I grab his face in my hands and study him. "I can't either."

We finish eating, and Trent cleans up the kitchen before telling me goodbye.

"Let's go out for dinner tonight," he tells me between sweet kisses.

"Are you asking me on a date, Dr. Laken?"

He grabs my ass. "You better believe it. I should be home around seven."

We say our goodbyes again, and I walk him to the door. I let out a relieved breath that everything is okay, and that he wasn't lying. Just as I step into the bathroom to wash my hands, I see his dirty clothes lying on the floor, and I pick them up to toss them into the hamper. Instantly, I stop walking.

My heart lodges in my throat when I smell smoke and gasoline.

I close my eyes tight and press his clothes to my nose, smelling the undeniable mixture of gas and smoke again, then replay the facts about the Bishop barn.

It was arson. Someone used gasoline to set the barn on fire. It happened early morning.

All the facts flood back, and I feel sick and drop the clothes on the floor. As I glance down, I notice something was spilled on the suede of his boots too. I pick them up and smell them, and it's gas. They fall to the ground, and I feel as if I'm losing my mind.

Is it possible Trent was the one who set the Bishop barn on fire? Or just a coincidence all the lies add up to it?

I think back to the previous lies about the child he kept secret, the bank account he lied to my face about, and now all of this...I don't know what to believe anymore. If he's responsible for this, what else is he capable of? It's a pretty hefty allegation to blame someone for arson, especially the man I'm supposedly set to marry in four short weeks.

For the first time in our two-year relationship, I'm actually scared of what this all could mean and don't know what to do. We just decided to actively try for a baby and hopefully start our family soon. How do things always go from great to worse in just a matter of minutes?

CHAPTER TWENTY

JACKSON

WITH EACH PASSING DAY, I know I'm another day closer to losing Kiera forever. Though I agreed to be in the wedding and I bought the stupid vest and hat like she asked, I second-guess my decision every single day. After I picked up the lame wedding wear, I hung it on the back of my bedroom door, and now it's a constant reminder that she's getting married to Dr. Douchebag soon.

When they first started dating, I was in a constant state of denial. I knew it wouldn't work out between them, but as the days turned into months and transformed into years, I realized how wrong I actually was.

Four weeks.

In four weeks, she'll be his.

The thought makes me fucking sick.

Just as I'm getting ready to fall asleep for the night, I get a call from my dad. Considering the time, I instantly know something's not right. Though he's as calm as can be when I answer, he tells me the equipment barn is on fire. Within minutes, I'm dressed and down there watching so much history be destroyed. The look on my father's face as generations of farm equipment melts in the heat almost destroys me. I feel sick as I watch the wooden barn fall and the flames grow as the reserve tank of diesel fuel catches

fire. There's no way we'll be able to save anything now and not
being able to stop this makes me feel helpless.

Soon, the volunteer fire department shows up along with
Pettigrew, who takes statements from us all. I try to help the men
put out the fire, but considering the equipment is also full of gas,
it's dangerous for us to get too close. Alex, Evan, and John rush
over, too, and we're trying our best to save anything we can, but
we're too late, and it's written all over our faces. Instead, we
stand and watch it all happen. I fucking hate this.

As I search around, I notice a line of burnt grass off to the side
that leads straight to the barn. It's a long enough line, exactly how
we used to start large bonfires in high school. I call Evan over.

"Look at this," I tell him, bending down to the ground.

His eyes go wide. "Arson?"

I nod. "Exactly. Someone did this shit on purpose." My jaw
clenches, and I'm so fucking mad, I can barely see straight.

Evan notices and squeezes my shoulder. "We'll find who did it
and make them pay."

"Who would do this to our family?" I finally ask. "Why would
someone do this?" I know there's no answer to my questions, and
my words linger as wood cracks and pops behind me. Eventually,
Dad leaves, disgusted by it all. Alex goes to complete his morning
duties and offers to feed the horses at the B&B too. I tell him how
much I'd appreciate it if he did. Evan heads to work, and John
goes to get the B&B ready for our morning guests. I stay with the
volunteers, and eventually, Dad sends ranch hands over as the
sun rises. The cleanup will start as soon as the insurance
investigation is complete. It's all a fucking mess.

The loss I feel is indescribable. History and family heirlooms,
irreplaceable items are now gone forever, and I can't help but
question the reasoning. As the sun slowly rises, pinks and
purples splash across the sky. We try to contain the fire, so it
doesn't spread, but the barn was one of the largest on the
property, so we might be dealing with this for the rest of the
morning.

Soon, I hear a truck hauling ass down the driveway, and I let out a deep breath when I see it's Kiera. It's been awhile since she's been around because she's obviously avoiding me. But I get it. Right now, I don't want to see her because it physically hurts. I can't ignore she's here, though. Sucking in a deep breath, I tell the guys I'll be back and head over to her, crossing the pasture.

I can't take my eyes away from her, and I think back to all the summers we spent together, laughing, getting in trouble, and even drinking. We'd sneak out and meet at our spot, start a fire, and shoot the shit. She was one of the guys. Kiera was my best friend who knew everything about me and all my secrets except one—the way I felt about her. A smile touches my lips as I think back to all the good times we shared over the years. The sound of her laughter used to give me life. There were so many lonely nights when she was away at college that I'd almost do anything to hear it, though I was determined to give her space.

By the time I'm closer, the smile has long faded from my face, and I don't know why she's even here. Not after how I destroyed her fiancé's face without any regrets. If his sorry ass showed up on this property right now, I'd do it again without thinking twice. My jaw ticks just thinking about it.

The tension between us grows quickly, and the conversation is short, but I want to know why she's here, so I ask. We've always been upfront with one another, not holding anything back but our feelings.

"Why are you here, Kiera?" I finally ask. She looks at me like I slapped her and gives me some reason that I don't care to hear. The rest of the conversation goes downhill quickly, and Colton soon walks up, interrupting us, thankfully, but he's pushing every single button I have, which only pisses me off. Not able to be around her any longer without saying everything I feel, I walk away, cursing under my breath. I know I looked like a total asshole just now, but maybe it's better this way. When I hear her truck driving down the road, I breathe a little easier.

"You didn't have to be such a dickhead back there," Colton says to me with his arms across his chest.

I roll my eyes at him. "Mind your own damn business."

Colton pretends to check a nonexistent watch. "Yep, still an asshole."

"You know how I feel about all this. It's best if we keep our distance these days. Especially when she's acting weird and running to Trent's rescue. He's a pussy who needs his woman to save him." I crack my knuckles, thinking about the fight and bashing his face in again.

One of the firemen walk up and interrupt our conversation, which I welcome.

"I think we're done here. Not much more we can really do. It's going to burn for the rest of the day I'm sure, but it's contained," he says.

"Brett, right?" I ask, holding out my hand to give him a handshake and a thank you. "We appreciate y'all so much. It's so impressive how fast you got here. I'm sure Mama's gonna wanna have y'all over for lunch one day. Just wait for the invitation." I chuckle.

"We're a hungry bunch; she can feed us anytime." He looks over his shoulder at the rest of the men who came to help. He gives me a smile before they leave.

I allow the rest of the ranch hands to go back to their regular duties. As Colton goes to walk away, I grab him by the shirt and shake my head. "You're with me today, ass munch. Payback is gonna be a bitch."

His groan makes me smile. "And today we're fixing the septic tank over at the ranch hand quarters," I add.

"Are you fuckin' kiddin' me?" Colton's eyes go wide.

"Apparently, y'alls turds are the size of logs, so now we get to fix the shit, *literally*." I want to laugh, but I'm not joking.

We make our way across the property, and unfortunately, Colton doesn't stop with the Kiera questions.

"Why don't you just tell her how you feel?" he asks as we get out of the truck and walk toward the small shed that has the tools I need.

"How do I feel? Apparently, you know, and everyone else knows, so please inform me." I'm being an ass, but that seems to be my normal today. I'm just not in a good mood.

"You love her, Jackson. Everyone knows that. *Everyone*. And you're so goddamn stubborn about it." He grabs a wheelbarrow and begins to stack bags of the bacteria we need to throw in the tank to unclog the pipes.

"So let me get this straight. I'm supposed to go confess my undying love to her a month before she's supposed to get married and just a few weeks after I kicked the living piss out of her fiancé?"

I wait for his answer. He's got nothing. "Easier said than done."

We head over to the septic tank and get to work, making sure no lines are busted, and there's no debris. After we empty it, and everything checks out, we clean it, which makes me want to barf.

"How did we get volunteered for this?" Colton asks.

"I think it's payback for the Nicole thing," I admit.

"You suck," he tells me as we continue.

"I know," I say, pouring the two large sacks of bacteria in the tank and wait. We run the pumps and stick around for an hour, and everything seems to be working okay. Thankfully.

I figure out where Dad and Alex are and drop Colton off with them because I'm tired of him jumping my ass about Kiera. He's been riding me about this all day, and I finally just started ignoring him because it's too damn late. I've accepted it. Everyone needs to understand that because I do.

After I run home and wash the smell of shit from my body, I head over to the B&B with dread hovering over me. Ever since the Nicole thing happened, it's been a fucking nightmare walking through the door. As soon as I enter, John's jaw ticks.

"Glad you're so happy to see me." I force a grin.

"Can I help you?" he asks as he flips through the schedule book.

I lean my body against the desk. "Just wanted to see what my baby brother was up to today."

He groans, which causes me to laugh.

"I'm gonna take the rest of the day off," I tell him. "I need to get my mind straight after everything that happened this morning."

"Okay," John says. "I think your afternoon schedule is clear."

"Yeah, tomorrow will be busy, though. But I should be back by then."

He goes over all the lessons I have scheduled, and a guest walks up and asks a question, giving me time to sneak out. As I head out the front door, I walk past Nicole.

"No hello or anything?" she says as she pulls weeds from the flower bed in front of the B&B.

I stop walking and turn on my heels. "You think you deserve one?"

She laughs and acts as if the allegations are a joke, a game or something, but I don't think it's funny. I probably shouldn't speak to her and should pretend she doesn't exist, but that's not my style.

Standing, she tugs the gloves off her hands and walks to me. "You're not mad, right?"

I chuckle sarcastically. "Nicole, I'm way past mad. I'm fucking livid. You used me."

She bites on the corner of her lip. "How does it feel?"

Crossing my arms over my chest, I just stare at her.

She continues with a glare. "I just gave you a little taste of your own bitter medicine. It's called karma, Jackson. It was payback for all the women you left high and dry over the years." She takes another step toward me. Before long, Nicole is standing only inches away from me.

If I would've known she was a psycho, I would've never brought her home.

KENNEDY FOX

"You're fucking crazy." My voice stays low so no one can overhear my words.

"I'll make a deal with you, Jackson." Her eyes meet mine.

My heart is thumping hard in my chest. "I don't make deals with the devil, sweetheart."

She releases a maniacal laugh. "I'll drop all this, the raise, the charges, the threats, but I want another night with you."

I study her for a moment, waiting for her to say she's joking, but the words don't come. My eyes go wide. "Wait, you're serious?"

"I've had a thing for you for the past five years. You've always been so fucking wrapped up in Kiera and your one-night stands that I've always been invisible to you. For once, I felt like maybe I had a real chance and that maybe you thought I was pretty. I hoped what we shared that night meant the same to you as it meant to me. But when we woke up in the morning, and you looked at me like I was another mistake, it fucking hurt, Jackson. I wanted to hurt you the same way you hurt me. You're a jokester, and you're fun, and any woman would die to be with you, but you're only worried about yourself and your dick. You never think about how your actions affect anyone else, and that's not fair. So yeah, maybe I took it to the extreme, but do you really blame me?"

There have been women over the years who have stalked me and refused to let me go. But I've never heard truths so raw.

"Nicole, I didn't mean to hurt you, and I didn't know any of that, okay. I'm really fucking broken, and I don't do relationships. I know it's cliché as hell, but it's not you, it's me. You're a pretty girl. You deserve someone who can commit to you, and I'm not that man," I admit, trying to find common ground.

"It's because of Kiera, isn't it? Because you're not over her."

I roll my eyes, tired of hearing her name all day.

"She doesn't want you, Jackson. And the rumor is Trent doesn't want her speaking to you either. I heard that once their married, you won't even be able to be friends anymore. You're going to have to move on."

Out of everything she's said, those words almost break me. I've easily avoided any rumors that swarmed around town about Kiera and Trent. But I've heard the whispers at the feed store. I'm not a damn idiot. "I've gotta go."

"This isn't over," she says as I walk away.

"Yes, it is," I harshly bark over my shoulder as I head toward my truck. I really need to go for a drive and get the hell out of here. I need to clear my goddamn mind. Even Kiera's and my friendship is slipping through my fingers, and if that happens, it will fucking destroy me.

CHAPTER TWENTY-ONE

KIERA

Is it really possible the man I'm about to marry is capable of this?

Was it to get even with Jackson for pressing assault charges against him?

Could I see Trent doing something like that? No. Yes? *Maybe*?

The fact there's any doubt in my mind at all tells me all I need to know.

I need to get out of here.

Rushing to the bedroom, I pull out a duffle bag from the closet and start stuffing clothes and toiletries inside. I need to get to the bottom of this, and I can't do that here. If Trent lied to me before, there's no reason he wouldn't again. I kept thinking wedding stress was the cause of our relationship being rocky the past few months, but what if this is Trent's true colors? I honestly don't know if I can do this anymore. I'm not sure I know the man I'm going to marry.

I'm so busy running from the closet and dresser to the bathroom that I don't even hear Trent come back into the house. One second, I'm holding my hairdryer, and the next, Trent is standing in the bedroom doorway, startling me enough to drop it. It lands with a clunk, and Trent's brows pinch together as he studies me.

"What are you doing?" He takes a step toward me, and I hold my hand out to stop him. "Kiera, what the hell is happening?" His eyes scan to the open bag. "Are you leaving?"

"Trent…" I try to steady my breathing, but I feel like I'm suffocating. "I-I can't marry you."

"What?" His voice raises. "We were just talking about starting a family not ten minutes ago. What happened?"

My chest rises and falls rapidly, nerves hitting me hard in the gut. "What are you even doing back here?"

"I forgot my wallet," he answers immediately as if he had his reason ready to go.

"It's in your jeans you left in the bathroom," I tell him, my body shaking. "The jeans that smell like gas and smoke."

"I don't understand. Why are you packing your stuff, Kiera? Talk to me, please." He comes closer, not giving me the space I need.

"I don't trust you, Trent. You've put this doubt in my mind, and without trust, our relationship will never work."

He squares his shoulders and crosses his arms over his broad chest. "Is this about Jackson?" he asks, and it feels like a knife to my stomach. "You're spinning things around in your mind and making them bigger than they are because you have feelings for him, don't you? That's what this is really about." His lips go into a firm line as if he's scolding me like a child.

"What? No!" I'm annoyed he's even bringing Jackson into this conversation when it has nothing to do with him. "It's about the bank statements, the fact that you have a child you neglected to tell me about, losing your temper with Jackson and punching me instead, the way you talk about the Bishops even though you know they're like my second family, and finally…your clothes."

He searches my face and crinkles his nose. "What about them?"

"On the same day the Bishops' barn burns down, you come home smelling like smoke," I explain bravely. My palms are sweaty, and my knees start to buckle. Trent and I have had

219

arguments in the past, but nothing to this extreme or serious. Seeing him lose control around Jackson proved there was a side to him I hadn't known before.

"What are you saying, Kiera? Are you insinuating I did it?" His tone is harsh and edgy. "Do you think I'm a monster or something? That I'd risk the lives of others just to get back at your stupid boy toy?" He rambles off the questions in a deep, aggravated growl. "Because if that's what you're saying, then I know you're fucking Jackson."

"Trent!" I gasp, pissed at his accusation. "Enough about Jackson!" I nearly scream. "*Your* actions have me second-guessing us. I'm saying it's put doubt in my mind enough to tell me that you and I shouldn't be getting married."

"Kiera, listen…" He reaches for my hand, but I pull it away. "I already apologized to you about lying about Maggie and the bank statements. I know I fucked up in that regard and explained how I was scared. I've lived up to that mistake. The wedding planning has put on a little more stress than normal, and I'm the first to admit I haven't been taking it well, including how I've been acting about the Bishops, but you can't blame me for being skeptical of Jackson, considering his reputation."

"And what about *my* reputation? Do you even consider that I'd never cheat on you?" I ask, remembering the way I felt for cheating on Tanner when I was only sixteen years old. It was just a kiss, but guilt consumed me for months about it. Aside from the fact that Jackson and Tanner were best friends, I never spoke a word of it to anyone. Instead of waiting for Trent's answer, I keep going. "Tell me why your clothes reek of gas and smoke," I bluntly demand.

He inhales and exhales deeply, brushing a hand through his hair as if he's already frustrated with me. "Before I left the Millers, they were getting ready to burn some brush and branches that broke off from the last bad storm we got. Mr. Miller is well into his seventies, and I didn't want him to accidentally set himself on fire, so I offered to help and stayed a while to make sure it didn't get out of control."

Doubt settles in my gut, but I know his story is plausible. Lots of people burn stuff on their ranches around here, so I know it's not uncommon. But how likely is it the same morning of the Bishop fire that Trent was helping the Millers burn brush?

"And you spilled gas on your boots?" I ask, raising my brows.

"Yeah, I did. The Millers have this old ass gas can that sprays out like a shower hose instead of in one smooth stream. I wiped them off with a rag right away, but as you noticed, the smell sticks and lingers. I was wearing my work gloves so you'll probably smell it on those too." Trent's shoulders relax, and I can see he's being genuine. His voice softens, and a part of me feels guilty for thinking he was capable of being involved.

Could I be using my unresolved feelings for Jackson as a reason to spin things in my mind to be bigger than they are? I know having feelings at all for another man isn't right, but it's the kind of feelings that never go away because they're unconditional in a sense. Jackson's been a part of my life longer than anyone, and it'd be impossible to just forget about them overnight. But is it possible they're why I've felt doubt in the first place?

Fuck, I'm so confused.

When I don't respond, he continues as if he can't stand the silence between us. "Do you need me to call her and put her on speakerphone to prove it?" He digs into his pocket for his cell and starts scrolling through his contacts. "She's really a sweet, old woman. Calls me her honey pie because she says I'm sweet like honey."

"No," I stop him, and he immediately locks his phone. The fact that he was willing to do it and prove his story makes me feel bad that he even had to offer. We're supposed to have an open and trusting relationship, and though there've been secrets, I don't believe he kept them to be malicious. I know he's not perfect, but I have so many mixed feelings that I can't sort out with him right in front of me. "Why didn't you tell me you stayed to do that?"

He shrugs. "I don't know. I didn't realize it was something I needed to mention, honestly. I didn't even know about the Bishop fire until I spoke with you on the phone and didn't think about how my clothes smelled. I came home and took a shower right away because I helped with the delivery and had blood on my skin and under my nails."

I chew on my lip, wondering if it's possible. Trent's a Southern gentleman, and it's not unlike him to help people with random chores and jobs.

"Kiera, please…" he pleads, his dark eyes begging for me to believe him. "I'll do whatever it takes for you to trust me again. I know I need to earn it back, and if you want, I'll go to counseling, or we can do couples therapy. Whatever you need, babe. I can't lose you."

Guilt settles in because I hate fighting with him especially with how soon the wedding date is approaching. I love Trent, but lately, I seem to have to be remind myself of that more and more.

When I'm unable to respond, he kneels in front of me and takes my hand in his palms. "Baby, please. You have to believe me. I'd never do anything to purposely screw this up with you." I swallow hard as I look at him, seeing the sincerity written all over his face. "I'd do anything to prove to you that you're my entire world. I want to marry you, have a dozen babies, a horse ranch, and anything else your heart desires. Let me give those to you." He brings my hand up to his mouth and presses a soft kiss to my knuckles. "I love you, Kiera. I will never keep anything from you again. I swear on my granddaddy's grave."

His words bring comfort, and I want more than anything to believe them. I want to have babies and horses and everything this man in front of me is offering. I really hope all the stress and tension will disappear after the wedding, and we can finally move on and start the life I've dreamt about since meeting him. If Trent's willing to put in the work, I have to be as well.

Trent surprised me with a weekend getaway for just the two of us. We need to get back to our happy place and really spend some quality time together to reconnect. It's been tense between us since our blowup, but I promised to try to move our relationship forward again.

"I'm really glad we're doing this," Trent says, holding my hand and lifting it to his lips. He kisses my knuckles and keeps our fingers interlocked.

"Me too," I reply honestly, smiling at him. "It'll be nice to have a couple of days off at the same time for once."

"I agree, babe. I know our schedules have been extra crazy lately, but I've already booked and planned our honeymoon during Christmas since I knew we'd both be able to take some time off."

"You did?" I squeal, having no idea. "Where are we going?" I nearly bounce in my seat.

He kisses my knuckles again. "It's a surprise, but I promise you're going to love it! Ten days in paradise, just you and me, darlin'."

Oh my God. I'm shocked. "I'm so excited!" A vacation like that is just what we both need, and even though it's over the holidays, I can see why he booked it for then. We're able to take more days off without our clients getting upset.

"It's only a few months away, but I promise it'll be worth it." He winks at me, sending butterflies to my stomach, and it's just the sign I needed.

Three amazing days pass by in a blink, and we're already

driving back home. A weekend at the lake cabin was just what we needed to replenish our relationship. We were able to focus on each other and get back on track as a couple. A part of me will always have lingering reservations of how he kept a major secret from me, but I know with time and effort, he'll gain my full trust back. I'm not naïve enough to think it'll happen overnight, but I'm optimistic.

"Are you excited, darlin'?" Trent asks as I brush my teeth.

I smile as I think about what today is. I've dreamt about my bridal shower since I was a little girl. Emily and Jessica planned everything, and between them, I know they're going to make it extra special for me.

I look at Trent's reflection in the mirror as he leans against the doorframe with his arms crossed over his chest. He's sexy as hell in a blue button-up shirt and black slacks, and it's hard not to notice how delicious he looks when he dresses up.

"Yeah, I am," I say after rinsing out my mouth. "I'm excited to see everyone and eat carbs."

Trent laughs, taking a step toward me and caging me against the bathroom counter as I turn to face him. "You deserve to be showered, babe. I want the whole afternoon to be about my beautiful bride." He leans down and presses a sweet kiss on my lips. "I'll be there later to help clean up so your mama and the bridesmaids don't have to do it all themselves."

"You're so thoughtful," I say, smiling as I gaze into his eyes. "I'm sure they'll all be tipsy from the champagne by then too."

Trent chuckles and gives me another quick kiss. "I have to meet my dad and brother for lunch first, and then I'll meet you there."

"Sounds good." I place my hands on his cheeks and pull him in for a deep, sensual kiss. "Two weeks until I'm Mrs. Trent Laken. Can you believe it?"

"Not soon enough." He wraps a hand around my waist, then slides it down to my ass and squeezes. "See you soon. Love you."

"Love you, too," I call out as he heads out.

Once I'm finished getting ready, Emily picks me up and drives me to the old bank building in town we now use for events and parties. She's in a great mood, which puts me in an even better mood.

"You look amazing!" She beams. "You're seriously glowing."

"Thank you! I feel amazing," I admit.

"Are you pregnant?" she blurts out.

I turn and look at her, squinting my eyes. "Uh, no."

"Okay, just checking. I plan to serve you lots of booze."

I laugh, grateful for my best friend always looking out for me.

"It's gonna be a blast, I promise."

"I have no doubt!"

All the bridesmaids pitched in to help decorate, but I know Emily and Jessica took the reins in making sure it was pure perfection. Since Trent and I both work with horses, they made sure to weave that into the bridal theme with little plastic horse toys on the tables and cake. It was super cute.

"Kiera…" I hear my name and spin around to Mama Bishop holding her arms out for me. "You look breathtaking."

I let her embrace me in a tight hug and wrap my arms around her. "Thank you, Mama B. I'm so glad you could come today."

"Of course, sweetheart. I wouldn't miss it for anything." She pulls back and looks me up and down. "You're going to make a stunning bride. I sure hope that man of yours knows how lucky he is." She gives me a look and then winks.

"He does," I tell her.

After eating and playing some games, Jessica makes me sit at the front to open the gifts. Most of it is household items with some sexy lingerie and toys weaved in. We all get a good laugh out of it when my mother holds one up and asks if it's a back massager.

Trent shows up shortly after, and it puts a wide, goofy smile on my face to see him even though I just did this morning. My bridesmaids comment on how great he looks and have no problem giving him orders on cleaning and loading the gifts up in his truck.

I look around and think how special this day has been and how lucky I feel to have so many friends and loved ones here to help us celebrate. We kept it girls only, so none of the Bishop men are here, but it doesn't go unnoticed how I miss Jackson and wish he could've been here too. I just wish I had his blessing. Even though he's in the wedding party, I know what he thinks about me marrying Trent, but I also know it's not because he wants me for himself. It's because he doesn't think any guy is good enough, especially not Trent. Then again, I could be engaged to the Prince of England, and Jackson would still think he's wrong for me.

"So don't forget, next weekend is your bachelorette party! We have all the reservations set in place, and oh my God, it's gonna be so much fun!" Jessica squeals while telling me the details. I basically gave her and Emily permission to do whatever as long as it wasn't illegal.

Part of me still wonders if it was a bad decision or not.

"I better prepare," I tease, hugging Emily goodbye since Trent is here to pick me up.

"You better bring my bride home in one piece next weekend," Trent warns with a teasing grin.

"Oh don't worry." Jessica waves him off. "Nothing unusual. Strippers, gin, and fireworks."

Trent arches a brow, not impressed. His arm is wrapped around my waist, and he squeezes my hip when Jessica speaks.

"She's kidding," I tell him, all of us laughing.

Once everything is cleaned and loaded up, Trent and I say our last goodbyes and head home.

"Damn, I think we have a whole store in here now." Trent and I look around at all the bags and boxes on our kitchen table and counter. There's so much.

"Pretty much." I chuckle. "I'll be writing thank-you notes for weeks." I sigh, hoping I can fit it into my busy schedule before the wedding.

"Don't worry about that right now," Trent says. He leans down and lifts me, hauling me over his shoulder and smacking my ass with a loud crack. "Tonight we play naked Twister in bed."

I laugh, kicking my legs so he'll let me down, but he's way too damn strong and keeps me pinned against his body as he walks to the bedroom. Once we're inside, he kicks the door shut and gently places me on the bed.

Trent immediately starts showering me with kisses, and I lock my legs around his waist, pulling him down against me.

"I'm going to give you everything you ever dreamed of, Kiera. *Promise.*"

His words nearly have me choking up with emotion. He's been working really hard to repair our relationship, and it hasn't gone unnoticed. It's starting to feel like the early days when we just started dating, and those memories make me emotional and happy all over again.

"I can't wait."

CHAPTER TWENTY-TWO

JACKSON

PRESENT DAY

Mama is going to kill me for ducking out last minute.

Hell, they're all going to. Maybe even take turns reaming me a new asshole. Either way, I know I'd deserve it, and it's a pain I'll accept to avoid watching the woman I'm in love with marrying another man. The wrong fucking man.

Once I'm in my truck and flying down the gravel driveway, I know there's only one place I want to go to right now. Kiera and I went to our secret place more times than I can count during our teen years, and it was special because no one else knew about it. At least I know I can hide out there and none of my brothers will be able to find me.

Until I'm ready to be found, at least.

I park my truck and grab my flask before I step out. Leaving my keys and phone inside, I walk to our spot that still has our makeshift firepit with moldy hay bales surrounding it. I should throw them in the fire and bring new ones out here, but I know I'm the only one who still visits. Kiera stopped joining me years ago.

This spot was where I always imagined I'd finally tell Kiera how I truly felt. Every time I talked myself into doing it, figuring she'd either laugh at me or tell me I wasn't good enough for her, I chickened out last minute. Then as soon as Tanner was in the picture, I knew my time had come and gone.

And now it was really over.

Things would never be the same. They haven't been since Trent barged his way into her life, and even if I was naïve to think it wouldn't amount to anything, I only have myself to blame for my heartache. Now they're married, and soon they'll have babies, and she'll have everything she's ever wanted.

Too bad I couldn't have given that to her.

I take a swig from my flask, grateful it's still half full and I can drink away the pain. Hopefully, I can numb everything inside me so I can't feel the way my heart is shattering. I left shortly before I was supposed to walk down with Mila, which means Kiera is already at the altar, probably saying her vows and promising to be with Dr. Douchebag forever.

I take an extra-long swig, begging the alcohol to quickly take me under.

Remembering I have a blanket in my backseat, I walk back toward my truck and grab it so I can cover the bale of hay. Just as I sit down, I hear a truck roaring up.

"What the hell?" I mutter, then roll my eyes when I see it's Evan's truck. *Fuck.* How the hell did he know where I was? I already know what bullshit he's going to say, so I take another long swig and mentally prepare for his ass chewing.

The truck pulls up next to mine, and as soon as the door flies open, I brace myself for what's to come.

"You arrogant, self-centered asshole!"

I stand as soon as I hear Kiera's voice. She's walking toward me with tears in her eyes, holding the front of her dress up as she stomps her boots against the grass.

"What the fuck?" The words are mostly to myself, but I'm so shocked I can't say anything else. I'm almost speechless. I blink to make sure she's really standing in front of me and take a deep breath. "What're you doing here, Kiera? Aren't you supposed to be getting married right about now?"

She closes the gap between us and pushes her hands against my chest as hard as she can. I barely stumble back, which only seems to piss her off more. "What the hell were you thinkin'?" she yells, pushing and swatting at me, and after a moment of letting her take her anger out on me, I grab her wrists and hold her in place.

"Kiera, stop," I demand firmly, looking into her tear-filled green eyes. "Why are you here? Isn't your husband and everyone waiting for you?"

Her chest rises and falls as she tries catching her breath. I watch as she licks her lips and stares up at me. "I couldn't marry him."

All the air is sucked out of my lungs, and it takes me a minute to process her words.

"What?" I ask, releasing her arms. They drop to her side, and she shrugs in response. "You left?" My voice cracks with sudden emotion that the whiskey was supposed to take away.

"Why, Jackson?" she asks, ignoring my question. "Why would you wait fifteen years to tell me how you felt?"

I blink again, taking a step back before stepping closer. "What are you talkin' about?" After I kissed her last night, she told me I was too late and stormed off, so I'm genuinely confused at her outburst right now.

"Your letter," she confirms. "Why would you wait till my wedding day to give that to me? You know how much I want to hate you right now? This should be the happiest day of my life, and you decide this was the right moment to *finally* confess your feelings for me after all this time? First, you kiss me the night of my wedding rehearsal, and even after I tell you that you're too late, you decide to give me a letter on the day I'm supposed to get married! I waited years for you…*years* for you to tell me those exact words you wrote on paper and now—"

"Wait," I stop her, holding up a hand. "What letter?" I have no idea what she's talking about and even though I've been drinking all morning, I know I didn't give her anything.

The fire in her eyes tells me she's ready to blow up at me, but I'm confused as fuck right now.

Kiera bends and reaches inside her boot, pulling out a folded-up piece of paper. "This one." She smacks it in my palm. "It's your handwriting."

I open it up and scan my eyes down the paper. *Oh my God.* It's my handwriting all right, but I didn't give this to her. "I threw this in the trash," I mutter to myself. "How'd you get this?"

Brushing a hand through my hair, I'm just as surprised as she is about this. She was never supposed to read this.

"I found it in my purse this morning. It came in an envelope with just my name on it."

I sigh. "Motherfuckers."

"What?" she asks, panicked. "Please tell me someone else didn't write this and pretend to be you." She tilts her head up as if she's trying to hold back more tears. "I can't believe after all this time I'd assume you'd ever say those words to me. I should've known...I should've fucking known that you'd never—"

"I wrote it," I blurt out, grabbing her attention back to me. "I wrote every damn word, Kiera."

"You did?" she asks, breathlessly.

"Of course I fuckin' did. Tanner and John told me to write a letter to you and get all my feelings or some shit out so I could finally let you go. I'd been drinking and decided they were right. But I tossed it afterward." I scrub my hands down my face, contemplating kicking their asses or hugging them for this stunt. "One of them must've grabbed it that night. It's the only way it ended up in your purse."

"Did you mean what you wrote? That you're letting me go? That you would never be good enough for me?"

The pain is evident on her face, and I have to look down at our feet to avoid it from burning into my eyes.

"Jackson, answer me," she demands. "Did you really think I needed anything other than you? The fancy dates, the flashy cars, and dinners—I never wanted any of that."

"It's what you deserved," I tell her matter-of-factly. "Someone who could give you more than I ever could."

"You're so goddamn stupid." She shakes her head at me, closing the space between us, and then places her palm against my chest. "I was in love with *you*. When Tanner asked me out, I wanted you to fight for me, to give me a reason to say no. But you never did. Not once."

"I couldn't…" My voice cracks again before I can finish. Inhaling a deep breath, I continue. "I knew I'd only hold you back, Kiera. You went off to college and found a career that you were destined for. I didn't want to keep you here when you wanted to go off to school and experience life outside of this small town. I only ever wanted what was best for you. I wanted you to be happy."

"And you thought I'd be happier without you?" She removes her hand, taking a small step back. "Why were you the one to make that decision for me, Jackson? Didn't you understand how much I loved you? You let me go and broke my heart more times than I can count. I didn't want to be in love with you, but I couldn't stop. Even when I had guys chasing after me, I only ever wanted you."

"Kiera…" I don't know what to say that I haven't already. She turns around, and I'm afraid she'll walk away for good this time. "I'm sorry, okay?" I grab her arm, pulling her back. "I never wanted to hurt you, and I know that I did, which is why I drank and did so much stupid shit. I didn't want anyone or you to know how much I hated myself that I couldn't give you more."

"Jackson…" she says just above a whisper, bringing her body flush against mine. "I loved you when I was fifteen years old, and I still love you. Regardless of your stupidity, the pain you've put me through, the emotional roller coasters I felt over the years— I'm in love with *you*. I couldn't care less about all the materialistic things you think I deserve. I only ever wanted you to love me back." The tears in her eyes are fucking destroying me. "I couldn't marry him when my heart had already belonged to you."

"Are you kiddin' me?" Her words send an electric spark through me I've never felt before. I can't keep lying to her or myself. "I've always been in love with you, Pippi. I never fucking stopped." Before she says another word, I wrap a hand around the back of her neck and crash our mouths together in a desperate kiss. I taste her and slide my tongue between her lips, wanting and needing more of her. It's a kiss for the goddamn record books because nothing could fucking top this. Kiera kisses me as if her life depends on it, and by the way it makes my body feel, I know she's the only girl I ever want to kiss for the rest of my life. My arms snake around her waist to hold her in place because I'm not letting her get away this time. I pour years of longing into this kiss, wanting her to feel every ounce of regret I feel for pushing her away.

"Kiera…" I whisper against her lips, resting my forehead on hers. This feels so right. Something inside me finally breaks from holding back. "I love you. More than anything. Always have, always will."

She pulls back slightly, her hands covering her mouth as tears pour down her cheeks. I'm not sure if she's smiling or preparing to murder me, but I take my chances.

"I'm sorry I waited so long to tell you. I've always loved you," I tell her sincerely, cupping her cheek.

"I honestly thought the day would never come," she admits, dropping her hands and revealing a wide smile. "I mean, your timing kinda sucks…"

"Fuck, I know." I lean back and tilt my head toward the sky. "I really screwed this up for you."

"I'm pretty sure everyone is freaking out. I basically just walked out on my own wedding."

"Wait…when did you read the letter?"

"About five minutes before we left the house. Then as soon as I saw you weren't standing up there, I knew exactly where to find you."

"You left *during* the wedding?" I gasp. "Holy fuck, Kiera."

"You're not helping right now." She playfully swats at me. "I just left a man at the altar. I've probably just broken his heart and humilated him in front of everyone we know."

Hearing the remorse in her voice and seeing the fear of what's to come written on her face, I hate that shit is about to get really messy for her—for *us*. I want to be with Kiera more than anything, but I know this isn't going to be easy.

But hell, when has it ever been easy?

"What do you need me to do? I'll do whatever you ask to help get you through this. I'm sure your parents are freaking out."

"I just need you to be with me right now, okay?" She rests her palm on my face and pulls our mouths together for a soft kiss. "I'll go back in a few hours when everyone's gone."

"They're going to worry about you," I tell her, though spending some uninterrupted time with her sounds amazing.

"Emily knows," she says. "She ran after me to give me Evan's keys. I'm sure she's handling everything."

And just like that, Emily is my new favorite sister.

I smirk as I pull her lips back to mine. "Remind me to thank her later."

"Stop being so damn cocky." She laughs, melting her body into mine, and it's a feeling I never want to be without again.

"It's the charm, baby. It can't be stopped." I kiss her jawline, and my lips linger along her ear and neck. Kiera noticeably shivers in my arms, and though we'll be going back to a shitstorm, I can't wipe the smile off my face.

"Jackson," she whimpers. "Truth or dare?"

I freeze in place, my mouth on her collarbone. "You can't be serious."

"You know the rules," she teases, and when I bring my eyes to hers, I see she is.

"I was just kissing your neck, my dick is hard as fuck, and you want to play a twelve-year-old's game?"

Her eyes lower to my crotch, and the corner of her lips tilt up in a devilish smile.

"Play the game or face the consequences," she reminds me with a smug grin.

At this point, I'll do whatever she asks me if that means I can go back to kissing her.

"Fine," I say, shaking my head in disbelief. "Truth."

"Are you sure about this?"

"Well, it's gotta be better than dare. Lord knows what you'd make me do." I chuckle, remembering all the shit she used to dare me when we were kids.

"No, no." She shakes her head at me. "Are you sure about *this* —you and me? I know you just confessed your undying love for me, but I can't just be another notch on your bedpost, and everyone is going to be betting against us when the shit hits the fan. Rumors, speculation, all of it. You have any idea what's about to happen?"

"Kiera…" I hold her hands in mine and look into her eyes so she can see my sincerity. "I don't care what other people think, say, or do. I only care about you and what you want. I'm sure people will speculate, the rumor mills are probably already in motion, and people will be waiting for me to fuck this up—but I'm all in, Pippi. I want whatever you're willing to give me, good and bad. I never wanted anyone else, and I know I did a shit job of showing that, but I've never been surer of anything in my life that *you* are it for me. You always have been, and if you're giving me a chance to finally get this right, I'm going in one hundred percent."

It's the sincerest thing I've ever said, and I meant it with my whole heart. Kiera is my life, my world, and I'd do anything to make her happy. She's looking at me with tears in her eyes, and her bottom lip quivers as she stares at me. I hope she can see how much I want to be the guy she deserves, and I'll spend every day proving myself to her that I am.

"That's..." She puts a hand to my chest, right over my heart. "That's the Jackson I always knew. The side you never shared with anyone but me. The sweet, kind, and compassionate side. Everyone thought I was crazy for being in love with you, but they didn't know you like I do."

I grab her hand and bring it to my mouth, pressing a kiss to her knuckles. "That part of me was only ever reserved for you."

CHAPTER TWENTY-THREE

KIERA

I'M LIVING IN A DREAM.

It's the only explanation for today's turn of events.

Leaving Trent at the altar was something I never thought I was capable of doing. Jackson finally confessing fifteen years' worth of love to me and promising me the world is something I'll never forget for the rest of my life. My emotions are boiling over, and I'm not quite sure how to react to it all. I'm pretty sure I'm in a state of shock as Jackson tells me he loves me. I waited years for this very moment, and now that he's standing in front of me saying the most beautiful words to me, I don't want to ever leave. We're in our own perfect bubble, and when it's just him and me, things are the way they should've always been.

Except I know as soon as I go back home, a shitstorm will be waiting for me. It's my fault that Trent is heartbroken, guests are confused, and my family is completely humiliated. I know deep down that marrying Trent would've ultimately ended badly, considering how the past few months have been. I was in deep denial. I realize I was so willing to forgive him and look past his flaws because I wanted a family, but at the end of the day, my heart always belonged to someone else. I just never imagined I'd hear the words I've dreamed about all this time.

Jackson had nothing to do with the choices Trent made or how he lied to me. But him kissing me last night and then me receiving that note this morning made me realize I was making the wrong decision. The feelings I felt couldn't be ignored.

"I think it'd be best if we didn't come out and tell people about us right away, though," I say. Worrying how hurtful that might sound, I continue, "Until the shock wears off. I'm already going to be apologizing to Trent and our families for weeks, but I know nothing I ever do or say will make up for what I did. It's kinda unforgivable."

"So you want to wait?" he asks.

"Well, I want to wait until we're seen together in public or admit anything to anyone. Is that okay?" I ask nervously. "Just out of respect for Trent, ya know? He's already going to be hurt enough and super pissed. I don't want to add fuel to the fire. Time is needed for things to settle down. After it's all blown over, then we can start telling people we're together."

"So…we're together?" he teases with a mischievous grin. Wrapping his arms around my waist, he pulls me to his chest and buries his face in my neck. I inhale his scent of whiskey and soap, and I want to cling to him for hours. "Or would you rather wait another fifteen years?"

"Jackson!" I pull back and slap at his chest. He makes me teary-eyed one moment and laughing the next. That's the Jackson I know, though. "That's not even funny!" I say, chuckling at his antics.

"Oh come on. I'm hilarious, and you know it." He tilts my chin and softly kisses me. "I'll do whatever you ask me to. But if Trent thinks for one second he can win you back, I'm stepping in."

"Well, he probably will. I mean, I don't see him just walking away, which is why I need you to be the bigger person here. Let me handle it, and once the dust clears, we can make it known it's only you and me," I tell him.

"How long are we talkin' here? Like a day or two?" he mocks.

"A month. At least."

He groans in disapproval but doesn't argue.

"But…" I add with a cheeky grin. "We could always sneak around. Might be kinda fun if no one knows. Feel like we're teenagers all over again."

"Hmm…" he contemplates, pulling me closer. "I could probably get on board with that. We have years of acting like teenagers to make up for."

"We sure do," I say. "You can sneak me into your bedroom once the sun goes down, and we can make out in the stalls, so no one sees us." I grin at him, knowing he'll definitely be on board with this idea.

"You've always been my best kept secret, Pippi." He winks. "But if Trent flatout asks me, I'm not lying. I won't answer, but I won't say no either."

"He won't ask you," I say. "Least I don't think so. He'll probably ask me because he's already made comments about it in the past, but if he's smart, he won't bring it up again."

Jackson snorts, rolling his eyes. "Trent's not smart. If he were, he'd keep his distance."

Now I'm the one snorting and rolling my eyes. "What is with you men and all your caveman tendencies?"

"I gotta brand you, baby. Make sure everyone knows you're mine now." Jackson slides his hand down to my ass and squeezes. It makes me yelp in surprise. He's teased and flirted with me plenty before, but having his hands on me—the way I've always imagined and dreamed—is making it damn hard to control myself around him.

"Down boy," I tease, pushing him away.

"Don't worry. I've waited this long. I'm sure I can wait a bit longer. Maybe."

"Well, I mean…I'm not saying we have to be celibate."

"No, but we're gonna take this slow, baby." His eyes are so warm and caring that I nearly get lost in them. "You're not just a notch on my bedpost, Kiera. As much as I want to rip this wedding dress off you and christen the back of Evan's truck, I don't want to rush this with you. I'm not screwing this up. Not this time."

"Wait…" I try to wrap my mind around what he just said. "How do you know Evan and Emily haven't already done it in the back?"

"That's the part you're focusing on?" He laughs. "Because they're both germaphobe freaks. I mean, maybe. But I'm pretty good at knowing that stuff."

"You and your brothers have a strange relationship," I tease. "Also…" I continue, contemplating my next words carefully. "You're gonna make me wait to have you. Is that what you're saying?"

"Yes, ma'am. I'm not just a wham-bam-thank-you-ma'am kind of thing," he mocks lightheartedly, grabbing my wrists before I can push him again. He takes my hands and wraps them around his waist and secures me against his chest. "We kinda skipped the whole dating thing, so I want to do this right. You deserve that, Kiera. Let me give that to you. Please." He dips down and kisses the top of my nose so soft and sweet.

"Okay," I give in. "But you'll only be encouraging your own blue balls."

"Fuuuuuuck." He groans, tilting his head back. "Okay, so there'll need to be some rules."

"This is sounding less appealing by the minute," I quip, laughing when he gives me a death stare.

"No being a cock tease," he says, arching a brow at me. "You can't be a temptress and then stroke my dick and walk away. No playing dirty."

"Then you can't be touching my ass, looking at my tits, or making inappropriate comments about my body."

"That's been a part of our conversations since we were teens." He bursts out laughing when I give him an unimpressed expression. My lips in a firm line, not amused by him not taking this seriously. "Alright, alright. No teasing and tempting each other until we agree it's time."

"Thank you." I smile, victoriously. "Look at us; already making compromises like a real-life couple."

"Yeah, well, you've always been the one person I can't argue with or deny. No taking advantage, though." He winks, and I mold to his sturdy frame again, kissing his eager lips.

His hands cup my cheeks, holding us in place. I fist the shirt under his vest and pull him closer until it feels like I could climb inside him. Soon, his hands are sliding down my backside, and when he grips my ass cheeks, he hauls me up until my legs wrap around his waist and my arms around his neck.

His mouth against mine is desperate and heated as his tongue slides in and out with mine. I've waited years for this, and there's no way I'll ever be able to stop now. His movements are so calculated, and the way his lips move effortlessly over mine makes my entire body shiver with eagerness. It makes me second-guess this whole waiting thing and wanting to succumb to him right now.

Jackson walks us to the back of Evan's truck, and pulls the latch one-handed, so the gate falls down in one smooth motion. I chuckle against his lips as I cling tighter to his body, so he doesn't drop me. He turns and sits down, positioning me to straddle his lap.

My dress ruffles around my knees and hangs down Jackson's legs. He tightens his grip on my ass and pulls me roughly against him, showing me exactly how aroused he is right now.

"Jackson…" I murmur against his lips. "You aren't playing fair."

"I know, baby. Never said I was a saint, and I live to break the rules." He moves his lips down my jaw and neck.

I laugh against him and press my palms to his chest, putting distance between us. "Then I better get off your lap."

Jackson helps set me down, and before I can suggest something else, he's walking away toward our secret spot. Moments later, he returns with a blanket, and I watch as he fans it out on the back of the truck. Luckily, Evan has a smooth surface, so lying down won't be painful. Jackson helps me back up, and soon we're lying down with his arm around me and our bodies molded together.

We lie in silence for a while, enjoying these stolen moments before reality has a chance to pull us apart again. Looking up at the sky, I think back to all the times we spent out here as kids.

"Do you remember when we were like thirteen or so, and we snuck out here at like two in the morning, and there was that raccoon…"

"Ricky!" Jackson blurts out. "Ricky the raccoon…that bastard. Nearly bit me a dozen times."

We're both laughing, remembering the incident. He visited us so much, he eventually got a name.

"I think he thought this was his spot," I say. "He chased after us so many times, I lost count."

"Pretty sure Dad shot him that summer."

"Oh my God!" I squeal. "Why would he shoot a poor, innocent raccoon?"

Jackson grunts in response, knowing damn well Ricky wasn't innocent. "Kept getting into the trash and Dad had enough of it being scattered all over the yard. Grabbed his shotgun and—"

"Okay, I get the picture," I cut him off. "Poor Ricky. Rest in peace."

Jackson snorts, rolling over to face me. There's a smile plastered on his face—one I haven't seen on him in years—so genuine and happy. "That's one of the reasons I fell in love with you. You were always so compassionate about everything. Animals and people. Also why I wanted to impress you with my awesome riding skills." He lifts the corner of his lips and smirks. "Turns out I was smitten by you before I even knew what those feelings meant."

"Who knew it'd take almost two decades for you to figure it out?" I tease, getting a laugh out of him.

He leans in slowly, cupping my cheek, and when he brings our lips together, he kisses me with such tenderness, I melt against him. "Thank you," he whispers against my lips.

I open my eyes and stare at him. "For what?"

"For giving me a chance to prove to you I can be the guy you deserve."

Jackson and I lie in the back of the truck for the next few hours, watching the clouds while reminiscing about all the stupid things we did as kids. Eventually, I get the courage to head back to my parents' and face everyone.

"I think I should go back, so they don't get overly worried," I say, leaning up on my elbows and glancing down at my wedding gown. It's such a gorgeous dress too.

Jackson sits up, pushing his messy hair out of his face. I've always secretly loved when he does that. He has amazing messy hair.

"Do you want me to go with you? I can drive you back in Evan's truck, and I'll grab mine later," Jackson offers.

I give him a sad look, wishing I could have him by my side for support, but I know I need to do this alone. "No, I have to do this on my own. Apologize to my family and explain why I couldn't go through with it. I'm sure Trent is waiting to hear from me, too. If you're with me, they're going to think it's your fault, and I don't want anyone blaming you. They need to know this was my decision because Trent just wasn't the right one."

"I'm sorry…" he whispers. "I know this isn't going to be easy for you. I wish I could be there to hold your hand and give you the comfort and support to get through it." He kisses my knuckles again, and I already love this new side to Jackson that I know has only ever been for me.

"I'm sure people are going to assume, but I'd rather the whole town not form their own opinions based on us driving back together. So I'll tell them I was having second thoughts and didn't go with my gut, but when it came down to it, I just couldn't marry him. And that's the truth."

"You were having second thoughts?" he asks, furrowing his brows. "And you were going to marry him anyway?"

"You're seriously not going to judge me right now, are you?" I pin him with a glare.

"No, I'm just askin'."

"There were some signs I ignored, and then when the truth came out, I forgave him too easily. I can explain it to you later because it's a long story. But ultimately, the past few months have been rough between us. I figured all couples go through rough patches and that was one of ours. He kept making promises and vowed to never lie or keep things from me again, but when it came down to it, I didn't fully trust him."

"So if I had shown up and walked down that aisle, you would've gone through with it?" he asks.

"I don't know...I want to think I wouldn't have. You kissing me and your note aren't the reasons Trent and I weren't working out, but it was what I needed to realize I was marrying the wrong person. I didn't want to disappoint my family so close to the wedding after all the money and effort they'd put in, and I think that's part of the reason I overlooked so many of our issues. Then when I walked down the aisle, something didn't sit well in my stomach. It was supposed to be the happiest moment of my life, and as soon as I looked at John for confirmation on where you were, he just shook his head and shrugged as if he knew I was making a mistake. Trent wanted a trophy wife, but he kept secrets from me, and ultimately, his actions are what broke us apart."

"Wow…I wish you'd felt comfortable enough to come to me during those times, but I know I haven't exactly been a good friend to you. That's my fault one hundred percent."

"It probably wouldn't have mattered. I was naïve and living in a fantasy world. Love makes you blind, and when I finally opened my eyes, the signs were clear as day. I just want to be able to explain that to my family and Trent before they all point fingers at you."

"I understand, baby. Just know I'll be supporting you from afar. Call me anytime, night or day, and I'll be there. And if you need me to come punch Trent in the face for you, I'll do that too." He grins, but there's a hint of sadness in his tone. I know this isn't easy for him either, considering he needs to stay on the sidelines for now.

"Thank you." I kiss him. "I'll call you as soon as I can, okay? I need to get home and get out of this dress, though."

Jackson helps me off the tailgate and walks me to the driver's side before pinning me to the door for one last sensual kiss. "Good luck."

My heart pounds as I drive down the gravel driveway to my parents' house. I see the large, white tent in the distance and notice several trucks are still parked nearby. A quick glance tells me neither Trent nor any of his family are there, and I exhale with relief. I know he deserves an explanation, but I'd much rather do it after I speak with my family.

I park Evan's truck in the first open spot in front of the house and turn it off, but don't get out. People are in the tent, probably eating the food so it doesn't go to waste. Music echoes in the distance and a part of me is happy that they continued with the reception. Knowing my family and the Bishops, they're drinking and having a good time while they wait for me to return.

After a few minutes, I decide to step out and walk up the porch. Through the screen door, I can see no one's in the kitchen and figure it's safe to enter. As soon as the door slams behind me, my mama comes walking in from the living room.

"Oh thank God." She rushes toward me and wraps her arms around me. "I've been so worried. Emily said you took Evan's truck to go find Jackson but wasn't sure where you went. You didn't answer your phone."

"I'm sorry, Mama. I didn't have my phone. I found Jackson. He's fine, too."

She squeezes me tightly before pulling back to study me. "Are you okay?" She's inspecting me to make sure I'm emotionally okay.

"Mama, I'm fine. I promise. For the first time in the past few years, I'm thinking clearly." I flash her a smile, so she knows I'm being truthful. "I just couldn't marry Trent. He wasn't...*the one.*"

The corner of her lips tilts up into a relieved smile. "I know, baby." She pats my arm. "Let's get you changed, and we can talk."

Mama helps me out of the dress, and I change into something much more comfortable. I grab my phone and see it's almost dead from all the missed calls and text messages—most of them from Trent. He's left me five voicemails and guilt surfaces as I contemplate on how I'm going to face him.

Kiera: Can I come over and talk? Please let me explain.

I don't bother listening to his messages, knowing they're probably full of anger and hate. While I wait for his response, I head out to the tent with my mama and brace myself for what's to come.

Emily spots me immediately and rushes over. She wraps her arms around me and inspects me similar to how my mama did. "You okay?"

I nod and smile. "Yeah. I'm great."

She grabs my hand and pulls me to where the other Bishops are sitting and drinking. They look just as relieved to see me, but they don't berate me with questions right away, which I'm grateful for.

Members of my family stuck around, and I decide to go to them and apologize for the events. They ask if I'm okay and why I left. I give them a quick, condensed version about Trent and me not being right for each other and how I couldn't go through with it when I wasn't one hundred percent sure about our relationship. They listen and nod, though I'm certain most of them are skeptical. Even though that's the truth, I purposely leave out the parts about Jackson kissing me and the note.

An hour later, I check my phone and see Trent's message pop up.

Trent: Fuck off, Kiera. Your shit's on the lawn. Might want to come get it before it burns just like the Bishop barn did.

My eyes widen in shock, and then all my suspicions are confirmed.

He was always a monster. I just didn't want to see it even when the signs were there.

CHAPTER TWENTY-FOUR

KIERA

I FEEL as if a black cloud is hanging above me. This isn't over yet, and the dread of going to Trent's to grab my shit off his lawn is causing panic. I thought I'd have a little time away at least, or he'd have time to calm down. But that's not how Trent does things. It's usually to the extreme. I understand how mad he is, and how he wants me out of his life, so now is as good a time as ever to move all my shit out, I guess.

If I were left at the altar, I'd be just as hurt, but going through with the wedding would've hurt us both a lot worse. Having to go through a divorce and a possible legal battle while being fed lies–it's almost frightening what could've happened. We didn't sign a prenup, and I'm not so sure he wouldn't have fought to take half of everything I worked for over the past decade. I'm so unsettled and mad at myself for not standing strong a month ago when I told him I couldn't marry him. All this could've been avoided, but he wouldn't let me go. And a part of me didn't want to.

I should've figured it out sooner or actually listened to the internal alarms that've been going off, but I didn't, so here I am. The girls circle around me and notice something's wrong. I tell them what Trent's message says, minus the reference to the

Bishop barn. The wound is still too fresh to discuss that. The silver lining in the storm clouds is Jackson. I think I'm still in shock from it all.

"You're not going alone," Mila tells me. She looks over her shoulder at Evan, John, and Alex who are drinking and laughing at Colton as he makes a fool of himself on the dance floor. I'm actually glad none of the food or beer is going to waste and that some people are still enjoying themselves. As soon as John sees the look in Mila's eyes, he takes it as his cue and walks over.

"Round up your brothers, you're all going to be Kiera's bodyguards." Mila doesn't give John a choice.

"Is everything okay?" he asks, looking back and forth between us.

"Trent threw all my stuff in his yard, so I need to go get it."

John shakes his head. "He's such a damn baby. I'll get everyone together."

"I know. And it doesn't help that he's mad either." I let out a deep breath, happy Mila volunteered them to join me. It makes me feel a lot safer knowing they'll all be there.

John walks across the dance floor and tells them all what's going on. Within moments, I'm surrounded by four big guys, and I know they're enough to keep Trent straight.

"I'll drive, considering I'm the only one who's sober," Evan states, holding his palm out.

"I owe you one for letting me take your pride and joy," I tell him, handing his keys over. I actually forgot I still had them.

He lets out a hearty laugh and pats me on my back as the posse follows. We all load up in Evan's truck. My mind races as we pull out of the ranch and travel ten minutes down the road. It's almost as if time is standing still as we turn onto the country road that leads to Trent's land. I've driven down this road every day for a little over a year, and it's almost bittersweet to know I'll have no reason to come down here again.

Alex leans forward in the seat. "So, you and Jackson?" he asks with a grin.

"Leave her alone." John elbows him. "Don't you think she's gone through enough today?"

"There were just too many red flags I couldn't ignore any longer," I admit truthfully.

"Impeccable timing, though," Colton says with a laugh. "At least you didn't go through with it. Could've been a huge ass mess. Oh, speaking of, I think that means Jackson owes me a shit ton of money."

I laugh, remembering the stupid bet and turn to look at him. "How'd you know it wasn't going to happen? I'm pretty sure you're the only one who thought that."

He shrugs. "Just a gut feeling. I saw the way you looked at Jackson. There's no way you'd go through with that wedding when I could see your burning love for someone else."

Alex lets out a big aww, and it's followed by laughter.

"Well, at least I don't have to say I'm divorced now." I try to make light of what happened, even though it's a messy situation. I should've listened to my gut, but that's easier said than done, and I now realize how naïve I was. The man I fell in love with wasn't the same man I was going to marry, and the thought alone sends shivers down my spine.

Soon we're pulling up to Trent's place, and as promised, my shit is thrown on the front lawn. My clothes, toiletries, basically everything. He's had hours to do this, so it doesn't surprise me that everything's there.

I let out a deep breath and unbuckle. Evan gets out of the truck, and I follow him. As I'm walking past all my stuff, I notice photos that were taken of Trent and me together torn in half, and only my half is there. I shake my head and look around at my things on the ground. This is so damn disrespectful and childish, but I know this is his way of lashing out, to somewhat try to get me back for what I did to him.

The guys pick up my things and place them in the back of the truck just as the front door swings open. Trent's face is red, and I can tell he's been drinking and crying. The way he looks breaks my heart, and I'm truly sorry I let it go this far.

"Trent…"

"Shut the fuck up, Kiera. Don't say a goddamn word to me." His voice is full of poison, and by the way he's looking at me, I know I'm the last person on this planet he wants to see.

"I'm so sorry," I tell him, but my words seem to glide right past him.

I walk up the steps, hoping I can explain myself and let him know what happened, though I doubt he wants to hear it.

"You're sorry, Kiera? You're a piece of shit. Do you have any idea how I felt being left at the altar? Having to speak to everyone after you left? You embarrassed my family and me, and I don't think I'll ever be able to forgive you for that."

"I understand." I open my mouth and close it, trying to find more words that could even begin to explain how sorry I am that this happened, but nothing sounds like it will ever be good enough because it won't.

"Do you? Do you really understand it? Reverse the roles, Kiera. You're nothing but a skanky ass whore. And I know you're fucking Jackson. I knew you were cheating the entire time. I tried to look past all your insecurities. Everything. Because I loved you, but now you're dead to me, Kiera."

His words are a slap in the face, but I don't have the energy to fight him right now. I've told him over and over again that Jackson and I were never more than friends, which was the honest truth. He's living in a delusional world if he truly thinks that.

"This is because of *you*, Trent. It's always been because of the way you act. The way you lie. The way I can't trust you. This has *nothing* to do with Jackson," I scream at him, disgusted that he's still stuck on this. With every argument we've had in the past few months, he's somehow found a way to sneak Jackson into the conversation instead of taking responsibility for what *he* does.

Trent takes a step forward, rearing back and pushes me off the porch with every bit of strength he has. "Get the fuck away from me, you stupid bitch."

The shock of it all rocks through me. I stumble backward, missing the step, and fall to the ground. John rushes to me, searching my face.

"Are you okay?" he asks, helping me up. "I'm about to kick his ass for that."

"Don't." I grab his arm. "He's not worth it, John. I'm okay." I dust myself off and suck in a deep breath. The only thing that's broken right now is my damn pride.

Trent looks at me and John together, and I watch as his face contorts into rage. "You're a slut who lied to me for the past two and a half years. I should've never trusted *you*. And then you have the audacity to bring that motherfucker on my property with you?"

John stands and crosses his arms over his chest. "I'm not Jackson, asshole."

"I know you're upset, Trent. But when you settle down and you're not so mad, maybe we can talk about what happened."

Trent's lips are in a firm line. "You need to get the fuck off my property before I call the cops for trespassing. Don't you ever come back here either, Kiera. I have nothing to say to you. I never want to see you again."

My eyes meet Trent's before he turns his body, walks inside, and slams the door shut. When I turn around, the guys are all standing next to each other like superheros ready to fight the bad guy. Trent's lucky they didn't all jump his ass when he put his hands on me. But he would be stupid to even try to fight back. Having them with me may have even frustrated him more, but I had no other choice, especially considering how his temper has gotten away from him in the past. There's no way anyone would've let me face him alone anyway.

We walk back to the truck, and my shoulder throbs where Trent pushed me, but as sick as it is, I feel as if I deserved it. Though his words were hurtful, I understand the place they're coming from, and the guilt consumes me. I honestly don't think he'll ever forgive me for what I did, and I'm okay with it, because I made my choice.

"It's over now," Evan says as I buckle.

"Yeah, until the rumor mill starts," I tell him.

"It's already started," Alex admits. "But who cares, Kiera? You did the right thing. Trent's a psycho. He just has this look in his eye like he's got a few screws loose somewhere or something."

"He's just upset is all," I say, looking out the window, realizing I'm still making excuses for his actions. The silence draws on as we head back to my parents' house. Considering I rented my house out to a nice family when I moved in with Trent, I guess that means I'll be living with my parents until I figure something out. Great. There are so many things I didn't think about when I left that I'll have to deal with over the next few weeks. Being over thirty and living with my parents—didn't see that one coming.

We pull into the driveway, and Evan parks close to the front door of the house. They all get out and grab armfuls of clothes and things that Trent threw out like it was trash. I open the door and lead them to my room.

"Just set it wherever it'll go," I tell them, grabbing some plastic tubs to try to lessen the trips. Considering there's five of us and I didn't move every little thing into Trent's, it doesn't take that long.

"If you need anything else, let us know, okay?" John says with a hand on my shoulder, searching my face.

I give him a small smile. "You know I will. Thank y'all for everything and for sticking by me even when I make a complete mess of things."

Evan chuckles, then gives me a hug. "Family always sticks together, Kiera."

Alex and Colton do too.

"You made the right decision," Colton adds. "And made me a very rich man."

"Shut up." I laugh, seeing them out the door. "Y'all take all that food home and eat it for the next week."

My parents come in through the back door and thank the guys for helping me.

"You going to join the after party?" Mama asks.

"No, I kind of just want to be alone."

She wraps her arms around me and gives me a big hug. "I know it hurts right now, but with time, you'll realize you made the right decision. Okay, honey? You're probably emotionally exhausted. It's been a strange day."

"I'm sorry I did this to y'all," I finally say.

Dad shakes his head. "I'm still proud of you, Kiki. You followed your heart, regardless of the consequences. It takes a strong woman to do that."

"Thanks, Dad." I look at my parents and am so grateful they understand and aren't mad at me after all the money they spent to make this exactly what Trent wanted.

I eventually make my way through the hallway and walk into my childhood bedroom that's as messy as my life. Letting out a deep breath, I open my closet and push my old prom dresses to the back and start hanging everything up. Once my bed is cleaned off, I crawl on top of it and close my eyes. When I glance over, I see my wedding dress hanging on the back of the door and I get up and shove it in the closet because I can't stand to look at it. Today was supposed to be one of the happiest days of my life, and while it partially was, it wasn't for the reasons I expected when I went to sleep last night.

I think back to Jackson's words, to the confessions we made today, and I'm so fucking happy I can barely contain my emotions. Tears pour out of me, and I let it all out as I ride the emotional roller coaster. I cry tears of sadness for Trent and how badly I hurt him, but tears of happiness follow soon after. Though I loved Trent, I wasn't *in* love with him. After the newness wore off, deep down I knew, I just tried to hold on to the thought of us as much as I could, not wanting to give up. I hope one day he can find happiness.

Soon I'm being pulled from my thoughts by a text message. I slip my phone out of my pocket and see it's from Jackson and realize I totally forgot to text him.

Jackson: Everything okay?

Kiera: Yes. I picked up all my stuff from Trent's. It's over.

Jackson: Good. I'm here for you if you need anything.

I smile thinking about him, thinking about the letter he wrote to me and what this all really means.

Kiera: Thank you. I'm emotionally drained. I think I need sleep.

Jackson: Have a few shots of whiskey and call it a day.

Kiera: Good idea! I'll call you tomorrow.

Jackson: Sounds good. Sweet dreams.

I lock my phone and roll over on my side, allowing sleep to take over. I didn't realize how tired I was until I hear a knock on my door. The morning sun gleams through my window, and I know it's the next day. I slept like the dead.

"Are you feeding the horses, or do you have Alexis doing it?" Mom asks.

"She's taking care of it." I roll over and look at her. "But I'll probably head over there just to keep my mind busy."

"Well breakfast is ready if you're hungry."

I rub my eyes. "Thanks, Mama. Gonna take a shower first."

After I scrub all the leftover wedding makeup from my face, I get in the shower and stand there for at least ten minutes allowing the hot water to run over my skin. Today's a new day, but the guilt of everything still hasn't left. Only time will be able to heal those wounds.

After I get out of the shower, I get dressed and eat breakfast with my parents. It's almost weird how natural it feels to be here with them. I haven't lived at home since I was eighteen, but as I sit here, it feels as if I never left. Once we're done eating, I help Mama clean the kitchen, then head to my bedroom when I get a call from Addie.

"You have to tell me what happened. You left me on a damn cliffhanger yesterday," she says.

I let out a laugh. "You're never going to believe it. I'm not sure I do."

I explain the letter, tell her about what Jackson said, and how Trent pushed me off his porch. "Please don't tell anyone about Jackson and me. We've agreed to keep it a secret and to take it slow, whatever that means."

"I have no friends, so your secret's safe with me," she says with a smile. I know I can trust Addie. She knows everything about me and is sealed tight as a vault. "But damn. This is really happening. It's like it all happened so fast."

Now I'm the one to laugh. "Fast? It took almost two decades and a possible wedding to make it happen."

"And do you regret it?" Addie waits for my answer.

I think about it all. Jackson and my friendship, the kiss we shared when we were teens, how I never gave up on him when everyone else did. He was always the one. There's zero doubt in my bones, no inkling of distrust, and I know the decision I made was the right one. My life isn't perfect, but it's mine, and I wouldn't change a thing.

"Hell no," I tell her, and I mean it. "I have zero regrets."

CHAPTER TWENTY-FIVE

JACKSON

"SLOW? YOU'RE TAKING THINGS…*SLOW*?" Colton squints his eyes as if he's not sure he heard me correctly.

"Yes," I confirm. "Kiera isn't just a random hookup or a girl I just met. I want to do things…right. She deserves to be taken out and showered with all that romance crap."

Colton laughs, nearly howling. "And you know shit creek about that."

I glare at him, warning him to shut his damn mouth. "Clearly."

We continue walking to the equipment barn that burned down. All that's left is black ash on the ground. Until the insurance pays out, we're borrowing equipment from a few of the other ranches near us. It's still so damn depressing to look at, but it's inevitable since it's on our way to our trucks.

"So what's your plan, bigshot?" Colton taunts, opening the passenger door and hopping in while I do the same on the driver's side.

"Well since she doesn't want us to be seen in public just yet, I can't take her out for a real date, so I figured I'd cook for her and make it special at my place," I explain, cranking the truck and shifting it into gear. We're done for the day, and I'm eager to see

Kiera tonight. We have to sneak around like a bunch of horny teenagers, and although I respect her decision and understand why we have to keep things between us on the downlow, it still sucks.

After all this time, Kiera and I have finally confessed our feelings, and I want to announce it to the whole damn world and let everyone know she's mine now. However, I'll do whatever she asks me to do because honestly, it doesn't matter. Being with her and seeing where this goes are all that matters.

It's not easy to see each other now. She's living with her parents since she still has a tenant in her old house. We've talked every day, but we haven't been able to find time to be together between our schedules. I'm up at the ass crack of dawn for work, and she hasn't officially told her family about us yet, though I suspect they know. She's told me some details about Trent involving a secret child she never knew existed, and it gave me relief knowing his dumbass actions factored into her decision not to marry him.

"But you don't know how to cook," Colton blurts, taking me out of my thoughts.

"Thank you, Captain Asshat. I was going to call Emily and see what she recommended. I know Kiera's likes and dislikes, but I have no clue what's an appropriate meal for a dinner date."

"Well, aren't you lucky that you have a good-looking friend who's a pro in the kitchen." He gloats, smirking from ear to ear.

"You cook, huh?" I ask, turning down the road to the ranch hand quarters.

"Pretty damn well too."

"Okay, well as soon as Emily gets back to me, I'll text you, and you can give me some pointers."

"You're gonna need more than pointers. I'll come over and show you."

I park in front of his house and narrow my eyes. "So now we're cooking together?" I arch a brow, giving him shit.

"You wanna make a good meal or poison her?" he counters,

opening the door. When I don't respond, he continues. "That's what I thought." He smirks before jumping out. "You still owe me fifteen hundred bucks."

"What?"

"The bet. Kiera didn't get married, and now you owe me." He flashes a smug smirk.

I roll my eyes as he shuts the door, and I think about his offer to help while I drive to my house.

Guess it couldn't hurt to have some assistance. Kiera already has so many assumptions about me and my previous "dating" life, and I'd love nothing more than to prove to her that she's so much more than any of those other girls. I've never wanted to try at a relationship before, which she already knows, but I still don't want to screw this up.

Once I'm back home and showered, I send Emily a text.

Jackson: What would you suggest for a dinner date meal idea? I want to cook for Kiera, but I need suggestions.

Emily: You know her better than I do, Fabio.

What is it with everyone calling me dorky ass nicknames lately? It's like they all know I'm a love-sick puppy and enjoy giving me shit for it.

Jackson: True, Scooby-Doo. But I want to make something "date" appropriate.

Emily: Hmm, yeah. You know nothing about actual dates, so let me think...

I groan inwardly and wait impatiently for her response.

Emily: Okay, I got it. So easy even you couldn't screw it up.

Jackson: Thanks for the confidence.

Emily: Shrimp scampi with linguine pasta. It's delicious, and Kiera loves shrimp, so it's a win-win! Also, it doesn't take too long to make either. Then, while you're eating, you can bake an apple pie in the oven, and it'll be ready by the time you're done.

Jackson: Apple pie? I can't make a pie.

Emily: Good thing your mama is the best pie baker in the county!

She's got a point there. I'll call Mama later.

Jackson: Okay. Thanks, Em. Appreciate the help.

Emily: No problem.

Emily: Oh and Jackson…if you hurt my friend, I won't think twice about sneaking into your house in the middle of the night and using a chainsaw to your balls.

Jesus.
I cup my junk at the imagery.

Jackson: I promise to cut off my own balls if that ever happens.

Emily: Good. I'll hold ya to that.

Jackson: Oh, Em? I never thanked you, but I wanted to say thank you for being there for Kiera when she left the wedding and always being there for her. I know it hasn't been easy, and I'm sure it's not easy on any of you either.

Emily: Honestly, I always knew you were a better pick for her. She told me all about you when we first met in college, and I always wondered what it'd take for you two to finally get together. Never imagined it'd be like this, but I can't stay I'm not happy for you guys. I just don't want to see my friend get heartbroken by you again.

Her words nearly gut me, and I'm sure I've unintentionally hurt her over the years when I pretended my feelings didn't exist.

Jackson: She deserves the whole world, and it's exactly what I want to give her as long as she'll let me.

Emily: You're a good guy, Jackson. Keep it that way.

Jackson: You got it, sis. Thanks again for your help.

Emily was always a blunt, tell-it-like-it-is woman, and if it's possible, I like her even more now. She's exactly the type of woman to keep Evan in line and type of friend to support Kiera. I'm glad she's in all our lives.

I look in my fridge and realize it's nearly empty minus a six-pack of beer, half a carton of eggs, and random condiments. Fuck. I'm gonna need to go shopping.

Sitting on the couch, I call Kiera and wait anxiously until she answers.

"Well hello, Cowboy." Her sweet, honey-laced tone has a direct line to my dick, making me hard.

"Do you have any idea what your voice does to my cock?" I groan, shifting and adjusting my jeans. "If we're taking things slow, you're gonna have to start sounding like a dude on the phone."

Kiera laughs, and it does nothing to tame the hard-on in my pants. "Maybe I can help you with that." Her voice goes soft, almost seductive. "Why don't you relieve the ache while I tell you all the dirty ways I—"

"For the love of God, stop…" I blurt out, growling at her. "You're breaking the rules."

"Technically, we said no being a tease, and I'm not even there so…"

"You're a little minx," I tell her. "Changing the subject. How was your day?"

We text throughout the day when we can, but we're often both so busy that we sometimes go hours without being able to check or reply. Considering I used to spend days or even weeks without talking to her or even seeing her, I'll take what I can get for now.

"Not too bad, I guess. One of my clients who knew the Lakens abruptly picked up her horse and said she didn't want me to train him anymore, so that stung a bit."

"I'm sorry. Their loss anyway," I tell her honestly.

"I know. It just sucks." I hear her sigh and wish I could take the tension away. "I know it's only been a week or so, but I hate that everyone knows or thinks they know the details of what happened between Trent and me and why I left."

"Small-town rumor mills," I say. "They're gonna say whatever they wanna say regardless if you tell them the truth, so you might as well try to ignore it altogether. Eventually, they'll get bored of you and move on." I try to comfort her, but I know Kiera takes the rumors to heart more than I ever have. She prides her business and herself on having a good reputation, and it's partly why I agreed with keeping things between us private.

"You're right," she says, and I can hear the smile in her voice. "How was your day?"

"Same ole, same ole. Colton says I owe him since he won the bet, so I only think it's fair you offer up half," I tease, wanting to get her mind off the rumors.

And it works because Kiera bursts out laughing, which makes me smile wide. "Funny. I didn't tell you to make the stupid bet in the first place."

"Well, I had no choice. If I bet that you wouldn't, you'd say I wasn't being a supportive friend or some bullshit."

"Mmm…I'm sure that's why." I imagine her rolling her eyes. "Guess that'll teach you to place bets."

"No shit," I grumble. "Colton's a bastard for even startin' it."

She laughs again, and it brings me back to all the times of when we'd just be together hanging out, and things were so simple and easy.

"Kiera, come over," I say. "I need to see you."

"What if someone sees me?"

"Drive your dad's truck and park at the B&B guest parking lot. I'll come pick you up from there."

"I don't know…" She hesitates.

"I promise, no hanky-panky. I'll only grope you over the shirt."

"Jackson!" She chuckles. "Okay."

"Meet me there in ten."

"Better be on your best behavior, Cowboy," she warns.

"Scout's honor, Pippi."

Too anxious to wait, I head over to the B&B right away and park in front of John's house instead. When I see her truck's headlights, I get out and start walking over to meet her.

I spot her before she sees me and just stare at how damn beautiful she looks. Her blonde hair is pulled up in a messy ponytail, and she's wearing tight jeans that show off her perfect ass. Instead of letting her know I'm here, I sneak up on her and wrap my arms around her waist. Before I tell her it's me, she jerks her arm back and elbows me right in my gut.

"Fuck," I curse, stepping back and holding out my hand to grab her arm.

"Oh, shit!" She gasps when she spins around and notices it's me. "You ass!" she shout-whispers.

"What?" I try to catch my breath. Goddamn, she put all her weight into that.

"You don't sneak up on someone like that! I thought you were a creeper!" Her eyes soften when she looks down at me holding my stomach. "Shit, are you okay?"

"Yeah, fine." I blink until my vision clears.

She steps closer and cups my face with both of her hands. "You're so cute when you're trying to be tough." She smirks, and it drives me wild.

"I am tough," I retort, smirking. Before she can stop me, I wrap my arms around her waist and push her against the truck. I crash my mouth against hers and capture her bottom lip between my teeth, groaning at how amazing she tastes. "You owe me now."

She chuckles against my lips but doesn't push me away. Instead, she fists my T-shirt and pulls me toward her as I deepen the kiss. Our lips move and mold together as if we've been doing it for years—our bodies in perfect sync, and I don't want it to ever stop. She arches her hips and rubs against my cock.

"You're seriously testing my willpower," I murmur against her lips. "I'm going to come in my damn pants like a virgin if you don't stop."

"I'm sorry," she says, chuckling. She flattens her hands and pushes away. "We shouldn't be out here, just in case."

"I doubt anyone's going to recognize us anyway." It's pitch black, and the only light flickers from the moon and the porch. "Let's go." I grab her hand and drag her across the lot to my truck and help her into the passenger side. Before I shut the door, I smack a kiss on her lips.

"Are you always so charming?" she asks as soon as I slam my door shut.

"What do you think?" I grin.

"What are your first date moves?" she asks as I drive us to my house. "Tell me."

"You've lost your mind," I tease.

"Oh, c'mon! What are your infamous Jackson pickup one-liners?"

I look over at her, and she's biting down on her bottom lip, hiding her shit-eating grin. Fuck, it's so cute when she does that.

"What makes you think I have one-liners? I just flash a smile and clothes magically melt off."

Kiera snorts, rolling her eyes. "You're such an ass."

Reaching over, I grab her hand and pull it into my lap where I'm still hard. "You don't mean that."

"You're breaking the rules," she says, throwing my words back at me.

"You started it, Pippi."

When we arrive at my house, I lead her inside and immediately cover her mouth with mine.

"Jackson…" Kiera warns breathlessly.

"This is as slow as I can go," I tell her, wrapping my hands around her waist and holding her securely against me. "I can't not kiss you now that I've had a taste."

"That's not what I was going to say…"

I pull back slightly and look in her eyes. "What then?"

She swallows and looks down as if she's embarrassed. "I appreciate you doing this my way even if it's something we both *really* want. I have to contain my personal image as much as I can now before I lose all my clients."

Placing two fingers under her chin, I tilt her head up so she looks at me. "I'll do whatever it takes, baby. I've said it before, but I'll say it again." I dip down and quickly kiss her lips. "I'm in love with you. Nothing's going to ever change that."

I see her eyes gloss over and know she hears the sincerity in my voice.

"Don't make plans for this weekend."

She squints, pursing her lips together. "Why?"

"I want to make you dinner. If I can't take you out, I'll have to improvise."

"Really? You're going to cook?" Her teasing tone doesn't go unnoticed, making me groan.

"Why is that the first thing everyone says?"

Kiera laughs, wrapping her arms around my neck and pulling me down to her mouth. "Sounds perfect. It's a date."

"Stir that," Colton orders, watching me over my shoulder. "Slowly," he says when some of the sauce spills out.

"Fuck," I mutter, brushing a hand through my hair and feeling the sweat above my brow.

"You're really nervous," he says.

"No shit."

"Jackson Bishop. Nervous for a date?" He chuckles, and he makes me want to nut punch him.

"You gonna help me or give me a hard time?"

"Calm down, princess. Let me do it before all the sauce spills on the stove." He motions for me to move out of his way, and I gladly let him take over. "Go finish getting ready, and I'll continue setting up."

"Setting up?"

"Yeah, I brought some china and candles."

My brows rise, both shocked and impressed. I want to give him shit for having china because if the roles were reversed, he would, but considering he's saving my ass tonight, I keep my mouth shut.

A half an hour later, I'm dressed in my Sunday best that I normally despise wearing, but I know Kiera's going to like it. She's always commented how much she loves it when I dress up, though I feel silly since we aren't actually going out. Dinner is done and staying warm in the oven. The table is set, completely over the top, but I actually like it. Colton made it look like a real fancy restaurant and even brought a wine bucket to set on the side for the bottle of red I bought from the store. I don't drink wine unless it's the only option, but I know Kiera loves it.

"Thanks, man. I appreciate your help." I slap him on the back. "Wish me luck."

"Good luck keeping it in your pants." He smirks. "I'll stop over tomorrow to pick up my stuff unless plans change and you actually do get lucky, then I'll wait till Monday."

"Bye, asshole." I open the door and nearly push him out.

"Don't forget to light the candles when you serve the food! It brings the whole setting together."

I shake my head and laugh. "Okay, cupid. Go away now."

Once he leaves, I run around the house, making sure everything is clean and picked up. I don't ever worry about a clean house when I bring girls over, but Kiera is *the* girl. I want it to be perfect for her.

I drive over and pick her up promptly at seven. I'm making sure we have a proper date, even if it makes me feel dumb and corny as hell.

"You look stunning," I say as soon as she opens the front door. She's wearing a simple purple dress that hugs her curves and ends right above her knee. It's tight on her waist and gives me a gorgeous view of her tits. It accentuates her stunning eyes that I could get lost in.

Her parents are gone tonight, so I was able to pick her up. Leaning in, I pull her closer and give her a heated kiss. "Mmm, you smell and taste amazing too."

"You look quite handsome yourself." Her gaze falls down my body and back up to my face, and when she looks into my eyes again, she's biting down on her bottom lip. "Too handsome actually."

"You ready?"

She inhales a deep breath and smiles. "Let's go."

I can't stop looking at her as I drive back to the ranch. She left her hair down in beachy waves, and I love when she does that. It reminds me of when she'd braid her hair and then take them out, making her hair all wavy.

As soon as we step into the house, she inhales the smell and moans. "Mmm, whatever that is smells amazing."

"I can't take all the credit," I admit bashfully. I'm never insecure on dates, or hell, I wouldn't even call them dates. However, Kiera makes me nervous as hell with how much I want to impress her and show her that she's the only girl I've ever wanted. "Colton's culinary skills came to my rescue."

I lead her to the table and pull her seat out so she can sit. Once she's comfortable, I find a match and light the candle.

"Can I assume Colton gets credit for the table too?" She playfully smirks.

"He does."

"I like that you cared enough to ask him for help," she says as if she could sense that I feel stupid for not knowing how to arrange something like this myself. "It's beautiful."

"Well, I hope you like what we made too. Emily's suggestion," I tell her, taking the dish out and stirring it once more. "Oh, I should open the wine." Turning around abruptly to grab the bottle from the bucket, I nearly knock the bread off the table. "Shit." Luckily, Kiera catches it before it could fall to the floor.

She smiles at me but doesn't say anything.

Once I have our wineglasses filled and our plates dished out, I remember the music Colton recommended. Digging into my pocket for my phone, my elbow bumps the edge of the table and my wine glass shakes. Instinctively, I pick it up, and my palms are so damn sweaty, it slips from my grip and spills on my shirt before I can steady it.

"Fuck," I mutter, squeezing my eyes shut. "Sorry."

When I open my eyes, Kiera's clearly trying to hold in a laugh and has her lips tucked into her mouth. As soon as she sees I'm watching her, she places an elbow on the table and covers her mouth with her hand.

"Guess I'll just take this off," I say, hoping she gets my hint. Slowly, I unbutton my shirt, and she's nearly drooling as I slowly undo each one until my chest is fully exposed, and I pull it down my arms.

"That's not fair," she pouts, keeping her gaze on my chest. "You can't be flaunting your abs and tattoos during dinner."

"That's payback for laughing at me," I tease. Her eyes meet mine, and she glares.

"I did not laugh!"

"Oh really? You think I don't know when you're lying?"

She releases a groan deep in her throat. "Damn you." She chuckles. "Better hope you don't end up spilling anything on my dress then, because I won't think twice at removing it."

I raise a brow, intrigued by the idea. "Really? Considering my record already, I'd say it's a safe bet I'll have my pants off before dessert." I flash her a knowing wink, but she only smirks and shakes her head at me.

My nerves finally calm as we settle into natural conversation. Being with Kiera has never made me feel uneasy before, but now that our feelings have been laid out, I can't seem to relax. The tension and anticipation of being with her have me all kinds of worked up.

Halfway through dinner, I remember to put the apple pie that Mama made in the oven and serve it while we're set up in the living room watching a movie.

"Your mama makes the best damn pie," Kiera says, moaning around a forkful.

"Oh, you have some right here…" I lean in and stick my tongue out to lick sugar off the corner of her mouth. "Mmm… you're right. Delicious."

Kiera looks at me with hunger in her eyes, and I know she's thinking the same thing. Cupping her cheek, I pull her mouth to mine and kiss her slowly. She leans in, letting me take control, and when I slide my tongue between her lips, she caresses it with hers.

"Fuck, Kiera…you have any idea how many times I've thought about doing that?" I lean my forehead against hers and feel her pulse beating rapidly in her neck. "So many goddamn times."

"I hate that we've lost all those years we could've been together," she says softly. "But I know you weren't ready, and if I'm being honest, I don't think I was either, even if I didn't know it. We both needed to experience life outside of each other and grow up. I'm not so sure we would've stayed together if we'd dated when we were that young."

"I think you're right, baby," I agree. "That doesn't mean it was easy, though."

"The journey to happiness never is, Jackson," she says, pulling back with a smile, then laughing. "I've called you Jackson for so long, I don't know that I can call you anything else…"

"Well, considering the names you've called me in the past, anything beats 'dick, asshole, bastard, or idiot'…I mean, after a while the cuteness factor wears off."

Kiera bursts out laughing, tilting her head back as she covers her mouth. "Oh my God. But I mean, you can't really blame me. All those names were quite fitting at the time."

"You're probably right." I wink, reaching down to grab our plates, then place them on the coffee table. "However, if you need help getting inspired for something new…" I take her hand and place it over my cock that's straining against my slacks. It's painfully hard, which is nothing new when I'm around her. "Maybe add some colorful adjectives such as 'Big Dick, Thick Daddy, or Sexy Bastard'…take your pick." Instead of pulling away like I anticipate, she wraps her fingers firmly around my dick and slowly moves her hand up and down.

"Well if I'm going to agree to any of those, I'm going to have to see for myself which one is the most fitting…" She bites her bottom lip as she increases her speed.

My head falls back, groaning in painful pleasure. I know she's only teasing me, and I'll end up with blue balls, but I don't have the willpower to stop her. "Fuck…you call me anything you want as long as you're doing that."

Unable to take her teasing any longer, I pull her onto my lap and kiss her fiercely. My fingers weave into her hair, and as I arch my hips between her legs, she grinds down on my cock. I push her dress up and feel how wet she is for me. Our breathing quickens as she moves her body against me, rotating her hips and pressing her pussy against my erection.

Our lips never separate as they move in perfect harmony like they were always meant to, but I can't think clearly with her body grinding on top of mine like this. Kiera's hands move through my hair and around my neck, pulling us impossibly closer. Her body tenses as I hold her against me. Just because we agreed to no sex right now doesn't mean I can't give her the release she's begging for.

"You need to come, baby. You're trembling," I say against her mouth. "Use my cock as your personal vibrator until you do." She doesn't say anything, but nods and she keeps her eyes closed. "Fuck, I can't wait to feel that beautiful pussy wrapped around my dick. You're going to ruin me in more ways than one, sweetheart. I just hope you'll be ready for it…"

"God, Jackson." She moans, increasing the speed of her hips. "I'm so wet."

"Come against me, Kiera. I wanna watch you."

"Kiss me," she demands.

Pressing my lips to hers, I slide my fingers up her body, pull her dress down just enough, and squeeze her breast in my hand as she releases another sultry moan. Kiera has the best damn tits I've ever felt. I've seen them plenty of times when she'd wear low-cut shirts or bathing suits, but nothing compares to feeling them in my palm.

As her body tightens again, I grip her hips and push her back and forth against me to help build up her orgasm, and within seconds, she's shaking against me and releasing the sexiest moan I've ever heard. When she throws her head back and arches her back, I dip my head and wrap my lips around her taut pink nipple. It's hard, and I swirl my tongue around it before sucking it between my lips. Fuck, they taste good too.

Sixteen-year-old Jackson would be coming in his pants by now. However, this is all about Kiera and her pleasure—not mine. Another first for me.

Her eyes meet mine as she's trying to catch her breath. I keep my gaze on her as I glide my hand down her body and inside her panties. She gasps when I slide a finger against her slit, then bring it up to taste her arousal between my lips.

"Goddamn." I moan. "You taste so fucking sweet, Kiera."

"That was intense…" she admits. A cute blush on her cheeks tells me she wasn't expecting that. It's actually adorable on her, and I love that I'm the reason for it.

"It was a true testament to my willpower, that's for sure." I chuckle, wrapping my hands around her ass and hauling her body up higher on my hips. My dick is screaming at me for not giving in. "But I can wait. I'll just start taking some very cold showers."

Kiera laughs, biting her bottom lip as if she's contemplating something. Before she can decide, I shift out from under her and set her back down.

"Okay, let's watch a movie before I change my mind and fuck you against this couch."

CHAPTER TWENTY-SIX

KIERA

It's been three weeks since the wedding failure of the century, but it seems like a lifetime has passed since then. I help Alexis feed the horses, and then we do a quick rundown of what we plan to accomplish this week. Every Monday we meet so I can make sure we're on the same page, but Alexis is great because she doesn't need to be micromanaged. I should probably give her a raise after everything she's done in the past month. Once I go through my list, she reminds me I need to deliver a horse over to the Flitwicks.

"Shit, I totally forgot about that," I tell her. "I'll do it first thing this morning."

She gives me a smile, and before she walks away, I stop her. "What is it?"

Alexis shakes her head. "I don't even want to say."

I place my hands on my hips. Though she's worked for me for the past five years, we've had a pretty open relationship. We don't hang out outside of training, but we usually get straight to the point.

"Fine," she says. "I was at the feed store yesterday and Sandy, the woman who works the counter, asked me when you were going to announce your pregnancy. Of course, I was completely

confused by her statement, but then she said something about
you being pregnant with Jackson's baby, and that was the reason
you walked out on the wedding. Because you couldn't face being
under the eyes of the Lord knowing you were carrying another
man's baby."

"Oh for fuck's sake. Seriously?" I shake my head; the rumors
are getting more ridiculous with each passing day.

"That's what I said, but she was pretty convincing. I can't go
anywhere without someone wanting to know what you're up to
these days. But trust me, I haven't said a word. It's no one's
business what you're doing," Alexis adds.

"I'm not pregnant with Jackson's baby unless it's an
immaculate conception. Not sure if they realize this or not, but
two people have to have sex for a person to get pregnant, and
we're not." I'm so damn frustrated and humiliated. My
reputation has been dragged through the mud, and when I
thought it couldn't get any worse, this happens.

"I believe you," she says. "I do. I know y'all aren't anything
but friends."

I don't correct her. I don't tell her that Jackson and I are
secretly seeing each other since we promised not to tell anyone.

"Thank you." It's all I can offer right now. I give her a smile,
and we say our goodbyes. I head to the barn and load up the
Flitwicks' mare, then drive it across town. Lately, small things
have been slipping my mind, and I know it's because of
everything that's happened. After I drop the horse off, I decide
since I'm so close to the Bishops, I'll head over there, hoping
Jackson doesn't have any last-minute lessons. I'm already
addicted to him and can't seem to get enough.

I pull up to the B&B and park in the back. Of course, if anyone
sees me here with the trailer, they'll just assume I'm picking up a
horse, which is normal. It makes it hard to sneak around the place
when most people's families stay at the B&B, so I never know
who's on-site or who's watching me.

I park, get out of the truck, and walk toward the barn. As soon as I enter, I see Jackson carrying a bale of hay over his shoulder. I place my hands on my hips and watch his every move. Eventually, he notices me, drops the bale on the ground and brushes the extra hay from his shirt before taking off his work gloves. He comes to me, pulls me into his arms, and kisses me sweetly.

"I'll never get used to that," I say across his soft lips.

Jackson grabs my ass, and I yelp. "You'll never get used to that either."

"Mmm," I hum against his lips. "Why did we wait so long to do this?"

He pushes back and searches my face with a shit-eating grin playing on his lips. "Because you're stubborn."

I scoff. "Oh, whatever. You're the stubborn one with impeccable timing!"

"Better late than never, sweetheart." He pulls me back into his arms and kisses my forehead. "You always smell so damn good."

"Just imagine how I taste." I brush my lips against the softness of his neck and tug his earlobe into my mouth and suck.

"I already know. But damn girl, you play dirty. And as much as I want to get in your panties, your ploy isn't going to work."

Jackson has been holding himself back from me since we agreed to do this, and I'm getting impatient. Just having him touch and kiss me is driving me mad, and based on the bulge in his pants, I know he feels exactly the same.

I hear chatter behind me, and I rush away from him. A few guests from the B&B walk into the barn. My lips are swollen, and my hair is a mess, and Jackson looks just as guilty as I do.

"Howdy," he says to the older couple, bending over and picking up the bale of hay to cover the anaconda in his pants. I hold back laughter as the couple peeks in the stalls and pets one of the horses.

"If y'all want, I'm doing a few lessons this afternoon. I think there's room on the schedule," he tells them. I stand back and watch him work his magic until they agree. Eventually, they walk back to the B&B, and I rush toward Jackson.

Heat courses through me, and I need him like I need sleep. Forcefully he presses me against the stall door, his warm hand slipping under my shirt until he's palming my breast. I let out a desperate moan, wanting him more than I've ever wanted anything.

"Fuck, Kiera," Jackson whispers across my lips, devouring my mouth with his. "You know I have zero self-control when it comes to you."

I fist his messy hair, and the only thing that breaks us apart is a throat clearing behind us. Jackson glances over his shoulder, then stiffens, lowering his hands from my body.

John shakes his head, but the smile on his face doesn't fade. "Whatcha doin' in here?"

Jackson narrows his eyes at him. "I wanna ask you the same question."

"Oh hey, Kiera. Didn't notice you there with my brother's face eating yours." He chuckles as Jackson grows frustrated.

Jackson grunts, annoyed. "What'd I ever do to you?" It's a rhetorical question that has me laughing.

"Remember that time you caught Mila and me in the barn, and you just stood around awkwardly?" John smirks at his own smartass comment. "Payback's a bitch. Take care, Kiera," he says before walking away.

"We'd probably be banging on the barn floor if he wouldn't have walked up," Jackson says adjusting himself.

I let out a sigh, trying to catch my breath. "Damn him then."

"Waiting is going to be worth it, sweetheart. I promise," Jackson tells me, taking my face between his hands, then kissing me gently.

My eyes flutter open, and I take a moment to study him, noticing how happy he is with me. The feeling is mutual. Being with Jackson like this is a dream come true, and while I want him now, I know waiting is the right thing to do.

"I have a lesson in thirty minutes, but I'm free for a few hours afterward," he says as he opens my truck door for me. I climb in and roll down the window.

"Have you ever thought about us training together? As a couple?"

Jackson smirks and lifts an eyebrow, then glances down to his junk. "You want me to teach you how to ride bareback?"

"You're so damn dirty." I swallow hard, wanting to give him a kiss, but knowing anyone could see us without the barn shielding our secrets. "I want to kiss you," I admit.

"I know," he whispers. "Soon."

I drive around the pasture and reposition the truck and trailer. Instead of giving Jackson a kiss, we do a side friend hug thing that's awkward through the window, and I drive away. Before I pull out of the B&B, I realize I don't have my phone. I park in the front and walk back toward the barn with a smile on my face that quickly disappears the moment I see Nicole.

"Fuck," I whisper under my breath. I've done my best to avoid her because I know I won't be able to keep my thoughts to myself. I really try to bite my tongue.

"Whore," she says under her breath as I pass her, and that's all it takes to set me off.

I turn around and walk back toward her with a purpose in my step. She mouths off something else, but I'm already pushing her to the ground. She falls so easily, or maybe I just have too much pent-up anger inside me.

"Say it again, but to my face this time," I say above her, cracking my knuckles. She's already started way too much shit with the Bishops and needs to learn how to keep her mouth shut. It's one lesson I might teach her today.

"You're just pissed because I fucked your boyfriend. How does it feel to have everyone else's sloppy seconds?" Nicole seethes.

I lose control. She tries to push me away, but I topple her, fist in the air ready to beat her face in. "Maybe you should learn how to shut the fuck up."

Moments later, I feel strong hands pulling me away from Nicole.

"Whoa, girl," Jackson says, wrapping his arms tightly around my waist, lifting me off her, and holding me back. I let out a loud groan, and Nicole stands up, brushing dirt from her clothes.

"Trent's lucky he got rid of you when he did," she says.

"Nicole!" Jackson yells and points for her to go on. She rolls her eyes then walks away. Once she's out of sight, Jackson releases his strong hold on me.

A smirk plays on his lips. "You don't have to fight for me, Pippi. I'm already yours."

I shake my head, not amused. "She called me a whore."

Jackson tucks loose strands of hair behind my ear, and I look up into his blue eyes. "And we all know that's not true. Don't worry about her. She's just trying to make things messier than they already are, and she's jealous. But you can't be acting all cavewoman, okay? I don't want her to drag you through the mud, too, baby." He quickly leans in and kisses my lips, helping me relax.

I sigh and release a breath. "You're right."

His eyebrow pops up. "I'm always right."

How does he have the ability to make me laugh when I'm raging pissed? "Shut up. Oh, I forgot…"

Jackson holds up my cell phone. "I found it on the barn floor. Thankfully, I did. You might have destroyed Nicole if I wouldn't have shown up."

"She needs to watch her ass." I grab my phone, then quickly look around and plant another quick kiss on his lips. He pulls me back and kisses me again, much longer this time. I melt into his touch and don't want to leave, but I know his lessons are starting soon.

"I'll call you later," I tell him, holding up my phone before I walk away. "Go be a cowboy."

He chuckles. "I hate to see you go, but I love to watch you leave," he shouts the corniest line I'm sure he could think of, yet I think it's stupid adorable.

"You're relentless."

Just for fun, I make sure to shake my ass just a little extra for him as I walk back to my truck. After I leave the Bishop ranch, the anger is streaming through me. Nicole better be glad Jackson broke us apart because I would've gouged her eyes out. I can't believe she'd say those horrible things to me. I always liked her, well, until she started all this stuff with Jackson. Now she's on my shit list, which seems to be pretty long these days.

As I'm traveling down the old country road, my phone buzzes, and I see it's Mom, so I hurry and answer it.

"Hey honey, can you stop by the store and pick up some hamburger buns? I just noticed the ones I have are moldy," Mama asks.

I feel like a teenager doing my parents bidding again, but I don't mind. "Sure. I'll stop on the way back to the ranch."

Considering I still have the horse trailer on the back of the truck, I park on the side of the grocery store, then walk inside. Dixie Chicks blares on the radio, and a smile instantly touches my lips as it brings me back to my teenage years. I walk through the store until I find the bread aisle, then stand there for a second listening to the song as I look over the hamburger buns. I'm lost in my thoughts when I'm interrupted by the sound of a throat clearing beside me. I didn't even realize Trent's mother was in the store. *Fuck.*

My patience is really being tested today. First Nicole running her mouth and now this? I put on a fake smile and tell her hello because my mama taught me manners, and that's the nice thing to do. Hopefully, she'll grab what she needs and move on, but I have a feeling I won't be that lucky.

"Kiera." If looks could kill, I'd be lying dead on the grocery store floor. She looks so disgusted as her glare meets my eyes, and I'm not really sure what else to say to her.

"How've you been, Mrs. Laken?" I'm trying to make small talk so I can excuse myself from the awkwardness and get the hell out of here. Sometimes, living in a small town really sucks. It's hard to fade into the background when everyone knows everything. Then, of course, there's always awkward encounters like this one.

"After you broke my son's heart? Can't say I've been good at all."

The answer I was expecting. She's never treated me like a part of the family, and I always felt weird around her. I'm sure she's glad I didn't marry Trent; she never thought I was good enough.

"I'm sorry," I say, grabbing some sesame seed buns.

She looks me up and down. "I heard about your pregnancy. I'm not sure if I should say congratulations or not."

My mouth falls open as I stare at her. "I'm *not* pregnant." My voice seems to echo through the grocery store. Heat hits my cheeks, and I'm so embarrassed. I hate that I'm in this situation.

She gives me a sarcastic smile and nods. "But you're already showing."

I huff, and just as I'm getting ready to tell her where to go, a familiar voice interrupts us.

"Nancy," I hear Mama Bishop say. She's smiling big, showing her teeth, but she's eyeing Trent's mom like she might rip her hairpiece out. I look up and say a little thank you to God because I've been rescued by a Bishop—*again*.

"Rose," she replies in a voice laced with venom.

"How've you been?" Mama asks as sweet as can be as she pushes her buggy closer to us. The tension in the room is suffocating.

"I can't say it's been rainbows and butterflies. Not since this one ruined my son's life," she replies.

Mama Bishop laughs, and her smile never fades. "Pulling out all the dramatics, are we? Well, see, if your son would've been taught how to control his temper, then maybe Kiera here wouldn't have been so worried about what he was capable of especially after he gave her a black eye. I've always said, when men can't control their actions, it's because of the way they were raised." Mama Bishop sounds like she's speaking sweetly to a child, but her words are so damn salty that my eyes go wide with shock.

"Don't you even," Mrs. Laken says, huffing, pushing her buggy away.

"See you around, Nancy. Take care, ya hear?" Mama Bishop says, giving Trent's mother a five-finger wave.

I cover my mouth, trying to hide my shock, but it's impossible. "Thank you," I tell her, wrapping my arms around her neck. "She cornered me, and I… I didn't know what to do."

"She's a snake. Trusted that woman about as much as I trusted her son," Mama Bishop says, looking me up and down. "You okay?"

"I'm fine." I smile. "Just shocked by how she acted. I'm not used to being the center of all this attention and the rumors." I shake my head.

Mama Bishop's sparkling blue eyes meet mine. "And now you see where her son gets it from, don't you? About the rumors, that's exactly what they are. I've heard half a dozen of them, and honestly dear, I've never rolled my eyes so hard. You live your best life, sweetie, and don't worry about all the people running their mouths. Time will prove them all wrong. Keep your head high. You made the right decision. Also, you should come by for dinner sometime this week," Mama Bishop offers.

"I'd love that." I smile, and we exchange another hug. I love Mama Bishop. She's always had the best advice for me and treats me as her own. Today she rescued me from the wicked witch of East Eldorado, and I'm so damn grateful at least a few people in this town still have my back. After we say our goodbyes, I rush to the counter with my hamburger buns. Even the woman at the counter treats me strange, but I'm sure she's heard the rumors as well. Although it's not true, I'm sure my name has been added to a handful of women's shitlists because they want Jackson. Well too bad; he's mine. I smile at the thought and walk to my truck.

On the way home, my heart drops in my chest when I think about what Nancy said about me be pregnant and already showing. I think about what day it is and try to remember the last time I had my period. I break out into cold sweats and hear Trent's mother's voice on repeat as I try to count the days in my head.

As soon as I park, I open the calendar on my phone, and that's when I realize I'm late by almost a week.

"No," I whisper, dread coating my body. I break out into hives as my heart races and double-check the dates again. I'm definitely late.

I seriously can't be pregnant.

As much as I wanted to start a family, this can't be happening now. Not when I know it wouldn't be Jackson's.

CHAPTER TWENTY-SEVEN

JACKSON

THE NEXT MORNING after my daily duties are complete, I head over to the grocery store to pick up some essentials. The temperature is starting to drop, which isn't unusual for early November, but I hope it holds off for a little while longer. I'm not ready for freezing temperatures yet. My fridge looks sad again, and I ran out of eggs and bacon—basically one of the only things I can cook. I text John, letting him know I'm running to town, and ask him if he needs anything, but he doesn't. I grab a heavier jacket and head out. After I fill my truck up with diesel, I stop at the only store in town that has food.

I run in quickly, grab some eggs and bread, and as I'm looking over the bacon, hands run over my body. When I turn around, I make eye contact with Amanda, one of my crazy one-night stands who stalked me for a month after I broke it off. I take a step away from her.

"Can I help you?" I ask, hoping an inkling of recognition didn't flash across my face. It's times like this I'm thankful as fuck to be a twin.

"Jackson, baby." She leans over and whispers in my ear. "I know it's you."

I shake my head and pull off my best John impersonation.

Years of practice, plus it helps to have the same face. "Sorry, no. I'm John. It happens all the time, though. Who are you? I'll tell my brother you said hello."

She giggles and playfully slaps my arm. "Stop it, Jackson."

When I don't break character, her face drops. "I'm sorry. Can you tell Jackson that Amanda Turner said hello? And I still think about our night together often."

"I'll give him the message." I nod, then pick up a slab of bacon. I see her watching me, so I head over to the baby aisle and grab some wipes and whatever else I can carry in my arms. It's the best way to throw my exes off my scent, and I don't feel guilty about it at all.

Once I pay, I walk out to my truck and hop in. Just as I'm driving off, Amanda walks out of the store. Though the windows are up, I can still hear her yelling. "I knew it was you, Jackson! Asshole!"

I peel out, happy to have gotten the fuck out of there without seeing anyone else. I laugh all the way back to the B&B because it works every single time. I drop my food off at the house and pull out my phone and text Kiera. Usually, our days are so packed with work that it's hard to stop everything and be together, but I need to see her.

Jackson: Truth or Dare.

Kiera: Dare.

Lately, it's been her answer, and I love it.

Jackson: Dare you to take the next few hours off and come see me.

Kiera: But…

I smile, knowing either way I win. Seeing her doing the chicken dance butt-ass naked would make my day.

Jackson: You know the rules.

I see her text bubble pop up and disappear several times, but she doesn't send anything. I know she's contemplating what to do, and I love that I can catch her off guard even from a distance. I tuck my phone in my pocket and head over to the barn and saddle up a horse with a smirk planted on my lips.

Within twenty minutes, I feel warm arms snaking around my waist as I'm organizing bits and halters in the tack room. "Why is Ghost saddled?"

I turn around and pull Kiera into my arms. "Because we're going for a ride."

"Seriously?" she asks. I notice her hair is in braids, and it drives me wild. She's also wearing gloves on her hands and headwear to keep her ears warm.

I grab the pigtails in my hands and tug. "Nice look, Pippi."

She gives me a wink. "Keep tugging on them, and you might lose your pants."

Her words make me rock hard, as always. Taking it slow is becoming more difficult every single day especially when she tests me by being dirty. I'm sure she's hoping she'll push me over the edge, and if she keeps it up, she just might.

I interlock my fingers with hers, leading her over to Ghost. "I'll let you take the saddle."

"Do you remember the last time we rode doubles?" she asks.

"I'll never forget it." We were sixteen, and I was getting ready to cut out a few new trails for the B&B, but I wanted them to be interesting and not the same old boring flatness. Kiera wanted to see what I had in mind, so I pulled her onto the horse with me. She sat behind me, her arms snaked around my waist, and I never wanted her to let go.

I place my foot in the stirrup and pull myself up, then position myself behind the saddle. In one swift movement, Kiera joins me and takes the reins.

"Where to, Cowboy?" she asks over her shoulder.

"I'm thinking of clearing another trail. I wanted to get your thoughts on it. Since it's early November and most of the trees are dead, thought it'd be a good time to make it happen." I grab the reins from her, and she places her hands on the horn as I lead her off the beaten track.

Kiera is quiet as can be as we ride down the green trail. Soon I'm leading us off the path and down another. My chest is against her back, giving her all the warmth she could ever want. She leans against me, and I can't help but think something's wrong. Usually, she's got a million things to say, but right now, there are no words coming.

We climb down an area that's somewhat cleared until we're crossing a wash that leads to a part of the property that almost looks like a prairie in the summer. There are a few smaller trees bunched together. "I was thinking of putting a picnic table over there." I point out.

She nods. "It's a nice ride. Lots of things to look at. In the summer, it's going to be really pretty, I think, especially with the rolling hills."

I kiss her neck, and soon Kiera is repositioning her body where she's on the saddle backward facing me. It's sexy as fuck. I lean forward, capturing her mouth.

She breathlessly whispers across my lips. "I need to tell you something."

I pull back and watch as her eyes flutter open. "What is it?"

Her mouth falls open, and she closes it. I don't rush her and give her all the time she needs. After she sucks in a deep breath, she rubs her hands across her face.

"You're starting to worry me, Kiera," I admit, thinking the worst, thinking this is the moment that she says this isn't working. It'd crush me.

"I'm late, Jackson."

"For what?" I stupidly ask before it dawns on me. "Oh." My mouth slightly falls open, and the thought of what this means hits me full force.

"I'm so fucking scared I'm pregnant. I don't even know what to do." A tear streams down her cheek, and I kiss it away.

I search her face, though the thought of her having Trent's baby makes me absolutely fucking sick. "It's going to be okay. I promise. No matter what happens, it's all going to work out." I say those words, but I'm not sure I believe them.

I can tell she's freaking the fuck out, and all I can do is hold her as her emotions pour out.

"Don't cry, sweetheart." I try consoling her.

"I'd have to tell him. He'd be in our lives forever. We'd never be able to have a real relationship as long as Trent was in the picture. He'd make my life and our child's life a living hell, and it would just be another way for him to manipulate and control me."

I push back from her, placing my arms on her shoulders. "But you don't know for sure, right?" I try reasoning with her.

She shakes her head. "I'm trying to wait it out, hoping I'll start soon, but I'm nearly a week late, and I'm pretty regular. There's no way I can just walk into the grocery store and buy a pregnancy test with the rumors already floating around that I'm pregnant with your baby. This is a big fucking mess. Why can't anything ever be easy?"

My heart is breaking for her, for us, for our future. "I'll go buy one for you."

She snorts. "Um, no. That's a really bad idea. It would be adding fuel to the fire if you did that. Someone would see you."

I smile, realizing she's right, but I don't really give two shits what anyone says about me.

Kiera effortlessly slips off the saddle, and I follow behind her. I grab the reins and tie Ghost to a nearby tree. I take her hand and lead her over to a few stumps by the wash. I take a seat, and she sits on my lap. Her arms wrap around my neck, and I hold her, soaking in her sweet scent, taking in every small detail about her. It's quiet, and all I can hear is our shallow breathing and the rapid beating of my heart. A brisk breeze rushes past us, and Kiera shivers. I lean back to pull off my jacket and wrap it around her.

"I'm not going anywhere, Kiera. Regardless of what happens. Regardless of the outcome. I'll raise that douchebag's baby as my own and love it as my own because it's a part of you. Just know that."

She nods as she searches my face and tears pour down her cheeks. The mood is serious, the air is still, and then her words pierce straight through my soul. "I love you, Jackson Bishop. I love you so damn much."

I pull her into my arms and kiss the fuck out of her, not ever wanting this moment to end. "I love you. I've always loved you. Nothing or no one will ever change that. We'll work through it. I'm here for the long haul."

Her kisses are soft and sweet and emotional. I pour everything I am into her, hoping she understands that I mean every single word. I've never felt this way for any other woman, and no one has ever been able to compare to her. Her mouth is hot and greedy, and I know that if I don't stop, this will lead to a place it can't go, not yet, especially now.

I don't want to lose Kiera. I've waited this long to be with her, to have her just like this, and though the thought of her having Trent's baby makes me sick, I'd accept it. Shit, I'd have to, but I know his dumb ass wouldn't ever let go of her. I know he'd use the child against us in some way.

The last two years of them being together have been tucked away in the back of my mind because I hate the fact he was with her so intimately. He never deserved her like that and obviously took her for granted because if he didn't, they'd still be together. The slight anxiety of what all this could potentially mean streams through me, though I'm trying to be strong for my girl.

She stands, and I follow. "Promise me you're not going to let this stress you out."

"Too late for that," she says, and I wrap my arm around her shoulder, tucking her close to my body. We walk to Ghost and climb on, and I know the conversation is over. On the way back to the barn, we make small talk but don't chat about anything important. We're both too lost in our thoughts about what this could mean for us.

When I woke up this morning, this was the last news I could've ever expected, but I don't want it to ruin what we *finally* have.

Eventually, we make it to the barn, and Kiera slips off the saddle, and I follow. She stands back and watches me move around the barn. Every chance I get, I look over my shoulder and shoot her a wink or a smirk, just to make her smile. I take off the saddle and quickly brush Ghost, then lead him to the pasture to let him loose.

"Do you have plans for the rest of the day?" I finally ask, not wanting her to go.

"Not really. Told Alexis I was going out for a house call. She's taking care of my afternoon training." She stands on her tiptoes and kisses my chin. My afternoon is basically free, and I need more time with her, like always. I can never have enough.

"Come with me." I grab her hand but let go as soon as we're out in the opening. I hate that we're still sneaking around, but until the rumor mill dies, it's for the best. My reputation is already ruined, but I don't want Kiera's to be too. Though she's done a pretty good job of messing it up herself, which I'm grateful for, I still want to protect her from all the lies and speculation.

"Where are we going?" she asks, following me.

I let out a laugh and look over my shoulder. She runs up beside me. We walk across the pasture toward the shed, and I grab the keys to a utility vehicle. I know we just got back from a small adventure, but I know a place that will instantly make her happy. Kiera hops in beside me, and we take off. Before long, we're pulling up to our secret spot, and I watch a small smile touch her lips.

"Ahh, the memories," she says with a grin.

"I brought some extra firewood out here when the temperature started dropping." I bend over and set it in the old rusted fire ring. I spend some time trying to light the kindling with some flint, and eventually, it begins to burn. Before long, the wood is popping and cracking. I hold Kiera in my arms on the fresh bales of hay I brought. We watch the flames lick toward the sky in silence, and it's comforting. Just being with her like this is enough.

For the rest of the day, we don't talk about the possible pregnancy, and it's almost as if it wasn't mentioned, though I can tell it's on her mind. I try to push the thoughts away, but I know it's not the end of this, not until she knows for sure if she is or isn't pregnant. We sit there, holding each other until the fire burns out. Though I don't want our time to end, I know we'll need to head back soon because the sun is lazily hanging in the sky. It's getting harder to watch her leave me and go home, but I know that's a part of taking our time.

We make our way back to the shed and park the side-by-side. Before I get out, I lean over and brush my lips softly against hers. "I love you," I tell her again. The words should feel foreign, considering I've never whispered them to another woman, but they feel like home—natural—as they pour from my heart.

"I love you," she says, and hearing those words make me feel whole.

"My mama is cooking tacos tonight. Do you want to come over?" she asks as she gets out of her seat.

"Your parents know about us?" I ask.

"Not officially."

We haven't talked about who actually knows and who doesn't. My brothers have speculated, especially after Kiera took Evan's truck to find me. Mama hasn't outright asked me yet, though I'm sure she knows too. I've only allowed them to give me shit about it without admitting anything.

She lets out a big hearty laugh. "But it's the only rumor going around that actually has any truth to it."

"I'd love to but can't. Mama's cooking for the family tonight. If I skip, she'll have a hissy and talk about wasted food and all that. You know how she can be. If you want, you can join us."

Kiera's pigtails are messy. She takes one out and rebraids it as she walks to the side door. "Same. If I skip, Mama won't be happy, especially because I made her cook homemade refried beans for me and it took her all day, basically."

"We love our ruthless mamas, though." I stand and hang the key on the hook by the door, then meet Kiera outside. She's so goddamn beautiful standing in the warm glow of the late afternoon sun. I take a moment to study her, to drink in her curves, and watch how the loose wisps of her hair blow in the breeze. This woman is mine, and I'll be damned if I let anything come between us.

"You're beautiful," I say, touching the small of her back.

She playfully rolls her eyes. "Thank you. But if you want to get in my pants, all you have to do is ask."

"Once I get in, I'm not ever getting out, so be careful what you wish for."

I walk Kiera to her truck, hating she has to go.

"I'll see you tomorrow?" I ask, hopeful.

"Yeah. And Jackson?" She stops me as she cranks her truck.

"What, sweetheart?"

"Thank you. Thank you for understanding me. And for loving me at my worst," she whispers.

I swallow hard, wanting to keep her here with me forever. "I've always loved you, Kiera. *Always.*"

CHAPTER TWENTY-EIGHT

KIERA

I WAKE up with an unsettled stomach and cold sweats. Rushing to the bathroom, I dry heave over the toilet, but since I haven't eaten since last night, I have nothing to release. I stand, resting my hand on the cool wall, hoping this is over, but I couldn't be so lucky. I continue to try to empty my stomach, wishing I had something to give, but it's all for nothing. Once the sensation has slightly passed, I quietly sob, hoping I don't wake my parents.

Is this what morning sickness is like?

I'm nine days late—*nine days*—and I'm officially freaking the fuck out. This really can't be happening, not right now, not ever. For the past decade, I've wished for a baby, and I can't help but think that I'm finally getting what I always wanted at the exact wrong time. Stopping my birth control was one of the stupidest things I ever did, and the regret of it all floods through me in full force. But I really thought, at that point, Trent and I would be together forever.

I turn on the shower and step inside. The hot water pounds against my sensitive skin, but I stand there and take it. Nausea blankets me again, and I ride it out under the stream. After it passes, I get out of the shower, slip into my robe, and hide in my bedroom.

I sit on the edge of the bed with my face in my hands, praying that I'm just sick, but too many signs are pointing the other way. I text Alexis and let her know I'm not feeling well and won't be working today. Of course, she's as understanding as always.

After a few moments, I crawl under the blankets, but I can't get settled. My heart is racing, and my stomach hurts, and I just want to know what's going on with me. Today is Emily's day off, and I find the strength to text her. I try to find the words to say, but my eyes fill with tears as I think about telling anyone my dirty secret. Instead of describing it all, I settle for the bare minimum. It's a little past six, and I know she's awake. The woman is an early bird if I've ever seen one.

Kiera: Em. I need you. I feel like shit. And I'm stressed out.

Her text bubble instantly pops up.

Emily: What's wrong? Why don't you come over and let me check you out?

Sometimes it's great having a best friend who's a doctor.

Kiera: Are you sure?

She's pregnant, and if I'm sick, the last place I need to be is around her.

Emily: Absolutely. I'm immune to sickness so don't even worry about that.

A small smile touches my lips because it's as if she can read my mind.

Kiera: I'll be there as soon as I can. Warning: I'm a hot mess.

Emily: Welcome to the club. No rush, take your time.

With what little strength I have, I get dressed and drive over to Emily's. Somehow, I avoid my parents, which I'm so thankful for. My head is pounding, and I try to rehearse exactly what I'm going to say to her. Out of any one of my friends, I think she'll be the most understanding in this situation. Once I pull up to her house, the sun is sparkling over the horizon. I suck in a deep breath, find my courage, and get out. The front door swings open before I can knock, and I smile.

"Oh man," she says, looking at me. Between bawling my eyes out and trying to puke all morning, I know I look terrible.

"Are you running a fever?" she asks, looking as cute as can be with her little baby bump.

I step inside. "No, I just feel sick to my stomach."

"You know there's a stomach bug going around, right? Or maybe you ate something bad?"

Emily grabs her stethoscope and plays doctor. After she checks my vitals, and everything seems normal, she hands me some Tums. "You look okay to me. You probably just need some rest and relaxation."

Instantly, I burst out crying but try to keep quiet because I know Elizabeth is still asleep. I cover my face with my hands, and Emily comes over to me and pulls me into her arms. "Okay, what's wrong? Who do I need to kill? Jackson's a dead man."

I shake my head. "No, he doesn't deserve to die this time."

She noticed how I added 'this time' to the end of it because there were many instances where she would've hurt him in the past. "Then what is it?"

I search her face, somehow finding calm and peace in her soft smile.

"I'm nine days late, and I don't know what to do," I finally squeak out.

Her eyes go wide, and the grin doesn't falter. "That's what you've always wanted. I know there are all those rumors going around, but who cares. I'm sure Jackson would be happy as can be."

I haven't told anyone about the nitty gritty of our relationship because we aren't rushing anything. By Emily's reaction, I know she doesn't understand the full detail of what this really means.

"He's not," I continue speaking before she can threaten to kick his ass. "Because it wouldn't be his."

The look on her face tells me she fully gets it now, which only makes me cry harder. Emily holds me and tries to comfort me, but nothing she says makes me feel any better. I know I'd love this baby with all my heart, and who knows, maybe Trent will just pay me off and not care to see this kid either. I could only be so lucky.

Emily stands and decides she's going to make some tea to help settle my stomach. "You know there are many reasons why women miss their periods, right?" she says from the kitchen. "And the stomach aches can easily be explained. I bet you anything it's all stress induced."

"I know," I tell her as she hands me the cup of chamomile she made.

"Have you taken a pregnancy test yet?" Emily finally asks.

"No. I can't go into the store and buy them because the rumors are already spreading around that I'm knocked up. I've been hoping I'd wake up—"

"Do you realize how much stress you've been under the last month? Let's think about this. You left your fiancé at the altar. You started dating the man you've loved since you were a kid. You're constantly overworking yourself training. You're living back with your parents. And you've had to hear all the nasty rumors going around about you. Add that, along with the stress of possibly being pregnant, and it's no wonder you're upset. Stress can cause women to miss complete months. And what you're going through is a lot to deal with, Kiera. But you need to take a pregnancy test so you can know for sure, and then you can start dealing with it instead of internalizing it the way you are. I've got a few extra in the bathroom from when we were trying, and they were all accurate for me. If you're pregnant, you'll finally know, and then can decide what to do." Emily has always been a voice of reason.

"I don't think I'm ready to find out just yet," I tell her, taking a sip of tea.

She grabs my hand and squeezes. "I'm not letting you leave until you pee on a stick or ten."

Just being around Emily is already making me feel better, or maybe this tea is working. "I might pee on a dozen just to make sure the results are right."

"When we were actively trying, I bought those suckers in bulk. I should buy stock in the company, considering my bathroom cabinet is full of pregnancy tests." She laughs. "I've got you covered, trust me. I've got every brand that claims to be the most accurate. You can have them all."

I let out a breath. "Well, that makes me feel better."

Emily lifts her eyebrows. "So you and Jackson haven't…?"

"Had sex?" I ask, knowing exactly where this conversation is going.

She nods.

"Nope. Not yet. We're taking our time."

She looks just as shocked as I am. "Does Jackson actually know how to take it slow with anyone?"

A chuckle escapes me. "Right! That's what I was thinking. I waited all this time, and he's basically put a chastity belt on me. I swear to you, Em, if I'm not pregnant, he's going to have a hard time keeping me off him."

"I can't even imagine the blue ball situation he's going through. I've got to give it to him, though, for not hopping in bed with you the night of your wedding," she adds with a wink.

"I'm not trying to rush it or anything, but I think it's time I've had a ride on the wild stallion if you know what I mean. I've fantasized about it for over a decade."

Emily is smiling. "He probably just wants your first time together to be perfect. I'm sure it's driving him crazy too."

"He deserves to be driven crazy. It's payback." We sit in silence for a moment. "Jackson was amazing when I was freaking out yesterday about this."

"How'd he take it?" she asks.

"I can tell it bothered him, but he didn't say as much, only gave his support. I just know how Trent is, Em. I know how he would hold this over me for the rest of my life. After the way he acted, throwing all my stuff on the lawn and pushing me, I can't imagine him being in my life at all, especially not as the father of my child. But there's no way I could *not* have the baby, either. It's been eating me alive."

Emily stands up. "We're taking a test right now."

I shake my head. "Just ten more minutes. I don't have to pee yet. I might need some more tea."

"You're avoiding this." She crosses her arms over her chest. That's one thing about Emily, she's always told me what she thinks and doesn't hold back, which I appreciate.

"I really can't pee under all this pressure. And maybe I slightly am, because I know if it says positive, my entire life will change. Jackson and I won't have a fair chance in hell."

Emily sighs. "He'd follow you to the moon and back, Kiera. You know that."

"I hope he would." I feel small. I feel like I'm losing control of everything. Eventually, Emily sits beside me, and I try to make peace with all of it. If I'm pregnant, I'll still love my baby, and I know Jackson and I will figure it out together.

Emily hands me a bottle of water and tells me to chug it. I think she might be more stressed about this than me. I drink half of it before my bladder decides it wants to cooperate.

"Ready?" she asks, standing again.

"I guess." I let out a sigh and follow her to her bathroom. Emily bends down and pulls out a small storage container full of pregnancy tests along with a cup to pee in. "Damn. You weren't joking!"

There's every brand of test on the planet. She hands me the cup and opens five pregnancy tests. "No matter what it says, we'll work through this, okay?"

I nod and swallow, but I can't seem to get rid of the lump that's lodged in my throat. It makes me feel sick all over again. I stare at the tests, knowing that the results could change my life forever.

Emily gives me a quick hug and then walks out of the bathroom. I know she's standing outside the door waiting.

"You're making me pee shy!" My voice echoes off the walls of the vast bathroom.

"Sorry," she says, and I eventually hear her walk away.

I look down at the cup in my hand, then back at the tests on the counter. When I finally get the courage to pee, I'm not wasting a drop. I sit and wait. I run water, hoping that will help too. Eventually, Emily comes back and knocks on the door.

"Well?" she asks.

"I seriously can't pee. I'm too nervous."

The door swings open, and she places her hands on her hips.

"Kiera Young." She points at me. "You better pee in that cup right now." She glances at my panties around my ankles as I hold the cup tight in my fist.

At this point, all I can do is laugh. "You have a really scary mom voice…just saying."

She shakes her head and laughs. Right as she opens her mouth to say something, the urge hits me.

"Get out!"

Emily quickly shuts the door, and I finally fill the cup. I dip each stick, place them all on the counter, then hurry and walk out. My heart is racing so hard in my chest, and my mind wanders to a dark place. I don't wish one way or the other but feel some sort of relief getting an answer.

Emily is in the kitchen eating yogurt. "Want some?"

I shake my head. "Shouldn't you be eating chocolate or something instead?"

"I can't stop craving strawberry yogurt. It's so weird; like I want to eat it by the gallon." She empties the small container, then sets the spoon in the sink.

"How long does it usually take?" I lean against the counter, trying not to let my nerves get the best of me.

"Only a few minutes." Emily's eyes sparkle.

"This is going to be the longest wait of my life," I admit. Watching the clock on the wall, I feel uneasiness in my stomach.

The seconds pass on, but each tick feels like hours. When the clock shows at least three minutes have passed, Emily comes to me. "It's time."

I tuck my lips in my mouth. "Will you go look first?"

Emily grabs my hand. "We'll go together."

She leads me to the bathroom, and we stop outside the door.

"Everything is going to work out for the best, right?" I ask.

"Absolutely." Emily pushes open the door, and we step inside. The five tests are lined up on the counter. Emily glances down at each of them and then pulls me closer, but I can't seem to look.

She hands me all five, and when I see their readings, the tests drop out of my hand and bounce on the floor. My emotions take over and tears stream down my face. I have no words.

Emily pulls me into her arms and gives me a big hug. As I cry on her shoulder, the only person who comes to mind is Jackson. I need to tell him.

CHAPTER TWENTY-NINE

JACKSON

Fuck. Fuck fuck fuck.

It's the only thing I can think when I see Kiera's text.

Kiera: Can I come over? I took a pregnancy test.

I know I told her the results won't affect the way I feel about her, but that doesn't mean I'm still not scared shitless. A pang of jealousy hits me when I think about her being pregnant with Dr. Douchebag's baby and not mine. I want her to only have my babies. *Damn.* It's the first time I've ever wanted to think about having kids, and now it might not happen that way.

Jackson: Yeah, baby. I'll be here.

I want to be as supportive as I can, knowing this won't be easy for her either. Grabbing a beer from the fridge, I guzzle it down in three long sips. Whatever the results are, it doesn't change how I feel about her, and I will be there for her through it all. If Trent doesn't want to take responsibility, I won't think twice about taking the roll. Hell, even if he does want to be involved, I'll be right by the kid's side doing all the things dads do regardless.

By the time I've finished my third beer, there's a knock on my door, and I brace myself.

This is it. It could change everything.

Reluctantly, I open the door, and when she tilts her head up, I see her tear-stained cheeks. Immediately, I pull her inside and against my body as she cries. She wraps her arms tightly around me and clings to my chest.

"Shh, baby. It's gonna be okay." I try to comfort her. Rubbing her head, I hold her close and try to keep my own emotions controlled.

Finally, Kiera pulls back and wipes her cheeks. "I'm sorry."

"Baby, don't be. Don't worry—"

"I'm not," she cuts off my words, and my heart pounds. "The tests were negative."

"What?" I'm taken aback because I was completely expecting them to be positive.

"Yeah, I took five pregnancy tests, and they were all negative. I'm not pregnant."

"Holy shit," I mutter, grabbing her face in my palms, crashing our lips together. I taste the salt from her tears and lick them up. "Why were you crying?"

"Honestly, I'm not sure. I was just overwhelmed with emotion that they came pouring out as soon as I read the tests. I think I had just convinced myself I was, and that it was going to change everything, so when they showed negative, I finally broke down with relief."

"I know I already told you, but just so you know, if they had been positive, we'd have done this together." I rub my thumb along her jaw, giving her reassurance.

"You're truly one-of-a-kind, Jackson Bishop." She smiles up at me with her arms wrapped around my waist.

"Well technically, I'm two-of-a-kind." I flash her a wink, and she playfully swats at me.

"You really know how to ruin a sweet moment."

I press a kiss to her nose and smirk. "You still love me, though."

"I do."

Taking her hand, I lead her into the living room and pull her onto my lap as I sit on the couch. "So what do you say I grab us some food from the B&B, and we go to our spot and eat it under the stars?"

She twists her lips from side to side as if she's truly contemplating it. I thought it was a good plan, but she obviously thinks it's lame.

"Actually...I have a better idea." Kiera looks at me with lust in her eyes, and as soon as she shifts her body to straddle my lap, I understand exactly what her little idea is. Wrapping her arms around my neck, she pulls our mouths together in a deep, heart-shattering kiss, and it's enough to drive me crazy.

"Kiera..." I warn, feeling my dick getting hard between her legs and not wanting to jerk off in the shower again once she leaves. Pulling back slightly, I study her face. "As much as I want you, rubbing against my cock is only going to torture us both so we better st—"

"Fuck?" Kiera says the word as if she's talking about the weather. She crosses her arms to the hem of her dress that's pushed over her hips and lifts it over her head. My mouth opens, and I lick my lips, wondering if this is some kind of twisted setup.

"Don't test my willpower right now, Kiera," I growl, holding her hips in place, so she stops moving. The last thing I want to do is come in my pants like a teenage boy going through puberty. My eyes gaze at her luscious breasts that are peeking out of her lacy bra, and I imagine my dick sliding between them.

"I don't want to wait any longer," she says, reaching back and unhooking her bra.

Fuck me.

Removing it completely from her body, her beautiful tits are right in front of my face, begging to be touched and sucked. I wrap my palms around them, pushing them together and diving in head first. Pulling one hard nipple into my mouth, I swirl my tongue around it and taste how fucking sweet she is.

"Fuck, baby." I groan, moving to the other. "Are you really sure?" I pull back, studying her face and looking into her eyes. "I'm okay with waiting if you want."

She inhales sharply as if she's just as worked up as I am. "We've waited long enough, don't you think? Fifteen years of pent-up sexual frustration. A girl can only hold out for so long."

"What am I gonna do with you, Pippi?" I chuckle when I bring our mouths together and kiss her again. "You have any idea how long I've waited for this? Pictured this moment? It's going to be record-breaking, sweetheart."

"You sure sound confident, Cowboy," she taunts, rocking her hips against me. "I'm ready to see what all the fuss has been about."

Reaching behind her, I smack her ass hard. "You're gonna pay for those comments. Don't think I'm letting you off the hook." I flick her one-sided braid that has me thinking dirty thoughts. *Very* dirty thoughts.

"Good," she says sensually. "I want it *all*."

"I should grab a condom," I remind her before things get too heated. She gives me a look that has me questioning her. "I'm clean. I've always used a condom, but I figured with you not being on birth control—"

"I want your babies, Jackson," she whispers softly. "I want your sweet, messy-haired, cocky attitude babies. That's if you want mine, too."

I hold her face in my palms. "Are you kiddin' me? You're the only one I've ever thought of having kids with, but for the record, they'd be sassy, blond-haired spitfires just like their mama."

She chuckles against my mouth before sliding her tongue between my lips. I grab her hips and pull her to my chest, wanting to devour every inch of her. I've never felt this kind of need before—desperate and hungry—as if I'll explode if I don't taste her right now.

Wrapping my hands under her ass, I stand and lift her with me. She wraps her legs around my waist with our mouths still fused together. It's a sensation so strong, I need to remind myself to take my time with her. Kiera's not another meaningless fuck. She'd never be that, but that's all I've ever had before. I want to cherish every second and watch her unravel with me deep inside her. No more games. No more waiting. No more insecurities. Kiera's mine, and I'm about to claim her as such.

I walk us to my bedroom, and as soon as I kick the door shut, I press her against it and push my hips between her thighs as our mouths stay connected. I'm rock hard, and I want to sink so goddamn deep inside her, she'll be feeling me for days.

"You're mine, Kiera. *Mine.*"

"Always."

Releasing her, she lands on her feet, and my eyes instantly zoom in on her gorgeous body. I kiss her jaw, neck, and between her tits. Making my way down her body, I fall to my knees. As soon as I get to her panties, I hook my fingers through and slide them down as I continue kissing between her legs.

Reaching behind her thigh, I place her knee over my shoulder and bring my mouth to her pussy. Inhaling her scent, I slide my tongue up her wetness and flick her clit before drawing it between my lips.

"Jesus, Kiera…you taste so fucking sweet." I press a finger to her entrance and twist it, thrusting in and out as I feel her tighten around me. I continue sucking and licking while my finger pulses inside her.

"Oh my God…" She releases short, shallow breaths as she digs her nails into my shoulders.

Sliding and flicking my tongue against her pussy has her grinding her hips against my mouth, and when she weaves her fingers through my hair and fists her hands, I know she's close. I wanna taste her release on my tongue so damn bad, but I also want to feel her on my cock.

"You gonna come for me, sweetheart?" I look up at her and lick my lips at the sight. She's looking at me with hooded eyes, biting her bottom lip.

Nodding, she arches her back, pushing my tongue deeper inside her.

"Oh my G—...*yes, yes*..." Kiera's moans encourage me to fill her deeper and suck harder, and then I feel her entire body tighten and shake as she breathes heavily and releases the sexiest sound I've ever heard.

I lap up her pussy, tasting her arousal and drowning in her scent.

Lowering her leg, she nearly collapses from the high, and I hold her up when I stand.

"I don't think I've ever come that hard before..." she admits shamelessly. Her eyelids are heavy, and I love that I did that to her.

"Is that so?" I smirk, then bring my mouth to hers for a heated kiss. "Don't be surprised if you find me between your legs every morning."

"Don't be surprised if I never leave your bed." She chuckles, wrapping her arms around my neck and pulling me in closer.

"That doesn't sound like a fucking bad idea."

"Good. Now take off your clothes, Cowboy."

I grin at her bossiness. "Yes, ma'am."

Slowly, I unbutton my shirt and watch her gaze narrow in on my abs and tattoos as soon as I toss it aside. Next, I undo my belt and jeans. She's watching me, but I'm watching her, so damn mesmerized.

Kiera's nearly panting. "Do you enjoy torturing me?"

"In general, yes..." I tease, sliding my jeans down and kicking them to the side. "That's just a fraction of what I've felt over the years." I close the gap between us, letting her feel my erection through my boxers.

"Imagine the way I felt…" She pinches her lips together, hiding a mock smile as she shakes her head at me. "I've wanted to lick your tattoos since I first saw you shirtless after you got them done."

My brows raise. "Which ones?"

Now hers raise. "Is there more than you've shown me?"

"Yes."

"Then I guess it's time I go explore…" She flashes a devilish look. Standing on her tiptoes, she brings her lips to my collarbone and begins feathering kisses across my chest. "I've always loved these script ones."

Kiera lowers her body as she slides her tongue down my stomach, and it takes all the willpower I can muster not to haul her back to her feet and take her right against the door. The way she's teasing me, flicking her tongue out and circling it around my belly button, has my cock in agony.

"I think it's cute you and John have matching tats," she says, looking up at me as she kneels in front of me.

"It would really help my pride if you didn't use the word cute near my dick."

She rolls her eyes. "Adorable?"

I shake my head.

"Well, if I say sexy, then that means I'm calling John sexy, and I don't think—"

"Fine, adorable. But don't tell John that."

"I'd never." She grins. "Are the other tattoos I haven't seen before matching?"

"Yes," I reply. "But we don't have everything the same…"

She lifts a brow. "Such as?"

I lower my eyes, telling her exactly where she needs to look. I can tell she's nervous, so I grab her hand and place it over my dick through the fabric of my boxers. As soon as I begin moving her hand up and down my shaft, she takes over and loops her fingers inside. Sliding them down my legs, I kick them off and wait for her to notice.

"Is that…" Her eyes widen, and suddenly, I'm self-conscious and worried she hates it.

Before I can answer, she wraps a palm around my length and licks her tongue up the very sensitive vein that's throbbing and begging for release.

"Holy fuck, Kiera…" I have to rest a hand on the door behind her to hold myself up. That one little movement shoots electricity through my body. She rotates her hand around as she moves it up and down, tightening her grip as she holds her tongue out to circle my tip.

"Play with your tits, baby."

Peeking up at me with lust-filled eyes, she obeys. I love that she's so eager to oblige.

Suddenly, my world tilts and everything goes hazy the second she wraps her lips around my cock and inhales it deep into her throat. She swirls her tongue along the tip and sucks on my piercing.

"I'm not gonna last long if you keep doin' that," I warn, torn between stopping her and fucking her throat fast and deep.

Slowly, she pulls back, sliding my cock out of her mouth. "Fuck, you look so goddamn beautiful like this." I need to touch her. "Come here." I help her to her feet and claim her mouth.

I lead us to the bed and slowly drop her to the mattress. Towering over her, my hands explore her soft skin. My fingertips rub circles over her breasts, then slide up to her neck.

"I want to fuck you so hard, but at the same time, I want to go sweet and slow. I want to give you everything, Kiera." I lean my forehead against hers, our breaths mingle between us.

"Yes," she whispers. "I want all of you, Jackson. Everything you can give me."

"Listen…" I say, pulling back slightly so I can look into her eyes. I tilt her chin up and rub circles with the pad of my thumb along her jawline. "I don't want you to ever doubt that I've wanted you for years. I don't just love you. I'm *in* love with you. I hated seeing anyone else's hands on you, and it's why I blocked those feelings out and why I couldn't be involved with anyone. I never wanted to. I told myself that if you got married, I was gonna let you go. I would've died with my emotions trapped in my chest as long as you were happy. I would've come to your housewarming parties, barbecues, anniversary dinners, baby celebrations. All of it. I would've supported you while silently dying inside because all I ever wanted was for you to be happy. I would've let myself be miserable knowing I ultimately chose it, so before we continue, I just need you to know the feelings I have for you have only ever been reserved for you. I don't want you to ever second-guess that, no matter what happened in the past, because I want your future, Kiera. You mean everything to me."

Her eyes are glossy, and this moment turned into something more emotional than I intended, but after all this time, I needed to get the words out.

Kiera rests her hand on my cheek and smiles. "I've never felt more loved than when I'm with you. Never felt happier than I do at this moment. The past doesn't matter anymore. Only right now does. You *are* my future, Jackson. There's zero doubt about that."

I smile at her in amazement. "Fuck, you're perfect." Closing the gap between us, I claim her mouth and greedily take everything she gives me. Her hands roam down my back, scratching her nails along the way. It has me releasing animalistic noises and groans, and I need to claim all of her.

Pulling slightly back on my knees, I stroke my shaft a few times before lining my cock with her entrance. Sliding it up and down her slick pussy, I'm ready to consume every inch of her.

"Let me know if my piercing hurts you, okay?" I whisper, pushing my tip in. It's not a big loop, but it can feel a little weird at first for a woman who's never experienced it. I look up at her for approval, and when she nods, I push in even farther. Closing my eyes, I groan. "Shit, you feel amazing already."

Obviously not appreciating how long I'm taking, Kiera digs her heels into my ass and forces me forward. I push in the rest of the way effortlessly, and as soon as her body adjusts to my size, I slide out and back again.

Kiera's back nearly flies off the bed as she arches into my hips. Fuck, she's so tight around me. Leaning over her, I rock my hips against hers, and soon, we're forming a fast and hard rhythm.

"You feel amazing," I whisper just above her mouth. "*We* feel amazing."

"Yes…" she replies with a moan. She closes her eyes and bites down on her lip.

"Look, baby. This is a fucking sight to see."

She does as I say, and when I wrap a hand around the back of her neck, I pull her up just enough to see our bodies connecting.

I pound against her, hard and deep, wanting her to feel every inch of me. Her pussy squeezes me so goddamn tight, I have to remind myself to slow down.

"I never knew it could feel this way," I tell her softly.

"It's because it's you and me, Jackson. It was always meant to be this way," she says with so much certainty, it has me grinning like a damn fool.

"You're fuckin' right, baby." I tug on the end of her braid, and she sucks in her lower lip before she pops it back out. Damn, I love it when she looks at me like this.

We're both smiling, but as soon as I increase the pace and hook her leg over my shoulder, her breath quickens, and she's nearly gasping for air the faster I drive into her.

"Yes, oh my God…" Her head falls back, and her arms stretch out to the side, grasping for the sheets. "Don't stop," she begs. I can tell she's close, so I reach between us and rub circles over her clit. Her moans grow louder, and when she clenches her legs and bucks her hips, I know she's veering over the edge.

"That's my girl. Come on my cock, Kiera." And she does just that. Her head tips back as she releases a loud, drawn-out moan echoing my name. I smirk down at her when she fights to fill her lungs back up with air.

"Christ, babe. You look so sexy when you come." I bring my

lips to hers and kiss her tenderly. She's still out of breath, and it makes me chuckle.

"I'm sure you've heard this a million times before, but that was seriously the most intense orgasm of my life. I'm pretty sure I died and floated out of my body."

"That's quite the orgasm…" I tease.

"It was…earth-shattering, soul crushing, life changing. Take your pick. All of the above."

"Okay, now you're just trying to stroke my ego." I give her a smirk and push my hips against her slowly.

"Trust me, you don't need your ego stroked."

"So, the piercing…you like it then?"

"Um yeah, I'm thinking it can stay." She gasps when I move inside her again.

"Glad to hear it. It feels really good when you squeeze your pussy around it."

"Yeah? Like this?" The corner of her lips tilts up in a knowing grin as she tightens her muscles around my shaft. She enjoys taunting me.

"Mmhmm…" I press my mouth to hers, sinking deeper. "Hope you're ready."

"For what?" She furrows her brows.

"Me."

CHAPTER THIRTY

KIERA

JACKSON'S MOUTH on me drives me wild, but the way he moves inside me is a feeling I never expected. He's tender and sweet yet crazed and rough at the same time. He looks at me like I'm the only woman in the world who matters, and he says things I could've never imagined. He bares it all for me, and if my heart wasn't already bursting from how much I love him, it would've at this moment.

In one swift movement, Jackson rolls us over until I'm on top of him. He's still inside me, and he's like a sex magician with how well he uses that glorious cock. With his hands around my hips, he angles his body to align with mine perfectly and thrusts into me.

"Holy shit." I gasp, falling forward and catching myself on his chest. My palms are flat against him as he rapidly and repeatedly drives into me.

"Fuck, baby...fuck," he says between gritted teeth as his head falls back. He's hitting me so damn deep, I swear he has a G-spot detector in his cock that continues to tap it over and over.

"Jackson," I whisper, wanting him to look at me. His eyes flicker to mine in an instant, and I bring my mouth down to his. "Mmm...yes, right there." I moan. His hands slide up my back, giving me the reins to control our rhythm. I rock back and forth, pulling him in deeper with each thrust.

Straightening my body, I continue moving my hips as I lean back and rest my hands on his legs behind me. I increase the speed, feeling his buildup inside me. His eyes pop open, and he immediately brings his thumb to my clit, adding pressure and making circles.

"Kiera, Christ…" He moans, gripping my leg with one hand. "Ride that cock like you own it, baby. It's all yours."

Leaning forward, I put my hands on his lower stomach to push my hips up slightly so I can sink down hard on him again. "It's about fucking time."

Jackson smirks before bringing a hand around and smacking my ass. "So goddamn sassy." He leans up on his elbows and watches our bodies join with admiration in his eyes. It's so damn sexy and intimate; something I've never felt before. I have no insecurities when it comes to Jackson, and I want him to see all of me.

He manages to sit up and pulls a nipple into his mouth as I continue to move my hips, and the pressure is building so rapidly, I'm sure I won't survive another intense release like before.

"C'mon, baby. I can tell you're close." He coaxes me, and it sends heat straight down my spine. Is it bad that I'm thinking how much I've been missing out on all this time? I can't remember when I orgasmed more than once during sex, or hell, even once at all.

And it sure as hell wasn't for lack of trying—on my end at least.

"I am," I whisper. "So close."

Instantly, Jackson takes over. He squeezes the skin right above my ass and pulls me against him so fast I think I'll snap his dick in half. I don't have time to question it, though, because soon I'm soaring so damn high I'm flying to the moon.

The release jolts through my body, rocking me to my core. I

KEEPING HIM

gasp for air, my eyes clenching tight as I ride the wave of pleasure. When I look at Jackson, he's grinning like a damn devil.

"That makes two…" he taunts. Before I can retort, he wraps an arm around my waist and pulls me underneath him. "Whaddya say we get you to five before breakfast?" He winks.

My eyes widen, uncertain if he's joking or not. Before I can ask, he pats my thigh.

"Flip over, baby."

I'm not even sure I have enough strength to hold myself up at this point, but when Jackson positions himself against my entrance and pushes his weight over my body, I realize I don't need to. With my ass raised in the air and my chest to the mattress, Jackson slides inside me in one smooth motion and begins driving hard into me.

Jackson grunts and moans—our bodies slapping together in perfect harmony. I feel him so deep inside me, all around me, and I consume every inch. With both arms raised in front of me, I squeeze the sheets between my fingers and widen my hips for him. He slaps my ass and pounds into me, jerking me forward slightly. His hand slides up my spine, and when I squeeze my pussy muscles around him, he fucks me uncontrollably.

With both palms pressed hard into my shoulder blades, Jackson slides out of me slowly, then slams back in with so much force, my entire body moves up the bed. I scream in pleasure, never feeling this kind of intensity before. His balls slap against my ass so fast, I wonder how that doesn't hurt with how quickly he's thrusting our bodies together.

"Oh my God…" I can't hold back any longer. Moans and screams and begging for more, Jackson delivers it all. "Right there, please don't stop. More," I plead, and when my body quivers with a gush I've never felt before, Jackson slides out and slaps his cock against my ass cheek.

"Holy shit." His tone makes me look over my shoulder. He has a huge smile plastered on his face, and I wonder what the hell just happened.

"That was…I—" I'm at a loss for words.

"You just squirted all over my dick. Jesus, babe." He looks impressed. Meanwhile, I feel mortified.

"I…what?" I furrow my brows. "Are you sure?"

He chuckles, aligning himself to my entrance again.

"So fuckin' sure. It was hot as hell, too."

I shiver, feeling the haze that captures my body after the high. Did that really just happen? I smile to myself, thinking about how many firsts I'll get to experience with Jackson. Perhaps we didn't miss out, after all.

"Three." I hear the smile in his voice. "Over halfway there, gorgeous."

I can't even imagine my body going through two more orgasms. Hell, they can't even be considered orgasms at this point. They're explosive bursts of intense pleasure that have the power to take down an entire village.

Just when I'm about to tell him I'm tapping out and that my legs are boneless jelly, he picks me up and drags me to the edge of the bed, flipping me over, so we're facing each other.

"Did you think I was done with you?"

Inhaling, I'm still breathless when I try to speak. "I should've known better."

He flashes a crooked grin and kneels between my legs. He reaches toward his nightstand, and I sit up on my elbows to see what he's doing. Opening a drawer, I narrow my eyes when I see him take something out.

"Wh…what is that?" I try to hide the fear in my voice, but considering my brain cells have all been ping-ponged, I'm pretty sure he hears it.

"Do you trust me?"

"That seems like a really unfair question at the moment."

"Kiera."

I swallow. I do trust him. There's no one I trust more than him.

"Of course I do," I tell him, arching my neck so I can see what's in his hand.

"Good girl. Then lie back." He presses his palm to my stomach until it's flat and then rubs circles around my clit. It's so damn sensitive and swollen, my hips nearly buck off the bed faster than when I flew off an unbroken horse. "You need to relax, baby. I want to try something."

Oh my God. This is it. This is where I learn about all the weird sex fetishes Jackson's into. Honestly, I should've known. I mean, half the town knows he's a kinky bastard in the bedroom. I just never imagined—

Holy shit.

"Don't tense," he tells me as he swirls a cool lubricant over my pussy.

It slides down my ass and at first, I think his finger is lingering down there to rub it around, but then I feel an indescribable pressure, unlike anything I've felt before. Instinctively, I squeeze my butt cheeks.

"Kiera…I need you to relax, baby. Trust me, okay?"

I'm really trying to.

I inhale a deep breath and focus on relaxing. He pushes in deeper, invading an intimate part of me that's never been touched before. Within a few seconds, I feel it settle inside me, and Jackson presses a kiss to my inner thigh.

"Doing okay?"

"I think so." I bite down on my lip, unsure.

"I promise, you're going to love it." He winks, bending down to grab something else.

Oh hell, now what?

And then I hear a buzzing noise.

Oh sweet Mary.

He gently presses the vibrator to my clit, and my hips fly off the bed so fast, I don't know how Jackson manages to grab me so quickly. My hands reach for his messy sex hair, and I'm almost certain he's trying to kill me. Death by orgasmic seizure.

"Jackson!" I screech, my head falling back as all the muscles in my body give out on me.

"Lie back, baby," he tells me softly. I feel the tip of his cock at my entrance and think there's no way I'm going to make it to five. My body has never had three orgasms in one night, not even when I give them to myself. How the hell would I ever survive *five*?

Jackson rests the vibrator against my clit as he slides in deeper. He bends my knees and spreads my legs wider. Every part of me feels full, and when he starts thrusting, my hands dig into the sheets so hard, I'm quite sure every nail breaks off.

"How's that feel?" he asks in a rough, gravelly voice. Jackson's towering over me as he rocks his hips, and I already feel my body teetering over the edge.

"It's damn intense," I admit, my hips arching to meet his thrusts.

"You look so fuckin' beautiful, baby. I want to make you feel as good as you deserve." He leans down to kiss me, making the vibrator press harder against my clit.

"Oh my God…" My breathing quickens as the build surfaces.

"Feels amazing, doesn't it?"

I nod, biting down on my lip to keep from screaming. I'm not sure I'd have a voice left if I allowed myself to scream the way I want.

"Don't hold back from me, Kiera," Jackson says as if he'd just read my mind. He pulls back slowly, then rams back in. It's so much more intense with the other part of me full. My clit is throbbing, and there's no holding back now.

I open my mouth and release the most unholy scream of my life, fisting Jackson's hair and grinding my hips against him as fast as I can while I ride out the craziest orgasm I've ever had. Just when I feel my body soaring back down, it hits me like a lightning bolt and I. Wasn't. Ready.

My body, my voice, my everything is uncontrollable as the electricity zaps me to a level that nearly makes my insides go numb. It shoots up my spine, and I'm certain I'm having a seizure at this point because I can't stop shaking, and when all my muscles contract at the same time, I hear Jackson groan so loudly I'm positive he's dying too. With one last thrust, he releases everything inside me and tosses the vibrator away before collapsing on top of me.

For a long moment, we lie there, neither of us moving or speaking. Mostly, we try to catch our breath, and I can only hope he doesn't need CPR because I'm pretty sure all the air has been sucked out of me for eternity.

When my muscles have come back to life, and my heart has steadied to a normal, healthy rhythm, Jackson pushes himself up and smiles down at me.

"Five."

Waking up in Jackson's embrace for the first time has me smiling from ear to ear. Before I even open my eyes, I feel his strong arms wrap around me as his steady breathing whispers in my ear. His palm rests on my stomach, holding me flush against him, and moments later, I feel his morning wood pressing against the lower curve of my back.

I stifle a chuckle, not sure if I should be surprised or impressed that after the night we just had, Jackson's cocked and loaded already. I can still feel him between my sore thighs, but I can't deny the way my pussy aches to have him there again.

"If this isn't the best fucking way to wake up," he murmurs against my skin before feathering kisses along my neck. His hand moves down my stomach and reaches between my legs, sliding a finger slowly through my wet slit. "Mmm, yes…waking up to this, even better."

I chuckle as I arch my hips into his hand, needing the pressure deep inside. Instead, Jackson teases me by slowly brushing his finger over my clit, but not going further.

"Don't torture me," I beg. Jackson's lips brush my ear, sending a shiver down my spine. God, I can't believe this is real.

"Do you remember when we were like seventeen or so and we went fishing, and when you casted your line, you released too soon and got that fish hook right in my thumb?"

Laughing, I shake my head at him. "How do you remember that?"

"I remember a lot, Pippi. Mostly because it was with you." His cute confession has me turning around in his arms so I can face him.

"That's pretty adorable," I say, then kiss him.

"Adorable or not, teasing you is my payback."

I scoff. "That was years ago! And it was an accident!"

His hand rounds my body and slaps my ass. "Accident, right," he taunts. "I still have a scar to prove it."

"It's your battle wound, you poor baby." Before I can stop him, he's on top of me with my arms above my head. I laugh, wiggling underneath him, but his hold is too strong.

"Stay still," he demands. He parts my legs with his knee and starts kissing his way down my body. Right when he's about to kiss my sweet spot, my stomach growls loudly.

Jackson peeks his head up from between my legs, locking his eyes on mine with a devilish smirk. "Sounds like someone's hungry for breakfast. I know I am." He winks and then disappears between my thighs, hooking my knee over his shoulder. As soon as he slides his tongue inside, I'm gasping for air.

With Jackson, nothing feels awkward. All the insecurities I have with my body vanish because he makes me feel so comfortable and like I'm the most beautiful woman in the world. I know his past, and a small part of me wonders if I'll be enough for him, but it's confirmed this connection isn't one-sided.

"You look so gorgeous when you come," he whispers after my release. He crawls up my body. "Taste damn good too." Before I can respond, he presses his lips to mine.

"Now that you've feasted, time to feed me, Cowboy."

"You got it. Coffee and pastries at the B&B." He winks, making me laugh.

"You seriously need to start grocery shopping regularly. John's going to start pickin' up on your tricks."

"Pfft..." he says, rolling to my side, weaving our legs together. "Most of the guests think I'm him anyway, so they won't utter a word."

Shaking my head, I grin. "So I have to ask..." I pause, finding the courage. "Did you really mean what you said about making babies with me?"

Jackson's brows shoot up instantly. "Fuck yes, I did. I hope we made one last night. And if not, we'll try again later."

"You're crazy, you know that?"

"Crazy about you." He smirks. "I don't see any reason we shouldn't. I already know you're the *one*, and I know you want a family. And I want to give that to you."

"You sure are somethin' else, Jackson Bishop." I gaze into his eyes, sinking deeper into his hold. "I already know you'd make a great dad. Makes me even more excited."

"Well considering none of my brothers know how to wear condoms, I've gotten some experience under my belt. Being the cool uncle has had its perks."

I laugh at how serious he looks about it too. "I probably won't be able to train horses while I'm pregnant or at least for part of the time. It'd be too dangerous. Plus I wouldn't want to risk it."

"You wouldn't need to. I can take on your workload, and Colton can cover my bitch work. It'd be good for him anyway."

"Speaking of Colton," I say, starting to laugh. "The other day

319

he told me to remind you that you still owe him fifteen hundred bucks for losing your bet."

Jackson snorts. "I just bet him double or nothing yesterday."

I furrow my brows, confused. "On what?"

He blinks and looks like he's contemplating his next words. "On whether you'd say yes or no to my question."

My eyes widen, wondering what the hell he's up to.

"Okay…" I start, urging him to just let it out.

Instead, he cups my cheeks and pulls me in for a sweet kiss that quickly turns heated. We're both panting as he rests his forehead against mine. "I want to wake up to you every damn morning. I wanna roll over and be able to kiss you, and I even like hearing your cute, little snores. Secrets be damned. You're mine now, and I don't care what anyone says."

I part my lips, feeling relieved he wants this as much as I do. He wants our relationship to move forward, and even though we weren't announcing it to dim the rumors, I'm ready to scream it to the world now.

"So you want me to stay overnight from now on? Well according to the gossip, I've already been sleeping over anyway." I roll my eyes.

"No, baby." He plucks my lip with his thumb and smiles. "I want you to move in with me. Here. Permanently."

"What…really?" I don't mean to sound shocked, but I am. Jackson moving this fast is something I would've never anticipated, but considering I know I'm the only woman he's ever asked to move in with him, I know it's not something he planned on a whim. "Wait…" I squint my eyes. "Colton really bet you double or nothing that I'd say no?"

"Yep…but I might've led him to believe you already knew you were pregnant with Trent's baby, and he said there was no way I'd go through with asking you, and when I said I would, then he said there was no way you'd say yes."

I push against his chest and laugh. "You don't play fair."

"You know better than anyone I don't." He grabs my wrists

and kisses my knuckles. "So, are you going to make me lose three grand or do me the honor of moving in with me?"

"Well, Cowboy...when you put it like that." I smirk. "On one condition, though."

"Name it."

"Whiskey Fridays will have to retire because I'm not waking up to a pile of drunk guys or girls on the floor."

"That's an easy compromise," he says, matter-of-factly. "Lately, Whiskey Fridays were just me, Colton, and Braxton drinking and shootin' the shit anyway."

"Who's Braxton?"

"One of the new ranch hands. He's from Alabama, and Colton's training him."

"Oh, haven't met him yet."

"And you won't," Jackson says. "He's twenty-five and thinks he's God's gift to women."

I grin, shaking my head at the irony. "Sounds like someone else I know."

"No, I said he *thinks* he is. I actually am." He flashes a smug grin, and I pull his lips back to mine, kissing it right off his face.

CHAPTER THIRTY-ONE

JACKSON

THE PAST FEW weeks have been nothing short of amazing.

After I helped Kiera move all her things from her parents' house into mine, it seemed like everything was the way it was supposed to be. The way I feel about her is much more than a childhood crush—it's real, it's *everything*.

I know we were going to take our time and do this right, but damn, we already know everything there is to know about each other. We've been codependent, and there aren't any secrets between us. Her moving in was the next logical step, plus I selfishly just wanted her in my bed every night. I wanted to come home and know she was there waiting for me, and vice versa.

I roll over and watch her sleep so peacefully in my arms. Her blonde hair cascades across the pillow, and it takes everything for me not to wake her up. Though it's Thanksgiving morning and our day is going to be packed full of family, we still have daily tasks to take care of. But truthfully, I'd rather make love to her from sunrise to sunset. I can never get enough. Sometimes I have to pinch myself to make sure this is real. I dreamed about having her like this for so long that it's almost unbelievable. *Surreal.*

Kiera's eyes flutter open, and a soft smile touches her lips. "Morning," she whispers.

I lean over and press my lips against hers. "Mornin', beautiful. Hungry?"

She opens her arms and pulls me back to her. "Hungry for more of you."

"I'm your buffet. Eat all you want." I laugh against her lips before she slips below the blankets. Her fingers peel off my boxers, and soon she's throwing them from under the covers. Fingernails scratch down my legs, causing shivers to rush over my skin. The anticipation of having her again is almost unbearable.

As soon as her warm mouth licks up my shaft, my eyes practically roll in the back of my head. Kiera takes her time, licking and sucking, before taking me all the way to the back of her throat. I move the blankets from her body so I can watch my queen take full control.

"Mmm," she hums and flicks her tongue against the tip before she takes me in her mouth again and begins pumping me harder and faster. I thread my fingers through her hair as she varies her speeds, driving me wild and pushing me to the edge. She knows exactly what I like and want, and constantly uses it to her advantage in the bedroom.

Gently, Kiera brushes her fingers across my balls, and I know if she keeps this up, I'll lose it at any moment. Just as I feel my body tense, Kiera stops, climbs up my body, and slides my hardness inside. Her head rolls back on her shoulders as she releases a moan. She's soaked, and I love the fact that pleasing me arouses her. Hell, I love everything about her.

I dig my thumbs into her hips as she rides me like a horse, but I steady her. Her green eyes meet mine as she bends down to claim my mouth. Our bodies rock together in fluid movement as if we're one entity, and I don't know how much longer I'll last. I've never been a one-minute man, but with Kiera, I'm ready to come as soon as she gets naked.

"Jackson," she moans loudly, scratching her nails down my chest, picking up her pace. I thumb her clit, adding just enough pressure to have her begging for more. Kiera's eyes tightly close, and her entire body trembles and shakes. Before long, our bodies are moving together in perfect harmony as the orgasms blast through us. There's not enough air in the room for us to breathe. I wrap my arms around her and hold her until we come down from the high. I brush her messy hair from her face and kiss her.

"I just want to stay here all day," she whispers.

I smile against her skin. "I know. But we should probably shower, then feed the horses."

Kiera pretends to snore, and I tickle her until she jumps up and rushes to the bathroom. "First!"

I chase her into the shower where she turns it on and lets the warmth run over us. Taking my time, I wash every curve, making sure my hands cover each inch of her smooth skin. After she's clean, she takes the soap from me and returns the favor.

"Don't put too much shampoo," she tells me, reminding me of the last time I washed her hair.

"I'm a pro now," I remind her, putting a dot in my palm, then begin to massage her scalp. She presses her body against my chest, wrapping her arms around my waist. Once her hair is washed, she leans back, and I rinse the soap out and add conditioner. "I could get used to this every morning."

"It could be our new routine." I lift an eyebrow at her. "Sucking, fucking, then getting squeaky clean, all before the sun rises."

"Add in coffee and breakfast, and it's a date."

"Done deal." I hurry and wash and rinse my hair, then we step out of the shower. After we're dressed, we quickly kiss each other goodbye.

"I'll be back in an hour," Kiera tells me before we go our separate ways. Though we live together, her horses and business are still ten minutes down the road. I haven't brought it up yet, but eventually, we'll get married, and she'll need to decide if she wants to keep the business at her parents or move everything to the ranch so I can help easier. With ten thousand acres, there's plenty of room for us to build whatever we want. A smile touches my lips when I recognize I'm already planning our future. Before Kiera, that thought would've never happened.

I walk to the barn and hurry to distribute the feed into buckets. John walks up and helps me, knowing we need to be at Mama's in just a few hours for Thanksgiving lunch.

"How are things goin'?" he asks, knowing more than anyone about Kiera and my relationship. We've snuck around in town, and we haven't really announced she moved in, though her parents know, and of course, John, and anyone else who notices her truck parked overnight.

The day I showed up on the front steps of her parents' house to help her move, her mother welcomed me with a hug, and so did her dad. They're like my second family though Kiera spent more time over here than I did over there. When we were twelve, Kiera broke her arm and ever since then I promised them I'd take care of her until the day I died. I'm still keeping that promise true, and it's not one I ever intend on breaking.

"I understand now why you had that constant love-sick look on your face when you met Mila," I tell John.

"Shut the hell up. I did not." John picks up as many buckets as he can, and I'm really thankful for his help so I'll finish sooner.

"You still do," I tease him. "Like you're pussy whipped or somethin'. Catch a glimpse in the mirror every once in a while."

"Why when I can just look at your dumb ass every day?" John quickly says with a chuckle.

We pour grain in all the feeders until the horses are fed and meet back in the barn. "I bet you didn't think it could ever be like this with Kiera," he tells me as we put everything up.

"Not in a million fuckin' years," I admit. He flashes a smug grin as if he always knew.

John gives me a big hug, and it slightly takes me off guard. "Happy for you, brother. I'd say happy you found someone, but she's been in front of you since you were shitting your pants."

I let out a big laugh. "What are you talking about? I'm still shittin' my pants."

We walk out side by side, and I glance over at him. "Thanks, John."

"You deserve to be as happy as the rest of us." He gives me a smile and a head nod before walking back toward the B&B. Every holiday, the kitchen staff does a big lunch, and John usually goes in and helps get it all set up before heading over to Mama's. It's become a Thanksgiving tradition. The only difference this year is I'll be bringing a date, unlike the other times when I was the awkward Bishop who'd constantly get ragged on for being single. But then again, no one was ever good enough to meet the family. Luckily, no introductions are needed today.

After I head back to the house, I wait around until Kiera returns, which doesn't take her very long at all. She basically charges me with kisses as soon as she walks in, which I happily accept.

"I saw my dad before I left, and he asked me when we were getting married." Her cheeks redden. "I told him to stop, that I've had enough weddings for the year."

I pull her into my arms and smell her hair and skin before I place my lips on her forehead. "I'm ready whenever you are."

She slaps my arm and takes a step back. "Where's Jackson Bishop, and what have you done with him?"

I playfully unbutton and unzip my pants. "He's in here."

"After all this time, I don't know how you still manage to shock the shit out of me," she admits, standing on her tiptoes and painting her lips with mine.

"If you keep this up, we'll never make it over to my parents'."

She shrugs. "You say it like it's a bad thing. But I know your mama would come over here and drag you out with her bare hands, so we better get goin'."

I nod, agreeing, then slap her hard on the ass as I walk past to grab my keys, making her yelp.

"Come on, before I swing you over my shoulder and carry

you over there like a caveman for the world to see that ass is mine."

Laughing loudly, Kiera runs past me. I chase her out the door, and for a moment, we're sixteen again, having the best time of our lives. We drive to the main house, and Kiera sits close to me with her fingers interlocked with mine.

"I'm actually kinda nervous," she admits as I park.

"Why?" I'm thrilled to officially tell them, though I'm sure they know.

"Because we've crossed the boundary line. We're a thing now. You don't think they'll think it's weird?"

I burst out laughing. "Hell no. Not sure if you realized it or not, but *everyone* knew I had a thing for you, except for you."

Kiera scoffs. "Excuse me? You apparently didn't know either because it took you five million years to finally make a move."

I glance down at my crotch, then back at her. "Trust me, I knew. There wasn't a point when I didn't if you know what I mean. I've had blue balls since before I knew what that even was because of you."

"Hmm. Well. I knew I had a thing for you first." She smirks, before planting a quick kiss on my lips and getting out of the truck.

"No, you didn't," I call after her as she runs up the steps. "When? When did you know?"

She taps her finger on her lips as if she's thinking about it. "When I was thirteen, I started to see you differently and really wasn't sure, but I knew for certain when I was fifteen, and those feelings developed even more. Do you remember the time we were at our spot, playing truth or dare, and I asked you who your crush was?"

I think back to that moment. We spent so much time out there, and I've drunk gallons of whiskey since then, but I remember.

"I wanted you to say me. I wanted you to kiss me that night." Kiera's eyes are shining so brightly. "And you said Miss Whitman." She deadpans, making me grin.

I take a few steps forward, closing the space between us. Her breath hitches when I tuck loose strands of hair behind her ears. "That night was when I almost told you how I felt. And I wanted to kiss you, just like this." I place my hands on both sides of her cheeks and lightly brush my lips against hers, then become greedier. Breathlessly, she parts her lips and allows our tongues to tangle together. Kiera melts into my touch, and I feel as if I have decades of lost time to make up for. The only regret I have in life is not telling Kiera how I felt sooner. As we're lost in each other, the front door swings open, but I don't care. I finish what I started.

"Hey Kiera," Mama greets. "Jackson, think you can get your tongue from down her throat so she can come inside from the cold?"

Kiera's eyes bolt open, and she pulls away just as Mama steps aside and opens the door wider.

"Hey, Mama B," Kiera says, giving her a big hug as soon as she enters.

Mama gives me a wink as I follow Kiera with my hand placed on the small of her back. As soon as we enter the kitchen, Emily instantly stands with a huge smile on her face. Kiera and she exchange hugs, and Em gives me a wink and a thumbs-up. The only person who knew I was bringing Kiera today was Mama because I knew it'd be rude not to say something, though she cooks for an army anyway. So everyone else is surprised to see her. Dad gives Kiera a big hug and says his hellos as he sits at the head of the table. Mama is busy playing hostess, giving hugs to every person who enters the room.

Mila and John walk in with Maize and are soon followed by Alex and River along with Riley and Rowan, who's sleeping peacefully in her car seat. Riley and Maize grab each other's hands and sit on the floor, having the most interesting kid conversation about the dinosaurs and trucks Riley pulls out of his pockets. They're gonna get into so much trouble when they're older. I'm already calling it.

"Mama, you're gonna need a bigger dining room soon," I tell her as everyone enters the room.

Mila and River gravitate toward Kiera, and before long, we're all laughing and having a good time and making jokes. John and I help Mama set the table, and she opens the oven for me to grab the turkey. It's so damn heavy I don't know how she even got it in there by herself. I set it in front of Dad, and John hands him a knife to carve it. Mama places all the sides on the table, and my mouth waters just smelling it all. Candied yams, green beans, homemade mashed potatoes, macaroni and cheese—and that's just on one-half of the large table.

Once Mama says grace and all our plates are piled a mile high, the room gets quiet as we eat. I place my hand on Kiera's lap, and she places hers on top of mine. I love having her near and being able to touch her. We exchange side glances and smiles, and I notice everyone is looking at us. I've tried to ignore it, but I can't any longer.

"What?" I finally say with a smirk.

"Just wondering when you're gonna tell us." Evan clears his throat. I look at Emily, thinking she would've told him something because I know she and Kiera talk, but I guess she kept our secret.

"Tell you what?" I play dumb, taking a bite of mashed potatoes.

"That you and Kiera are living together!" Alex exclaims.

Mama turns and looks at me. "Seriously?"

"John knew." I shrug, and I'm honestly kinda shocked she didn't. "Thought you all did. I mean, we live really, really close to each other."

"Don't you bring me into your trouble," John adds. "I've had enough of that the past thirty something years."

The room erupts into loud chatter, and Kiera explains the whole story to them, from the very beginning, about the note and everything, because it's easier to start there. "So yeah, we're not hiding anymore. It's easier to just be out in the open about it." She

329

loops her arm around mine and leans into me. I dip down and kiss her.

"Oh my heavens. This is the best news I've ever heard. Eventually more grandchildren. Eventually another wedding. I'm one happy mama right now." Mama beams.

I watch John whisper back and forth with Mila because regardless of what most people think, I'm overly observant. He shakes his head, and she nods, and I can tell they're quietly arguing about something.

"Whatcha talkin' about over there?" I look at the two of them with my eyebrows raised, and I notice Mila's barely touched a crumb on her plate.

I narrow my eyes at her, then realization sets in.

"Oh my God," I say, and she knows I know.

"See, even he knows!" Mila tells John loud enough to draw everyone's attention to her. As everyone is staring, I grab Kiera's hand and squeeze it.

"So…" Mila takes a deep breath. "We're pregnant!"

Mama instantly stands up and goes to Mila, wrapping her arms around her. Tears stream down both of their faces. River, Emily, and even Kiera have the sweetest smiles on their faces.

"You know what they say." Evan leans over. "More babies, more problems." Emily slaps the shit out of him, but we can't stop laughing. They both look tired, and they still have some months to go before baby number two is born.

As the chatter continues, I lean over and whisper in Kiera's ear. "I love you."

She whispers it back, and it brings me so damn much joy, I barely know how to contain it. All is good in the world right now. For the first time in my life, I really know what true happiness is —it's family and love—and as I look around the table, I'm grateful to have an abundance of both.

CHAPTER THIRTY-TWO

KIERA

THE MORNING FOG rolls over the hills as I drive to my parents' land. I've got my heater blasting because a cold front blew in last night. Frost covers everything, and I can't say I'm excited for December. Though my training facility is only ten minutes away, each morning I have to climb out of bed and leave Jackson, it feels like I'm being forced to drive across the universe. Eventually, we'll need to discuss our future, though I'm completely content with living in the present, for now. However, the quickies in the barn would be a lot easier if we worked closer together.

Jackson and I have effortlessly sunk into our little morning routine. We wake up with morning sex, have a delicious breakfast, which is usually pork and eggs, then finish it off with a to-go mug of coffee followed by kisses. Each day I wake up next to him holding my body close to his, I'm so grateful he's mine.

I've never felt this way about another man, and I knew deep down in my heart, I never would. This piece of me was always reserved for Jackson—locked up tight—and only he ever had the key. But I have to admit, being with him like this is much better than my fantasy of it all. Every day, he surprises me with his smart mouth or jokes, and I can't seem to get enough. I'll never get enough of him, and I don't ever want to.

After pulling up to the main barn, I start feeding the horses on this side of the land. I see Alexis across the way and wave with my free hand. I lay out hay, then do a quick check of all the troughs to make sure there's no ice in the water. I need to make sure my babies are getting well hydrated in the cold. I do my bi-monthly inventory check before I head to the feed store to pick up some more alfalfa and grain. I'll pick up a few horse treats too.

As I head back to my truck, I make a mental note of everything I need to do today. Frost crunches below my feet, and each time I exhale, my breath causes smoke. I tuck my hands in my jacket pockets and walk a tad faster. I don't particularly care for the cold.

I head down the old country road that leads to town until I arrive at the feed store. It's actually pretty busy for being so early in the day. I park and walk inside with a pep in my step. As soon as I enter, Charlie, the owner, gives me a big hello and a smile. I grab the things I need, and he gets some of his helpers to load the back of my truck up with the alfalfa and grain as I pay.

"How've you been, Kiera?" It's a simple question, one I'm asked often, but I always feel as if people are trying to confirm rumors or not.

"Gettin' along pretty good," I tell him, trying to keep it short.

"That's good. Glad to hear it." He hands me my receipt, and I make my way back outside carrying a sack of horse treats. A woman passes me and looks me up and down. I'm actually used to it these days. It's been two months since I walked out on my wedding, but some people act like it was just yesterday. I really can't wait for something else to happen in this small town, so I don't have to be the center of all the whispers in public.

I pass the two teenagers who loaded my truck and thank them for their help. As I'm walking across the parking lot, kicking rocks, I hear steps walking behind me. Considering I'm pretty aware of my surroundings, I glance over my shoulder and see Trent.

My heart drops.

I haven't seen him since the day of the wedding, and I've done a pretty good job of avoiding him at all costs. I knew I'd eventually run into him, but I wasn't expecting it today. I see the scowl on his face as he watches me, and I turn around and keep walking forward. Still hearing his footsteps behind me, I stop at my truck, turn around, and cross my arms over my chest.

"What the fuck? Can't even say hello?" he barks.

I just glare at him. I'm past being friendly especially after he felt the need to lay his hands on me. Frustration is written all over his face, but the difference this time is I don't have to care.

"What do you want, Trent?" I'm unamused. I don't feel completely threatened because people are around. If he lays his hands on me because he can't control his temper, I'll scream.

He continues walking forward until he's a few feet away from me. "Heard about you and Jackson, but somehow it's not surprising. I knew you were fucking him the whole time because you're nothing but a cheating whore."

I've been called so many names over the past few months from his fan club that it barely fazes me anymore. "Are you done?"

He takes another step forward. I can smell his cologne, and it leaks off him like poison. The smell makes my stomach turn. As I look up into his eyes, standing tall, I can't believe I ever felt a thing for him. The blinders are off, and I see him for what he is—a manipulating asshole.

"Just know this. Your little boy toy needs to watch his goddamn back." His words are nothing more than empty threats.

My lips are in a firm line. "Fuck off, Trent. Leave me alone."

He pretends like he's going to hit me, hoping I'd flinch of course, but I don't move. I grew up playing with boys and am not intimidated by him—especially in a public place. Over his shoulder, I can see people looking at us, and I know I need to end this conversation soon. The last thing I want is for any sort of log to be added to the rumor inferno of Trent and me.

I roll my eyes at him and get inside my truck. I crank it and back out of the feed store driveway. Before I pull away, I catch a glimpse of him in my rearview mirror, and he's seething. I couldn't be happier to get away from him.

On the way back to the barn, just the thought of him approaching me pisses me off. The audacity of him, with his empty threats, has me wanting to turn around and tell him exactly what I think. But I don't. Because I'm better than that, and I'm actually moving on—something I wish he'd do too.

After I make it back to the barn, I unload the supplies, then do a walk around to make sure everything is still okay. With ice sticking on the ground, I won't dare risk training, so today is basically a wash. Plus the weather isn't looking too great for this afternoon either. I text Alexis and tell her she can head home for the day and make a mental note to check the weather for tomorrow too. In the winter, several of the locals pay me to board their horses so while I'm not training every day, there's still a lot of upkeep when it's cold.

I lock everything up, hop in my truck, and can't get to the Bishop ranch quick enough. As soon as I turn under the iron Circle B sign, a smile touches my lips. It's always been home to me, but now since I've moved in with Jackson, it really is. After I park at the house, I go inside and grab an extra jacket because the temperatures are slowly dropping, then head to the barn where Jackson is.

Once I make it over there, I lean against the vast opening of the barn and watch Jackson clean the stalls. He's so wrapped up in his thoughts that he doesn't notice me. Plus, it helps that his back is turned. Not often do I get to watch him like this, so I don't dare interrupt him.

I soak him in. His messy hair falls across his face, and though it's cold outside, he's got his sleeves rolled up. It gets hot quick when working, so I understand. I lick my lips, studying his broad shoulders, and watch the muscles in his forearms flex as the rake goes back and forth in fast, brisk movements. I imagine his strong hands on my body, and I instantly crave him.

"Take a picture, it'll last longer," he says over his shoulder, and I can tell he's smiling.

I grin, walking toward him. "Maybe I will."

Jackson turns around, drops the rake, removes his gloves, and pulls me in for a kiss. Next thing I know, my legs are wrapped around his waist, and his hands are holding me by my ass. He takes two steps forward, pressing my back against the stall door. We're greedy and hungry for one another; it's an insatiable craving that will never be met. We have years to make up for.

"Fuck me," I whisper. The likelihood of someone walking in is high, but the thought of possibly getting caught turns me on that much more. Jackson sets me on the ground, undoing his pants as I undo mine. Two swift movements and he's inside me, fucking me against the stall door. My hands are threaded through his messy hair, and I tug and pull as our mouths wage war. His hot breath brushes against the skin of my neck, and I hold on to him for dear life as he fucks me hard and quick.

"I can never get enough of you," he tells me, pumping deeper inside me, kissing along my collarbone.

"Good." I pant breathlessly, knowing I'm quickly unraveling with each calculated movement. He continuously fills me with his length, our bodies joining together. Jackson doesn't slow down, keeping steady the entire time as he claims me as his. My mouth falls open, and moments later, the orgasm rocks through me, causing me to moan loudly.

He doesn't slow, keeping me steady in his hands until he finds his own paradise. As his warmth fills me, his lips greedily take mine. Once we catch our breath and come back to reality, Jackson sets me down, buttons and zips his pants, then grabs a few paper towels from the tack room.

A smirk touches his lips. "Glad you stopped by. Can we make that a daily thing?"

"I might be able to work you into my schedule. Gotta make up for lost time somehow." I run my fingers through my just-been-fucked hair.

"Are you goin' now?" he asks, picking up his gloves and the rake that was lazily lying on the ground.

I shake my head. "Nope. I took the rest of the day off and sent Alexis home. The ground is too icy, and I don't want to risk an injury."

His arms snake around my waist. "So you should make yourself useful and help me clean these stalls."

My head falls back with laughter. "I don't think so, Cowboy."

Taking a step back, he shrugs. "Welp, I tried."

"Jackson." I grab his hand. "I saw Trent at the feed store today."

He searches my face. "And?"

"He told me to tell you to watch your back, along with some other colorful words."

Instead of being pissed, the reaction I fully expected, Jackson bursts into hearty laughter. "I need to watch my back?" He's hunched over laughing so hard that I start giggling.

"If he comes within twenty feet of me, I will beat his face to the point he's completely unrecognizable. His threats are empty. He's nothing more than a big ole pussy. And he's an idiot. Did he touch you?"

"No, he didn't. I *know* you'd destroy him. But I wanted you to know; no secrets. I'm sure there were people who saw us chatting in the parking lot, and I didn't want it to get back to you like I was sneaking around or something." I remember all the times Trent accused me of doing something I wasn't, and I don't want Jackson to ever feel that way.

"Babe, I'm not worried about you leaving me for anyone. I know how you feel. There are zero doubts in my bones about it."

I smirk, thinking about how much different it is being with Jackson. I don't have to explain myself to him, and I'm not in a constant state of defense. There are zero trust issues or secrets, and I'm so grateful Jackson rescued me from that toxic relationship. "Damn, I love you. Have I told you that today?"

He nods. "I'm pretty sure you did this morning when I was buried between your legs."

A laugh escapes me. "Do you really want me to help you with stalls?"

"Nah, sweetheart. I was just kiddin'. But if you want, you can see if John needs anything. I think Nicole called in this morning, so he's been dealing with it all alone."

I give him a quick kiss on the lips, and when I walk away, he pulls me closer and deepens the kiss, his tongue swiping against mine. "I love you too."

It's becoming harder to walk away from him, but I pull myself away. Before I walk out of the barn, I look over my shoulder and give him a wink, knowing he's watching me. I tuck my hands in my pockets as I walk up the path to the B&B. Happiness instantly fills me.

John is standing on a ladder with a box placed on top, and he's putting ornaments on a ten-foot Christmas tree in front of the large window panes in the common room. My face lights up.

"Oh my God. I freakin' love Christmas," I say, and he turns and looks relieved to see me.

"Please tell me you came to help. I forgot to put the tree up over the weekend, and Mama about ripped my head off when she found out."

I nod. "Actually, I am. You can thank Jackson."

"Sometimes I really love my brother." John climbs off the ladder and brushes his fingers through his hair. Boxes of ornaments and decorations are almost stacked to the ceiling in the corner. My eyes widen when I realize how much of it there is.

"I've got to get all of that put out today, or I was threatened with my life." He grins.

I walk over to the boxes and open them up. Garland, glass nativity scenes, holly, lights, fake poinsettias, and countless ornaments fill each of the boxes. I unzip my jacket and place it on an extra coat hook by the door and try to come up with a game plan.

"Where should we start?" I ask, looking at everything and feeling a bit overwhelmed with it all, but I'm happy to help.

John crosses his arms over his chest and studies it all. Jackson and he have the same look when they're deep in thought. "What if we start with each room downstairs and complete them, then do the tree last. I think the tree might take the most time since we have three boxes of ornaments to put on it."

"Sounds like a solid plan." I notice on the side of the boxes each room is marked. I open the common room box and begin placing the lighted garland around the fireplace. There's an entire winter wonderland scene with fake snow that I set up on the mantel.

John puts on some Christmas music and laughs. "Just for inspiration."

I grab another box and carry it to the dining room. There's a small, two-foot tree tucked in the box with a stand, and I set it up, plug in the lights, and place the western ornaments on it. I hang holly around all the windowsills and grab a small stepladder to hang the mistletoe at the dining room entrance. Once it's complete, I take a step back, feeling proud of what I accomplished.

When I turn around, I see John has changed out the large pictures on the wall with winter landscapes. Rugs are replaced with more Christmas themed ones, and red and green throw blankets are tucked on the back of the couches in the common room.

"It looks amazin'," John says, passing me with another box in his hands. He sets it on the counter and begins setting glass Christmas cowboy boots around and shoving a handful of candy canes inside. I grab one, open it up, and crack a piece of it off and place it in my mouth.

"So how's Mila doin'? She feeling okay?" I ask him.

"Yeah, she's doing okay. Having some sickness, but nothing too major—at least not yet."

"I'm so excited for y'all. Maize is going to love having a little sister or brother. I bet you're just over the moon about it." I smile at him, knowing how hard things started out for him when baby Maize was left in his hands.

"I really am. I'm glad I get to be here to experience the pregnancy this time and watch her belly grow. I'm not gonna miss any of it," he says, proudly.

"You're a great dad, John." I smile at him. "Just thought I'd tell you that."

"Thanks, Kiera. I can't wait till the day Jackson becomes a dad. Hope you don't mind, but I've kinda put a hex on him to have triplets after all the shit he's stirred up in the past."

I burst out laughing. "Please take that back, okay? I want a lot of babies, but not all at once."

"I'll see what I can do." He winks with a grin.

"I'm gonna start on the tree now," I tell him.

He nods and smiles. "Go for it."

I sing along to "Rudolph the Red-nosed Reindeer" as I string the lights around the massive tree. John comes back and grabs another box, and I continue, dancing around, making a fool of myself. A few guests notice how much fun I'm having and ask if they can help to decorate. Before long, there's a group of us passing ornaments around, and we're all laughing and having a good time. Most of them are over the age of sixty and are so thankful to help. I'm just happy I can be one reason their stay at the B&B is enjoyable.

I climb up the ladder, and John walks up and hands me the ornaments for the upper half of the tree. Just as I turn around, I see Jackson walking through the back door, and when our eyes meet, I can't stop smiling. John asks me a question, but realizes I'm not paying attention to anything he's saying. He turns around and spots Jackson, and so do the guests.

"Howdy, y'all," he tells them.

I climb down from the ladder and see John is holding the tree topper in his hand. I look at it then look at him. "You should do the honor," I tell him.

"You sure?" he asks.

"Absolutely." I smile as Jackson places his arm around my shoulder and pulls me close. He bends over and kisses me, and even in the smallest instances like this one, I'm so happy we don't have to hide the way we feel anymore. John climbs up the ladder, places the angel on top, clears everything from in front of the tree, then looks around.

"Okay, I'm gonna plug in the lights," he announces. Everyone crowds around the tree as John does a big countdown. The guests are loving all of this. As soon as it's plugged in, the tree is like a shining beacon in the room with its twinkling lights. Some gasp and clap, and I'm actually impressed by how beautiful it looks. The glass ornaments sparkle and shine, and the music playing in the background catapults me into the Christmas spirit. I think helping John do this might be my new tradition.

"We should put the tree up at home." I snuggle into Jackson's arm.

"Only if we can do it naked," he whispers in my ear.

I smile, blush hitting my cheeks. "Deal."

I look up at Jackson, soaking him in as he says something to John. At this moment, I'm not paying attention to anything but him. There was a point in my life when I thought I was losing Jackson Bishop, but as he holds me close, I know he's always been mine. It just took us some time to get here, and I plan on keeping him forever.

CHAPTER THIRTY-THREE

JACKSON

CHRISTMAS IS IN TWO WEEKS, and I'm proud of myself for getting most of my shopping done early. When you live in the middle of nowhere, the internet is a beautiful thing. I want to make sure it's really special for Kiera, considering it will be our first one to spend together as a couple, and I've had everything sneakily shipped to my mama's.

This morning, Colton's responsible for my duties, and I'm being forced to work at the B&B because John's taking Mila to a doctor's appointment in San Angelo. Though John has a daughter, this is his first time being involved with the pregnancy, so he's excited about the entire process. I expect to be covering many more shifts shortly, but I couldn't be happier for them.

I kiss Kiera goodbye, and before I make my way over to the B&B, I send Colton a text reminding him he needs to feed the horses by six, but I don't get a text back. I shove my phone in my pocket, and when I pass the barn, I realize none of the lights are on, which is frustrating, so I send him another text. No response.

Knowing I have an extra thirty minutes before I really need to be at the B&B, I climb in one of the side-by-sides and make my way over to the ranch hand quarters. I'm actually kinda pissed I have to drag him out of bed, but considering they had a party last night, it somewhat doesn't surprise me. Halfway to my destination, I realize I should've driven my truck because it's cold as balls outside.

By the time I pull up to Colton's, I notice all the lights in the house are on, except for his bedroom. Considering he lives with a group of guys, and Dad starts earlier than I do, it doesn't surprise me that most of them are awake and already gone.

I park and hop out of the seat, walk up the steps, and open the door. It seriously stinks like guys and feet, and I'm reminded why I moved the fuck out as quickly as I could. The place is trashed, and beer cans and empty liquor bottles line the countertops. The house is empty for the most part, so I go to Colton's room and crack open the door. He's sleeping peacefully, but that's about to change really quick.

Considering I've been woken up a dozen shitty times in the past by John, I take a page from his playbook and grab a pitcher from the cabinet, then fill it with ice cold water. As I carry it back to a snoozing Colton, I'm smiling the whole time. I flick on the light, which doesn't bother him in the least, then in one swift movement, I dump the water on him.

As if someone lit a fire under his ass, he bolts up out of bed wearing only his boxers and socks. "Fuccccckkkkkkkkk!" he screams.

A roar of laughter escapes me as he tries to tackle me but fails miserably.

"Time to wake up, ya bastard. You're already behind schedule," I say, stepping out of his way and watching him crash into the wall.

Colton rubs his hands over his face, trying to wake up or sober up, then turns to me. "I hate you. It's rude to wake a man up like that."

I shrug. "Learned it from John. Hurry your ass up. You got horses to feed and some lessons to teach today. I'll wait five minutes for you."

He groans, and I can tell he's hungover from last night, and I feel like I should be giving him a medal of honor or something for following in my footsteps. Many mornings, I woke up and fed the horses still drunk from the night before or even worse with a hangover. It's almost like a rite of passage or something for my job.

Colton changes out of his wet boxers and slips on some jeans and a T-shirt. He struggles to put on his boots, then grabs a heavy jacket. After he takes a banana from the kitchen, he gives me a dirty look before walking out the door.

"You act like you're mad or something," I taunt.

"Imma get you back. Just you wait," he threatens with a smug grin.

"I wouldn't if I were you. I play dirty," I admit.

He shrugs and begins peeling his banana. When I look over, I can't stop laughing.

"What?" he asks, chewing.

"Dude, there's no proper way to eat a banana in public. You basically just deepthroated that thing like a champ. I'm impressed."

He shakes his head. "Bullshit!"

"Okay! Well, if ranching doesn't work out for you…"

He breaks a piece of banana off and pops it in his mouth. "You're an asshole."

"That's what they say apparently," I tell him with a grin as I park the utility vehicle outside of the barn. "You got this?"

He gives me an animalistic grunt and walks into the barn and flicks on the lights. I turn and make my way to the B&B since I'm in charge today. It's a slight change of pace being inside when it's so cold out, and I welcome it, though I'm dreading being around Nicole. Since our incident, things have been rocky, and I've been forced to walk on thin ice so as not to set her off. Though she wanted another night with me, I refused. I might have a man whore reputation, but I'm not going to whore myself out over threats. Everyone is worried but me, mainly because I know she needs this job more than anything because the market around here is slim to none.

I walk in through the back door, and the B&B looks like Christmas threw up inside it, which it kinda did, but Mama loves for it to be over the top. It makes most people happy, and honestly, I don't mind it. The tree and lit garland cast a warm glow throughout the common room. All is quiet so far, so I turn on the lights, open the blinds so the sun can shine through when it rises, then make some coffee. As it brews, I check with the kitchen staff about breakfast. When I walk in, homemade dough is being peeled off by the handfuls for biscuits. Sausage patties are in large cast iron skillets as white gravy is being whipped up in a pan. There are four people who cook for the B&B every day, for every meal, who Mama knows from church. They could seriously start their own restaurant.

"This looks delicious, Mrs. Jackie," I tell one of the main cooks.

"Make you a plate when it's done, darlin'."

I smile. "Don't have to tell me twice." Breakfast at the B&B is so good a group of locals will drop in every once in a while and buy a plate. It's always a big, extravagant, homemade Southern meal, and I eat here whenever I can. It's been less frequent lately, though, because I've been having breakfast with Kiera or, rather, having Kiera *for* breakfast. The thought of it has me grinning from ear to ear.

I hear footsteps in the main room and step out and see one of our guests filling a coffee mug full. I hurry and grab the fresh cream and set it out.

"Good mornin'," I offer.

"Mornin', John," the older woman greets.

"Oh, I'm Jackson. The other brother."

Shaking her head, she chuckles. "Oh, that's right. I forget there're two of you. Don't know how your mama tells you apart."

I pour myself a cup of coffee and take a sip. "Honestly, there are times when she doesn't. But don't tell her that. She swears she knows who is who." I let out a laugh and greet others as they come downstairs.

Checking the time, I realize Nicole's late for her shift. Considering she's been walking on thin ice and believes she can do whatever she wants, I decide to write her up. Yesterday, when John gave me the rundown of everything that needed to be done, he mentioned Nicole has been coming and going as she pleases. He mentioned he'd already given her a warning but told her the next time she'd be written up, and here we are.

Even though we're a family run business, it's important that if we decide to fire someone, we have our ducks in a row, especially considering what happened between Nicole and me. As breakfast is being laid out, Nicole walks in without a care in the world. Thankfully, she doesn't have an attitude, but as soon as she sees me, she makes up some excuse about a flat tire.

"Sorry, John. Shit happens." She shrugs before she's interrupted by a guest to help change sheets upstairs. She sets her purse behind the counter and walks away. I'm half tempted to tell her it's me, but then again, I kinda don't give two shits. Her attitude and how she doesn't take this job seriously really pisses me off, especially considering she used to love being here. At this point, it's personal.

Just as most of our guests sit for breakfast, I open the schedule book and hear Nicole's phone dinging at an ungodly pitch in her purse. At first, I try to ignore it, but it keeps going off, one text message at a time, which is annoying as hell. Not able to take it anymore, I grab her purse and search for her phone. I wouldn't normally dig through a woman's bag like this, but phones are supposed to be on silent for a reason. It's distracting, and I don't know where she is to tell her to come turn it off herself. Once I find her cell, I'm just about to click the side button to silence it, and that's when I notice all the text messages are from the same person—Trent Laken. A lump the size of a basketball forms in my throat, and I can't seem to swallow it down. Why the fuck is Nicole talking to Dr. Douchebag? I can't see the full text messages, only previews because her phone is locked, but what I can see is more than unsettling.

Trent: It's important that everything goes off without any...

Trent: Did you do it yet?

Trent: Let me know so I can make sure there are no...

Trent: The plan is in place.

Trent: Fuck Jackson Bishop. He'll get what's coming to him.

Trent: I can't wait to see the look on her face when...

The last message catches me off guard. They're planning something, and I need to get to the fucking bottom of it right now. Anger rolls over me in waves, and I'll be damned if she's conspiring with Trent against Kiera and me. This is the last straw. I grab her phone and take the stairs two at a time. Nicole is chatting with a guest in the hallway, and as soon as I see her, I grab her arm.

She tries to get loose, but I keep my grip tight, so she doesn't get away. The fire inside my blood has anger seething out of my ears. I drag her down the stairs and into the office. I shut the door, lock it, and stand in front of it, so there's no way she's escaping until this is discussed. Trent can talk about me all he wants, but to even insinuate anything about Kiera is too fucking far.

"What the fuck, John?" she asks, glaring at me.

"I'm *not* John," I tell her between gritted teeth and watch her face transform from annoyance to anger. She's pissed.

Good. Now we're on the same page.

"What the hell do you want, Jackson?"

"I want a goddamn explanation, Nicole." I pull her phone from my back pocket and hold it in front of her face. She sees the text messages from Trent, and I watch as her expression is replaced with defeat or maybe even regret. She knows she's fucking busted, and I won't open this door until I find out what's going on.

"I don't have all day." I hand her phone over.

She looks down at the text messages, then opens her mouth and closes it. She's got nothing because I've literally backed her into a corner.

Another moment passes and tears begin to stream down her face before she starts hyperventilating. "I'm so scared, Jackson."

I try to understand what the fuck she's talking about because she's not making any sense.

"Trent." She sobs. "He's lost his damn mind."

With my back firmly pressed against the door, I stand there and watch her cry uncontrollably. "I could've told you that."

"I'm afraid for my life. After he caught the barn on fire—"

"What?" I search her face. "*Trent* caught our barn on fire?"

She nods. "Yes. Before that, when he was still with Kiera, I saw him in the grocery store, and we chatted. He told me if I could tell him when Kiera was with you, he'd pay me a few hundred dollars each time."

My mouth falls open. "You didn't."

She covers her face with her hands. "He manipulated me, Jackson. He made me believe he just wanted to surprise Kiera. After the two of you got into that fist fight, he basically threatened me and told me if I mentioned this to anyone, he'd track me down and end me."

"You have to go to the police, Nicole. You're the only person who can end this. Seriously."

"And now…"

I wait with bated breath for her next words.

"And now he's going to hurt Kiera. He hasn't gotten over it. I've tried to stop him. I've tried to lead him on, making up stories about how she's no longer coming around the property anymore."

My heart is pounding hard in my chest. "His text message said he couldn't wait to see the look on her face when…what? When he does what?"

Nicole swallows. "She's planning to pick up a horse tomorrow, and when she does, he's going to be there and follow her. I don't know what his plans are after that. Possible kidnapping? He mentioned taking her away."

I instantly text Kiera.

Jackson: Please come home now. Trent has lost his mind. I think you're in danger.

When she doesn't text back, I call her. When she doesn't answer, I begin to think the worst. I know I'm supposed to be watching the B&B, but I can't stay here when Trent is acting this way. I call Kiera two more times and leave panicked voicemails. Nicole just sits there and watches me.

The next phone call is to the police. I punch in 9-1-1 and am instantly connected. Nicole looks alarmed, which doesn't make me feel good at all about this situation.

"What are you doin'?" she asks, smearing the runny mascara on her cheeks even more.

"I'm getting the police involved right now."

Nicole stands up and grabs on to my arm, trying to take my phone. "No, please. He'll kill me, Jackson. He's already threatened me. Do you know why I was late this morning?"

I look at her. This is all happening too fast, and I'm going into panic mode. I'm wasting too much time already.

"Because I was worried that Trent was stalking me, and I was scared to leave until the sun came up."

"And this is why they need to be involved, Nicole. You need to be truthful and tell them what's going on or I will. You're in danger. Kiera is in danger. And apparently, I've been threatened too. I'm not playing these fucked-up games."

I open the door and walk out of the office. I feel as if I can't breathe as I explain to the operator what Nicole told me. The fact that Trent is capable of arson shocks the shit out of me. I know he's crazy and fucked up, but I didn't realize how deep his hatred for me really ran. Now that Kiera and I are together, and are open about it, I feel as the fuse to destruction has been lit.

"I need an officer to meet me down at my girlfriend's property right now. Her life's in danger, and I can't get ahold of her." I hurry and spit off her address as I head to the back door.

"That's not needed, Jackson!" Nicole begs. "It's supposed to happen tomorrow!"

I look at her and shake my head. I walk outside, send a quick text to Colton to watch the B&B, and sprint to my truck. Nicole continues to follow close behind me.

"Please!" she begs, and I can hear the hysteria in her voice, which only unsettles me more.

She continues crying and yelling, making a scene, trying to stop me, and I know leaving is the right thing to do. By the time I make it to my truck, she's still behind me. She completely breaks down as she forces herself in front of me, her last effort to make me stay, but it's no use. "Please, Jackson."

"Why are you trying to stop me, Nicole? Sorry, but I don't trust your ass as far as I can throw you. You need to get the fuck out of my way."

She steps aside, realizing her words are falling on deaf ears.

I shake my head and open the door. "This shit ends now. I have to know Kiera is okay."

CHAPTER THIRTY-FOUR

KIERA

Fuck, it's a cold one today. To make matters worse, Alexis texted me this morning and said she's too sick to come in. I'd been working her a lot lately, so I can't even be mad about her needing a day off.

"Hey, Champs," I say, rubbing my bare hand up his dark nose. He grunts in response, and I smile. "Ready for your breakfast?"

I've boarded six additional horses in the past two weeks and enjoy taking care of them during the winter months. Most of them I trained and are sweethearts, so they aren't much extra work for me. It makes me think of the possibility of building a larger barn on the Bishop property near our house. It'd be a dream to build something that's ours, something we can both work in and be proud of. I'd love to have a dozen extra stalls and a bigger tack room for my saddles and accessories.

I sigh. Hopefully someday.

At the rate Jackson and I are moving, I have a feeling that day is sooner than not.

I smile when I think of him and how much has changed in such a short amount of time. I don't regret it at all, knowing that everything lined up and happened the way it was meant to.

However, a small part still wishes we hadn't wasted all these years fighting it.

But that's all in the past now. I only care about our future and being happy for the rest of our lives.

I'm lost in my thoughts as I fill the water buckets outside. I recently upgraded to heated ones to help keep the water from freezing, so Alexis and I didn't have to work as hard, but it still takes an eternity to fill up. I hear crunching in the distance and think Jackson must've stopped by, but when I turn around, I don't see his truck.

Damn, I miss him. Hell, I always miss him. It's a sickness really. No matter how much time we spend together or how many times a day I see him, it's never enough. My hunger for him is an endless pit. Obsessed and possessed. It's the only way to accurately describe it, yet I don't even want to be cured. He owns every part of me and not having him in my life would feel empty and incomplete now.

My feelings for him were always present, sitting on the sidelines, waiting to be called out for the big game. I might've benched them while I was dating Trent because I thought he was the one I was supposed to marry, but as soon as Jackson made his feelings clear—the game was off. These past two months have been surreal, and even if we're moving a hundred miles an hour, I don't even care. It doesn't scare me like it would in any other relationship because deep down, I've always known he's the one. I want to build a horse training barn near the house, get married, and have lots of Bishop babies.

I smile at the thought. My mind often wanders while I'm working—thoughts all leading to Jackson. I still can't believe it sometimes. I've waited so long that it feels like it can't be this easy, can it? Jackson has never had a relationship in his life, and I always wondered if we ever did get together, if he'd even be able to handle something serious.

Turns out he *definitely* can. And to make things unimaginingly better, he's still the same ole Jackson he's always been, except intensely affectionate. We might be in our thirties, but we can't keep our hands off each other like a bunch of love-sick teenagers.

Thinking about all of this makes me want to text him a sweet message. I reach in my back pocket but realize I left my phone in the barn. *Crap.*

The hose is still running, the bucket not even halfway filled yet. While I wait, I head into the barn to retrieve my cell and contemplate what I want to send.

Something dirty. Or sweet. Maybe I'll send him a boob shot from my collection. I took them with the intent to tease the shit out of him.

Snickering at the thought, I step into the barn, the thin layer of ice crunching under my boots. I walk to where I left my phone, and it's not there. *What the hell?* I could've sworn it'd be there. Maybe it's in the back.

When I don't find it in the back of the barn either, I figure it must've fallen out of my pocket on the way out to the pasture. Making my way out of the barn, a sudden cold chill goes through me.

I should get my other jacket, I think to myself. Champs starts neighing and thrashing around his stall.

"What's the matter, boy? You—" I stop midsentence when I see a dark figure out of the corner of my eye. Turning my head to get a better look, I gasp at the sight of Trent standing in front of the barn door.

"Hello, Kiera." His voice is distant and cold, making me tremble at the sound of it.

"What are you doing here?" I try to keep my voice level, but I'm anything but relaxed. Taking a small step back, hoping he doesn't notice, he steps forward.

"Do you miss me?" he asks, his tone dripping with ice. "Do you?"

"Trent, I think you should go." I try to plead with him. His eyes are empty as he stares at me. "I'm going to call the deputy if you don't get off my property."

His lips widen into a wicked grin, obviously not fazed by my threat. "Is that so?" He reaches in his pocket and holds up my cell phone. *Fuck.* "Going to be pretty hard to do, don't you think?"

"Trent…" I tread carefully. "You need to go. Now."

"Not yet, babe. We need to talk."

I cross my arms over my chest to stop my body from shaking. "There's nothing to talk about. Nothing you say is going to change anything," I say firmly, hoping he gets the point.

"Wrong." He reaches behind his back and under his shirt before he exposes the revolver in his hand.

"Oh my God," I mutter. "Why do you have a gun?" I step back.

My heart hammers in my chest as horrible thoughts race through my mind. I can't believe this is happening. Trent has never shown this side to me before, and he looks almost manic. Who the hell is this guy? There's no way I was that blind to almost marry him.

Instead of pointing the gun at me like I anticipate, he shocks me when he puts it directly to his temple.

"Trent, wait…"

"You…" he stammers. "You did this to me."

Slowly, I step closer. "Trent, put the gun down. Please."

"Don't you dare," he spits out. "Don't you dare pretend to give two shits about me now. You tossed me aside like last week's trash after everything I gave you!" he screams, nearly making me jump out of my skin. "I gave you everything, you little bitch!"

"Trent, please," I beg, tears blurring my vision. "Let's talk. Put the gun down." I hold my hands out, slowly creeping forward.

"I have nothing now," he says in the saddest voice. "I lost you, and I have no fucking purpose. If I can't have you, I'd rather be dead."

"Don't say that." I manage to step closer without him

stopping me and can smell the faint scent of bourbon. Great, he's drunk too.

"It's true, Kiera. I loved you. Without you, life just isn't worth it." He unclicks the safety, and my heart beats into overdrive. "And you'll have to live with that for the rest of your life."

"Trent, please." I'm nearly in front of him now. "I do love you."

"Don't fucking patronize me," he snaps.

"I'm not, I swear," I quickly spit out. "I made a huge mistake leaving you. I thought Jackson was who I wanted because of our history, but I was wrong." The words taste like venom in my mouth, but I have no choice if I want to get the gun out of his hand.

"You really mean that, babe?" His grip loosens on the gun just slightly.

"Yes, I swear. I love you. We can repair our relationship, can't we?" I look into his cold eyes and try to find the faintest glimpse of the Trent I once knew, but he's nowhere to be found. He's gone completely insane.

I take the final step to reach him and slowly ease his arm down. "Put the safety on, baby."

He obliges and watches me. I nod to give him reassurance. Just when I reach for the gun so I can slowly remove it from his hand, a piercing siren screams in the distance along with gravel crunching under tires. We both turn to look, and my heart drops when I see Jackson's truck racing toward us. The deputy is speeding behind him.

Fuck, fuck, fuck.

Before I can move a muscle, Trent roughly grabs me and pins me against his chest, holding me hostage in his firm embrace. He presses the barrel hard into my temple and hisses.

"Don't fucking move or your boy toy gets the first bullet," he threatens, and my body shakes with sobs.

"Trent, don't…"

"If you really love me, you'd want him out of the picture once and for all." His voice is completely void of any emotion, and I'm terrified by what that means. I have no idea what he's actually capable of, considering who I thought he was just a few months ago was entirely wrong.

"You'll go to jail," I tell him. "Then we won't be able to have any kind of future." I hope it's enough to make him think clearer.

"Get your hands off my—" Jackson stops mid-scream when he realizes Trent has a gun to my head.

"Laken, drop the gun!" Deputy Pettigrew shouts, pointing his weapon right at us.

Oh my God, this cannot be happening.

I feel like I can't breathe. The air is being completely sucked out of my lungs as I try to process what's happening right now. One click and Trent could end me. End Jackson. End all of us.

I'm more worried for Jackson than myself, knowing he's not just going to stand back and watch Trent threaten me. I know how to play into Trent's trap and ease us out, but Jackson won't. He looks like he's ready to plow Trent down, regardless of the consequences.

"Take another step, and I'll blow her fucking head off," Trent shouts. I cringe, the pain slicing through my body as he pushes the gun harder into my skull.

"Trent, I'm warning you..." Deputy Pettigrew says calmly. "I'll shoot you if you don't drop your weapon."

I feel his chest rising and falling with evil laughter. "You think that's going to scare me? You'll shoot Kiera before the bullet hits me, so I know you're full of shit."

"Put your weapon down," Pettigrew tries again, but honestly, it's no use. Trent's at a level where he doesn't care about anything, including his own life.

"I'm taking my woman and leaving...and you're going to let me." Trent forces me to walk toward Jackson's truck. "Bishop," Trent spits his name out like it's lava. "You're going to give me your keys, and we're driving out of here.

"Not a fucking chance!" Jackson's ready to attack, but Deputy Pettigrew holds up his hand to signal him down.

"Otherwise, I'm going to make you watch me fuck her and then put a bullet between those sparkling green eyes. Once I'm done with her, you'll be next. Except I think I'll be aiming lower on you…" Trent pushes me forward. His lips graze my ear, and the touch sends shivers down my spine. I swallow. "You better cooperate, or you'll be responsible for four deaths, sweetheart."

"Trent, please don't do this…" I whisper, pleading for our lives. "I'll go with you willingly, just leave them alone."

"You hear that, Jackson?" Trent cackles. "Your girl wants to come with me. Guess your magic dick wasn't so satisfying after all."

Jackson's eyes narrow into deathly slits. He knows exactly what to say to work Jackson up, to give him one reason to shoot.

"Jackson, don't!" I shout without thinking. Trent growls, and when I hear the safety click, I panic. "I want to go with him," I force out of my mouth. "Trent and I are going to be together. Just let us go."

I speak with my eyes, knowing Jackson will be able to read between the lines. Deputy Pettigrew, on the other hand, isn't allowing it. I find myself wondering if he's already called for backup, and if so, why aren't they here yet? Did he call them off? If Trent hears them coming, he'll shoot for sure.

"Alright, fine," Jackson says, digging into his pocket and retrieving his keys. "Here." He tosses them to the ground, and they land halfway between him and us.

"Stay back," Trent warns. "You too, pig." Deputy Pettigrew has his gun out still but hasn't moved a muscle. I hope to God one of them has a plan, and they aren't going to actually let me get into the truck with him.

Trent pushes me forward until we're within reach of the keys. "Bend down with me on three," he whispers in my ear, and I know exactly why. If I cover him, Pettigrew won't be able to get a clean shot on him since I've been his personal body shield. "Grab the keys and hand them to me." He's holding me with one hand and pressing the cold metal to my head with the other. I swallow again, unable to get the razor blades out of my throat. I can't think of anything else but Jackson and how Trent won't think twice about shooting him.

"One…two …three …" I lower my body with his, slowly extending my arm out to reach for the bundle of keys. My adrenaline peaks as I lean my body forward just enough where he has to loosen his grip on me to allow me to pick them up.

Once I hold them securely in my palm, I fist my fingers to keep them in place.

"Good girl. Now put them in my left hand," he orders. Looking up from my eyelashes, I stare at Jackson and hope he can read me to understand what I'm about to do next.

I love you, I mouth.

When I lean back, Trent's focus is on grabbing the keys. His left hand slightly opens to take them, but instead of handing them over, I muster up every ounce of my strength and jab my elbow directly into his gut, exactly how Jackson taught me when we were younger.

He jerks back with an *oomph*, falling to his ass, making me fall with him. Then the whole scene unravels within seconds. Jackson tackles Trent, fighting for the gun. I want to scream, beg for them to stop, but I can't find my voice. I open my mouth, but just like in my dreams, nothing comes out.

Deputy Pettigrew grabs me and pulls me to my feet. "Get inside my squad car. Now!" he orders, but I can't move. I'm frozen as I watch Jackson and Trent wrestling on the ground. Jackson's easily stronger than Trent, but that doesn't matter when Trent is in this state of mind. He's gone completely psychotic.

"Kiera, get out of the way…" Pettigrew warns, but my gaze is glued to Jackson. I feel so helpless and want to know why no other officers are out here to help control the situation. "Cover your ears."

My eyes snap to him as Pettigrew raises the gun over his

head. Just when it dawns on me what he's planning, I step back, unsure of how this will turn out.

"Laken, this is your last—" The gun goes off before the deputy finishes his threat. He lowers his arm, then looks back at me then at his gun.

Oh my God.

He's not the one who pulled the trigger.

"Jackson! No! *Jackson*!" Screams pour out of me, and just as I run toward him, Pettigrew grabs me and pulls me back.

I hear muffled sirens in the distance, but all I can see is my whole world crumbling around me. Falling to my knees, Pettigrew loses his grip on me, and as soon as I'm free of his hold, I stumble to my feet and rush over to where Trent is lying on top of Jackson.

"Jackson! Oh my God! Please, God no!" I scream and sob as I reach for him.

Jackson slides out from Trent's lifeless body and grabs me with one arm. He manages to sit up and holds me to his chest as I bury myself in his neck.

"It's okay, baby. It's over. It's all over. Shh…" Jackson's voice is calming, but I'm anything but calm. Everything happened so fast, I can't even think.

"Are you hurt?" I pull back to examine his face and body, inspecting every inch. There's blood on him. "Are you bleeding?"

"No, baby." I turn to look at Trent, but Jackson blocks my view with his hand, pulling my gaze back to him. "Don't look, Kiera." It's all he needs to say because I already know.

Half a dozen squad cars pull up with their guns raised as they rush over toward Trent. Jackson holds me tightly in his arms as I sob. He pets my hair and kisses my face.

I know I'm in complete shock, but nothing could've prepared me for when they took Trent's body away. Deputy Pettigrew gave his statement explaining that Jackson was only acting in self-defense and protecting me. There won't be any charges pressed, but it needs to be said for the record. They want my statement next, but I'm too shaken up to even speak. They allow Jackson to take me home as long as I agree to come in the next couple of days.

Once I agree, Jackson carries me to the truck, and we drive home. We shower in silence together, kissing and holding each other. Once we're clean, he puts me to bed and holds me as I cry myself to sleep.

CHAPTER THIRTY-FIVE

JACKSON

ONE MONTH LATER

My eyes lazily open, and I blink when I feel the warm wetness between my thighs. Looking over, I see the empty side of the bed and realize Kiera didn't wait for me to wake up to start our morning tradition.

Smirking, I rest both arms behind my head and arch my back as I feel her mouth consume every inch of me. *Fuck.* She's so goddamn good at this. Her hand is wrapped around the base of my shaft, rotating up and down as her tongue licks circles around my tip. She knows that drives me fucking insane.

"Baby…" I groan desperately. Arching my hips, she gets the hint and speeds up. She's a master at getting me off in minutes due to the quickies we squeeze in between our work schedules. Speaking of which, today is a special day, and there's a lot to do for my plan to properly work. "Get on your knees," I demand, reaching for her.

She finally brings her head up, gasping for air. The corners of my mouth tick up in a pleased grin, and I notice how breathtaking she is.

"Turn around," I tell her, getting to my knees so I can take her from behind. She happily obeys and sticks her plump ass out for me as she arches her back low to the mattress. "Fuck, this view is perfection," I say, talking about her backside. I give it a little slap, and she moans. She has no idea what's in store for her—right now and later.

I stroke my cock a couple of times before positioning myself at her entrance and thrusting inside her. I love it when she's at this angle because it allows me to be so damn deep and it gets her off within minutes. Feeling her bare makes me lose it usually after she does, but it doesn't stop us from going back at it shortly after. We're completely insatiable for each other, never able to really feed that hunger for long before we're both starving for more. Every day I get to wake up next to the love of my life is another day I won't waste without making love to her.

"Jackson…" she whimpers, widening her hips and pulling me impossibly deeper inside her.

I squeeze her hips tightly, moving her back and forth on my dick. The fading bruises on her waist are from the countless times of giving in to her demands to go harder and faster.

"What do you need, baby?" I ask, grabbing her ass cheeks and opening her wider.

"Harder," she begs. I smile wide. My girl likes it rough, and it's my pleasure to give her whatever she wants.

Instead of holding her hips and bruising her all over again, I have another plan.

"Straighten your legs," I tell her. "So I can straddle you from behind."

Kiera does exactly that, her pussy putting my cock in a deathly vise grip between her clenched cheeks. I cover her body with mine, wrapping a hand around her throat and pulling her head back until my lips touch her ear. My other hand lies flat on the bed next to her shoulder, holding me up just enough to slide in and out of her.

"Wanna know how many times I've jerked off to the image of your luscious ass?"

"Hmm?" She pulls her bottom lip between her teeth. "A billion?" she teases.

"Pretty fucking close." I chuckle.

Slowly, I pull back, and without warning, I push inside her in one hard thrust. I repeat the motion, tightening my grip on her throat. "I want to fill you up, sweetheart. Put all my babies inside you then fuck your tight cunt again with more."

Kiera shivers underneath me and gasps. "Yes…*please*."

I thrust—no, *ram* inside her over and over, plunging my hips against her as hard as I can until she's clasping my dick so tight it sends us both over the edge in a sweaty, heated daze.

Rolling over, I pull Kiera to my chest as we both gasp for air. After several minutes, Kiera looks up at me with a frown.

"What's wrong?" I furrow my brows, brushing my fingers lightly over her shoulder.

"Are you concerned that I haven't gotten pregnant yet?" Her question catches me off guard, and I'm not sure how to answer. I don't know much about what it takes to knock a girl up besides the obvious, but considering I've spent half my life trying *not* to get a girl knocked up, I haven't a clue what the average timeframe is.

"Well, it's only been a few months. Don't these things take time usually?" I try to offer some kind of comfort.

She shrugs, lowering her eyes. "Sometimes, yeah. But we do it like…every day. Sometimes twice. You'd think if I were capable of even getting pregnant it would've happened by now. Maybe my eggs are all dried up, and my window of opportunity has come and gone. I'm an old lady."

I hate the sadness in her voice and want to offer any kind of encouragement I can. Rolling her over so she's on her back and I'm halfway on top of her, I tilt her chin up so she looks into my eyes.

"I'll do whatever it takes to knock you up. Day and night of hardcore fucking if I have to." I grin, and that gets a laugh out of her.

"Oh, what a sacrifice," she taunts, wrapping her legs around my thighs.

"Yeah, but for you, I'll do it." I wink. "Seriously, sweetheart." I lean down to kiss her gorgeous pink lips. "Don't worry, okay? It'll happen when it's supposed to."

"How do you know?" she asks with doubt in her tone.

"Because I just have a feeling, okay? Trust me."

She groans, rolling her eyes at the way I waggle my brows at her. "The last time I trusted you, it took over fifteen years." She deadpans, but I see the slightest smirk on her lips.

"I'm never going to live that down."

"Oh hell no. Never *ever*." She wraps her arms around my waist and slides her hands down to squeeze my butt. "I'm just glad you finally came to your senses."

"Ya know…" I give her a look. "I'm getting an awful a lot of blame here when *you* could've at any time told me how you felt. So I think you deserve half the blame too." I dip down to her neck and inhale her sweet scent. "You were single for a long time before…" I linger, not wanting to say his name aloud. "So…what made you just stand around and keep quiet?"

Kiera narrows her eyes at me as if she doesn't appreciate being put on the spot. "For starters…" Her tone lowers, sounding accusatory, and it makes me laugh. "I appreciate the upheld tradition of a man asking a woman out, so for the most part, I was just waiting and hoping you were getting my signals. However, when you started dating all the single women in town, I figured you weren't asking me out because you didn't think of me that way." She pauses, thinking for a moment. "Also, you'd make random comments that made me believe you just didn't see me as anything more than a friend, so instead of making a fool of myself, I kept my feelings buried."

"I'll be the first to admit I was a selfish dumbass who pushed you away anytime I felt you getting too close. I still believe you deserve better than me, but now that I've had you, I'm not ever letting you go. You had your chance to find a rich lawyer, so you'll just have to settle for me now," I tease, plucking her bottom lip with my thumb.

Kiera places both palms on my cheeks and forces me to look up at her. "Being with anyone else besides you would've been settling," she tells me sweetly. "This is exactly the life I wanted, Jackson Bishop. I love working with horses. I love living here. I love your family. I love that I'm still close to my parents. I love *everything* about you and me. There is absolutely *no* settling, and if I have to remind you of that for the rest of our lives, I will. Do you understand me now?"

Fuck, she's adorable when she gets all serious. Gets me hard all over again.

"I do, baby. You've never given me a reason to doubt you. I just wanted to be able to give you the world."

She squishes my face, pulling me in for a kiss. "You already have. I love you."

"I wove you too," I mutter between my smooshed lips.

It makes her giggle. She drops her hands and wraps her arms around my neck. "We should get ready for work." She sticks her bottom lip out and pouts. "Though I'd much rather stay in this warm bed with you all day."

"Hmm...I could make that happen." I wink, rolling to my back and taking her with me until she's on top.

"Sorry, Cowboy. Horses need to be fed." She gives me one more peck before crawling off me, and as soon as her feet touch the floor, I'm off the bed and racing her to the shower. "Dammit, Jackson!" she squeals when I wrap my arms around her waist, pick her up, and set her down behind me.

I'm in the shower seconds before she is, but it doesn't even matter because I have her pinned to the wall as soon as she gets in.

"You're relentless." She laughs against my mouth as I kiss her.

I help her wash her body and rinse her hair, and she does the same for me. It's more than just being together naked. I cherish these moments, and it still feels like a dream that she's mine.

"So do you have a busy schedule today?" I ask as she finishes getting ready.

"Sorta." She bites down on her lower lip. "I have a new horse arriving today, some paperwork to get done, and I have an accountant meeting later."

"Well if you can squeeze me in for dinner, I'll wait for you." I wrap my arms around her waist and pull her close, then kiss her on the nose.

"Why? You wanna feast on me for dessert?"

"How'd you even know?" I smirk.

"I've known you all my life, Jackson Joseph Bishop. I know all your tells," she says matter-of-factly.

"Guess so." I hold back a grin, knowing there's one secret she won't see coming.

Once she leaves, I put my plan into action.

"Don't forget. You need to pick her up at exactly five," I remind Colton.

"For the hundredth time, I know." I hear him groan into the phone. "After I'm done with all my shit, I pick her up at six and bring her over."

I grunt. "I'm going to junk punch you."

"Oh c'mon, I'm just messin' with you. You know I won't let you down."

"I know."

We give each other a lot of shit, but truthfully, he's a good friend. After the whole incident with Trent and Nicole last month, he picked up a lot of my slack while I took some time off to be with Kiera. She was pretty distraught, and no matter how much I tried to get her to open up and talk, she kept saying she wasn't ready. I didn't want to push her, so I just continued to be there in any way she'd let me.

After Trent's death, Nicole was arrested and plead guilty to being his accomplice. After the police went through her phone and text messages, we learned she helped him with the barn fire as well. That day of the incident she tried to convince me that

Trent's plan was the next day when all along she knew it was happening right then. Luckily, she'll be paying for that for a long time behind bars.

Shaking my head and trying to clear my thoughts, I can't focus for shit while doing my daily tasks, but I know I have to get them done, so I push away the distractions of what's to come tonight. Though I never in a million years thought this would be my life, I'm not going to let the opportunity pass me by.

At exactly five, I'm already showered and changed and ready for Colton to bring Kiera home. The moment I hear his truck pull up, I head to the door to greet them.

"What the hell?" I hear Kiera cursing at Colton. It makes me laugh as soon as I see him carrying her over his shoulder.

"Here she is, boss." Colton sets her down on the steps and winks.

"Jackson, what are you doing?"

"Okay, well to be fair, I didn't tell him to bring you here all caveman style." I shrug, reaching for her and bringing her mouth to mine.

"It was the only way she'd listen." Colton shrugs, then tips his hat. "Later."

I take Kiera's hand and lead her into the house. "You gonna tell me what the hell is goin' on?"

"No, ma'am," I smirk, bringing her to the shower. "You have thirty minutes. Get cleaned up. Wear jeans and boots."

"John, is that you?" Kiera snaps her fingers in front of my face, giggling. "Because I know my Jackson enough to know this isn't his forte."

"I take offense to that." I swat her ass. "Now move it, woman."

Forty-five minutes later, she finally comes out of the bedroom dressed with her face and hair done. I smile, taking all of her in. "Did you dress up for me?" I tease, pulling her in for a kiss. "Fuck, you smell good." I bring my lips to her neck and feather kisses toward her ear. "Screw it. Let's get to dessert now."

Chuckling, she manages to push me off her, then demands I tell her what's happening.

"I made us a light dinner because I fully plan to feast on you later."

"You made dinner?" She nearly gasps.

"You really know how to kick a man down, don't you?" I lead her to the dining table where I have a Caesar salad and steaks waiting.

"Truth or dare?" I ask her when we're halfway through our meal.

Kiera narrows her eyes, tilting one side of her mouth up in suspicion. "Truth."

"What color panties are you wearing right now?"

"Panties? You only told me to wear jeans and boots?"

"Kiera Young, don't make me come over there and make you pay the consequences."

"You wouldn't dare." She arches a brow.

"Afraid you wouldn't be able to beat the champ at my epic chicken dance?"

"Considering you were wasted and naked, I don't think anyone could."

"Good. Now answer me."

She stabs a piece of her steak and shoves it into her mouth. "Ud."

"What?" I burst out laughing as she tries to speak with a mouthful. It makes her laugh, and soon we're both chuckling while she tries swallowing down her food. "That was very ladylike."

"I think thirty-plus years is enough time to show you the real me," she teases. "I said *red*. My panties are red. Happy now?"

I stab the last piece of my own steak and smile. "Sure am."

An hour later, we're in San Angelo at a rodeo bar I haven't been to in years. She has no idea, though, because I made her wear a blindfold.

"This is ridiculous," she whines, holding her hands out in front of her.

I cup her face. "Trust me?"

Her shoulders relax, and she sighs. "Yes, of course."

"Good. Then just let me lead you."

I'm getting looks left and right as I guide Kiera through the busy bar scene. "Why's it so loud in here?" she shouts, thinking I'm next to her, and it makes me laugh.

"Truth or dare?" I whisper in her ear when I'm behind her. My hands are on her hips, holding her back to my chest.

Kiera turns her head toward my voice. "Are you freaking kidding me right now?"

Chuckling, I squeeze her tighter. "C'mon, baby. Play along."

Her shoulders sink, and she audibly sighs. "Fine. Dare, I guess."

"Perfect answer."

"I'm regretting it already." She groans.

"No, ma'am. Are you ready?"

"I don't know. Am I?"

I undo her blindfold and slide it down her face.

She immediately shakes her head. "No! No way! That's not fair."

Spinning around, she puts her hands on her hips and scowls.

"Kiera Young, I dare you to ride that mechanical bull."

She closes her eyes as her head falls back. "You're the worst!"

Laughing, I grab her hand and drag her up to the guy operating it. "Put it on the fastest speed you have."

Kiera smacks my arm and yells in protest. "You tryin' to kill me?"

"Oh, c'mon babe. You're a top-rated, multi-award-winning horse trainer. Surely you can ride the bull for a lousy eight seconds." I wink, but she doesn't find the humor in it.

She steps onto the mat, then turns around to point a finger at me. "You better not record me, or your balls will feel hell later."

I hold my hands up, showing her I'm phone free. "Don't worry. Everyone's already here anyway."

She starts scanning the crowd, and when her eyes lock on Emily, River, Mila, and her cousin, Addie, she tries holding back a smile. "I'm gonna get you back *so* much worse, Jackson Bishop!" Her threat is adorable.

The operator waits until she's climbed up and situated herself. She holds tightly with one hand while leaving one arm down.

I cup my hands around my mouth and shout, "You got this, Pippi!" She takes her free hand and flips me off.

I watch as the operator presses the button, and soon, the bull is moving. Kiera waves her arm in the air as she squeezes her legs to the sides, holding on as tightly as she can. Within seconds, the bull is turned up another level, and Kiera goes flying with a scream.

We all clap and cheer as she gets to her feet and adjusts her jeans. The girls are screaming wildly, so Kiera gives the crowd a little bow before she walks off the mat and comes charging for me.

"I hate you so much right now."

I wrap my arms around her and kiss her sassy mouth. "You killed it! I even got to see those red lacy panties I love so much."

She pushes against me and laughs.

The girls rush over, and Kiera glares at them. "You're all on my shit list!" she teases, letting the girls hug her anyway.

"Hey, Jackson lured us here with free margaritas," River explains.

"Yeah, he's sure good at that," Kiera says, locking eyes with me. Even though Emily and Mila are pregnant, they didn't want to miss out.

"Was that a sneak peek into what it looks like when you're on top of Jackson?" Addie blurts out, making Kiera blush. "Gives a whole new meaning to riding a cowboy…"

"Okay, she's had enough margaritas for all of us…" Emily takes the glass out of Addie's hand and gives it to River.

"Alright, well you enjoy ladies. I'm taking my woman out for dessert."

"You wanna explain to me why we drove an hour so I could ride a mechanical bull?" Kiera asks when I drive us out of the parking lot. I try to hide my smirk but fail miserably.

"You'll see soon enough."

I see her studying me out of the corner of my eye but don't give in. Eventually, I get her off the topic, and we discuss a few of the horses she's training. Once we're back in Eldorado, I tell her to put the blindfold back on.

"You can't be serious." She groans.

"Kiera."

She grinds her teeth. "Fine. But if you make me do something even more outrageous, I will castrate you."

"You'd only be punishing yourself," I taunt.

I drive us out as far as I can to our spot. Part of the reason I had to kill time and brought her to that bar was so Colton could get everything set up for me. Plus, I really wanted to see her ride that bull.

"Okay, baby. Take my hands and jump down," I direct after I open her door.

Her nose wrinkles. "It smells like a campfire."

I smile as I take her hand and then walk us up the short path. I had Colton start a bonfire and set up Tiki torches around the area, and now that it's pitch-black, the flames light up everything perfectly.

"Okay, turn around and face me." I place my hands on her arms. "Stand here."

"Is this where you reenact your naked chicken dance for me?"

"You wish."

She smirks.

I shift around her body, so her back is to me now. The fire and torches are behind me, and soon she'll know exactly what's happening. I'd be lying if I said I wasn't a tad nervous, and although my palms are sweaty, I've never been surer of anything in my life.

"Kiera…" I whisper in her ear, wrapping one hand around her waist. "Truth or dare?"

The corner of her mouth ticks up slightly. "I have a feeling it won't matter what I choose at this point…"

"Still gotta pick one, sweetheart." I graze my lips under her ear.

"Okay. Fine." She sighs. "Truth," she says just like I knew she would. I smile at how well I know my girl.

"Will you marry me?" I whisper just loud enough for her to hear.

"What?" she asks slowly.

I reach inside my pocket and bend on one knee. "Turn around."

Kiera pulls the blindfold off, and when she spins toward me, her eyes widen, her jaw drops, and she nearly crumbles to the ground. I take her hand while she covers her mouth with the other hand.

"Kiera Georgina Young…" I start, and she immediately shakes her head at me. I know she hates when I use her middle name. It was something I often teased her about when we were little kids. "I know you haven't been ready to talk about what happened last month, but I just need you to know that I was ready to take a bullet for you the second I saw he had you. I had never been more terrified in my entire life, and you know me better than anyone to know that I don't scare easily. I thought I was going to lose you. I felt so helpless at that moment, and when it was finally over, I knew I didn't want to waste any more time without you as my wife. I was ready to propose to you the next day, but we needed time to heal, so I didn't want to rush anything. However, today seemed like the perfect day to finally ask you because this day over fifteen years ago was the night I knew I was in love with you. Playing truth or dare with you had always been my favorite game even if I pretended it was stupid back then. I looked forward to spending any time I could with you, and I love that even after all these years, we can still laugh, tease, and taunt each other. I can't imagine not having you in my life, baby. I love you doesn't sound adequate enough for how I feel, but I love you more than anything in the world. You'd make me the luckiest man in the universe if you'd be my wife."

"I-I can't believe this," she whispers with tears in her eyes.

"You know what happens if you don't answer the question..." I tease, smiling.

She nods frantically. "Yes, yes, yes!" She wraps her arms around my neck, tackling me to the ground. I hold her face in my hands and kiss the fuck out of her, then kiss her cheeks and tears away.

"Give me your hand," I tell her once we're both sitting up. "Your left hand." I chuckle when she nervously gives me the right.

I slide the ring on, and she gasps. "Jackson, it's beautiful." She slides it around her finger. "I can't believe you did this..." I can tell she's in shock, and it makes me so damn happy she had no idea this was coming today. "It's so perfect."

"It's a double halo split shank ring with a full carat diamond."

Kiera looks at me as if I'd grown a third eye.

"Well, that's what I was told anyway."

"You could've given me a Ring Pop for all I care, and I would've been happy." She kisses me again.

"Only the best for my girl," I tell her proudly.

"This is more than I could've ever imagined." Kiera looks at me again. "Seriously..." She pokes me in the chest. "Are you really John? Blink twice if you're being switched against your will."

"Har har, you're so funny." I roll my body over hers until she's pressed to the ground.

"Did you really fall in love with me on this exact date?" she asks, looking up into my eyes.

"You bet your ass I did. Even if you did burn my clothes and make me run back home naked."

Kiera's head falls back slightly as she laughs the memory. "Yeah, shrinkage is a bitch."

"Feisty, sassy, and sexy—I knew at only fifteen you were the one."

"Yeah? How'd you know?"

I roll off her and pull her up until we're both on our feet. "Let's sit," I say, leading her to the hay bales. Once we're able to warm up near the fire, I angle my body and look at her, grabbing her hand in mine. "I might not have known what it was back then, but I knew I felt something that wasn't like anything I'd ever felt before. As I got older, I continued to deny it; my own insecurities kept me from telling you, but now that we're here, I can confidently say it was that night that stayed with me after all this time."

"We have shared so many memories," Kiera says softly.

"Hundreds," I confirm. "And I wanted to make another memory out here that will stay with us forever."

She's smiling wide and looks so damn happy. "We'll be ninety years old telling our great-grandchildren."

I chuckle, nodding in agreement. "And when they ask me how I knew you were the one and how we continued to love each other after all those years, I'll tell them this…" I clear my throat, inhaling deeply. "It's never felt this good before. Because it's never been this right before. I've never felt so desperate to be with someone before you. I've never wanted anything more with anyone because I knew I could never give myself to anyone but you. It's because it was always *you* who had my heart, Kiera. Those feelings I felt were locked up and safeguarded, and I wasn't willing to let them out for anyone other than you."

Kiera's crying by the time I finish, and I pull her close and kiss her cheeks.

"You're a beautiful man, Jackson Bishop. Inside and out. You're the exact person you always said you weren't, but I knew.

You never cease to amaze me, and I can't wait to spend the rest of my life with you."

Reaching behind one of the hay bales, I grab the cooler Colton left for me.

"What's that?" Kiera asks.

I open it up and take out a bottle of whipped cream and Mama's famous apple pie. "I did promise you dessert after all." I flash her a look that tells her exactly what I mean.

"You thought of everything."

I hold Kiera in my arms, and we make love on the blanket I told Colton to leave out. It's slow and sweet, and we share a connection I never knew existed until her.

"I love you," I whisper as we lie under the stars. She's pinned to my side with her arm draped over my chest. "I promise to give you the best life possible." I place a kiss on her forehead, and she smiles, knowing I never break my promises.

CHAPTER THIRTY-SIX

KIERA

FIVE MONTHS LATER

It's hot as hell in June, but it's the perfect day for an afternoon indoor wedding. My nerves have the best of me because I've imagined every detail of this day since I was a little girl from the dress down to the groom. But the good news is I'm not planning on running anywhere but straight into Jackson's arms. For once, everything is right, perfect, and the way it should be. Butterflies and excitement swarm through me.

It's happening. It's finally happening.

The guest list for the ceremony is small and intimate, the way I always wanted it to be. I didn't listen to a single person's suggestion and made sure that today was how Jackson and I wanted it, come hell or high water. This time, there won't be a big show for the whole town to experience and whisper about for months to come. There won't be any runaway brides, rumors, or speculation.

Only family and very close friends were invited because of the size of the chapel. Emily and Addie will be standing up in the front with me as I say my vows, staying true to keeping the wedding private. Mila and River didn't mind at all and volunteered to help me in other ways, though the planning of it was surprisingly stress free. Apparently, when you're marrying the person you're meant to be with, everything from the cake to the reception is trivial and easily falls into place.

As my mama helps me zip up my dress, Emily, Mila, River, and Addie surround me with eager smiles on their faces. It's nothing extravagant with sequins or a long train. It hugs my body in all the right places, but it's simple and perfect. Instead of everyone gasping over my expensive luxury dress, they'll be seeing me for me. I even did my own makeup this time, taking the classy Meghan Markle approach, and kept it light and natural. My hair falls in beach curls along my back with my bangs clipped to the side, just the way Jackson likes it. A small crown and veil sit on the top of my head, and I'm so happy with the whole look. It's me—not a made-up version of myself, trying to impress everyone —and it's exactly how I envisioned when I'd marry Jackson.

I glance in the mirror, asking the girls and Mama if I can have some alone time to collect my thoughts beforehand. They all agree, but Emily lingers behind.

"You're not planning to run, are you?" she playfully asks, already knowing the answer to that question.

I pull her into a big hug. "Not this time. This time it's right."

When we break apart, she hands me a letter. I glance down at it, somewhat surprised.

"I promised I'd hand deliver it." Em gives me a sweet smile and leaves me to read it in peace.

My heart beats erratically as I sit down in the chair in front of the small vanity mirror. Sucking in a deep breath, I open the envelope and immediately recognize Jackson's handwriting. Before I even begin to read it, I start choking up. Already there's nothing I'd change about today, not a damn thing.

Kiera,

Before you walked down the aisle to say your 'I do's' the last time, you received a letter from me. I thought it'd be kinda like a tradition to give you another one. :)

On a more serious note, words can never truly express the way I feel about you, how deeply I love you, or what you really mean to me. I will never, for the rest of my days, be able to fully explain it, but I'll spend eternity trying and making sure you understand. Today will officially mark the first day of our forever, and there's no other woman in the world I'd rather spend my life with.

You are my everything, Kiera.

You're my best friend, my lover, and now you're finally going to be my wife. I'm still pinching myself and wondering what I ever did to deserve someone as kind and sweet as you.

When I was younger, I dreamed of marrying you.

I dreamed of you being the mother to my children.

Anytime I thought of my future, you were always a part of it.

Today those dreams will finally become our reality.

There was a point in my life when I thought I'd lost you forever, and the thought scared the shit out of me. A life without you isn't a life worth living at all, but I wanted your happiness above all things, and I still do. I know we will read our vows soon, but I want you to know right now, I'll do anything for you, baby. I'd rope the damn moon for you.

For every day I've known you, I've become a better man.

And I'll try every single day to make you a happy woman.

You've given me the greatest gift—yourself and your heart—and if I die tomorrow, I'll die a happy man knowing you love me the same way I love you. You bring joy to my soul, light to my dark days, and have restored my faith in love and true happiness.

A year ago, I wasn't ready to let you go, but I'd come to terms with it.

Sweetheart, today I'm promising I'll never leave your side.

Thank you for making me the happiest man on earth. Thank you for giving me a chance, giving us a chance, and loving me with every fiber of your being. We might have a simple life full of horses and kids on a ranch, but it's our life, and that's more than enough for me.

I love you so much. So damn much.
Always yours,
Jackson

P.S. Truth or Dare?
Dare you to marry me.

Tears stream down my face, and I try to wipe them away, but it's no use. His words speak straight to my heart, and I want him to know that he's my everything, too, and that marrying him will be the best thing that's ever happened to me.

A knock rings out on the door, and I hurry to wipe my face.

"Come in," I say.

The door swings open, and Mama Bishop enters wearing a lavender dress. When she sees my tears, I can tell she's alarmed.

"You okay, honey?" She walks in and closes the door. "Not having second thoughts, are you?" She smiles cautiously.

"No, ma'am. There's not an ounce of doubt in my body. Marrying Jackson is the only right thing I've ever done," I tell her confidently.

She glances down at the letter and smiles, knowing what happened before. I stand and wrap my arms around her.

"I'm so happy you're officially joining the family. But you know you've always been like my second daughter, Kiera, and I love you."

Tears well in my eyes again. "I'm an emotional mess. I'm sorry."

She chuckles. "As long as those are happy tears, they're welcome anytime, sweetie."

I sniff. "They are. I promise."

Carefully, she wipes away the tears that stream down my face and smiles. "Just wanted to come see you before we started. It's almost time. We've got about thirty minutes."

I give her another big hug, and she tells me again how pretty I am before she leaves. Soon my parents enter, and they're a big emotional mess, just like me. My mama wraps her arms around me, and so does my dad. They squeeze me so tight, and I'm so thankful to have them as my parents.

"I know we're really letting you go this time, Kiki," my dad tells me, his eyes watering.

"Daddy, please don't cry," I beg. "You're going to make me start again."

"She's right, Charles," Mama tells him. She gives me a grin and lets the girls in who were patiently waiting in the hallway. Their excitement is contagious, and soon I'm smiling and laughing again. I feel like I'm living in a dream state, but I'm trying to soak it all in because I never want to forget a single detail about this day.

Eventually, Evan knocks on the door, telling us we have less than ten minutes.

Emily looks at me. "Ready to officially become my sister?"

"You better believe it."

Emily grabs my hand and leads me out to my father. Dad turns to me with happiness, and I tell him to stop it before he starts a chain reaction. As I peek inside the chapel, seeing everyone waiting for me to come out, I can't stop smiling. Today is one of the happiest days of my life, and it's only going to get better from here.

It's still so surreal.

Emily walks down the aisle with John, and Addie walks down with Colton, and a minute later, the "Wedding March" begins to play. My father positions the veil over my face, and I suck in a deep breath and let it out quickly. "I love you."

"Love you too, Dad. Thank you."

It's time.

It feels like I've waited a lifetime for this very moment, or at least half a lifetime.

I walk up the aisle, and as I do, everything that surrounds me disappears when I see Jackson in the front of the room wearing a tuxedo, smiling at me. It's the most beautiful thing I've ever seen. The way he's looking at me like I'm everything completely takes my breath away. As I walk forward, I feel as if I'm gliding to the front to him. My father gives me away, and I take the few steps up to Jackson. Slowly, he removes the veil from my face, and I see tears on the brims of his eyes, and it almost makes me lose it in front of everyone. I never knew happiness like this could ever exist.

"You're so beautiful," he whispers, only loud enough for me to hear, and I want to kiss him now.

The pastor begins, and I'm not listening to a word he says as Jackson and I hold a silent conversation. I'm lost with him as he holds my hands, brushing his thumbs over my fingers. The pastor clears his throat, and the chapel erupts into chuckles. Neither of us was paying attention, and it's time to say our vows.

Jackson looks into my eyes and pulls his handwritten vows from his pocket. The paper shakes in his hand as he pours his heart out in front of our friends and family. I feel as if I can't find my voice when it's my turn to tell him exactly how I've always felt, though he knows by now. When tears stream down my face, he wipes them away with his thumbs. The pastor requests our 'I do's' and soon we're exchanging rings and being pronounced man and wife.

There's no hesitation from either of us, not an inkling of doubt.

When Jackson is finally allowed to kiss me, he pulls me into his arms and kisses me sweetly, before it becomes more heated and passionate. The pastor clears his throat again, but neither of us cares because right now, this moment is everything. When we break apart, my lips are swollen, and our smiles are contagious. As soon as we're announced as Mr. and Mrs.

Jackson Bishop, the entire room erupts into cheers and applause.

We make our way down the aisle, happiness radiating from us, and run down the steps of the church. The photographer stops us and has us pose in front of the double doors. The family feeds in, and we take pictures with them, then she takes us off to the side of the church in a big overgrown field. I can't stop looking at my husband, and the smile on my face is so genuine, it might possibly be permanent.

Jackson pulls me into his arms and feathers kisses up and down my neck as the flashes go off. It feels so natural being with him freely like this. After hundreds of photos are taken of us laughing and kissing and holding on to each other for dear life, Jackson grabs my hand and leads me back to the church. The photographer doesn't miss a single precious moment.

As everyone crowds around, Jackson picks me up and carries me to the classic Mustang he rented to drive us home. On the back, it says "Finally Married," and I let out a huge laugh because it's true.

As soon as we get in, we can't seem to keep our hands off each other.

"Let's get the hell outta here, *wife*," he whispers against my lips as we break and wave bye to everyone.

He interlocks his fingers with mine as we drive home to change clothes. Mama Bishop is holding a small reception at her house, and we're supposed to meet there in an hour. It was important to give everyone time to arrive, but all I want to do right now is be with my husband.

Jackson glances over at me. "I love you."

I squeeze his hand. "I love you more."

We pull under the Circle B ranch sign and travel down the gravel road, and my heart is so damn full when we park in front of the house. Jackson walks around the car, and when I step out, he picks me up and carries me up the steps to the porch, kicks open the door, then sets me down.

"I think I might be finally gettin' used to this caveman thing." I laugh against his lips.

He lifts an eyebrow at me. "Bedroom. *Now*."

I do exactly as he says, knowing I need him as much as he needs me.

Jackson takes his time, undressing me, kissing every inch of me. I remove his tux, and we're standing naked, touching, not able to keep our lips apart. His fingers lightly brush against my skin, and goose bumps cover me.

"We don't have much time," he tells me as he lays me on the bed.

My eyes meet his. "We have *forever*."

A smile touches his lips as he moves to me. Though we have somewhere to be, an event that's celebrating us, we decide to take our time. We make love like never before. As our worlds collide, the emotions I feel are indescribable, and by the look on his face, I know he feels exactly the same. Jackson moves in and out of me, our bodies joining, and we're as close as two human beings can possibly be. Right now, we're one. It takes no time at all before we're losing ourselves together, but in the end, Jackson finds me and pulls me back to reality with his mouth.

"Truth or dare," I whisper with a smirk.

"Truth," he says, searching my face.

I swallow hard, knowing I've got to ask this one question before we go to his parents' house. My heart pounds hard in my chest, almost to the point where I wonder if even he can hear it.

"What is it?" he asks, grinning, propping himself up on one arm, not taking his eyes from me.

I tuck my lips in my mouth, almost nervous. "You said truth, right?"

I somehow knew he'd choose that one this time. It was a gut feeling.

He nods, waiting.

"What if I told you I'm pregnant?" I wait patiently for his answer.

"I'd be thrilled to death." He runs his fingers through my hair, and my eyes flutter closed.

When I open them, Jackson is staring at me. A hint of a smile touches my lips.

"Well…" I linger.

He's searching my face. "What?"

"You're gonna be a dad, Jackson."

His eyes go wide as my palm holds his cheek. "Seriously. Like this isn't a joke?"

I shake my head with a smile. "I found out this morning. I was late and thought maybe it was stress induced, but I took a test or three, and they were all positive. We're *finally* pregnant. We're going to be parents."

Tears immediately roll down his face, and he devours my lips, then bends down and kisses my tummy. "I'm the happiest man right now. Today has been the best day of my life," he admits.

"I know," I whisper. "I feel like I might burst with happiness too."

My emotions spill over. I have everything I've ever wanted—Jackson Bishop and starting a family together.

"Also," I add, "John told me he put a hex on us to have triplets."

Jackson bursts into laughter. "That bastard would. Hmm. Maybe it'll happen."

I slap his arms. "Don't wish that on me. Bishop babies are the size of turkeys."

"Okay, so if not triplets, maybe twins?" He lifts his eyebrows.

"We'll see how potent your sperm really is," I tease with a laugh.

Jackson smirks. "I want this printed in the paper. Just imagine the headline, *The Infamous Jackson Bishop Settles Down and Knocks Up His Wife with Multiples*. It's stuff for the record books."

I pull him closer, wanting to taste his lips again. "Thank you."

"For what, sweetheart?" He wraps his arms around me.

"For making me your wife and a mom. You've given me everything I've ever wanted."

He leans over and kisses my forehead. "And just think, we're only getting started."

CHAPTER THIRTY-SEVEN

JACKSON

THE PAST EIGHT months have been one hell of an experience. Right after the wedding, I swept my bride away for a two-week honeymoon in the Cayman Islands. I originally scheduled it for a week, but once Kiera told me she was pregnant, I knew this would be our last chance to go on a vacation for a while. We spent most of the time in our room anyway, but not having any responsibilities and getting to just be together was exactly what we needed.

Watching my beautiful wife change and her belly grow with life inside has been indescribable. Between the cravings, hormone changes, setting up the nursery, picking out names, and buying enough baby things to fill one of the barns, I'm so damn excited the day has come to bring our babies home.

"I always knew you were gonna get payback for all the shit you gave us," John told me as soon as we announced we were having twins. He laughed his ass off, but I didn't find it as humorous with their horror stories. Though I was over the moon to start our family, I have no idea how to be a dad, especially to such a tiny human, nevertheless *two* tiny humans. However, after the shock wore off and we started preparing for our new bundles of joy, I was ecstatic. Kiera, on the other hand, blamed me for the back aches, muscle cramps, and spasms. Though I can't say her little fits weren't adorable, I know how uncomfortable she was toward the end of her pregnancy.

"What if my vagina never goes back?" Kiera groans as Emily and River assist her into the house. I offered to carry her, but she wanted me to bring the babies in, and all four of us walk into the house together. It was a special moment for her, and I wanted to do it her way.

We'd been having unprotected sex since our very first time, but getting pregnant wasn't as easy as it sounded. After six months, I was starting to worry my sperm was no good, but then Kiera surprised me with the best news on our wedding day, and it felt like it was supposed to happen like that all along.

"Your vagina will go back, I promise," Emily reassures her as Kiera takes a seat on the couch. "But no hanky-panky for six weeks," she warns, pointing a finger at me.

"I just pushed two babies out—no scratch that—two *Bishop* babies out. He's not getting anywhere near my vagina again," Kiera announces firmly. My boys came out over seven pounds —*each*. All the Bishop babies are born big, so it wasn't that much of a surprise. Except to Kiera.

"But they're the cutest little twins ever," River coos, kneeling by their car seats.

"You're right." Kiera smiles. "Totally worth the pain and wrecked vagina."

"Can we stop teaching my sons about vaginas? They're only five days old," I remind them all.

Emily snorts. "Look who's talking. Mr. Playboy himself doesn't want his boys to hear the word."

"The irony," River cackles. "You better hope they don't turn out like you."

"Oh, I already know I'm doomed. I grew up with three brothers, so I anticipate they'll get into all kinds of mischief." I kneel in front of Kane's car seat and unbuckle him. He doesn't even fuss and stays sleeping as I pull him out. He looks so small in my large hands. They both have dark hair, and according to theory, Kiera's horrific heartburn nightmares predicted it all along.

"Not to mention, you were the ringleader," Emily adds.

"Just for that, you don't get to hold him," I tease, handing him off to River.

"Don't you dare," Emily comes over to Knox and takes him out of his seat. "Don't listen to your daddy," she whispers to him. "Aunt Em will always get to hold you."

"You have your own babies," I remind her with a smug grin.

"Yes, but Ethan is eight months old, and these little guys are giving me baby fever all over again," she admits, and I snicker, wondering what Evan thinks about that.

"But at least all the babies are pretty close in age," River adds.

Right after Emily and Evan had their second baby, John and Mila had baby Mackenzie the following month. A few months before that, our friends Dylan and Jessica also welcomed a baby girl named Harper. It's safe to say these kids are all going to grow up together and hopefully form close relationships.

As I look down at my babies—my *sons*—I'm in awe. They're special in more ways than one. It's rare for an identical twin to have their own set of twins, but it's even rarer for an identical twin to have their own set of identical twins. Not only that, but they were also born on February 29th.

Identical twins born on a leap day. Damn special indeed.

"Do you need anything, baby?" I ask Kiera, wanting to make sure she's as comfortable as possible.

"No, I think I'm okay for now." She smiles when I lean down and kiss her.

"Don't worry about your vagina. The doctor reassured me he stitched ya up good. Nice and tight." I flash her a wink, and she scowls.

"You're the worst," she teases.

I shake my head. "You're the one who said you wanted to

have six kids. I was just getting a jumpstart to make sure we could get started as soon as you're healed."

"Six?" River gasps.

"Well hey, with twins, that means you're one-third of the way there." Emily chuckles.

Kiera laughs, holding her stomach. "Don't make me laugh. It feels like my insides are going to fall out."

"Was I this way when I had Riley?" River turns and asks me with a grin.

"From what I heard, yes. I think even worse, though."

She glares at me and scowls.

"They're seriously so perfect, Kiera," Emily says, gazing down at them. "They look—"

"All Bishop," Kiera blurts.

"Can't fight those strong Bishop genes," I declare with a proud smile.

"That only means one thing," River says.

Emily smiles and continues. "Heartbreakers."

Less than an hour later, the house is filled with more family all taking turns holding the twins. Kiera breastfeeds between, and I'm so proud with how she's adjusted to motherhood. She makes it look so damn easy, too. Meanwhile I'm internally freaking out about how I'm going to keep them alive.

"So I gotta say," Tanner speaks up, holding Knox. "I'm a little disappointed y'all didn't name a baby after me."

Kiera snorts. "Sorry, I didn't think naming one of my babies after an ex-boyfriend would reward me with bonus points in the bedroom." She gives him a teasing grin.

"Well, considering I'm the reason y'all finally got together, it would've been a small sacrifice." He winks. Kiera and I look at each other confused.

"Wait, what?"

Tanner and John smirk at each other.

"I'm the one who snuck your letter into Kiera's bag that day. You're welcome," he says proudly.

My eyes go wide, shocked. I always assumed it was John, but he never confirmed, and I never asked. At that point, it didn't matter, but hearing it was Tanner all along has me bursting out with laughter.

"You sneaky bastard!"

"Wait, wait, wait…" Kiera says between a fit of giggles. "Why would you of all people do that?"

"Well, for starters, everyone knew Jackson had a thing for you. It wasn't a secret to me, at least. Even when we were younger, but when we went out that night, and he told me I was part of the reason he held back all those years, I knew I had to jump in and intervene, or at least thought *you* needed to know," he tells Kiera. "I hoped that if you knew the truth about his feelings, you might not go through with your wedding, and well, let's just say—I was right." He holds up his arms like he's a champ.

"I don't know whether to smack you or hug you for stealin' that letter," I joke. "But right now, I'm gonna let you off, considering it all worked out in the end."

Kiera laughs, shaking her head. "When Jackson told me he wasn't the one who put that letter in there, I for sure thought it was John or maybe even Mama Bishop."

"Oh, if I was going to intervene, I'd have done it years ago, honey," Mama says matter-of-factly. "I've been telling Jackson long before that to get his shit together, but do you think he ever listened to me?"

We all laugh.

"I can only hope that Kane and Knox give him the same treatment." She snickers.

"Oh, come on. Don't wish that on me. I was good!" Kiera pleads with a laugh.

Shortly after, I push everyone out so Kiera can get some rest. The twins need to be fed and changed before bed.

"I'm proud of you, honey," my mama tells me when I walk her to the car. "You two are going to do just fine. But don't hesitate to call if you need help, okay?"

I wrap my arms around her for a hug. "You got it, Ma. Thank you."

Once I'm back inside, I bring the boys to Kiera so she can try tandem breastfeeding with her special pillow, and honestly, it's the craziest thing I've ever seen. "Your tits are ginormous."

"Can you stop staring at me like that? You aren't getting into my pants for two months, mister," she warns.

"Two months? Doc said six weeks."

She rolls her eyes. "Play your cards right, or it'll be three months."

Leaning over the chair, I kiss her lips. "Playing my cards right is what brought us here."

She smirks and looks down at the boys who are successfully eating. "You got that right, Cowboy."

Kiera and I eventually get into a somewhat decent schedule with the boys, though it's organized chaos to say the least. Knox is a night owl and Kane is an early riser, so it's safe to say we aren't getting much sleep. After two weeks, I'm forced to go back to work, and even though we have Braxton's extra help around the ranch and Alexis fully took on Kiera's workload, we need to start preparing for how we're going to juggle this all long term.

When Kiera entered her second trimester, she stopped training. It was too risky with the wild horses needing to be broken in, so I happily took on her clients because I didn't want her to lose them. She helped where she could by doing easy tasks that wouldn't have her straining herself, but once she hit the third trimester, she was mostly too uncomfortable to keep working outside in the heat. She liked helping at the B&B, so John let her stop in a few times a week to feel productive. Once she hit thirty-four weeks, she went on bedrest, and the twins came four weeks later.

After I took over Kiera's job, Colton took on my chores, including the B&B horse riding and lessons. It's been a smooth transition for the most part, but now I'm a new dad getting little to no sleep.

I managed to get the blueprints drawn up for the new training facility we're going to build on the ranch. It'll be huge, and I can't wait for it to be done because I know Kiera will absolutely love it.

Thankfully, the insurance money from the fire paid out. Though a lot of the equipment was sentimental and, therefore, irreplaceable, Dad was able to rebuild the barn and buy new machinery.

So much has happened, but the past eight months have been some of the best months of my life. Making Kiera my wife, finding out there were two heartbeats on the sonogram, waking up every day with a smile on my face—I didn't know it was even possible for life to get any better.

Then the boys arrived, and somehow it did.

A YEAR AND A HALF LATER

My alarm goes off with a piercing sound, and I'm quick to turn it off before it wakes the twins. I turn over and grab my beautiful wife, wanting to soak in these last few minutes before I have to get ready for work. There have been a lot of adjustments within the past eighteen months since the boys arrived, but I wouldn't change it for anything. I love being a husband and a father.

"Mmm…" She moans, crossing a leg over my my hip. Our morning traditions stopped long ago, but I'm no stranger to morning sex—especially when Kiera moans like that.

"Good mornin', gorgeous." I kiss her temple and grin when I feel her hand slide down my body.

"Hmm…looks like it's a very good morning." She pulls my dick out of my boxers and strokes it in her palm, adding pressure as she slides her hand up and down.

"Kiera," I growl. "You better finish what you start."

"Don't I always?" she taunts, her tone laced with seduction and hunger. "We have about thirty minutes before the boys walk in here demanding breakfast."

"In that case…" I'm on top of her before she can say another word, pinning her body down with mine. "Slide your panties to the side," I demand. She does as I say so I can position myself at her entrance.

"Mmm, God." Her head falls back with a throaty moan. I thrust deep inside her, jerking my body back and forth to drive harder against her hips. "Yes, just like that. Don't stop."

I know exactly what it takes to get my girl off. We're a pro at these quickies now, and though I miss the days when we could be together for hours without interruption, I wouldn't change this life for the world.

"Fuck, I love when your hormones get needy like this…" I whisper into her ear.

"It's uncontrollable," she says as if she's apologizing for it, squeezing her legs tighter around my waist.

"No worries, baby. I'm here for whenever you need it." I grin against her lips before claiming her mouth.

I continue driving into her, over and over until I feel her falling over the edge. She reaches for a pillow and screams into it, knowing she'll wake the twins otherwise. Her pussy squeezes my dick, and soon I'm releasing deep inside her.

Once we catch our breath, I reluctantly slide out of her and press my lips to her forehead. As soon as I roll off her, I place a hand over her belly and kiss it.

"Sorry, baby girl. Your mama likes to attack me, and I'm a sucker for pussy."

"Jackson!" Kiera swats me immediately. "Do you have to tell our daughter that every damn time?"

"I'm sure she's gonna learn it from her brothers eventually." I grin, and she rolls her eyes. "I'll go check on the boys quickly. You stay in bed."

I tiptoe down the hall to the twins' bedroom, and as soon as I open the door, I see two bright-eyed faces staring up at me.

"Do you two ever sleep past five a.m.?" I walk in, smiling. "Of course not, right? You're born ranchers!"

I grab them from their cribs and set them down. I can't believe they're eighteen months already, running everywhere and causing craziness wherever they go. It's a life I love so much, and I can't wait until we add a third precious bundle in about four months.

"Diapers, boys. Let's go." They each grab a diaper and I take the pack of wipes. We're working on some early potty training so we don't have three kids in diapers, but they're not overnight trained yet.

Once the boys are changed and dressed, I start making breakfast so Kiera can get a few extra minutes of sleep. We have eggs almost every morning, and the boys like theirs scrambled, whereas Kiera likes to dip her toast into the yolk.

"Alright, boys. Applesauce or grapes?" I ask with the fridge open, so they can pick their sides. They both pick grapes, and once I rinse them off, I set everything on the table.

"Well look at this sight…" Kiera's voice has me looking up from pouring milk into the boys' cups, and when I see her leaning against the doorframe with her arms crossed, I smile from ear to ear. "My boys take such good care of me." She walks over and kisses Knox and Kane, then comes to me and wraps her arms around my bare waist. "Smells delicious."

I bury my face in her neck and inhale the scent of her soap. "Yes, it does." Flashing her a wink, she gives me a knowing that look that tells me not to even think about it.

"Truth or dare?"

"Jackson," she warns, glancing over at the twins who are currently shoveling food into their mouths.

"You know the rules, Pippi," I remind her with a seductive grin, holding her tightly.

"Truth." She groans.

I lean down, bringing my lips to the shell of her ear, and whisper softly, so the boys don't overhear. "How do you feel about anal?"

"Dammit, Jackson!" Kiera tries pushing against my chest, but I don't budge. She's laughing. "You're exhausting."

I laugh with her, wrapping a hand around her neck and crashing our mouths together.

"Dammit!" a small voice echoes, and we both turn to look at Knox. He's the troublemaker of the two.

Kane starts giggling and right on cue, repeats after his brother. "Dammit, dammit, dammit!"

They're both in a fit of giggles, and although we're supposed to tell them not to say that word, Kiera and I can't help laughing at their cuteness.

"Boys, that's a naughty word," Kiera finally explains once she's able to compose herself.

"Dammit!" Knox repeats with a shit-eating grin on his adorable chubby face.

"Argh. What am I gonna do with you, Jackson Bishop?" Kiera shakes her head at me though I know she's secretly amused.

"Keep me forever?" I grin.

"I suppose I will...even if you gave me a run for my money." She flashes a cute smirk, and we both know what she's referring to.

"Couldn't make it easy for you, baby." I give her ass a smack.

"Trust me, you haven't." She snorts. "But I wouldn't change it for anything."

"It's a good life, Kiera Georgina Bishop." I wink, knowing she hates when I use her middle name.

"Promise me we aren't going to give our daughter my horrible middle name?"

"It's not horrible at all," I protest, noticing the way Kiera's eyeing down my chest, and when she notices my cock stirring, she looks up at me with an arched brow. "In fact, I think we should name our little girl after her beautiful mommy."

"Not happening." She shakes her head. "Now go shower before you start getting ideas…"

Kiera walks around me, swatting my ass, but I quickly grab her arm and pull her back. "You still didn't answer my question," I remind her in a low voice.

"I think…" She takes a couple of steps backward, tapping a finger to her bottom lip. Spinning around, she shakes her ass while she walks toward the fridge.

"Kiera…" I growl.

She looks over her shoulder and smirks. "I'll get back to you in about fifteen years."

EPILOGUE
KIERA

FOUR YEARS LATER

"Kaitlyn Rose Bishop! You best not be playin' in the mud in your brand-new dress!" I shout from the back door with my hands on my hips. "We have to leave in ten minutes!"

Knox and Kane are God knows where, and the party starts in twenty minutes.

"What's a pretty woman like you doin' out here screaming? The only time you should be screaming is when your legs are wrapped around my face." Jackson snakes his arms around my waist and softly speaks into my ear. He instantly makes me smile.

"Would you contain your children? We have to go soon, and Kaitlyn's out there in the dirt." I frown. "Go figure, I have a girl, and she's ninety-nine percent tomboy. I had to bribe her with three suckers, two popsicles, and she even got a five dollar bill out of me in order to get her to wear that dress."

Jackson chuckles against my neck, pulling me tightly to his chest. "Are you really surprised? She's just trying to catch up with her brothers. Not to mention, she's been raised on a ranch and around horses her entire life."

I turn around to face him, wrapping my arms around his neck.

"Well, I know. I was never a girly girl either, but that doesn't mean I wasn't hoping to dress up my little girl in bows and tiaras and play Barbies. She won't even let me braid her hair!" I stick my bottom lip out and fake a pout. "I do love that she's adventurous, though. She's a spitting image of you, too, of course."

"Nah, she's a perfect mixture of us. She has your gorgeous blonde hair and my blue eyes. She's sweet and witty and knows how to throw a punch. She's the exact replica of a future heartbreaker." He looks over my shoulder, his eyes go wide, and then he sucks his lips into his mouth.

"What?" I furrow my brows.

"And she's a total troublemaker."

I turn around and see my little girl skipping toward the house in her cowboy boots and her pink dress covered in mud. There's dirt in her hair and on her face, and she's smiling wide as she makes her way to the back door.

"Excuse you, young lady. Who said you could leave the house and play in your new dress?" I place my hands on my hips and give her my best firm look.

She looks up at me with the most innocent smile that she's mastered. "Daddy did."

Jackson chokes behind me, and as soon as I look over my shoulder, I see him narrowing his eyes and shaking his head at her.

"Is that so?" I ask, directing my harsh tone toward my husband.

"To be fair, she put her little fingers under the door while I was trying to pee and then asked if she could come in. When I told her no and to wait, she then proceeded to ask me where the baby horses come from and how they're made. I had no other choice."

I want to laugh at how damn cute his scared tone sounds, but to contain my disapproval for Kaitlyn's messy dress, I turn and give her a scowl. "March into the bathroom and clean your face and hands right now. I'll find you a new dress." I point my finger into the house, keeping the stern look on my face.

"Yes, Mama." She bows her head and slowly pads her feet against the floor as she walks inside.

Once I'm sure she's out of hearing distance, I turn and face Jackson who's unsuccessfully holding back a laugh.

"Oh, c'mon, babe. She's too damn cute to discipline." He gives puppy dog eyes, and just like always, it works. "And she's had me wrapped around her little finger since the day she came into this world, kicking and screaming. She's a daddy's girl," he states proudly.

"Trust me, I know. That's why our almost four-year-old has more horses than years she's been alive."

"Hey, you're the one who said you wanted a hundred horses, a big fancy training facility, and a big pasture." Jackson flashes his I-told-you-so grin and pulls me closer.

"Well you better go find your mini me's so we can get going. It's humiliating to always be the last ones to arrive." I pat his chest before walking around him to make sure our daughter hasn't somehow managed to make a mess in the bathroom.

Twenty minutes later, Knox, Kane, and Kaitlyn are fighting in the backseat as Jackson drives us over to his parents' house. I turn around to scold them, but quickly stop myself as I look at the three of them. Three Bishop kids. And they're all ours.

Finding out I was first pregnant the morning of our wedding took me by a happy surprise. We hadn't been preventing, but Jackson and I wanted to start a family right away. Though it didn't happen quickly, I now know it happened when it was meant to. It gave Jackson and me months to spend together with just the two of us and really transition our relationship from friendship to forever.

Looking at my children, I feel so blessed and happy how things turned out. At one point, I was certain I'd never get this, but as I listen to them bicker and poke each other, I've never been surer that this is the life I'd always wanted and more.

I slide my hand through Jackson's arm and lean my head against his shoulder. He glances down at me with a smile.

"I love you," I mouth, squeezing him.

"I love you too, Pippi." He winks before bringing his eyes back to the road.

Today's a huge occasion for the Bishop family, much like most of their parties, but especially since Jackson's sister, Courtney, and her family are visiting. The triplets turned ten a few months ago, and Riley turned ten last month, so we're having a huge birthday party for the four of them.

Ten years old.

I can hardly believe the oldest grandchildren are ten already.

Jackson parks the truck, and I'm quick to turn around and stop my kids from rushing out.

"Wait…" I hold a hand up, and the three of them freeze with their hands on their buckles. "I expect your best behavior today, ya hear me? There's gonna be a lot of people here, and Grandma Bishop wants a nice party. Do you understand me?"

The three of them nod their little heads and chuckle as they nearly fly out of the truck. Kaitlyn can't quite jump down on her own yet, so Kane lets her jump off onto his back and gives her a piggyback ride.

"Is it weird to say that I think your 'mom' voice is pretty sexy?" Jackson flashes a mischievous grin. "If I'm naughty, will you spank me?"

"You're always naughty…"

"Now you know why."

Laughing, I jump out of the truck and wait for Jackson. He takes my hand and presses a kiss to my knuckles. I still get butterflies whenever he does that.

"Life is sure an adventure with you," I say, pulling him down so I can reach his lips. "Not that I ever doubted it wouldn't be."

"And to think I almost let you go."

He's smiling, but I see beneath it. It's hard not to think about what would've happened and where we'd be if things hadn't worked out the way they did.

"Think you'll keep me?" He arches a brow with his infamous Jackson smirk, and it makes me laugh at how damn adorable he is. His blue eyes sparkle whenever he looks at me. After all these years, it still feels like we're only fifteen years old and sneaking out to our spot. There's never a dull moment.

I plant a sweet kiss on his lips, before we join the family. "I'm keeping you forever."

...And they all lived happily ever after.

Don't be sad that the Bishop Brothers is over because you see lots more of our couples in the second generation series, **The Circle B Ranch series.** These are the kids of the four couples and you can't miss these! Filled with angst, steam, small-town vibes, and of course, plenty of family saga drama!

If you haven't started at the beginning, make sure to read Alex & River's story in *Taming Him*, Evan & Emily's story in *Needing Him*, and John & Mila's story in *Chasing Him*.

CIRCLE B RANCH SERIES

Meet the Bishops second generation

Hitching the Cowboy
Riley Bishop, Alex & River's son

Catching the Cowboy
Rowan Bishop, Alex & River's daughter

Wrangling the Cowboy
Maize Bishop, John & Mila's daughter

Bossing the Cowboy
Elizabeth Bishop, Evan & Emily's daughter

Kissing the Cowboy
Ethan Bishop, Evan & Emily's son

Winning the Cowboy
Mackenzie Bishop, John & Mila's daughter

Claiming the Cowboy
Knox Bishop, Jackson & Kiera's son

Tempting the Cowboy
Kane Bishop, Jackson & Kiera's son

Seducing the Cowboy
Kaitlyn Bishop, Jackson & Kiera's daughter

HITCHING
the COWBOY

The Bishops Second Generation

Wedding bells are the last thing on twenty-two year old Riley Bishop's mind, but that's exactly what he hears after waking up in Vegas next to a woman he just met—his new *wife*.

He never saw her coming, but she might be worth the risk.

Zoey Mitchell is high on life, free spirited, and adventurous. However, learning she married a rowdy cowboy after a night of partying is not what she expected—even for her.

She's risking it all, gambling with her heart.

Deciding to give their instant marriage a chance, Zoey moves from her big city life to a small town Texas ranch. She has to know if their connection is based on more than just a wild one-night stand before announcing to her family that she got hitched.

One moment changes everything—*for better or worse*—and a secret could destroy them both.

ABOUT THE AUTHOR

Brooke Cumberland and Lyra Parish are a duo of romance authors who teamed up under the *USA Today* pseudonym, Kennedy Fox. They share a love of Hallmark movies, overpriced coffee, and making TikToks. When they aren't bonding over romantic comedies, they like to brainstorm new book ideas. One day in 2016, they decided to collaborate under a pseudonym and have some fun creating new characters that'll make you blush and your heart melt. Happily ever afters guaranteed!

CONNECT WITH US

Find us on our website:
kennedyfoxbooks.com

Subscribe to our newsletter:
kennedyfoxbooks.com/newsletter

facebook.com/kennedyfoxbooks

twitter.com/kennedyfoxbooks

instagram.com/kennedyfoxbooks

amazon.com/author/kennedyfoxbooks

goodreads.com/kennedyfox

bookbub.com/authors/kennedy-fox

BOOKS BY KENNEDY FOX

DUET SERIES (BEST READ IN ORDER)

CHECKMATE DUET SERIES

ROOMMATE DUET SERIES

LAWTON RIDGE DUET SERIES

INTERCONNECTED STAND-ALONES

MAKE ME SERIES

BISHOP BROTHERS SERIES

CIRCLE B RANCH SERIES

LOVE IN ISOLATION SERIES

Find the entire Kennedy Fox reading order at
Kennedyfoxbooks.com / reading-order

Find all of our current freebies at
Kennedyfoxbooks.com / freeromance